To

forgetting you, forgetting me

Never forget that You are amazing.

To Sue,

Never forget that
You are amazing.

Mom

forgetting you, forgetting me

International Bestselling Author

Monica James

Copyrighted Material

Forgetting You, Forgetting Me

This book is a work of fiction. Names, characters, places and incidents are the product of the author's imagination, or are used fictitiously. Any resemblance to actual events, locales, or persons living or dead, is coincidental. Any trademarks, service marks, product names or named features are assumed to be the property of their respective owners and are used only for reference.

Copyright © 2017 by Monica James
All rights reserved. No part of this work may be reproduced, scanned or distributed in any printed or electronic form without the express, written consent of the author.

Cover Design by MGBookCovers and Designs
Editing by Toni Rakestraw of Rakestraw Book Design
Formatted by E.M. Tippetts Book Designs

CreateSpace Independent Publishing platform

Follow me on:
monicajamesbooks.blogspot.com.au

Other Books By
Monica James

THE I SURRENDER SERIES

I Surrender

Surrender To Me

Surrendered

White

SOMETHING LIKE NORMAL SERIES

Something like Normal

Something like Redemption

Something like Love

A HARD LOVE ROMANCE SERIES

Dirty Dix

Wicked Dix

Dedication

This is dedicated to my readers…thank you for never forgetting me.

One

"THERE'S BEEN AN ACCIDENT."

It's unimaginable how one simple, ordinary word can change a person's life forever. One simple word, when merged with other simple, ordinary words can transform the best day of your life into the worst.

"Lucy? Lucy, can you hear me?" asks my best friend, Piper. The trepidation laces her tone, but I can't speak. I can't verbalize that yes, I can hear her, because the moment I do, I'll have to accept this horrible nightmare as being real.

"C'mon, Luce, please—talk to me!"

It's funny the things you remember and the things that you don't. But sometimes, those forgotten memories are brought back to life by a simple word, a certain smell, or sometimes, a single moment. Sadly for me, this is a memory, a moment I will never be able to forget.

This wasn't supposed to happen. This was supposed to be the best day of my life. The one day that was going to change my life forever. And it has. Just not the way I anticipated.

"Honey, it's Mom. Can you hear me? There's been an accident, and we need to go to the hospital." I flinch when she uses yet another word I don't want to hear.

"Simon, I think she's gone into shock. Can you lift her up?"

"Of course, Maggie." A moment later. "Daddy's got you." The world begins spinning around me, but I don't fight it. I want to tumble into the bleak, perilous vortex and never look back. Never look back on this day, which is the beginning of the end.

Was I too bossy? Or maybe I was ungrateful? Maybe it's because I didn't invite Mrs. Goldstein. Whatever the reason, I'm sorry. I take it back. Please give me a second chance. Please give *him* a second chance.

"Just buckling you up, sweetheart." The term of endearment transports me back to happier times, and I begin skimming back over my twenty-six years on this planet.

I fondly recall the time when Simon and Maggie Tucker welcomed me into their home. I was five. Although they weren't my birth parents, I never once felt like anything but their own. They showed me nothing but true kindness, and after being treated like a nobody my entire childhood, only being known as M in my foster homes, their unbending love made me realize I was the luckiest girl in the world. I felt like a somebody. And I was—I was their daughter. I was their daughter who finally had a name.

I go on to remember the time I met Piper Green in gym class. She had my back when I became the favorite target for dodge ball, and she's had my back ever since. Piper is my sunshine and without her, my life would be clouded with darkness.

I recapture snippets, small fractions of my past, slivers that have made me, me. But in this moment, one memory comes crashing to the surface, clearer than any others because it's my most favorite memory of all. It's of the day I met the love of my life, Samuel Stone.

I loved him from the first moment I saw him, and I have ever since. He was the captain of the high school basketball team, while I was just me, little Lucy Tucker. But Samuel saw something in me that not many people did. Not even me. He supported my ideas of wanting to change the world, no matter how farfetched they were. I know what it's like to be hungry, underprivileged, and unloved, and that's why I was determined to not allow another child suffer like I did. But if it weren't for Sam's constant encouragement, I never would have graduated top of my class with a masters in human rights. He helped me accomplish my dreams because he *was* my dreams.

He supported me no matter what, and he loved me regardless of my imperfections and now, it's my turn to do the same.

I know where we're headed, but knowing your final destination doesn't make what you're about to face any easier to digest. In this circumstance, I wish I didn't know. I wish I could wind back the clock by just a few hours because if I knew then what I know now, I would have appreciated and embraced every moment and not let go.

"You look so beautiful, honey."

"Thanks, Mom." The reflection staring back at me was surely not my own. My long, honey blonde hair was twisted high in an elegant knot. The hairdresser assured me it was the perfect style to support the tiara as she slipped it into my locks. The jewels felt so regal underneath my fingertips, but it all feels so insignificant now.

"You've got stunning green eyes, Lucy, and I'd die for these plump lips," said the makeup artist as she applied my final coat of mascara and thin layer of peach gloss. It's all so superficial, so unimportant. I violently scrub any trace of it off my face.

"Luce, stop it. You're hurting yourself." But what Piper doesn't understand is that it's the unseen bruising that hurts the most.

As I slipped into my tight-fitting gown, I remember the crystal beads catching the sunlight and reflecting tiny rainbows across the room. My white heels made me taller, but my small frame could never catch up to Samuel's towering, imposing six foot four frame.

The final touch was sitting in my mother's hands. She fingered the lace, tears pricking her hazel eyes. "I wish your grandmother was here to see this."

"She is, Mom," I replied, reaching out and stroking her arm.

She nodded and handed over the final piece which would make my outfit complete, which would take me one step closer to being Mrs. Samuel Stone.

The hairdresser pinned the veil in place and when that thin segment of lace became my view, I knew I was ready. Nothing could stop me now. I should have known something was askew when I didn't see Samuel. But I walked down that aisle, never feeling more beautiful, never feeling more proud. But I waited and waited, but my time never came. Every bride's worst nightmare had just happened. I was stood up at the altar. And when ten minutes became thirty, I knew something was horribly wrong. But I never foresaw it would have been this—anything but this.

As it was, my groom-to-be was late because he was in the wrong place at the wrong time. Samuel never stood a chance when a drunk driver slammed into his car head on. *Oh fate*, sometimes you can be so cruel. Why, on this day, and at that time? Why did you choose my Sam to suffer at the hand of your callousness?

So now, all my happy memories are plagued with new ones just formed—ones of my fiancé laying in a coma, his outcome unknown. In a blink of an eye, happiness can be snatched out from under you and all you're left with is this—this emptiness. You really don't appreciate what you have until it's gone.

As we pull up at St. John Memorial Hospital, I try and

refocus on all the pleasant memories, but I can't. All I can focus on is that beyond those doors lies the man I was supposed to marry. Lies the man who is my reason to live.

"Lucy, please, for the love of god, say something!" Piper shakes me, begging I speak. But there are simply no words.

As she continues rocking me, I know it's time to go.

Turning slowly, I look at my best friend, staring into her tear-stained eyes. I need to say something, anything, so I say the only thing that I can—the only thing that'll elucidate how I feel inside.

With a single tear tracing a path down my cheek, I profess, "I think I'm going to be sick."

★ ★ ★ ★ ★

April 8th 2011

Dear diary,

Today has been the best day of my life. Well, one of the best. Samuel and I finally did it— we moved in together! After eight years of dating, Sam has finally made an honest woman out of me!

Our dream home in Montana is everything I could ever wish for. I still can't believe I'm sitting in my bedroom, in my new home, writing this. Our property is absolutely amazing, and I can't wait to venture out on our twenty acres, hand in hand. Or better yet, ride our horses into the sunset. So corny, but true!

Our ranch, Whispering Willows, has incredible views of the Tobacco Root Mountains, and I look forward to sipping iced tea while enjoying the tranquillity from our decks and stone patios, which are surrounded by our beautifully manicured landscapes.

Cottonwood trees, quiet groves of quaking aspen, and gorgeous willow clusters give us the privacy we need to venture around undisturbed. Mom and Dad are about thirty minutes away, and so are Kellie and Gregory. It's perfect. It's my dream come true.

Every day I wake, grateful for what I have and who I've become. I don't like to separate my life into two parts because bouncing around from foster home to foster home in L.A. is a distant memory, but it's one I'll never forget. It made me into the person I am today. It showed me where I belong, and to whom I belong.

I know we're going to be happy here. I can feel it in my bones. This is the start of our new life together and I couldn't be happier.

I knew Samuel was 'the one' and as naïve as that makes me, I do believe in true love and our happily ever after. He is my soul mate, and there is no one for me but him. He's ingrained into my very existence, and I couldn't imagine my life without him. Not that I ever have to worry about that.

I know Sam feels the same way because I saw something which cements our future. I didn't mean to snoop, but the gleam from his grandmother's engagement ring caught my eye. The ring was sitting innocently in a box he had half unpacked. I debated with myself for all of three seconds before I quietly, like a thief in the night, slipped my hand inside and pulled out the most stunning ring in the world.

I felt beyond wicked, as I've never

been a rule breaker, but the moment I felt the smooth, one carat diamond and imperial white gold band pass under my fingertip, I was completely converted to a life of crime.

I didn't dare put it on, but then my newfound rebellion kicked in. I snuck a quick peek at the door before slipping it on my finger. I couldn't stop the tears—it was perfect. But just as quickly as I found the ring, I swiftly placed it back, not wanting Sam to catch me red-handed.

We've spoken about marriage and kids in passing, but Sam wants to focus on the family business, Stone and Sons, helping his dad on the wheat and barley farm. We're still young—we've got our entire lives ahead of us. But as I think of that beautiful ring and how it looked on my finger, I realize I want that future to come sooner rather than later.

I want nothing more than to be become Mrs. Samuel Stone. But all good things come to those who wait, so I'll sit tight, but not so patiently. Patience has *never been my strong suit, but I'll wait forever and a day for Sam.*

So here's to our new life together...I can't wait to see what comes next.

Two

THE STUNNED, GRIEF-STRICKEN GASPS OF visitors and patients reveal I look as mad as I feel. But I can't stop. After I finished throwing up all over my now ruined gown, a sense of urgency passed over me and nothing, not even Satan himself, could stop me from charging into the hospital, desperate to see Sam.

My heels strike in time with my hammering heart as I pound down the long hallway, frantic to find my fiancé. Piper and my parents trail behind, offering words of encouragement, but nothing will ease the knot of despair eating away at my very existence.

A pretty blonde nurse sitting behind a large counter raises her head when she hears my stilettos stab at the linoleum. Her horrified reaction confirms that I look like the bride from hell with my smeared makeup, vomit-stained dress, and lopsided bun. But my appearance is the least of my concerns. On any other day, I would make conversation and ask how her morning has been. But not today. I sniff back my torrent of tears. "C-can you p-please tell me where S-Samuel S-Stone is?" My breathless tone is shrill, unlike me; therefore, my sentence is comparable to gibberish.

"Sorry?" she says, pulling backward as I prop onto the counter, ignoring social etiquette and disregarding her personal bubble.

"Samuel Stone," I repeat, tugging at the pearls around my neck, as they're suddenly cutting off my air supply.

When she continues staring at me, no doubt thinking I'm completely unhinged, I slam my palm on the counter, tears pricking my eyes. "Samuel Stone! Where is he?" She's wasting precious time.

Just as I'm about to very uncharacteristically jump over the desk and strangle her, a warm, familiar hand rests on my arm, reminding me of my manners. "Sweetheart, I've got this. Go wait with your mother." I don't argue with my father, and nod a quick apology to the startled nurse. I'm appalled at my behavior. This isn't her fault.

I wait on the sidelines and watch as my father calmly uncovers the details. When he pales, I cover my mouth, turning into my mother's side. I know it's bad, my father's reaction says it all. "It's going to be okay, honey." My mom's words are empty, but the false assurance is her way of saying there's always hope.

But my hope is lost. I know nothing will ever be the same.

When my father walks over, looking solemn and grave, I hold my breath and internally count to five before I ask, "How is he?"

"He…" The pause is all the answer I need. "Let's just go see him, okay? Kellie and Greg are with him." I nod, my stupid veil practically highlighting what was within reach, but will never be.

The nurse buzzes us through a sectioned off ward to the left, most likely pleased to see the back of us. When we rush inside, the antiseptic odor burns my nostrils, but I don't care. I will scramble through heaven and hell to find Sam.

My heels pinch my feet, slowing me down, so I stop, lean against the wall, and rip them off. Nothing will stop me from seeing my fiancé. My feet sing in relief as I follow my dad with a now quickened step. He's looking overhead, ensuring we're going the right way. The moment we see Gregory Stone standing in front of the last door on the left, we know that we are. His downturned face, unfastened tie, and disheveled salt-and-pepper hair reveals that whatever is happening inside that room can't be good.

"Greg!" my father calls out. Our footsteps are in sync, reflecting our urgency to reach him.

As Greg raises his head, his grim expression brings on a fresh set of tears. His greenish-gray eyes—eyes so similar to that of his son's—meet mine, while his lower lip trembles. "I'm so sorry, Lucy."

I can't stop the avalanche of tears. Will I ever stop crying? "Is he okay?" I manage to choke out.

Greg sighs, placing his hands into his expensive suit pockets. "We don't know the extent of his injuries. He's in a coma. The doctors say the swelling around his brain is—" He halts, shaking his head. He clears his throat, fighting back tears. "It's too early to tell."

Why did he pause? What was he going to say?

I don't have time to question him however because Kellie emerges from Sam's room, still wearing her navy Chanel dress, her long blonde hair snarled. When she sees us, she bursts into tears. Her onset sets me off once again.

"Can we see him?" my mother asks, filling in the blanks for me.

Kellie dabs at her blue eyes with a tissue. "Of course, but only two people are allowed at a time. Doctor's orders."

My father looks over his shoulder and nods. "You girls go in. Piper and I will wait outside." I don't need to be told twice as I hike up my dress, the wretched long train a hindrance as I almost trip over it.

Once we sterilize our hands, my mother pushes open the door while I take three calming breaths.

One...

Two...

Three.

I take one step, then two, and enter the room which seals

this awful nightmare as truth. Lying in a single bed is the man I was going to marry. But that man, no, that can't be Samuel. That man is barely recognizable as that person is more machine than man.

A loud beeping pervades the otherwise still air in concert with my breaking heart. My gaze takes in the unfathomable sight of my fiancé hooked up to endless machines. Tubes and cords are coming from his nose, mouth, head, and out from under his gown. An IV drip is inserted into the back of his hand, the saline solution feeding his wounded body.

If it weren't for these apparatuses, it would appear that Sam is simply sleeping. He rests gently on the bed, his arms lying by his side, his legs covered with a stark white blanket. I don't know what I was expecting. Maybe to see bruises and contusions? But I know, just as an unseen iceberg is dangerous to an unsuspecting ship, it's what I can't see that will do the most harm.

"Honey?"

My mother's concerned voice whips me back into the now. I realize I'm slouched against the wall, unbelieving what I see. I don't bother wiping my tears away as I know new ones will just take their place. "I-I want to talk to his d-doctor."

She nods, brushing past me as she exits the room, leaving me alone with Samuel. It takes me a minute to feel confident enough to stand on my own, barefoot in my wedding dress, as I beg the love of my life to wake up.

Seeing Sam so still makes me physically ill. He's usually such a vibrant, lively person—a quality I adore about him. You'd never catch him lounging around, reading a book, or watching a DVD. He would prefer to be outdoors, working on the ranch, walking our beloved Border Collie, Thunder, or playing ball. His downtime would be reading the paper. But now, I don't even know if he'll ever be able to do any of those things ever again.

I need to touch him, feel that this is real. I stagger over, my hands wavering as I reach out and brush the backs of my fingers down his clean shaven cheek. He feels warm to the touch. His short, dirty blond hair sits in twisted tufts, and I gently run my fingers through it, trying to comb out the snags.

"Please come back to me, Sam," I plead, running my fingertip over his slightly parted lips, cringing when I brush over the clear tube. "Our life together has only just begun. I can't do this without you. I need you. You can't leave me. You're my f-forever." Every word chips away at the hole in my chest, and I'm afraid before long my heart will spill out onto the floor, exposing how it's broken in two.

I slip my hand into his, remembering the feel of his fingers squeezing mine. But now, nothing. Closing my eyes, I place my other hand over our union and press, my mind happy to pretend that the pinch was Sam's hand closing over mine. But I can't pretend forever.

The door opens and I look up. I see a middle aged doctor

in a white coat, holding a clipboard and talking quietly to our parents. When he sees me holding vigil beside Sam's bedside, standing in my soiled wedding gown, his mouth dips into a poignant frown. "Ms. Tucker, I presume?"

I nod, hating how if life was fair, I would be Mrs. Samuel Stone by now.

"I'm Dr. Kepler. I'm so sorry about what happened to Samuel. We're doing everything we can for him." We're all silent, waiting for him to decode what that means. "Samuel sustained very serious head injuries, and due to that trauma, his body has gone into a coma. The coma will hopefully give his body time to heal. It'll also hopefully help with the swelling so we can determine the extent of his injuries. As you can see—" he steps over to a machine "—we're monitoring his brain waves."

I look at the machine, studying a faint line limping up and down.

He follows the sluggish line with his finger. "This indicates that thankfully, there is some brain activity present, but it does indicate that Samuel may not wake and be the person he once was."

My father scoops me up into his arms. I lean against his shoulder, but his warm, familiar musky fragrance does nothing to soothe my pain.

"It's still very early days." I can hear the hopelessness in Dr. Kepler's tone. "Like I said, we'll monitor him closely. Once the swelling goes down, we'll have a better understanding of what's going on inside of Samuel's head. He may need surgery, he may not. He's young, fit, and healthy; the odds are in his favor. The rest is up to Samuel. Now, I understand his blood type is AB-negative. His blood type is one of the rarest in the world, so just for precautionary measures, I would like to have some on hand. What blood types are you, Mr. and Mrs. Stone?"

As they talk shop, my brain begins churning through everything Dr. Kepler has just said. It appears we wait, wait for my comatose fiancé to come to. But for how long? And who will Samuel be when he does wake? Peering back over at the near flat line on the monitor, I know that my Sam may never return.

I hear Dr. Kepler ask, his tone troubled. "The fact you have Type One diabetes, Mr. Stone, and seeing as you have a phobia of needles, Mrs. Stone, I need to know, does Samuel have any siblings? It may also be wise to have him or her on standby, just in case Sam needs a transplant."

When a stale silence permeates through the room, I slowly pull away from my father's cocoon, watching as Greg and Kellie uncomfortably avert their gazes. I know why, but this is literally a matter of life and death. Their differences now mean nothing because the only thing that matters is making Samuel well again.

Dr. Kepler looks on, confused by their sudden retreat, unaware of the big, fat elephant in the room. "Mr. and Mrs. Stone? Do you have any other children?" he questions once again. Kellie nervously tugs at her diamond drop earring while

Greg clears his throat.

I can't take it anymore. They're wasting time. With a surge of confidence, I step forward, all eyes swinging my way. Piper and my mother nod, egging me on. In a small voice, I declare, "Dr. Kepler, Samuel does have a brother."

Dr. Kepler looks relieved, while Kellie and Greg turn green.

I choose to ignore them as I add, "He has a *twin* brother. And they're identical."

★ ★ ★ ★ ★

August 4th 2004

Dear diary,

*Something amazing happened today at school. Samuel Stone finally spoke to me. *sigh* It was by far the most exciting thing that has happened to me all week. After admiring from afar for months, I FINALLY got to talk to him.*

I needed a copy of The Catcher in the Rye to complete a paper, which of course, I'd left to the last minute. I raced into the library during my lunch break, hoping to be hit with the creativity bat, but instead, I got hit with the reality bat when all copies of the book were out. I lent my copy to Piper, who was even more behind than I was, so I felt bad asking for it back.

While I was contemplating writing another paper on a different book, a fragrance which can only be defined as pure masculinity oozed through the air, leaving me gasping.

My questions were answered soon after when I ran straight into a solid wall of muscle. I yelped, apologizing profusely, but my apologies died in my throat when I was pinned to the spot by one of the hottest boys in school. His eyes were the most striking color—they were sea green, licked with a curving swirl of gray. He was tall—taller than I thought he was. And his face—total heartbreaker. At first, I didn't know which twin it was.

Samuel was the cocky, arrogant jock, while Saxon was the quiet, arty type.

When a coiled smile touched his lips, I realized I was creepily staring, so I quickly stopped being a weirdo and smiled. I wish some kind of coherency followed that smile because when I saw a tattered copy of The Catcher in the Rye clutched to his chest, I blurted out, "I need that."

My cheeks instantly reddened as I corrected, "I meant, I need that book."

I never thought a laugh could be sexy, but my opinion on sexy laughs soon altered when the hottie twin opened his mouth. "Well, in that case, here you go." He chuckled as he handed me the book.

I looked down at it, focusing on his hands; the flecks of dirt underneath his fingernails making him appear even more manly. When he waved the book, highlighting that I was once again staring at him like a creeper, I quickly reached for it, accidentally brushing against his fingers. A zing, a spark, an electrical current zapped through me, rendering me useless as I dropped the book to the floor.

Absolutely mortified, I lunged for it the same time he did and we ended up bumping foreheads. As he reached out to save me from face planting, I felt that spark, those butterflies once again taking flight within my belly, and it took all my willpower not to turn to putty in his hands.

This encounter was not how I wanted our first meeting to go, but his smirk made me feel…beautiful. I've never felt that way before. I know I'm only sixteen, but Piper has made it to second base with two guys, while I haven't even been offered a place on the team.

It was like I was in a movie. Staring into each other's eyes, nothing existing but us. I nervously licked my lips, my braces suddenly sticking to my dry mouth.

"You can keep it for as long as you like."

His deep voice reminded me where I was, and I smiled. "Thank you. I promise to return it asap."

"No worries, Lucy. I know you'll take good care of it." He knew my name! It took all my willpower not to break into a happy dance right then and there. And how did he know I'd take good care of it? Has he been watching me?

I wanted to subtly ask which twin he was, but his confidence had me guessing it was Samuel. When he shouldered his backpack and I saw an orange basketball wedged inside, I knew I was right, as Samuel was the captain of the basketball team.

The bell sounded, ending our weird, yet electrifying encounter. "I'll catch you around, little Lucy Tucker."

dies

He stood, obviously waiting for me to reply, but I didn't know what to say. I was still obsessing over the fact he knew who I was. He rewarded me with a dimpled smirk before turning around.

My mouth acted before my brain could join the party and I exclaimed, "What topic did you choose to write your paper on?" I wasn't going to copy him, I just…I needed to talk to him one more time. I needed to know this was real.

Turning over the shoulder, he grinned, and I swear, I've never seen a more striking sight. "Ask her if she still keeps all her kings in the back row."

I know the quote well, but somehow, it felt like the line took on a double meaning. I didn't bother replying, as I'm pretty sure my response would have been, 'I love you.'

He waved goodbye...that mysterious, dimpled grin the last thing I saw as he walked out the door. It took me about two minutes before I could breathe normally again.

August 5th 2004

Dear diary,

I've finished my paper, but I don't want to give Sam's book back just yet. The longer I hold onto it, the longer I have to gather the guts to talk to him. At lunch, I saw him enter the library, and like a complete stalker, I followed.

I watched the way he silently sat, contentedly reading whatever text book his head was buried in.

Piper's words came back to haunt me.

"Just talk to him. You've been obsessing over Samuel Stone for months. This is your in." She was right.

With that thought in mind, I pulled back my shoulders and sauntered through the library like I was Cindy Crawford. However, when he lifted those eyes and met mine with confusion, I stopped, my confidence nose-diving.

He stared at me, and like a love struck fool, I stared back. I should have averted my gaze, but I couldn't. I don't know how long I stood in the middle of the room because time stood still. I was staring into the eyes of my future.

When my future smiled and waved, I internally high-fived myself and waved back. I had come this far—what was a few more steps?

When I sat down next to him, I was cocooned in his fragrance. It took all my willpower not to take a big whiff.

"How's the paper coming along?" he asked.

I instantly felt bad for lying, but I couldn't give up this feeling, not yet.

"It's going slow."

Sam smiled and the earth stopped spinning. "I can give you a hand if you like?"

"Yes, I like," I replied a little too quickly. In no way was I referring to the paper.

Realizing that him helping me with a paper that was already written was not going to work, I quickly amended, "Actually, you're in my math class too, aren't you?"

He held up his math text book in response.

"Maybe you could help me with that instead? I think I've got English covered, but algebra is another story."

His laugh was deep, genuine. It sent chills all through my body. "Sure, I can do that."

He hunted through his backpack, producing a notebook and a pen. "What don't you understand?"

"All of it," I replied with a smirk.

That weird static began bouncing between us, and when he leaned forward,

I stopped breathing. "Well, you're lucky I've got a free period. What's your favorite number?"

"Seven."

"All right. Let's start with something familiar then."

All I could do was nod when he smirked. I don't know why, but being there with him was an occurrence I wanted to become familiar with—daily.

An hour later, I was no better at understanding algebra, but I was better at understanding my feelings for Sam were real. I was desperate to see him again, so I did something I've never done before.

"Did you maybe want to have lunch with me tomorrow?" My voice was high-pitched, completely uncool. Just as I was going to backtrack, embarrassed I let my fantasy of living happily ever after get the better of me, Sam nodded.

"Sure, Lucy. I'd like that."

"Really?" I didn't hide my surprise.

"Yes, really." His response made me smile.

I feel so comfortable around him. I think its love. 😍

August 6th 2004

Dear Diary,

Its official—I'm in love with Samuel Stone!

Our lunch date was just that— a date. I don't know if Sam was aware it was just that, but to me, it was my first date, and it was perfect.

We chatted about everything—well, I chatted, and he listened. Just when I thought I was boring him, he'd ask me another question, appearing genuinely interested in my life.

The entire school was watching us. All the girls were jealous that someone like Sam was talking to me. But he didn't even seem to notice or care. All he seemed to care about was me.

When the bell rang, I couldn't hide my disappointment. I just spent the best thirty minutes of my life talking to the boy of my dreams.

Just when I thought my day couldn't get any better, Sam reached into his pocket and pulled out a silver necklace. When he handed it to me, I think I actually choked on my raspy breaths.

So here I sit, fingering the silver seven around my neck, unable to stop smiling as I think about Sam nervously explaining how he saw this and thought of me. He played it off as a joke, saying it was a good luck charm to help me pass my test, but we both knew what this meant.

We both have weird, messy, inexplicable feelings for one another, and nothing has felt sweeter.

I'm never going to take this necklace off. It may (according to Sam) only have cost five bucks, but as long as I live, this will forever be my good luck charm.

August 10th 2004

Dear diary,

O M G! I went out for coffee with Sam!

I saw him in the corridor, basketball under his arm, and thought it was about time I gave his book back. I was wearing the necklace underneath my t-shirt, afraid Sam might have regretted giving it to me. But when he smiled and suggested I give him the book back over coffee, I knew things were never going to be the same.

We met at Starbucks, not the most romantic of places, but I was with Sam and I didn't care. We chatted about everything—he said he'd love to go horseback riding with me one day as his family owned a farm. I realized I must have chewed his ear off about my love for riding on our lunch date, and suddenly felt embarrassed. I just felt so comfortable around him—like I could be myself and tell him anything.

He mentioned Saxon, his twin brother. I don't know why, but I got the distinct feeling they don't get along. He said they look identical, but on the inside, they're nothing alike. I wanted to press, ask for more info because Saxon seemed really nice. He was painfully shy, and didn't really socialize with anyone, but the few times we spoke, he was actually really sweet and funny.

After Sam made it clear he didn't want to talk about Saxon, he told me it was his dream to get a basketball scholarship, and if he had his way, he'd leave Montana as soon as he turned eighteen. I tried not to look too disappointed, but the thought of him leaving left a gaping hole in my chest.

He completely surprised me when he said, "But things change. Maybe there's a reason for me to stay."

Could that reason be me? A girl can only hope.

Three

My confession has the room dropping to an unpleasantly cold temperature.

Dr. Kepler ignores the sudden discomfort. "Splendid news. As soon as he gets here, and he's willing of course, one of the nurses can take his blood. We can also discuss the details about organ transplants."

Greg clears his throat once again. "Our son, doctor…he's estranged. We haven't seen him in over a year. Last we heard, he was living in South Carolina. I doubt he'd be willing to help his brother out." Kellie sniffles.

"Oh." Dr. Kepler finally understands the uneasiness. "Well, if anything changes, please let me know." He excuses himself, most likely not interested in tangling himself in a family feud.

But that's the thing. There never has been a feud per se. Saxon and Samuel may be identical on the outside but on the inside, they're universes apart.

From the moment I met them, there was an invisible tension there. It just grew and grew the older they got. I haven't seen Saxon since he left his family's farm on Thanksgiving when there was the usual talk of Saxon taking over the farm with Samuel. Saxon has always wanted his own identity, to be different to his twin—it's just a shame that to find that individuality, he pushed all the people who love him aside.

Sam never spoke about Saxon, as I know it's a topic he prefers to steer clear of, but deep down, I can see it hurts to have his twin brother hate him for no apparent reason. But regardless of their differences, Samuel needs blood, he needs Saxon's blood. And I'm going to get it.

"Kellie, have you let Saxon know?" I ask, pushing down my sorrow and focusing on Sam's survival. She raises her blue eyes and guiltily shakes her head. I'm not usually this forceful, but when it comes to something I feel passionate about, I can't help but lead with my emotions. "May I use your phone to call him?" Kellie peers over at Gregory, who nods.

We may not like it, but we need Saxon. I choose to believe he's not all bad. He can't be. He's connected in the most intimate way to the most amazing, considerate person in the world. He's a part of Sam, and I can only hope that part will overthrow the malice.

All eyes are on me and I suddenly feel nervous. Saxon and I have never really had much of a relationship, and if I were to be honest, I would even go so far to say he's never really acknowledged me at all. I've always felt invisible around him. My attempts to talk to him proved fruitless because the more I talked, the more he pulled away. I know I'm not the type of person he would usually associate with, as the female company he's kept in the past have been polar opposites of who I am. They've all been tall, big breasted, and their lack of clothing matches their lack of maturity and wisdom—but that's the type of girls he seemed to be drawn to.

Samuel never judged his brother for his promiscuity and accepted him for who he was. That's the type of person Sam is. It's just a shame Saxon couldn't do the same, as he never really accepted me. But now is not the time to dwell on our strained relationship. Now is the time to act on a vow I was so ready to take.

In sickness and in health I remind myself as I step out into the hallway to make the call. My heart thrashes stridently while the blood whooshes through my ears as I listen to the dial tone.

Please pick up, I silently beg. He *has* to pick up.

The moment I hear his deep, rugged voice, I don't know whether to celebrate or cry. It's so much like Samuel's, but at the same time, it's not. "Whatever you have to say, I'm pretty certain I don't want to hear. Goodbye, Kellie."

"No, no, wait!" I screech on a rushed breath. "Don't hang up, Saxon! It's me, Lucy." When I'm greeted with silence, I yank the phone from my ear to ensure he's still on the line.

He is.

"Lucy?" He doesn't conceal his complete surprise.

"Yes, it's me. Lucy Tucker," I foolishly clarify.

"I know who you are, Lucy," he replies, making me feel even stupider. "What do you want?"

His clipped response is exactly what I needed to concentrate on the task at hand. Deciding to use the words my mother did, I take a deep breath before revealing, "There's been an accident."

Silence.

"Are you okay?"

I wasn't expecting that response. "Yes, I'm fine. It's Samuel." My voice breaks, my courage nose diving as my eyes fill with tears.

"What about him?"

Slouching against the wall, I sadly divulge, "He's in a c-coma. It was our wedding day today. I don't know if you knew?" We sent Saxon an invite, but we never got an RSVP.

"I'm well aware," he coldly replies.

"Oh?" Maybe our invite got lost in the mail. "Well, he was on the way to the church and…a drunk driver ran him off the road," I continue, taking deep breaths between each sentence. "It's bad, Saxon."

Another pregnant pause.

"Son of a bitch," he finally mutters.

"We need you here." I don't care that I'm begging.

"Why?" he spits, not masking his contempt.

I push off the wall, incensed. "Why? Did you not hear me? Samuel is in a coma."

"And what am I supposed to do about that?"

I can't believe my ears. "You're supposed to be here, supporting your brother, just how he would if the tables were turned!" My anger is spiking, which is a nice change from wanting to cry myself into oblivion.

He scoffs. "I doubt that. Look, Lucy, I'm sorry you're upset, but there's nothing I can do."

"That's where you're wrong," I blurt out. "Samuel needs your blood! And maybe a kidney!" I curse the moment the insensitive words leave my lips. "I didn't mean—" But it's too late.

"So if Samuel didn't need me, I'm guessing no one would have called?" My silence speaks volumes. "Did Kellie put you up to this?"

"What? No, of course not! Even if he didn't need your blood, someone would have called you," I reply, hoping I'm right.

"Don't count on it."

Rubbing my forehead, I know he's right. The fact Greg and Kellie were so reluctant to call Saxon reveals they were probably in no hurry to tell him. We're all in shock, but Saxon had every right to know the moment it happened. What he decided to do with that piece of information was entirely up to him—just as it's within his rights to say no if he doesn't want to help his brother.

"Okay, I understand." I sigh, hating that I've failed Samuel. "I'm sorry to have bothered you."

I want to kick and scream, beg him to change his mind, but I know Sam wouldn't want me to. No matter their differences, Samuel always respected his brother's wishes. When Saxon ignored Samuel's continuous contact attempts, Sam didn't press. He said everyone is entitled to their opinions and choices, just as Saxon is entitled to being a total jerk.

"I'm sorry, Lucy."

I don't know what he's apologizing for, but I accept his apology. "I can text you with updates—if you want me to, of course." As I look through the sliver of glass on Samuel's door, I give it one last try. "If you change your mind, not about the blood thing, but if you want to come see him, he's at St. John Memorial hospital. I know he would love to see you."

The line goes dead.

I run a hand down my face, attempting to rub away my epic fail.

The door opens and Piper steps out, looking how I feel. "How'd it go?"

"Awful," I confess. Today, I've gone through a range of emotions, but right now I just feel numb. "I have to see Samuel. He needs me."

Piper nods, but I can sense something is on her mind—the perks of knowing someone for the majority of your life. She has never approved of me dating Sam, and usually, I can respect her opinion, but not today. "Luce, you should go home. Before you bite my head off—" she raises her hands in surrender "—I just meant how about you shower, grab something to eat and a change of clothes, and then come back when you've had time to digest this."

I know she means well, but I'm not going anywhere. "I'm not leaving Samuel, Piper. They can kick me out, and I'll still loiter outside his door. Outside this damn hospital if I have to."

She doesn't argue, which surprises me. "Well, how about I swing past your place and grab you a change of clothes?"

Looking down at my current attire, I realize she's right. This isn't really appropriate hospital wear, and when Samuel wakes, I don't want him seeing me like this. A reminder of what was lost. "Okay, that'll be great. Thank you. Can you please pack a few days' worth of clothes? And maybe bring in some of Sam's stuff, too? That gown is so..." I can't finish that sentence without wanting to cry.

"Of course." She dabs at her eyes, her mascara running down her porcelain cheek.

I suddenly realize I didn't even compliment her on how beautiful she looks as my maid of honor. I remember how excited we were when picking out her pink pastel gown. The soft silk slid underneath our fingertips as we both agreed it was 'the one.' Her long brown hair is curled, hugging her heart shaped face, a face which I've loved for more than half of my life. She only needed a whisper of makeup as anything else paled in comparison to her natural beauty. "You look beautiful, Piper. Best maid of honor. Ever."

Her tears mirror mine. "You're the one who's beautiful, Lucy. Inside and out." We hug, not masking our sadness, and not ashamed for the world to know our sorrow. But through sorrow, I'll find strength, the strength for both Samuel and I to survive.

★ ★ ★ ★ ★

Hushed voices stir me from a very vivid dream. A nightmare, in fact.

I dreamt Samuel and I never married because he was in a coma. He was drowning in a dense pool of the unknown, and I couldn't save him. No one could. The only person who could save him was himself.

Just as I'm about to bask in Sam's signature fragrance and wake him up with a kiss, the low voice sounds once again. "That poor girl, can you believe her fiancé was involved in a car accident on the way to the church?"

Gasp. "No?"

"Ah ha. She came here in her wedding dress. Her entire family were dressed in their Sunday best with no place to go."

"Oh, that's terrible. Tragic. Have you read his chart?"

"Yes. Doesn't look good. When he wakes, he won't be the same man he once was."

"*If* he wakes."

No…no…no!

I demand my body to wake from this awful nightmare, but I can't because I *am* awake. This horrible reality is real—it's my reality. My mind allowed me a moment of reprieve, but now I'm back—back in hell.

I fake sleep as the nurses prattle on about Samuel's condition, each word tearing down the pillars of strength I tried so hard to build.

When they finally leave, I raise my weary head from the mattress and peer up at Samuel, who is illuminated by the soft glow of the light above his head. Slipping my hand into his still one, my engagement ring catches the light, confirming what I have to do as I vow, "They're wrong, Sam. You will wake and when you do, everything will be all right. I won't give up on you, on us. I promise." My eyes are dry, I can no longer cry.

I don't know whether he can hear or feel me, but I don't care. Squeezing his fingers, a new sense of determination hums through my body and I vow to prove those nurses, those doctors wrong.

Four

Day four is absolutely no better than day one, two, or three, especially since there's been no change in Samuel's condition. Dr. Kepler said this was perfectly normal and these things take time, but I was impatient. I was also a woman on a mission to do all I could to speed up any small progress Sam might make.

I had read that many people who came out of a coma confirmed they could hear and sense everything that was going on around them. They may not have been able to communicate, but they were very aware of the world moving around them. This fact cemented what I had to do.

Since my discovery, I made it my job to talk to Sam every chance I got. And if I wasn't talking, or reading, or singing to him, his parents, my parents, his friends—hell, even books on audio and my iPod were doing it for me. It didn't matter that there were no improvements. It just felt good to know I was doing something to help Sam. I've barely left his bedside, only taking a break when I needed to use the restroom or stretch out my legs. But I wouldn't have it any other way.

Today he's listening to a mix of Top 40 on my iPod. I figure if anyone can wake someone from a coma it's the annoying voice of Kanye West.

I'm sitting in the world's most uncomfortable chair doing a crossword puzzle. My aching muscles scream in protest as I tuck my leg beneath me, getting comfortable for another long day ahead. Just like I do every other day, I plan on replaying our future to Sam. I share my dreams and goals, and where I see us in fifty years. It doesn't matter that he can't reply because I know he feels the same way. I avoid talking about the past, as I only want to focus on our future.

"Okay, I need your smarts to help me with two across, nine letters. Phonological awareness consists of…blank…and analysis skills." I tap my pencil against the paper, racking my brain for the answer.

I peer up while I'm in the midst of asking for a little help, but I suddenly freeze, wheezing in utter disbelief. As the painful seconds tick by, I'm almost afraid to breathe. And I'm definitely too frightened to move. But when I see it again, I jar upright, rubbing my eyes.

"Sam?" I whisper, terrified that what I saw was my imagination playing a cruel trick.

Rising at a pace akin to a sloth, my eyes never waver

from Samuel as I beg him to do it again. I beg him to…move his eyelids. It was a mere flicker, but it was a flicker of hope. "Samuel, can you hear me? It's Lucy."

I stand, blinking in disbelief as I swallow down my panic and sheer anticipation at what comes next. Shuffling closer and closer, with arms rigid by my side, I furl my fingers into my palms, my nails imprinting crescent moons into my flesh. But I welcome the pain as it confirms that this is real.

"Sam?" The air is charged with a heavy undercurrent, weighing down my entire soul. I gasp and almost fall over my feet. I saw it. The flicker of hope shines brighter than before.

Diving for the call button, I buzz the nurse before skidding on the linoleum as I run towards the door. "I need a doctor!" I shout louder than I have ever bellowed before. The entire hallway looks my way, the nurses thankfully understanding that this is an emergency as they scamper off in different directions.

Dashing back into Sam's room, I sprint over to his bed, securing his hand in mine. "Sam, can you hear me? Squeeze my hand if you can." With everything that I am, I will him to give me a sign that he can hear me. Please god, give me a sign.

"What's happened, Ms. Tucker?" Dr. Kepler asks, rushing into the room.

"He moved his eyes!" I reveal, clutching Sam's hand. "Three times, I think! But definitely twice."

"Did he open them?" He reaches into his pocket and produces a pen light. He politely pushes me aside.

"No, but his eyelids flickered. That's a good sign, right? Right?" I ask again, almost begging when he doesn't answer.

I intently watch on, biting my nails as Dr. Kepler gently lifts Sam's upper eyelids and moves the light from side to side. "Samuel? Can you hear me?" he shouts, continuing his examination. "Samuel Stone, can you hear me?" Removing the ear buds, he claps loudly, inches from Samuel's temple.

The wait is excruciating and I bounce on the spot, looking over his shoulder, awaiting a sign. Nurses and another doctor come charging in, pushing me against the wall as they frantically talk about things I have no knowledge about. They tear off Sam's sheet, ignoring his modesty as they run a gadget which looks like a knitting needle along the soles of his feet.

The room is pandemonium for minutes, but when the panic dies down and they replace the blanket, tucking Samuel back in, I know the news is not good.

"Doctor?" I ask, beseeching him to tell me good news.

He sighs, writing something down on Sam's chart. "Ms. Tucker, nothing has changed."

"No, that can't be." I point to Samuel's bed. "There must be some mistake. I saw it. His eyes, they moved."

Tucking his pen into his top pocket, he shakes his head. "What you saw was a muscle spasm. It's quite common."

"But, but it's never happened before." The rational part of my brain is telling me to shut up and believe him because he's the doctor. But my heart can't, it won't accept it. "Are you sure?"

My lower lip quivers and I choke back my tears.

"I'm sorry. I really wish I had better news. He didn't respond to stimuli, light, or sound. His pupils show no response. And his brain activity is still inactive." He lowers his eyes, breathing heavily through his nose.

A hot tear scores my flesh as it rolls down my cheek.

"I really am sorry." He closes the door behind him, leaving me alone with my broken dreams. I feel a fool. Even though I know what I saw, it doesn't matter. A muscle spasm obviously means jack shit in the world of medicine.

A river of sadness cascades down my cheeks. I don't bother wiping them away. Peering over at a comatose Samuel, I irrationally feel angry at him for not waking up. I'm giving him my all while he's barely trying. But I know this absurdity is my emotions toying with my head.

I amble over to the window and press my forehead to the cool glass. I close my eyes. I remember the last memory I have of Samuel, the last words he spoke. 'I love you so much. Never forget, you're the reason why I smile.'

My heart breaks. Actually, it doesn't just break; it shatters into a million irreparable pieces. I don't know how I'm going to get through this. I've tried to be strong, but I can't do this. I can't go on without him.

I can't say goodbye. I can't.

"Lucy?"

A strangled sob gets tangled in my tears because that

husky, rugged voice—no, it can't be. I don't want to believe because the last time I had faith, it was premature and cruel. But that masculine, familiar bouquet, there is no mistaking that fragrance *is* infusing the air.

Nothing else matters but turning around. And I do. I spin around so quickly I almost fall flat on my face. However, when I see who stands before me, I know I'm seconds from tumbling like a leaf in fall.

It can't be, but it is.

Those sea green eyes, licked with a curving swirl of gray, belong to the one man I didn't even know I was so desperate to see. He shuffles his motorcycle booted feet uncomfortably while running his long fingers over his dark stubble. I know my staring is incredibly impolite, but I can't stop. I'm afraid once I'll blink, he'll disappear.

"Hi, Lucy."

Our body language tangos in an unfamiliar, yet familiar dance, and when he lifts his chiseled chin, I'm pinned with the stormiest stare of a man who exudes nothing but confidence and allure. The bright fluorescents reveal his eyes are akin to that of angry storm clouds, but they're also licked with a touch of a soft Russian blue floating in a sea of tranquil waters.

His dirty blond hair is longer on top with shorter sides. It's kicked to the left, the mussed locks falling over his eye and framing his jagged face. He looks rugged and dangerous, someone who oozes trouble. The colorful, intricate tattoo sleeve running down his right arm perfects the bad boy look. He is the complete opposite of Samuel.

"Saxon?"

When he nods slowly, his jaw firm, I gasp, crossing both hands over my mouth. My brain knows this isn't my Sam, but my heart, my whimsical center, won't accept it.

"Sorry for turning up unannounced. I should have called. Do you want me to go? I can leave if you want me to." He hooks a thumb towards the door.

I'm speechless as I'm experiencing my personal state of unexpected nirvana.

But Saxon mistakes my euphoria for disgust. "I shouldn't have come." He spins on his heel, racing towards the door.

Loud alarm bells sound in my ears; it's the wakeup call I needed. Looking over at Samuel, who is lying still and docile, I realize I need to touch the same life source that flows through his veins.

My shoes pound on the floor as I sprint towards Saxon, still wordless, but a mission firm in mind. The moment he turns, I throw myself into his arms, and just like I knew he would, he catches me.

Five

I DON'T KNOW HOW LONG I stay nestled in Saxon's arms. His heavy heartbeat is surprisingly comforting.

Everything about him is so familiar, yet so foreign. His scent is rugged, earth peppered with a trace of cigarettes, while Samuel's was always more refined, sometimes a little heavy handed with the cologne. His brawny frame is stronger, almost too firm, but he's always been the bigger brother. It's not a bad feeling, it's just…different.

I'm surprised at how easily I can compare and contrast the similarities and differences between them, considering I barely know Saxon. Although they are like night and day, and silence and sound, they are both my heaven and hell. Saxon is here to save my Samuel.

"Saxon?" Kellie doesn't hide her surprise at seeing her eldest son. Her clipped tone has us both pulling apart uncomfortably.

"Hey, Kellie." He turns around to face her, while I feel my cheeks heat. Now that I'm somewhat coherent, I realize I probably should have greeted Saxon with a handshake, rather than clinging to him like a spidermonkey. But I don't regret it. I feel closer to Sam for some unexplained reason.

"What are you doing here?" Even I cringe when I hear her unpleasant tone.

"I'm here to see my brother," Saxon replies sharply. "And I'm here because you need my blood."

Kellie's scowl transforms into a smile. "Oh, Saxon. I knew you would see sense." She rushes over to him, throwing her arms around him. I don't fail to notice the difference between our unions.

Saxon stands rigid, arms pinned to his side, while Kellie ignores his lack of feeling. Gregory strolls in a moment later, almost dropping the tray of coffees he holds. "Saxon?"

"He's here to help Samuel, Greg," Kellie exclaims, letting Saxon go and wiping the tears from her eyes.

Greg stands motionless, digesting what was just said. "Is it true, son?" he finally asks moments later.

Saxon nods with resolution.

I feel like I'm encroaching on a very private moment, but I don't dare move.

Greg's eyes fill with tears and in two long strides, he's across the room, throwing his arms around Saxon. The embrace has my heart feeling heavy.

Saxon's eyes lock with mine, but I can't decode what he's feeling. I know the last time he saw his parents harsh words were exchanged, but it appears they're pushing those memories aside. But when Greg lets go, Saxon stands stiff, appearing unmoved by the reunion.

I guess time doesn't heal all wounds.

As Kellie goes on to inform Saxon about the events of the past four days, he makes no secret that he's openly staring at me. I silently move off to the side and lean against the wall, unable to tear my gaze from Saxon.

His strong jaw line is coated with a dark scruff, which seems to highlight the pinkness of his full, slightly downturned mouth. A small scar licks the curve of his upper bowed lip and I wonder how he got it. His nose is straight, evenly sloped, but his eyes are what I'm mesmerized by. They're conflicted. They yearn for annoyance, but they're not, they look relieved, and I can't help but wonder why.

Realizing I'm staring, I pull out my cell and shoot a quick text to my mom, informing her of the latest news, including Sam's muscle spasm. The thought has me sighing aloud. How long is Saxon going to stay? Now that he's here, I don't want him to leave. If anyone can pull Samuel out of his coma, I know it's Saxon. They're identical twins, for god's sake. They're replicas of one another. Surely he can sense what Sam is feeling. Surely he's the one to bring my Sam back to me.

Dr. Kepler walks into the room, doing a double take when

he sees Saxon. "The twin brother, I assume?"

Kellie beams, nodding animatedly. "Yes, Doctor, this is my other son, Saxon. He's here to donate his blood. And also, an organ if needed."

I don't know if I'm just on edge, but Kellie's disrespect towards Saxon irks me. He's not just a walking donor, he has feelings too. His twin brother is lying in that hospital bed, comatose. I'd like to think that affects him just as it affects us all.

Kellie's comment appears to roll off Saxon's back however. "Just tell me where to go, and I'll happily roll up my sleeve. The sooner I get this over with, the sooner I can leave."

His remark churns my stomach. I need to talk to him; I need to beg him to stay. "I'll come with you," I offer a little too quickly. The entire room turns to look at me. "I need some fresh air," I add, which is a complete lie.

Dr. Kepler nods, giving us instructions on where to go. As he informs Greg and Kellie about Samuel's progress, or non-progress, I reach for my pink cardigan and walk out the door. Saxon's heavy footsteps follow me.

We walk side by side in silence, stopping once I push the call button for the elevator. Thankfully, we don't have long to wait, and I charge inside once the doors open. The silence continues on in the cart, grating on my already shot nerves.

I try not to make it too obvious as I observe him closely. So alike, yet so unlike Sam. Saxon has an air of confidence about him, a natural magnetic charm that have people turning heads the moment he walks into a room. But the thing is, I doubt Saxon realizes just how captivating he is.

"Thanks for coming, Saxon," I say, needing to drown out the static. "I know Sam appreciates you being here. So do I."

He nods, looking above him at the floors passing by, but doesn't say a word.

"Did you have far to come?" I ask, deciding to pose a question so he has to speak.

He digs his hands into his ripped jeans pockets. The action has me tilting my head to the side, attempting to decode some of the obscure artwork inked on his arm. I can make out a queen chess piece. "I rode my motorcycle from Oregon."

His comment has me lifting my head. "Oregon? Your dad said you were living in South Carolina."

He scoffs, running the longer strands of hair through his fingers. "He has no idea about my life."

I'm quiet, mulling over his revelation. "How long have you been there?"

"Over two years."

His clipped response is a sure sign he doesn't want to talk about this, but I continue to delve. "Do you like it there? What about work?"

His gaze is still rooted to the flashing floors as we descend. "It's as good as any other place I've lived. I work at a garage."

"Oh, you're a mechanic?" I remember he always liked tinkering around on anything that moved. "I remember—"

But he abruptly cuts me off. "Look, Lucy." He turns to face me while I jolt backward. "I'm not here for a social visit. I'm here to do my bit, and then I'm gone. Please don't feel obligated to talk to me, or try to get to know me. I'll be out of your hair soon enough and your perfect little life can return to normal."

My mouth falls open. "*Excuse me*?" He doesn't know me, and he certainly has no clue about my so-called perfect life. "Perfect life? You have no idea what you're talking about. Maybe if you had actually acknowledged me over the years and spoken to me, rather than grunt your way through my attempts at talking to you, you'd see my *perfect little life* isn't so perfect after all!"

He has the gall to smirk, angering me further. So much for our heartfelt reunion.

"So you and your bit can shove it, we don't need your help! Samuel needs people around his bedside who want to be there, not people who are keeping score of who helped who." I end my rant with an exasperated huff. I've never ranted before, well, not like this anyway. It feels good.

The elevator stops, the doors opening and allowing unsuspecting people into a spontaneous cage match. The rest of our journey is traveled in silence.

I wait with Saxon as he generously gives blood, trying not to scowl at him because regardless of his assholeness, he's still here, helping Samuel. The young nurse is shamelessly flirting with him, asking him a million and one questions as she labels the vials of blood she took. Unlike when *I* asked him about his life, he's answering her questions politely.

"So you ride a Harley, that's so cool," she gushes, watching him as he rolls his sleeve over his humongous bicep. "I'd love to see it."

"Sure thing. Any time you want a ride, let me know." He smirks cockily.

I lean back in my seat, crossing an ankle over my knee as I roll my eyes. So he's staying now? To give Nurse Bimbo a ride? I hate to think of what kind of ride he'll give her. On that note I stand, wanting to get back to my comatose fiancé who is far more interesting than watching the nurse make googly eyes at Saxon.

My chair scraping along the floor interrupts the love fest. "I'm going back to see Samuel." I half expect Saxon to push me out the door and lock it behind me, but I'm surprised when he stands too.

He appears to be weighing up what to say, which confuses me. "Okay, I'll come with you."

Nurse Bimbo doesn't hide her disappointment. "Oh, I have my break in ten minutes. Maybe you could wait for me?" I do a double take when I see a button on her scrub suit has mysteriously come undone. Some women really have no shame.

I've never been a girly girl. I've always been more comfortable in jeans and a t-shirt, rather than a dress and high heels. The only makeup I ever wear is a light dusting of foundation to cover my freckles, mascara, and lip balm, and on some days, that's too much. I'm a no-frills kind of girl, but I'm me—little Lucy Tucker. And I'm comfortable with that person.

Nurse Bimbo over here needs a spoonful of humility. Or maybe a mirror to wipe off her clown inspired makeup. I scold myself for such thoughts as I'm not usually a catty person. "Or you could just wait in here?" she suggests, leaving nothing to the imagination.

This awkward situation is suffocating me and I shuffle my feet, feeling like the third wheel. Saxon must be able to read my uneasiness because he doesn't take the bait, which again surprises me. "I better go." He unscrews the lid of a candy jar, pulling out a heart-shaped lollipop. "You were very gentle with me. Thank you." He accents his sentence with a wink.

I refrain from gagging as I push open the door, welcoming the medicated smell of the sterile hallway as opposed to Nurse Bimbo's overpowering floral stench. An exit has never looked more appealing and I scurry towards it, shouldering open the door.

The warm spring breeze butters my cheeks, and I relish in the warmer weather as it thaws out the constant chill. I ignore the fact that if all went to plan Sam and I would be in Costa de Galicia in the north of Spain, enjoying white sandy beaches and absolute seclusion from the outside world. But that's nothing but a dream.

Piper has been a life saver and made the dreaded calls,

informing all parties of my current situation. Of course there are no refunds, but the owner of the villa we planned to stay in has kindly rolled over our funds, stating we're always welcome to take a belated honeymoon when the time is right. Thinking about Samuel and his condition, who knows if and when that'll ever occur.

"I'm sorry."

A red lollipop dances into view, and I look down at it, cocking an eyebrow. "What's this for?"

"It's to apologize for being an asshole to you earlier," Saxon explains, waving the sucker.

"Oh, so it's bribery candy?" He chuckles, and the sound—it hurts. It's identical to Samuel. Pushing those thoughts aside, I scrunch up my nose. "Thank you but no thank you. I don't know where it's been." I make no attempt to conceal my disgust.

I continue walking but jar to a stop when Saxon touches my arm. "I'm just going to have a cigarette. I'll meet you inside."

Looking down at his hand on my arm, I frown; even his fingers are similar to Sam's. Will I ever be able to stop comparing the two? I doubt it. "I'll wait with you," I offer, not ready to leave this fresh air behind just yet.

We sit on a wooden bench, both quiet, our pensive thoughts filling the space between us. The landscape before us is beautifully green, filled with ponderosa pines and pretty, multi-colored wildflowers. The scenery should give one sitting before it a sense of peace, but the circumstances surrounding why they're here no doubt taint their views—just how it blemishes mine.

How many days, hours, minutes, and seconds will I sit here, wondering what comes next?

"Are you going to be all right?" Saxon asks, a nicotine cloud floating on the gentle wind.

Saxon's intuitive nature surprises me. He's never cared about my well-being in the past, but I suppose we've never been involved in circumstances such as this before.

Deciding to be honest, I raise my shoulders in a candid shrug. "I don't know. I've seen some awful things. I've lived them." I subconsciously pull at my cardigan, just as I do every time I think about my childhood. "But this, this is something that is beyond words. I remember travelling to Ghana on my internship. The injustice there was unbelievable, but those people, they still smiled regardless of their shitty conditions. And they fought for their survival because they had hope. They had hope that one day their luck would change. I look up to them. I am in awe of them because I don't have their mindset, Saxon. I can't smile and I don't have hope. I know if Samuel doesn't—" My voice wavers as I place a hand over my mouth. "If Sam doesn't ever wake, I won't be able to smile ever again. I know that makes me selfish and ungrateful, but I don't know how I'm going to survive without him. There are so many wrongdoings in the world, my situation is so insignificant, but…it's…just not…fair."

I'm sobbing by this stage, ugly tears and nothing less. I should be embarrassed that this is the second breakdown I've had in the span of an hour in front of Saxon, but I'm not. He pulls me into his warm arms, allowing me to cry on his shoulder once again without any judgment.

He can't go. In some weird, inexplicable way he makes me feel better. He makes me feel closer to Samuel and after feeling so detached from him for days, I need that intimacy to go on. "Why are you being so nice to me?" I snuffle into his shoulder.

A husky laughs rumbles in his chest. "Would you prefer I be mean to you instead?" A half laugh, half sob escapes me.

Pulling away, I wipe my eyes, sniffing back my tears. I take a moment not to compare Samuel and Saxon; I take a moment to appreciate the man in front of me. "Where are you staying tonight?"

Saxon doesn't hide his surprise. "At a motel. I was going to head home in the morning."

"You could always stay…with me?" I'm attempting to sound calm, but my heart suddenly begins to race. When his uncertainty is clear, I decide to be honest. "Please…don't go. Stay here. Stay here… with me." I don't know why, but I like having him close.

I'm expecting a refusal; I wouldn't blame him if he did. It's not like Samuel ever went out of his way to salvage their broken relationship. He didn't try hard enough to make amends. Saxon is here because he's the bigger man. He's a good man.

"Okay," he replies a moment later.

"Okay?" I question, my head snapping up. Wisps of hair blow in the breeze as he nods. "Thank you, Saxon. You'll never know how much it means to me." A ghost of a smile touches his lips.

Once again, my meltdown subsides; it appears that Saxon is my unexpected balm. Regardless of this tragedy, I'm going to try and see the light. I don't really know Saxon, but that's about to change. I'm hoping through this tragic loss, I can gain a new friend, a friend who gives me the hope I so need.

"We better go back in." He's right.

Quickly wiping my eyes, I cringe when I see his fitted gray Harley Davidson t-shirt is stained with my tears. "I'm so sorry about being such an emotional wreck. I promise it's the last time."

I start to get up but stop when he reaches out and holds onto my wrist. When I peer down, confused, he unlocks his fingers and slowly unwraps the heart-shaped lollipop, passing it to me a second later with a poignant smile.

This time, I don't object.

★ ★ ★ ★ ★

Saxon followed me home on his bike, much to the disapproval of his mother.

I've never had an issue with Kellie or Gregory, as they've

both treated me with nothing but love and respect. But her disrespect towards Saxon is showing a side to me that I don't particularly like.

I push down those thoughts however when Saxon strolls into the spare bedroom, freshly showered and looking ready for bed. "You didn't have to change the sheets. Believe me; I was lucky to even get a bed in some of the shithole places I've stayed at."

I want to press, ask why he chose to sleep there in the first place, but I don't. We're both dog tired, and I have a feeling the getting to know you part may take a little longer than a night.

"Okay, well, if you need anything, just let me know." I fluff his pillow one final time.

A happy bark sounds before excited toe tapping skids along the floorboards. "Hey, Thunder!" Saxon doesn't hide his excitement when he bends down and pats my dog on the head.

Thunder was a present to me from Samuel on my eighteenth birthday. He lived with the Stones while Samuel and I lived at home, but of course he came to live with us when we finally moved into our home together a little over three years ago.

Thunder makes himself comfortable as he jumps onto the double bed. Saxon laughs a deep, husky laugh, which sends an unanticipated shiver down my spine. I'm trying my hardest to not compare him to Samuel, but it's hard not to. Yes, his hair is longer than Sam's and he's covered in tattoos, but my brain still tricks me into thinking its Samuel standing before me. Wishful thinking, I suppose.

"Goodnight, Saxon," I say once I realize I'm absentmindedly staring at him.

I have no doubt he knows every second thought of mine is comparing him to Samuel, but he doesn't say a word. "Night, Lucy. Thanks again for letting me stay."

He doesn't realize I'm the one who should be thanking him.

When he pulls back the corner of the covers, I take that as my cue to leave. I shut the door, smiling when I hear him talking to Thunder.

The scalding shower is utter heaven, and when I turn off the faucets, I'm so ready for bed. Once I brush my teeth and run a comb through my wet hair, I pad into my bedroom, but abruptly pause in the doorway. Feelings of nostalgia hit me and I frown, saddened that once again I won't be sleeping beside Samuel.

The fact Saxon is sleeping two doors down makes me feel a touch better, and I close the door behind me, reassured. I slip under the covers, my eyes heavy with sleep as I turn to rest on my side. As I reach out to switch off the light, my leather-bound journals, which sit in a box near my bedside dresser, catch my eye.

I started keeping journals the moment I could read and write, and I've retained every single one since. Writing everything down was my form of therapy, my way of dealing with who I was. Some journal entries are too painful to read, detailing the horrific start I had in life, but most detail every happy moment I've shared with the people I love. Most entries are about Samuel, which is why they're sitting in my room.

I'm so afraid that as time goes on without any improvement, I'll forget my memories as they'll be plagued down with a horrible, pain riddled reality. I'm afraid I'll forget Samuel's uplifting smile, contagious laugh, and his generous heart. But most importantly, I'm afraid I'll forget how he made me feel time and time again. I'm afraid I'll forget what it felt like to be connected to another person in a way that shadows any memories I've ever made.

Tears stain the pillow as I reach down and rummage through my box of memories—the only things I have left of Samuel. I run my fingertips over the leather journal I seek before opening it up to a page I've read many times before.

★ ★ ★ ★ ★

December24th/25th 2011

Dear diary,

As I write this, the biggest smile is plastered on my face and I doubt it'll fade any time soon.

Christmas time has always been a special time for me. It was the time I became a Tucker, and as fate would *have it, it'll now be the time I was asked to become a Stone.*

Magic is truly in the air—I can almost touch it. My Christmas angel is sleeping soundly beside me, exhausted after a day that can only be described as magical.

It began with breakfast in bed, my favorite of buttermilk pancakes and strawberries. Once I was done stuffing my face, Sam and I went into town to finish off our Christmas shopping. Much to Sam's dismay, I got Saxon a small gift. Even though Sam hasn't spoken to him in months, I still want to show him that we care. Christmas is about giving and family. I don't think he'll be at our Christmas family meal tomorrow, but regardless, I'll send it if I have to.

Once we were done shopping, Samuel insisted I get a massage as he had a few things to take care of. Thinking back, I should have known he was up to something, but at the time, I was too excited at the chance of being pampered for an hour.

I floated out of the day spa, my body feeling so relaxed and my mind at peace. Once we arrived home, I told Sam I was going to take a nap. It was Christmas Eve and we didn't have any plans—well, none that I knew of. He kissed me on the forehead and said he'd wake me when dinner was ready. I fell into a deep slumber, only waking when the delicious smell of lemon chicken drifted up the stairs.

It was dark out, the full moon shimmering off the white blanket of snow which coated our entire yard. I stood in front of our bay windows for minutes, reflecting on my good fortune. Not a minute goes by where I don't appreciate what I've got, and who I've got. I'm surrounded by so many good people, people I love. And the one I love the most was spoiling me rotten when I smelled spring rolls.

I bounced into the kitchen to see Samuel pouring us two glasses of white wine. A feast was laid out on our marbled kitchen counter. My stomach rumbled in delight.

After we were done eating enough food to feed a small starving nation, we decided to sit in front of the fire and watch a DVD. Samuel let me choose the movie, which again, I should have guessed he was up to something. But I didn't.

My eyes grew heavy halfway through "Pretty In Pink," and before I knew it, I had passed out, using Sam as my cushion. I woke to soft butterfly kisses all over my face, then one big lick. No guessing who the lick was from.

Reaching down, I patted Thunder, burying my fingers into his soft mane. As I stroked his fluff, my fingers passed over his collar, feeling something dangling from it. I didn't recall seeing anything different, so I pried open my eyes, the orange hue from the fire warming me instantly. When Thunder saw I was awake, he jumped on me, giving my face another lick, and it was then that I saw what was hanging from his collar.

A ring.

The flames echoed off the flawless

contours, shooting sparkles across the room. Samuel gently unfastened the string from Thunder's collar while I watched, eyes wide. He offered me his hand and I accepted, slipping my trembling fingers into his. I sat, speechless, waiting for what came next.

He gulped, and I could tell he was so nervous, but he squeezed my fingers and smiled. "I had this long speech planned out about how you make me feel, but nothing was good enough. No words strung together could ever convey how you make me feel."

When he got up and then sunk to one knee, I allowed the floodgates to open and I cried happy tears.

"I love you, Lucy Tucker, so very much. Will you marry me?"

My heart soared and my body sang, it was by far the best moment of my life. "Yes," I sobbed. "I'll marry you, Sam."

If I've ever seen Sam happier, then I can't remember when. He slipped the ring on my finger, tears pricking his eyes. He scooped me up into his arms, kissing me passionately, taking my breath away.

I kissed him back, wrapping my arms around his nape, never wanting to let go.

We made love in front of the fire, our bodies frantic, our love frenzied. When we lay naked, sated and content, I placed my hand out in front of me, admiring my ring and all that it represents. I couldn't wait to be Mrs. Samuel Stone.

Sam nuzzled my hair, kissing me softly on the neck. "Merry Christmas." Our grandfather clock chimed on the hour, revealing that it was indeed Christmas.

Turning to look at my fiancé (yes, fiancé!), I smiled. "Best Christmas present. Ever."

Samuel's expression turned bold as he rolled on top of me, slipping a hand between us, coming to rest at the junction between my legs. "Babe, I haven't even begun." He emphasized his point by running his finger up and down my needy opening.

When he slid down my body, using his

tongue as his guide, I closed my eyes, appreciating that I must have been a very good girl this year as Santa brought me everything I wished for...and more.

Six

THE NEXT DAY, SAXON AND I are sitting by Samuel's bed, arguing over who would win in a fight between Batman and Superman. I'm rooting for Batman, but Saxon is detailing all the reasons why I'm wrong. The conversation is beyond ridiculous, but it's a nice change from sitting around and waiting, wondering if today is the day Sam might open his eyes.

"I cannot believe you're rooting for Batman," Saxon scoffs, leaning back in the plastic seat as he links his hands behind his head. His bulging biceps rival his hero. "Superman would win, hands down. The laser beams he shoots from his eyes would fry Batman in seconds."

I stifle a laugh behind my hand. I can't believe how passionate Saxon is about this. "Fine, Superman's inhuman powers are impressive. But..." I emphasize, hushing his rebuke as I raise my finger. "Batman is far more intelligent and cunning than Superman. He would invent some kind of kryptonite gadget and then it's bye-bye, Superman."

Saxon folds his arms over his broad chest, the bright lights emphasizing his ink. "We seem to be caught in a deadlock. The only way to remedy this is to watch every Batman and Superman movie ever made, read their comics, and then have this discussion once again."

I nod eagerly, as this means Saxon will have to spend more time defending Superman's title.

Last night was the best night's sleep I've had in days. I know it was a false sense of security, but it felt nice having Saxon there. I woke, afraid my house was empty, but the smell of coffee alerted me that Saxon was still there.

We rode in together in my Jeep, as I wanted to ensure Saxon left his bike at home so he couldn't sneak off undetected. I know I'm being selfish, but I can't help it. I meant it when I said he makes everything better.

"Sam's idiocy must be rubbing off on you," Saxon says, snapping my thoughts to the present. When I cock an eyebrow, he smirks. "Sam would always side with Batman. It's a fight that's still ongoing."

His comment has me wondering what went wrong between them. Sam never divulged why they never got along, and I didn't press. I could see how much it hurt him, so I let it be. Even when we were kids, Saxon made himself scarce. Whenever I came in the front door, I could put money on the fact that Saxon was leaving via the backdoor. I always thought he hated me because he was jealous that Sam was spending so much time with me. But now, I'm not so sure.

After yesterday, could it be Saxon felt Samuel was the favored child? Kellie didn't hide her favoritism and made it more than obvious she was happy to see Saxon only because he was here to help Sam.

My curiosity gets the better of me. "Did you hate me?"

Saxon chokes on his Coke, mid-sip. He thumps on his chest, coughing.

I probably should have led in with something a little more subtle, but time is precious. Samuel lying in that hospital bed is proof of that.

"Did I hate you?" he repeats when he can breathe again. I nod. "What kind of question is that?"

"An honest one?" I offer with a shrug.

He seems to weigh up his response before replying, "No, Lucy, I didn't hate you."

"Then why did you practically run towards an exit whenever I entered the room?"

His smirk lights up his face. "I hardly ran."

"Okay, walked briskly then," I amend, smiling.

He runs a hand through his hair, leaving behind a mussed, but stylish mess. "I guess I didn't want to be the third wheel. Sam made it clear you were his girl and that he didn't want his older brother cramping his style."

"You're older by two minutes," I state, rolling my eyes playfully. I don't buy his excuse, however. "Did Sam tell you that? That he wanted you gone whenever I was around?" I don't keep the surprise from my voice, as Sam always hinted Saxon kept away by his own will, not because Samuel asked him to.

Saxon pins me with those sea green eyes and I suddenly feel hot. "No, he didn't, but I knew." When he lowers his gaze, I know he's not telling me something. He reveals what a second later. "One of the joys of being a twin is that most of the time, you know what the other is feeling, thinking, wanting, without speaking a word. I'm linked to someone who shares my DNA; I'm bound to share his thoughts, whether I like it or not."

His comment has me leaning forward, sitting on the edge of my seat. "Did you know something happened to Sam before I called you?"

He exhales deeply, tonguing over the jagged scar on his lip. "I think so."

I *was* right. If anyone can drag Sam from this coma, it's Saxon. Excitement bubbles in my belly. "Can you feel him now?" I ask, hoping I don't sound bat shit crazy.

That excitement gets shot to hell however when he frowns. "It doesn't work that way, Lucy."

He's stalling and I know why. "Don't bullshit me, Saxon. Just tell me the truth. I can handle it."

I really wish I'd kept my mouth shut. He senses my resolve and sighs. "No, I can't feel anything. It's…quiet. It's the strangest, most disconcerting feeling. I've never felt this before. No matter how many miles apart we were, I could always feel him. But now, I feel nothing."

I'm trying my hardest to hold back my tears, but one betrays me and sneaks past my walls. I quickly wipe it away.

"I'm sorry, I shouldn't have said anything. I didn't mean to upset you. I'm probably wrong, anyway. It's not like I can read his mind."

"You haven't upset me," I correct. "You're the only person who has given me an answer I understand. The doctors keep treading lightly around me, telling me these things take time, but I can see it in their eyes. I know they believe his chances aren't good. And deep down, so do I." Looking down at my engagement ring, I can't help but feel cheated.

"Hey, don't talk like that." The seat creaks as he rises and walks over to me. He crouches down in front of me when I lower my eyes. "I believe that Samuel *will* wake up. He's too stubborn not to. You've just got to have faith."

When he kindly strokes over my thigh, I glance up, taken aback that Saxon is so…nice. I never doubted that he was nice; I just never realized he was so…intuitive. "You're a good guy, Saxon."

He grins, a dimple hugging his left cheek. "Depends on who you talk to."

No guessing who.

His hand is still on my leg, stroking me, and it feels nice.

Comforting.

"Saxon?" a stunned voice sounds from the doorway. It appears he has that reaction on everyone.

Piper doesn't hide her shock to see him crouched by my feet, stroking my leg. She's met the Saxon we thought we knew, and that Saxon wouldn't be consoling me, telling me to have faith.

He quickly removes his hand and turns his head towards the door. It takes him a second, but he remembers my best friend. "Hey…Piper." He stands, his towering height dwarfing mine.

"Hey yourself," she replies, making no secret she's checking him out. Piper had a major crush on Saxon when we were growing up, but he either didn't notice, or he simply didn't care.

I too rise, rolling my eyes at my friend's lack of shame. "Did you bring me something good to eat?" I ask, peering at the brown paper bag she holds.

Her gaze is still entwined with Saxon's as she replies, "Ah, yeah. I got you some bear claws, donuts, and other unhealthy, sugar-filled goodies." She tosses the bag my way, not caring if I catch it or not.

As strange as this sounds, Piper making puppy dog eyes at Saxon makes me feel a touch better. I've been surrounded by tears and gloom all week; it's nice to have some normality. If what Saxon says is true, I'll be here for the long haul. To avoid being admitted into the bed beside Samuel, I've got to stay connected to the real world and not lose my grip on reality. And at the moment, my reality is my best friend brazenly flirting.

When we were younger, she said it was her dream to marry Saxon because a) he was gorgeous and b) it would make us sister-in-laws. Looks like she's still dreaming.

"How long are you staying?" Piper asks, subtly pulling out her messy pigtails.

Saxon looks over at me briefly while I hold my breath. "I'm not too sure. I'll probably head back in a couple of days."

Couple of days? I hide my disappointment by sticking my head in the bag and retrieving the biggest bear claw in there.

"Where are you staying?"

"Um, with Lucy," he uncomfortably replies.

I tear into the sweet pastry, wondering why staying with me would make him feel uneasy.

"Oh, cool. Maybe I'll swing by one night."

Piper better make it one night soon, seeing as Saxon has no intention of staying. I can't believe he's actually leaving. After my confession yesterday, I thought he'd at least stay a week, maybe two. But it appears I was wrong about him. He doesn't care.

As I shovel half the claw into my mouth, I almost gag on it when Kellie and Gregory stroll through the door. Neither hide their surprise at seeing Saxon.

Kellie brushes past Saxon and Piper and gives me a big hug. My cheeks are puffed out as I try and swallow down my mouthful of food. "How is he?" she asks, rubbing my back.

I don't know why but once again, Kellie is grating on my nerves. Her soft, sorrow-filled tone reminds me where I am, and that Sam's progress is still nada. Of course I'll never forget, but being reminded 24/7 makes everything so much harder to digest.

"No change, Kellie," I reply into her shoulder once I've finished chewing. She lets out a strangled sob.

I subtly pull out of her grip, my gaze fixing on Sam. His strong jaw line is coated with a dark, five o'clock shadow, which is quite unusual for him, seeing as he's almost always clean shaven. I know it's only been a few days, but his face looks thinner, and his skin has a waxen, lifeless appearance. I don't want to admit it, but before long, I know he'll begin deteriorating before my eyes. My strong Sam will be a shell of who he once was.

These thoughts are giving me emotional whiplash, and I don't know how much longer I can deal.

"Would it hurt you to shave, Saxon? And get a haircut," Kellie says, tsking while attempting to comb a hand through his hair. He dodges her attempts to groom him. "I won't even touch on the subject of your clothes. Or tattoos."

Looking at his ripped blue jeans, motorcycle boots, and dark gray t-shirt, I think he looks fine. Sam was a little more conservative, nothing ripped and mostly button down shirts rather than t-shirts, but Kellie can't expect Saxon to be his doppelganger.

"How long will you be staying, son?" Greg asks, walking over to Sam's bed.

The dreaded question has me wishing for another bear claw.

"I'm not sure. I'll probably split tomorrow."

Tomorrow? I thought he said a couple of days.

I can't hide my annoyance as I huff loudly while clenching my jaw to stop my tirade.

Dr. Kepler walks in, not bothering to remind us about the two visitors at a time policy. He reads over Samuel's charts, the same, stone-faced expression as he jots something down while looking at the endless machines. However, I notice something different when he peers over at a machine longer than he usually does.

When he slips on his glasses and moves closer, I feel my heart beginning a steady climb. "What is it, Doctor?" I ask, following him as he steps closer and closer.

His response is, "Interesting."

"What's interesting?" Greg questions, the room falling silent as we all watch with bated breaths.

"How long has this line been this way?" Dr. Kepler asks, pointing to a yellow squiggly line.

I shrug, desperately trying to decode what that line means. We all look at one another, hoping someone has the answers Dr. Kepler seeks. However, when no one speaks, my hope gets trampled on, that is, until Saxon speaks up.

"It changed this morning," he says confidently. "When I was here yesterday, it was close to a flat line, fluttering occasionally. But this morning, I noticed it spiking more frequently."

I'm too caught up in the moment to reprimand him for not mentioning it to me earlier. "What does that mean?" I'm seconds away from dropping to my knees and begging him for good news.

He reaches for the call button. "I need you all to wait outside."

"What's going on?" Greg demands, standing his ground.

"Mr. Stone, I need you to wait outside for a moment," Dr. Kepler repeats. "We're going to run some tests."

"What tests?" Kellie asks, her hand wavering in front of her ruby lips.

He senses we're not going anywhere until he tells us what's going on. "It's too early to make any assumptions, but from what I can see, Samuel has increased brain activity. Like I said, we need to run some tests before I can determine what's going on."

A group of doctors and nurses storm inside, pushing us out of the way. I want to stay, watch every single thing they're doing, but I don't. Saxon is the first to leave, his heavy boots pounding on the floor. Piper follows soon after.

Greg is consoling a grief-stricken Kellie, while I stand by the foot of Samuel's bed, willing him to wake up and come back to me. Finally we leave, Kellie collapsing into a chair outside

Sam's room, Greg hugging her tightly. I don't know where to go, but I know I can't be in here. I can't listen to Kellie's cries, nor can I stand being on the outside as the doctors and nurses talk in a language I don't understand.

With a determined swiftness, I run down the hallway, not looking back, only forward as I shoulder open the door and soar down the staircase. My sneakers pound on the cement as I take two steps at a time. My mind buzzes and whirls the quicker I descend. By the third floor, I'm breathless and my legs ache. But I keep running, desperate to get outside, as that ache can't compare to the throbbing within my chest.

Once I kick open the door, I stop and bend forward to catch my breath, placing my hands onto my trembling thighs. The lack of oxygen to my brain is making me dizzy and I suddenly feel like I want to be sick. Rushing over to a trash can, I fist my hair to one side and attempt to purge out my sickness, but all I do is gag.

Please don't let this be a false sign. I couldn't take it if it were.

I vaguely feel a hand rubbing my back, telling me it's okay, but I can't concentrate on anything other than what Saxon said. He said the line moved yesterday and today. It hasn't moved any other day before, but it moves the day Saxon arrives. That's got to mean something. That's got to be a sign.

Wiping my mouth with the back of my hand, I stand upright, wavering on my feet, feeling nauseous and lightheaded.

Piper steadies me, but I shrug out of her hold when I see Saxon leaning against the brick wall.

"It's you," I state, wielding my finger at him like a crazy person. He stands tall, not backing down from what he knows is about to turn ugly. "Samuel is responding to *you*, Saxon. Don't you see, the day you arrive, he responds. Not on any day prior, just on the day you walked through his door."

"You don't know that. The doctor hasn't even confirmed if that's true yet," he denies, shaking his stubborn head, but his firm jaw reveals he thinks it, too.

"Either way, you can't go. Not now. Please, you have to stay." I charge over to him, ready to beg. His resolve reveals he won't budge, but neither will I. "Please, just stay a week. Or two. Don't give up on him, not yet."

My plea sends Saxon into a fury as he pushes off the wall. "Why should I stay, Lucy? Tell me, what has he—what have any of them done for me? I'm not the son my mother can proudly boast about to her country club socialite friends. I never have been. I'm a disappointment to my father because I refuse to allow him to control my life, and my brother..." He chuckles, but it's not a pleasant sound. "My brother is a stranger to me."

His rage has me reining in my anger because underneath his wrath, I can hear his pain. "I'm not here to apologize for any of them or their behavior. How they've excluded you over the years was wrong, but you've hardly made an effort, either. It's a two-way street."

He resembles an angry bull as his nostrils flare and he huffs raucously.

"But I'm here to beg for your compassion because I know you wouldn't let your brother suffer if you knew you could help him. If you knew that the simple gesture of you just being here by his bedside would wake him up."

"You don't know that!" he yells, spreading his arms out wide.

"Yes, I do!" I shout back, jabbing my finger into his chest. I can be as stubborn and as headstrong as he is.

Piper yanks on my arm, sensing my frustration. "Luce, c'mon, let it go."

But I'm not going anywhere. "I know that underneath your hard exterior lies a good man. I know that because I've seen it. You being here proves it."

"It proves nothing!" he retorts, leaning down, trapping me with his glare. His angry breaths fan out the wisps of silken hair around his face. "I told you, I was here to do my bit, and then I was out of here! I never made any false promises. You knew where I stood."

"Why?" I cry, shoving at his chest with both hands. "What has he done that's so bad that you won't stay? He's your brother!" I'm hysterical by this stage. This outburst is so unlike me, but nothing can stop me.

"Not by choice," he spits, his lip curling. "He may wear my face and share my DNA, but we're nothing, nothing alike."

"I know you feel something for him, Saxon. You told me so today. You told me you can feel him, that you share a connection." My fire is slowly fading, I can smell defeat.

"I also told you that I couldn't feel him, so if what the doctor is saying is true, we share no connection at all. He's dead to me, Lucy!" He grabs my wrist and slams it over his galloping heart. "I…feel…nothing!" He lifts my hand and violently strikes it against his chest between each jagged breath he takes. I suddenly realize he's no longer talking about Samuel, but rather, himself.

He won't surrender. He would rather let some bullshit feud get in the way of doing what's right. "Just go," I say, sniffing back my tears as I yank my hand out from under his.

The air is sizzling with a palpable tension, and if he doesn't leave, I won't be held accountable for my actions.

He starts, "I'm—"

But I cut him off. "Don't you dare say you're sorry. I don't want your apologies. They mean nothing."

His heavy sigh is weighed down like a lead balloon, but he's chosen to keep sinking, not accepting any help.

"If only you knew the whole story, Lucy, you'd understand." But I'm past caring. "You want me to stay and see my brother get better, but where does that leave me afterwards? You all return to your happy, perfect lives, while I go back to what?"

I can't answer that for him.

His exasperated huff slices at my resolve, but I won't back

down.

"Just go, Saxon." I turn my back, shaking my head in disappointment. Piper's lips dip into a sympathetic frown.

After a moment, Saxon's heavy footsteps grow quieter and quieter, indicating he's respected my wishes— he's gone.

★ ★ ★ ★ ★

I'm absolutely exhausted and it's only one o'clock. The moment we round the corner, Kellie yelps and comes charging towards us.

I look behind, fearing Saxon has followed us, but I see he's not there.

"Where's Saxon?" she cries. I scrunch up my nose, not sure why she would want to see him.

"He left," Piper answers for me, while the burn of defeat chokes me.

"No! Where did he go?" She looks over my shoulder, moving her head from side to side to search between the crowds of people.

"I think he went back home, Kellie," I reply, confused by her urgency.

"Shit!" she atypically curses, running back down the hallway and into Sam's room. Her odd reaction has Piper and I both following in hot pursuit.

When we step into Samuel's room, I'm hoping to see him

sitting up and welcoming me into his arms. Sadly, I don't. He's still attached to all the machines, and there are still a group of doctors in white coats observing him.

Kellie is pacing, while Greg runs a hand over his jaw, his eyes glued on the doctors. "What's going on?" I ask, rushing over to him.

My voice snaps him out of a trance. Looking over my shoulder, I know what his question is going to be before he opens his mouth. "Where's Saxon?"

"He left. What's going on, Greg?" I ask, this time not holding back my fear.

I'm seconds away from shaking him when he unevenly replies, "Samuel's brain activity has been mounting in a slow, but steady pattern."

My legs almost collapse out from under me. "That's good news, right?"

He nods. "They believe something, some stimuli triggered this response."

My breathing becomes deeper and deeper. "What stimuli?"

He looks defeated as he reveals, "They've looked over his charts and they believe it was some time yesterday, at around two o'clock."

I close my eyes, my worst fears confirmed.

"What happened at two o'clock yesterday? We think we know, but we need you to confirm it."

Everything is swirling around in my head, a torrential, wild river and I feel like I'm going to drown.

"Lucy? Sweetie? What happened?" Kellie begs, begs that I corroborate what we all know to be true.

The white noise is a steady rhythm, pounding against my skull. I wonder if it feels the same way for Samuel. Thoughts of Sam trapped within his body has me taking a deep breath. This is it. I know the answers—but it doesn't make a lick of difference.

"I think it's Saxon," is all I can say.

Seven

THE REST OF THE DAY is spent holding Samuel's hand, begging him to show any sign, no matter how small, that he can hear me. As expected, I'm faced with radio silence. Doctors and nurses wander in throughout the afternoon, their grim expressions saying it all.

Dr. Kepler confirmed that there has been no further improvement since this morning, and sadly, his current brain activity is stagnant. When I asked him if he believed it was Saxon's presence that triggered the response, he simply said the link between twins is a mystery that only the twins themselves can validate.

Seeing as one twin is comatose, while the other is a selfish bastard, I have to accept it as being a riddle I'll never solve.

As I ascend our pebbled driveway, it's no surprise that Saxon's bike is gone. We've all tried calling him countless times, and we've all come up with nothing. His silence speaks for him, confirming that he doesn't want to help.

Slamming my car door shut, I stagger to the front door, so many emotions plaguing me. At the forefront, I'm disappointed that Saxon turned out to be what I thought he wasn't—an asshole. I don't know what happened to turn him into an asshole, and quite frankly, I don't care.

Pushing open the front door, I slip off my Nikes and amble down the long hallway and into my bedroom. I have no appetite, except for sleep. I decide to have a shower, as I'm desperate to wash away the remnants of this disastrous day.

My shower is quick, as I feel my eyes grow heavy the moment the warm spray massages out the abundant knots in my body. Just as I'm done brushing my teeth, I hear a light rapping on the door. Reaching for the flannel robe off the back of the door, I tie the belt around my waist, covering my penguin print pajama bottoms and frayed Green Peace t-shirt.

I'm not exactly dressed for company, but it could be someone important at my front door. As I turn the porch light on, I gasp, as that someone *is* important, *very* important. My bare feet squeak along the polished floorboards as I race towards the door. Yanking it open, I don't know whether to kick him off my property or welcome him into my home.

"Can we talk?"

"I thought you said all you had to say this afternoon?" I bite back, folding my arms over my chest.

Saxon looks a mess. Most of his disheveled hair frames his downturned face. As if on cue, he brushes a strand behind his ear. “You have every right to be angry at me. I was a complete jerk.”

“Yes, you were,” I agree, seeing no point in being coy. “You seem to be making a habit of it. This time however, no lollipop is going to get you out of it. What do you want?”

He huffs, exasperated. “Can I please come in?”

I want to hate him, but I can’t, especially when those eyes remind me so much of Samuel’s. “Fine.” I step aside, opening the door wider.

He brushes past me, his signature fragrance somehow comforting me, but his confident swagger annoys me. I slam the door shut.

We walk in silence as I follow Saxon into the living room. I avoid looking over at the rug near the fireplace where many nights were spent snuggled in Sam’s arms. The moonlight streams in from the beautiful arched windows, highlighting the opulence in every corner. I used to love this room. Loved how the rustic feel complemented the elusive modern vibe. But now it just reminds me that I may spend the rest of my life appreciating it alone.

“I couldn’t leave knowing you were angry at me.”

“Well, guess what? You leaving guarantees I will be angry at you for a very long time. So save your apologies. Unless you’re here to tell me you’re staying, I have nothing further I wish to say to you." I tenaciously stand my ground, making it clear I'm serious.

Saxon interlaces his hands behind his neck, shaking his head with an infuriated sigh. "I don't ever remember you being this stubborn."

"Ha, that's because you don't remember me at all. Do I need to remind you of all the times you were blatantly rude to me when I tried to say hello? Or what about the times I asked how your day was and you replied by turning up the TV?" I have no idea why I'm dredging up old memories. I didn't even realize how much they bothered me until now.

Family is so important to me, considering my birth mom didn't give a damn about me. I started my life as Baby M. I was named that due to the fact I was dumped on the front steps of St. Margaret's church on a Monday night in the month of May. I was raised in the adjacent convent, but eventually, I was put into foster care.

For the first five years of my life, I was simply known as M. I didn't have a real name, just M. Or sometimes, stupid. I bounced from foster home to foster home, never really feeling like I belonged anywhere. Some places were okay, but most were awful. I draw my lapels over my body when thinking about my home when I was four. Those scars, both inside and out, will never heal.

When a meeting was set with Maggie and Simon, I crossed my fingers and toes that they were the ones. She looked like an angel with her long, curly auburn hair, and he looked like my Superman with his strong smile.

It was love at first sight.

The first song I heard playing on the radio while driving to my new home was the song I was named after. I remember a surge of excitement surging through my tiny veins and I danced, wiggled, and jiggled in my seat because I was free.

"Lucy in the Sky with Diamonds" by The Beatles is a song, regardless of how many times I've heard it before, that will always make me cry. As Simon and Maggie saw my first tears of happiness, they knew the name was perfect, and so did I.

I never sought out my biological parents because doing so felt like a big M itself—a big mistake.

So I suppose the reason why I'm so hurt at Saxon for snapping my olive branch in half time and time again is because regardless of the fact he hated me, I still saw him as family. And as much as I want to hate him now, I can't. How can I? He's the spitting image of my betrothed.

"I do remember you, Lucy. Someone like you is hard to forget," he reveals. His comment catches me completely off guard. "Anyway," he brushes off his openness quickly. "For what it's worth, I'm sorry. I hope one day you'll come to realize that I'm not the bad guy."

I want to stomp my foot in protest. "Well, how about you let that day be today?" At the risk of sounding like a broken record, I step forward, interlacing my hands. "Please stay. Show your mom and dad; show Samuel that you're not the bad guy. Whatever happened in the past—please, put it aside. I know I have no right to ask you this but if you were in Sam's shoes, I would be asking him the same thing. Family is forever. For always. You may not like it, but you're linked to Samuel. If he… dies—" the word slices through my throat "—I know a part of you will die with him."

Saxon's hard resolve dwindles, I can see it. This is the lucky break I was looking for.

"I promise you, if you stay, I will ensure that Sam—" I don't get to finish my sentence because Saxon suddenly grows pale.

"Saxon?" I cock an eyebrow, wondering what's wrong. "Are you all right?"

His breathing turns ragged as he presses a hand to his brow. "I'm fine," he states a moment later, but his pained tone reveals otherwise.

I nervously bite my nails as I watch him breathe steadily through his nose. What's going on? Has my persistent nagging given him a headache? I know it's given me one.

It feels like hours, but I know it's only seconds before he gradually gets the color back to his cheeks. "I think you need to sit," I suggest, raising my hands in surrender when he scowls.

He thankfully doesn't argue and stumbles to the couch, slumping into it with a grunt. He leans his head back against the headrest, closing his eyes.

"Do you want a glass of water?" From where I stand, I can

see the beads of sweat collecting on his brow.

He angrily whips his head around to glare at me. "I said I'm fine."

"Okay then, no need to shout, Mr. Grumpy Guts," I mumble under my breath.

My landline begins ringing, which I'm thankful for as I can speak to someone who actually wants to talk to me. I reach for the phone on the side table. The moment I pick it up, everything goes black.

"Sweetheart..."

I feel an electrical current singe straight through my body.

"Dad? What's happened?"

"It's Sam."

It feels as if I'm suddenly zapped with a trillion volts of electricity. Every hair on my body stands on end and an overwhelming heaviness takes residence within my soul.

"What about Sam?" I beg.

His silence butchers away at my last tether to this plane, and just as I'm about to scream, demand he answer, he whispers, "He's awake."

I peer over at Saxon, who nods slowly. Whether he heard my dad, or his random onset was brought on by Sam, I'll never know.

Somehow, it seems like we've looked into the same crystal ball and have both seen the future. In this moment, something shifts between us. I don't know what, but I can feel it—the planets have somehow all aligned.

When the noise abruptly becomes still and the bedlam twinkles to tranquility, I know—I can feel it. I can feel *him.*

★ ★ ★ ★ ★

He's awake.

Those two words have been playing on a loop the entire drive to the hospital. It appears the last few days, my world has been blanketed with words I had no idea could take on so many different meanings.

We leap out of the car, both unsteady on our feet. Saxon nurses his Gatorade while I cradle my coffee. Thankfully, I had the presence of mind to change out of my pajamas and into a pair of jeans. I still look a fright and it's no surprise when I stampede into the hospital, people shift away from the crazy woman.

We enter the elevator, both a ball of nervous energy. The moment we reach Sam's floor, I bolt out the doors, my sneakers skidding on the floor as I run towards Sam's room. My mom and dad are standing outside, both looking relieved, but also a little baffled.

"Lucy!" my mom says, meeting me halfway. We embrace tightly. She strokes my hair.

"Sweetheart, are you all right?" my dad asks, his eyes warm as he approaches.

"I am. I just want to see Sam."

I can feel Saxon behind me, waiting quietly and not demanding he see Samuel first. He has every right to see him… hell, if anything he has more right than me…but I know he won't go in before me.

"Can I see him?"

When my mother lowers her eyes, and my dad tenderly rubs my arm, I know something is very wrong. "What's the matter?"

"Lucy…"

"What?" My heart ascends to a deafening staccato.

"Sam…" my father falters. My dad has always worn his heart on his sleeve. This time is no exception.

"Dad, what?"

He pushes up his silver framed glasses, a sure sign that he's worried. "Maybe it's best you wait out here until you speak to Dr. Kepler."

Everything is too much. I need answers, and I need them now.

Pushing past my parents, I dart into Sam's room, my impatience overtaking my good sense. I come to a screeching halt when I see Dr. Kepler talking to Gregory and Kellie, while two nurses stand around Sam's bed. They're chuckling quietly while writing something down.

The already small room feels like a shoebox and I take three deep breaths before willing my feet to move. I can't see the bed as five people stand in my way, but the moment Dr. Kepler turns to face me, I see it—I see my Samuel.

He's sitting up and his eyes, his enchanting eyes, are open and vibrant. A smile paints his face as he chats with the nurses, laughing at something one of them said. He looks tired, a little rugged, but he looks well. He looks alive.

I have so many things I want to say, but I don't know where to start. But maybe in this circumstance, actions speak louder than words. Exhaling deeply, I take one step and then two, only to be stopped when Greg lightly takes a hold of my arm.

Why is everyone trying to stop me from seeing Sam? I understand he's still not fully recovered, but surely I'm able to give him a quick kiss and say hello.

"Lucy, there's something about Samuel you need to know." His stern tone has me gulping, a thousand angry butterflies taking flight within my belly.

"What do I need to know?" When he too pauses, I crack. "What's going on?" My loud tone interrupts the chatter from the bed, and I can sense all eyes are on me.

"Samuel has awoken, but…" However, Dr. Kepler doesn't have a chance to finish because a hoarse voice has my entire body breaking out into tiny goose bumps.

"Get over here. I missed you."

I've heard Sam speak countless times before, but those six words are the most important words I've ever heard him say.

Kellie smiles, but it's bittersweet.

"If you'll excuse me, Doctor, my fiancé needs me," I say, brushing off everyone's peculiar behavior because all that matters is being in Sam's arms.

I politely push past Dr. Kepler, my eyes focusing on Sam. The moment he sees me, he smiles, his trademark dimple hugging his cheek. Tears prick my eyes because I never thought this day would ever come.

"Oh, Samuel." I try and keep the emotion from my voice, but I can't. I'm just so happy to see him.

I take a step forward but abruptly freeze, as my brain is unable to process what the next thirty seconds entails. Sam's smile broadens and he sits up higher, motioning with his hand that I come closer. But when his gaze skates over my shoulder, I know he's not gesturing to me, he's gesturing to Saxon, who stands in the doorway.

I remain motionless, feeling selfish, as of course he'd want to see Saxon. He hasn't seen him in over a year. But what about me? Isn't he happy to see me? Have I done something wrong?

"Excuse me." I look up, not realizing my gaze is glued to the ground until Sam addresses me. "Could you please move? My brother is trying to get past."

My mouth opens and closes as I don't know what to say. I numbly step to the side while Saxon enters the room. I'm surprised when he stops and stands beside me. When he lightly rubs my shoulder, it appears he too is in on a secret I'm not privy to.

Sam smirks, the sight shattering my already broken heart into irreparable pieces. "Come give your baby brother a hug. Since when have you had long hair? And tattoos? You bad motherfucker!"

The walls begin closing in on me and I'm finding it hard to breathe. I need to know what is happening. No matter how painful, I know something is wrong.

"Samuel?" My voice is small, weak, pathetic—it's a plea that he acknowledges me.

Sam's gaze swings my way, and that's when I can see it. His once familiar, loving eyes are now blank, filled with emptiness and…nothing.

No, cruel fate, no—not again.

Stepping closer and closer, I rush to Samuel's bedside, reaching for his hand and brushing his fingers over my face. "Samuel, it's me, Lucy."

When his warm fingers trace over my cheek, down my jaw and then outlining the curve of my lips, a ray of hope beams bright and I scold myself for thinking such irrational thoughts. But when his hand drops to his side, the detachment clear, a tear breaks past the floodgates and I choke back a silent sob.

His expression turns gentle, but his stare is teeming with pity. The old Samuel would comfort me, tell me not to cry. But that old Samuel is dead. This person may look like my Sam, but it's not Sam at all. As another tear slashes at my flesh, he shifts uncomfortably and says, "I'm sorry, but I have no idea who you are."

★ ★ ★ ★ ★

May 1st 2008
Dear diary,

Today, Sam and I had our first real fight. It was awful. ☹

Piper said it was long overdue, seeing as we've been together for over three years. She was hopeful I would break it off, but it surprised me that she didn't press the issue.

We've had disagreements, but never a full blown screaming match like we had today.

It all started when I heard about an internship in Ghana. The Humanitarian Peace Foundation is an organization I admire, and when this opportunity arose, I jumped at the chance to gain a hands-on career experience and discover what it's like to live and work abroad. The internship was for eight weeks, and I had three days to decide if I wanted to go or not.

I discussed it with Mom and Dad, who of course supported me 100%. They would help with the costs, as my wage at Starbucks would barely cover it. I was so excited. I couldn't wait to tell Samuel. The drive over to his house was filled with mental preparation, as I was to leave in ten days.

I bounded up the stairs, unable to contain my excitement as I burst into his room. He was hunched over his desk, surrounded by marketing textbooks. The moment he spun around in his chair to face me, I ran over and perched in his lap.

"I'm going to Ghana!"

He didn't hide his shock, and I instantly felt a little guilty for not leading in with a 'Hello, I love you. I'm going to Ghana!'

I'll never forget the look on his face because it's a look I've never seen before. He was angry. Sam NEVER gets angry. "What do you mean you're going to Ghana?"

I explained my situation and almost fell off his lap when he responded with a, "You're not going."

I didn't realize this was up for discussion, so of course I leaped out of his lap, not impressed in the slightest. We argued for the next hour, both stubborn and headstrong. He was being totally irrational, and I didn't appreciate him standing in the way of my dreams. When I very loudly proceeded to tell him this, he got even angrier.

I was going whether he liked it or not, and I left his house, not intending to change my tune.

I came home sobbing harder than I've ever sobbed before. I was glad Mom and Dad were out to dinner with friends, as I didn't want them seeing me this way.

I didn't know what to do. I wanted to go, but I didn't want to lose Sam over it. I didn't understand why he was so angry at me leaving. His reasons were that it was dangerous, and he didn't like me being away for so long.

It was only eight weeks! This was such a good opportunity, and he was being incredibly selfish!

I pretty much listened to Fiona Apple on repeat, wallowing in my self-pity until there was a knock at my door. Raising my head, I saw Sam looking as bad as I felt. Our fight seemed completely petty, and I jumped up, forgetting I was mad at him.

He begged for my forgiveness, dropped to his knees, and interlaced his hands. "Lucy, I'm so sorry. I was a fucking idiot. I had no right to dictate your future. I just..."

When he paused, I dropped to my knees as well. I asked him what.

He peered into my eyes and confessed, "I thought I was your dreams. I'm afraid you'll see what's out there and forget about me. You're beautiful, smart, ambitious—I'm petrified you'll see the world and chase your dreams—dreams that don't include me."

Nothing has ever sounded so tragically beautiful before.

Before I could stop myself, I wrapped my arms around his nape and buried my face into his neck. His outburst made sense—he was afraid of losing me. For some stupid reason, he believed I was biding my time until something better came along. Didn't he know he was my something better? He was the reason why I believed in myself. Without him, I was nothing.

"Sam, my dreams are nothing without you. My life started the day I met you in that library. I fell in love with the kind, considerate boy who had no qualms lending me his most treasured copy of 'The Catcher in the Rye.'"

He lowers his eyes, tugging at his bottom lip.

"I will never forget you. I can't."

He finally looks at me and smiles. "I'll never forget you either, Lucy. Ever. You're a part of me, now and forever."

★ ★ ★ ★ ★

"What do you mean?" Words get caught in my throat. "It-it's me, Lucy. Your f-fiancée." He has to remember who I am.

His bewildered expression reveals that he doesn't have to do anything. "Fiancée? Is this some kind of joke?" He peers over my shoulder, cocking an eyebrow. "Sax, did you put her up to this?"

I can't take it anymore.

My legs feel like jelly and I crumble, not caring that I'll probably concuss myself in the process. However, before I can knock myself into oblivion, a pair of strong hands latch onto my upper arms. Samuel makes no secret that he's watching mine and Saxon's exchange with interest.

"How about we get some fresh air?" he suggests, his fingers tenderly punctuating his point by squeezing softly.

I nod because if I stay in this room for a second longer, I'm bound to suffocate. With my head bowed, I avoid the sorrowful stares of my family as Saxon leads me towards the door. We walk in silence down the hallway and into the elevator, his arm still wrapped around me.

The moment we step outside, I take a much needed deep breath, but still feel like a million hands are clutching at my throat, cutting off my air supply.

So many thoughts are pinballing around in my head, but one stands out clearer than any other. *Samuel doesn't remember me.* When he looked at me, his eyes were utterly void. There was no love, or affection, or recognition—there was nothing.

I turn into Saxon's chest, needing his comfort more than I've ever needed anyone's before. I don't cry. I simply stand numb.

"It'll be okay."

I appreciate Saxon's reassurance, but I don't believe a word. This situation is so far from being okay, I'm pretty sure it's bordering on being the worst thing that has ever happened to me.

"He doesn't remember me, Saxon. How is it going to be okay?"

His saddened sigh says it all.

"Did my parents say anything to you?"

"Let's sit," he suggests, breaking our embrace and placing me at arm's length. I'm afraid to know why he thinks this next conversation needs to take place while I'm seated. However, I slump onto the infamous bench.

As he lights a cigarette, I appreciate the way the sunshine catches the blond in his hair, contrasting the woven strands of brown. It suddenly hits me that Saxon is now more familiar to me than Samuel is. The person sitting in Sam's bed is a stranger.

"Your dad was sketchy on the details," he says after blowing out a ring of smoke, "but Dr. Kepler thinks Sam has some form of amnesia. He can only recall certain things, places, events. And people," he adds regretfully. "He has holes in his memory."

"And I what? Fell through one of them? How can he not remember me?"

He raises his shoulders in defeat, looking just as baffled as me.

Trying to get my head around it, I state, "He obviously remembers you. What about your parents?" He nods, taking a pensive drag of his cigarette. "My parents?" He nods once again.

"How is that even possible?" I run a hand down my face in frustration.

"He recognizes them, but can't place how he knows them."

"So basically, he remembers everyone but me."

"Lucy, no," he refutes, sensing my pain. "He doesn't remember a lot of things. Your dad said he doesn't remember going to college, or what he does for work. Or where he lives. He just knows the basics."

Too bad those basics don't include me. But I refuse to cry. "Do they know how long he'll stay this way?"

"No. They need to run some more tests. It'll take time."

"So what am I meant do to in the meantime?"

"Keep reminding Samuel of who you are. Who *he* is," he replies with conviction.

"And if that doesn't work?" I ask, wishing I was as positive as he is.

We sit, lost in thought, both endeavoring to guess what comes next. "Just have faith," he says, breaking the silence. It's the second time he's said this to me. I'm glad he's more confident than I am.

"So what happens now?"

"We wait."

"For how long?" I whisper, hating the hopeless undertone to my words.

"For as long as it takes." He draws the cigarette to his lips, inhaling languorously.

"And if he never remembers me?"

"Let's cross that bridge when we come to it."

I sit upright, brushing the hair from my brow. "So you're staying?"

He lowers his eyes. "I don't know, Lucy."

His response disappoints me as I can't believe after all that's happened, he would leave.

"Please don't make that face."

"What face?" I ask, a little more heated than intended. I don't know what it is about Saxon, but he brings out a fiery side of me that I didn't even know existed. Sam and I hardly fought, but with Saxon, it's a miracle if I don't throttle him the moment he speaks.

"The 'I'm going to murder you in your sleep' face," he clarifies, his tone light.

I know he's trying to make me smile. It works. "I promise you're safe. Just one more night? Please." I can't explain why I need him to stay. He offers me a sense of security I so desperately crave.

He doesn't answer. He simply butts out his smoke with his boot and grins. "Let's get back inside." He stands, offering me his hand.

The sun shines down on him, creating an illusionary halo as I look up and slip my palm into his. The moment we connect, I feel…better. I no longer feel like a nobody. Samuel may not remember me, but Saxon does. It appears Saxon has remembered me the entire time—*I* was the one who didn't remember him.

Eight

I DON'T KNOW WHAT TO expect when I walk into Samuel's hospital room the next day. I've opened myself up to all possibilities, all possibilities bar my fiancé flirting with Nurse Bimbo.

I should be relieved that most of the machines are out of Sam's room and he's only connected to an IV, but I'm not. In this moment, I would rather he be in a coma where he remembers me, than awake, and not remembering me at all.

Two buttons are now undone on Nurse Bimbo's uniform. It appears professionalism is optional in this hospital. I clear my throat very loudly, interrupting Nurse Bimbo taping a small gauze pad in the crease of Sam's elbow. She's leaning in way too close, while he appears that all his Christmases have come at once.

His eyes flick up and I hold my breath, hoping I'll see

recognition. But I don't.

He looks over my shoulder and smiles. "Hey, Sax. Please tell me you've brought some real food. I'm living on a diet consisting of air at the moment. I was in a coma. Not dead. You couldn't sneak me in some food could you, darlin'?" He has the gall to wink.

Nurse Bimbo laughs, fluttering her eyelashes, which resemble epileptic caterpillars. I curl my fingers, ready to dive forward and strangle her.

Saxon's gigantic frame shadows me, as he can no doubt read my need for violence. "Sorry, Sam. But I did bring something better." He nudges me and I ungracefully hobble forward like a wobbly puppet on a string.

Sam finally looks at me, but I wish he didn't. "Oh, hey… Leanne."

And suddenly, I'm Baby M again. "It's Lucy," I amend, trying to stay strong.

"Right. Sorry." He pulls an apologetic face. His guilt at not remembering me is clearly evident, but it doesn't ease the heartache.

He looks remarkably better than he did twenty-four hours ago and I wonder what triggered him to wake up. Dr. Kepler said he responded to stimuli, i.e. Saxon. So what triggered it this time?

My thoughts distract me from wanting to pluck out Nurse Bimbo's black extensions one by one as she flicks her hair over her shoulder. “I’ll come check on you later.” She stands behind her cart, placing Sam’s vials of blood into a tray.

“Feel free to bring some food with you,” he whispers from behind his hand in a conspiratory manner.

She giggles.

As she wheels her noisy cart past us, she makes no secret she’s checking Saxon out. “I can’t believe how alike you look,” she declares, while I raise my eyes to the ceiling. It appears one brother isn’t enough.

“That would be because we’re identical twins,” Saxon replies, not bothering to mask his apathy.

Both our mouths drop open—hers in shock, mine in humor.

She thankfully takes the hint and leaves. I’m still grinning moments later. That grin sadly disappears however when Sam opens his mouth. “I’m so bored. When can I go home? I can’t wait to get into my own bed and demolish Mom’s pot pie.” He runs a hand over his heavier stubble, oblivious to my internal meltdown.

Dr. Kepler chooses this moment to walk into the room. “Good morning, everyone. How are we all feeling?”

“Can I have a word?” I blurt out, indicating I’m bad, very bad.

Dr. Kepler nods, my desperate tone heightening the importance of my words. Saxon gives me a sympathetic smile as I follow Dr. Kepler out of the room and down the hallway.

"I'm sure you have a lot of questions, Ms. Tucker," he says, turning around.

Dr. Kepler is the kind of man who was born to be a doctor. His intelligent blue eyes show wisdom, empathy, and compassion—rare traits in a man of his standing. He's gone out of his way to inform us of Sam's condition, and not once has he made us feel stupid or meddlesome for asking endless questions.

Like right now.

"I do. The most important is how long will he stay this way?"

I can see the answer, the regret on his kind-hearted face even before he speaks. "We don't know. Like I told your parents and Samuel's parents, amnesia is unpredictable. It could be two days, two weeks, two years. And in some cases, possibly not at all."

"Not at all?" I almost fall over myself, unable to digest the finality of his comment. I brace my hand against the wall to stop my plummet. "But that's worst case scenario, right? Right, Doctor?" I press when he doesn't respond.

"No, Ms. Tucker," he says regretfully. "You need to understand. Sam may never regain those memories back. Segments may return, but it's like a jigsaw puzzle. He's missing some vital pieces to complete the entire puzzle. He may be able to get by with the pieces he has, but those missing pieces may always remain misplaced."

This day has just gone from bad to worse. “So I’m a missing jigsaw piece? He seems to have all the pieces except my piece. How is it possible he doesn’t remember me?”

He pushes his glasses up his nose. “I wouldn’t take it personally.”

But I do. No matter what anyone says to me, I can’t not take this personally.

“Let’s just focus on the positives and get him well. Dr. Yates, an expert in this field, will be coming in today to talk to Samuel. She’ll be able to test his cognitive responses and give us better insight into where Sam is.”

I nod as it’s too much to process.

“In the meantime, help him find the pieces by looking in the right places.”

His comment stirs a ray of hope. “What do you mean?”

“Bring in photographs, watch his favorite movie, wear his favorite scent, anything that may help him remember who he was. Try and evoke those feelings of familiarity by associating today with yesterday. Jog his memory to why he loved the things that he did.”

One of those things used to be me. I thank Dr. Kepler, taking his advice on board.

Sweeping my palms over my face, I scrub away my sadness, as I’m determined to make Sam remember me. Inhaling then exhaling loudly, I untie my long blonde hair and shake it out around my shoulders. Digging into my pocket for my

ChapStick, I apply a coat and smack my lips twice. This cherry flavor is my favorite and I never leave home without it. Maybe if I gave Sam a kiss, he'd remember the taste and smell. It's worth a shot.

Smoothing out my hair, I flick it to one side, hoping to give my flat locks some body. When I catch a glimpse of my reflection in the window across the hall from me, I understand why Sam doesn't recognize me. I currently resemble the living dead. *I* barely recognize me.

Looking down at my scuffed black Chucks, blue skinny jeans, and tattered Beatles t-shirt, I decide to make more of an effort tomorrow. No more grieving and feeling sorry for myself. If I want Sam back, then I've got to show him the girl he fell for.

Pulling my shoulders back, I stroll into Sam's room with a staged confidence because I'm burning up on the inside. Both Sam and Saxon turn when they see me enter. Sam looks completely and utterly untouched, while Saxon swallows. I don't know why, but the look makes me feel…pretty. My cheeks instantly blush.

"Did you bring any food?" Sam asks, sitting up to see if I bear any bags in hand.

My cheeks redden for a different reason this time. "No, I didn't. But I have food for thought." He cocks a brow.

Saxon stands off to the side as I walk towards Sam's bed. A whirlwind takes flight within when Sam narrows his eyes, indicating he's listening. It's a mannerism so like the old Sam. It hurts that I've grown to refer to him in this way.

Opening up my bag, I reach inside for my purse. Both brothers watch closely as I hunt through the pockets. Pulling out two tattered photographs, I run my fingertip reminiscently over the first one before flipping it around for Sam to see.

He stares at it for the longest of times, small lines etching along his brow.

"It's us at prom, Sam," I explain, remembering my blue silk gown and how handsome he looked in his tuxedo. I also remember what took place in the hotel room afterward. My cheeks heat at the memory of me losing my virginity to the man of my dreams.

He leans forward and takes the picture from my hand. His eyes are fixated on the image and I can see it. He's trying to remember this moment in time. I can only imagine how strange it must be for him to look at an image and have no recollection of it.

"We look happy," he says, which warms my heart.

"We were. We met when I was sixteen and you were seventeen."

"How'd we meet?"

His interest has me edging forward. "We met at school. In the library, actually. I knew then that I loved you. I felt the spark from the moment we spoke. The moment we touched."

The room is silent. Stale.

I unhurriedly take a seat on the bed beside him, ensuring I

don't smother or crowd him.

"And this picture." I pass him the next one. "Is us in front of our home."

He accepts, his eyes widening. "We live together?"

"Yes. On the day of your accident, we were going to get married." I leave out the details, as I don't want to overwhelm him.

"What?" he gasps, his face paling. He looks at Saxon for confirmation. "Is it true, Sax?"

I meet Saxon's eyes. He looks torn. "Yes, Sam," he replies a moment later. "It's true."

"How old am I? How old are *we*?"

Saxon swallows. "We're twenty-seven."

"What year is it?" His chest begins to rise and fall.

"2014."

"No. It can't be." Sam shakes his head violently, disbelieving.

"It is," Saxon confirms soberly.

"Where do you live?" he asks, sitting upright.

"In Oregon."

"Why?"

Saxon averts is gaze.

"Sax, why?" Sam presses, his tone incensed. "Why would you move so far away from me?"

"Things change," he replies, leaning against the wall and bracing his boot against it.

"What happened to our pact?" When Saxon remains quiet,

Sam continues. “We promised to move out together after high school and live the college life. We promised to party hard, pick up chicks, and live the wild life. We promised to hitchhike around the country together if we both didn’t get into the same college. We promised that one day, we’d get to sunny California and surf the biggest waves. We promised to never let anything, *anyone* come between us. Do you remember that?”

“We were eight,” Saxon refutes, but his argument doesn’t deter Sam.

“Do. You. Remember?” he repeats, pausing between each word for effect.

“Yes.” Saxon sighs, his cheeks puffing out.

“So what happened?”

Silence.

I suddenly feel my pulse spike because the air is charged with anger and accusation.

“I know,” Sam snarls, his irate gaze landing on me. “I know what happened. *You* happened. You took my brother away from me.”

“What? No.” I shoot up, latching onto his forearm. “Sam, no.”

But he shakes his head, tugging his arm out from under me. “There’s a reason why I don’t remember you.”

That’s my cue to walk out that door, but I don’t. I need answers. “Why?”

With nothing but venom lacing his words, he declares,

"Because maybe I don't want to." He holds up the photographs, flailing them in my face. "Maybe I want to forget these memories because I want to forget you."

"Sam, stop it!" Saxon rushes forward, standing at the foot of the bed.

"Why are you sticking up for her?" He points at me, his finger accenting his anger.

"Because she's done nothing wrong. You're upset and angry; we get that, but stop being such a jerk."

Sam shakes his head, aggravated. He doesn't hide his annoyance and jealousy that Saxon is taking my side. "Get out."

Sam's harsh words bring home the gravity of this situation. "What?"

"Sam…" Saxon's constant need to defend me seems to infuriate Samuel further.

"You heard me. Get out! And take your memories with you." Please, somebody, pinch me and wake me from this nightmare.

But when he begins tearing up the photographs, I know this nightmare is real. "No!" I dive for him, attempting to stop him. "Stop!" But my efforts are futile.

In seconds, my memories are torn and scattered to the floor. My happy memories are now replaced with bitterness and hate.

Hot tears cloud my vision as I slump to the ground, frantically gathering up the torn pieces of my past. Saxon drops besides me, helping me pick up the remains.

"Let me help you, Lucy." He places his hand over mine.

"No, I'm okay." I sniff, my lower lip quivering as I hold back my tears.

"Lucy—"

"You heard her, leave her alone." Sam's unsympathetic words are my undoing.

"You may have amnesia, but you're still an asshole!" Saxon yells, attempting to console me as he offers me a handful of my past.

"Well, fuck you, too." I know he's lashing out because he's frustrated, but his lack of feeling hurts.

I can't be in here a second longer. My sneakers skid on the flooring as I run out the door, ignoring Saxon's calls that I stop. But I can't. I need to get out of here before I choke.

Sadly, my plans to flee are ruined as I crash into someone. We both topple over, papers floating around us as they glide to the floor.

"I'm s-sorry," I cry, madly trying to pick up the paperwork. My fumbling fingers are like sticks of butter.

"Are you all right?" a kind, soothing voice asks.

"No," I reply honestly, giving up on helping the stranger. "I'm not. My life is a mess."

"I'm so sorry to hear that."

By some miracle, I'm able to see through my tears and read the nametag of my kind stranger as Dr. Yates.

"You're Samuel's doctor?" I exclaim, wiping my eyes. "Samuel Stone," I clarify when she appears confused.

"Oh, yes, I am. I was actually on my way to see him now."

Pulling it together, I help her gather the scattered sheets of paper. "I'm Lucy. Lucy Tucker. I'm Sam's fiancée," I reveal, handing her a pile of paperwork.

Her face softens. "It's so nice to meet you, Lucy. Were you just coming out of Samuel's room?"

I nod, chewing my cheek to stop another onslaught of tears.

"I take it things didn't go well?"

I nod again.

She peers down at her silver watch and smiles. "I have a few minutes before Samuel's appointment. Would you like to grab a coffee?"

When I meet her warm blue eyes, I instantly like her. "I'd like that. Thank you." We collect the rest of her things in silence before making our way to the adjacent coffee shop.

Once we've ordered our coffees, she leads us to a small garden table outside. I'm glad, as I need the fresh air. I cradle the paper cup, the warmth thawing out my internal storm.

"How are things going? I know it's early days, but if anyone knows Samuel, it's you."

Her words are a heavy burden to my already plagued heart. "*I* know Samuel. It's just too bad he doesn't know me," I reply unhappily.

She pushes her black framed glasses up the bridge of her small nose, emphasizing her big blue eyes. She's absolutely stunning and looks to be no older than thirty. She also doesn't look like a doctor. Her long black hair is tied back in an elegant knot, exposing the natural pink hue on the apple of her cheeks. Her porcelain skin is flawless. But beauty aside, I immediately feel a kinship with her because I know she's the one who'll bring my Sam back to me.

"I've read over his file briefly and it's not uncommon for this to happen. Parts of Samuel's brain were injured quite severely during the accident."

Her comment has me thinking about the driver who was responsible for Sam's injuries. I've been so caught up, I haven't even thought about him and the consequences he's faced with.

She goes on, "There are different types of amnesia, and my job is to determine just what form Samuel has so we can treat him accordingly."

"What type do you think he has?"

"I don't want to make any assumptions without a proper examination. There's no point speculating and worrying you unnecessarily. He's surrounded by the people who love him and sometimes, there is no greater medicine."

Her words prompt a thought. "Samuel is an identical twin. Would his brother staying help him remember?"

She sips her coffee, leaving a bright red stain on the rim her cup. "There's no denying twins share a special connection, especially when studies have proven that one twin feels what the other is feeling at the exact same time."

I remember Saxon's weird reaction seconds before we got

the call. I still believe he's the key.

She reaches across the table and strokes my hand. "We will get to the bottom of this, Lucy. I promise. I'll be working closely with Sam, not only in here, but at home also. Once he's discharged, he'll be under my care. You have my word that I'll try my absolute hardest to have Sam remembering again."

"Thank you so much, Dr. Yates." Her words are like a salve to my covert burns.

"Please call me Sophia."

I try not to celebrate prematurely, not wanting to jinx my happiness as I know we're a long way from things going back to the way they were. But Sophia's optimism and caring nature has me feeling like the old me. I can only hope she does the same for Sam.

"Shall we go back in?" she suggests, finishing her coffee.

I nod, even though I haven't taken a sip of mine.

We walk back to Samuel's room, both silent, but the silence isn't stale. A thousand thoughts are rolling around my head, but the forerunner is the fact I feel composed for the first time in days. To get through this, I have to accept that Sam's road to recovery is a long one. Although we haven't officially declared in sickness and in health, I take my vows very seriously and don't plan on giving up on him any time soon.

When we round the corner, I see Saxon braced against the wall, looking worse for wear as he scrolls through his phone. I've been awfully hard on him and I've also been unfair. It's his choice whether he wishes to stay or not. I've voiced my opinion on more than one occasion, so the rest is up to him.

He raises his head, his intense gaze falling on both Sophia and I. Now that I'm not looking at him through a veil of crazy, I can see his pain. Regardless of their strained relationship, I know Saxon cares for Samuel. I know that he cares for me. He's come to my aid on more than one occasion, and all I've done is yell at him.

Sophia stops and smiles. "Hi, I'm Dr. Yates, Samuel's doctor."

Saxon pushes off the wall and shakes her hand. "Hi, I'm Saxon, Sam's brother."

I notice they shake for a little longer than needed, not that I can blame Sophia as Saxon is ridiculously handsome. I can't say that he isn't, considering he's the spitting image of my fiancé.

"Lucy," she says, turning to face me. I notice her crimson cheeks appear pinker. "I'm going to talk to Samuel. Would you mind waiting out here for just a few moments?"

"Of course. Take all the time you need." Saxon doesn't hide his surprise at my newfound composure. She nods before entering Sam's room.

Saxon and I stand quietly, him peering at me, no doubt waiting for me to breakdown, or claw at the walls, screaming about the injustices of the world. I do neither.

"I'm sorry for being a complete bitch to you."

He fumbles over his words. "You…what…huh?"

I can't help but smile. "I haven't been fair to you. It's your choice whether you go or stay. I can't force you. And that's what I've been doing. You've got your own life to live in Oregon and honestly, my eyes have been opened these past few days." When he cocks an eyebrow, I elaborate. "I don't know what happened between you and Sam, or between your mom and dad, but I've seen the way your mom speaks to you. If I were you, I wouldn't want to stay either. Sam is being a total asshole, so really, there's no incentive for you to stay. There's no *reason* for you to stay."

Saxon's mouth moves with wordless animation.

"Thank you for being there for me, Saxon. I won't forget it."

I don't know why, but I do something totally unexpected. I step forward, stand on tippy toes, and kiss Saxon's stubbled cheek. The texture is rough, but it's also incredibly soft. I can't help but compare the feeling to Sam's.

I'm wrapped in his signature fragrance and the perfume has me closing my eyes, basking in the bouquet. I'll miss him, which is ridiculous. Collecting myself, I step away, ready to say farewell. "Bye—" But I gasp, unable to finish when Saxon places a finger over my lips.

I meet his eyes, confusion swirling in mine. "I'm staying."

"What?" I mumble in disbelief from under his fingertip.

"I'm staying," he repeats, sweeping his finger down my lip, releasing me.

I try not to fall forward. Everything is too much. "Are you staying because I told you not to?" I ask, baffled. Is this one of those reverse psychology things?

He smirks. "No, Lucy, I'm staying because I want to."

"But why?" I'm grateful, I truly am. I just don't understand why he would choose to stay. "What reason is there for you to stay?"

The space between us becomes stiflingly still and I feel beads of perspiration form at the base of my spine. He takes a confident step forward while I stand my ground, too baffled to move.

"Ask me again when all of this is over with," he replies, his voice heavy, driven with nothing but emotion.

My head feels like it weighs a thousand pounds as I nod.

I don't know why, but I feel like when I ask that question again, his response will change everything I believe in and love.

Nine

One week later

"Do you want to go for a walk?"

Sam looks up at me like I've just asked him to donate a kidney. "No, Lucy, I do not want to go for a fucking walk. I want to go home." I suppose I should be grateful he got my name right.

"Samuel! Language," Kellie scolds, looking up from her fashion magazine. "Apologize to Lucy."

"Sorry, Mom, and Lucy—" he looks at me guiltily "—but I just want to go home," he gripes, sinking against his pillows.

"I know, sweetheart, but the doctors say you need to stay for observation. There is still some swelling around your brain."

"I doubt the swelling is from the accident. It's most likely because I've got a headache from the constant nagging." He glares at me while I timidly return to browsing through my iPad.

Sam has made his feelings for me perfectly clear—he hates my guts. I don't know why he does, but it appears he can stand to be around everyone except me.

I'm trying not to meddle or hover, but I'm just so relieved he's okay. I need to touch him to make sure he's real, but the moment I come within reach, I recoil, afraid I'll lose a finger. Kellie even appears overprotective and sends me on ridiculous errands to keep me away. The only person who seems to want me around is Saxon.

How backwards my life has become.

"Hey."

I leap up from my seat the moment Saxon enters the room. He's holding two cups of coffee, and I'm really hoping one is mine.

"Please tell me that's an Irish coffee without the coffee," Sam says, looking hopeful.

Saxon raises his eyebrows to the ceiling. "Good to see you're Mr. Funbags today." He passes me the coffee without making a fuss.

I gratefully accept and cradle the cup, basking in the warmth, as there is a constant chill in the air whenever I'm in this room.

"Why does she get one and I don't?" Sam sulks, which looks as unattractive on a grown man as it sounds.

Saxon looks over at me fleetingly before addressing Sam. "Because she deserves it. She deserves a lot more for putting up with your bullshit."

Kellie's mouth gapes open in horror, Samuel flips him off, and I simply sip my coffee, hiding my smile.

★ ★ ★ ★ ★

Two weeks later

"Samuel, we really need your cooperation here," says the physical therapist, holding a skipping rope. "Before you can go home, we need to test your hand eye coordination, among many other things."

In response, Sam glares at the poor girl while flipping her off. "How's that for hand eye coordination?"

She looks over at Saxon and me, asking for a little help, but I shrug my shoulders, powerless to lend a hand. Two weeks in, and if possible, Sam appears to hate me more. He still hasn't remembered a thing. According to Sophia, his sessions seem to be going well. She said it'll be a slow process, as any brain injury takes time to heal. But how long?

"Sam, seriously, hurry up and answer the question. The longer you're a complete dick, the longer you stay in here, which nobody wants. This poor girl included," Saxon says, while the girl blushes.

Once again, Saxon has saved the day. He seems to be the only person who can talk some sense into Sam. I have given up trying because the moment I suggest something, Sam decides to do the opposite. I feel like I'm hindering his progress because he makes no secret that he can't stand to be around me.

I feel helpless and like I'm getting in the way. Kellie has suggested I go out and pamper myself on more than one occasion. She's either trying to get rid of me, or I look like utter shit. I wouldn't be surprised if it's both.

Saxon crosses his arms over his chest, daring Sam to argue. I don't know how he does it, but Sam accepts the challenge and yanks the rope from the stunned therapist's hands. She looks relieved that he's finally cooperating. And so am I.

That relief is short-lived when he turns to look at me and scowls. "I'll only do this if *she* leaves."

Sighing, I head for the exit.

★ ★ ★ ★ ★

Three weeks later

I didn't realize daytime TV was so sad. But I guess I didn't realize a lot of things, like how my life is a complete and utter mess.

I'm sitting on the couch sobbing as I watch an 80's Hallmark movie when the front door opens. Quickly wiping away my tears and hiding the dozen used tissues, I reach for my wine and try my best to appear composed.

Saxon pauses in the doorway when he sees me sitting huddled beneath a crocheted blanket, blotchy faced and in my pajamas at four p.m. Not a good look, I know, but I can't face another day of Sam hating me.

"This movie is so sad," I say, pointing to the flat screen, hoping to explain my tears.

Saxon cocks a brow when he sees the ridiculous, over the top acting, but doesn't say a word. He's holding two brown bags that I hope have more wine inside. "I'm making you something to eat," he says, ruining my drunken dreams.

"I'm not hungry, but thanks anyway." Just as I'm about to take a sip of wine, he snatches the glass out from under me. "Hey! I was drinking that."

"I think you've had enough to drink," he refutes, tossing back the rest of the wine to remove temptation.

He's right. I've drunk more in the past few weeks than I have my entire life. But I can't face the day sober because the harsh light of day hurts my heart.

Saxon looks at the crumpled note on the table while I draw the blanket to my chin, tears filling my eyes. "What's that?" He doesn't miss a thing.

"That is Sam's official 'fuck you' letter," I explain.

He doesn't bother asking me to elaborate, but instead places the groceries on the coffee table and reads the blasphemy for himself. It won't take long, as Sam was never one to mince words.

When his face hardens, I sarcastically quip, "Have you gotten to the part where he says he'd rather live in hell than with me?"

Saxon shakes his head, tossing the note back onto the table.

The note in question is the letter Sophia asked Samuel to write as a form of therapy. I was the lucky one, as I was the only person Sam decided to write a letter to. I was ecstatic, thinking that maybe he'd come around. But when I read what he thought of me, I wish he didn't write one at all. It was short and sweet and pretty much said, 'I can't stand being near you. I wish you'd get the hint and leave. P.S. I'm not coming home to live with you. P.P.S. Fuck you.'

I understand Sam is going through something awful and I'm trying not to take things personally, but I don't know how much longer I can stand this. I'm miserable.

Saxon has learned to read me so well, and I've come to rely on him more than I thought I would. We've spent every waking minute together, as he hasn't left my side. He's been my one and only ally as both Kellie and Greg seem to be giving me the cold shoulder, too.

He takes a seat near me and sighs. "Lucy, it'll get better."

"You can't promise that."

"No, I can't, but I do know that something will give sooner or later—either Sam or you," he wisely says. "Try and look at the positives."

"There are no positives," I refute.

Saxon runs a hand over his scruff, deep in thought. "He offered you an apple today without using your head as target practice." I half smile.

What would I do without him? "Promise you won't leave?" I selfishly ask.

Saxon's chest rises and falls as he exhales steadily. "I promise," he finally replies, and I smile, just like I always do whenever he's around.

"Thanks, Saxon." Without thinking, I shuffle over and give him a hug. He hugs me back and it feels nice that someone isn't repulsed by my presence.

I stay pressed against him, thinking about how drastically my life has changed. What my future holds, I don't know, but I hope Saxon will remain a part of it.

Just as I'm getting comfy, Saxon says, his lips pressed to the top of my head, "Now that that's settled, next thing in order is for you to shower because you smell, well…a little ripe."

His light tone reveals that he's joking, and for once, in so many weeks, I laugh.

It feels good.

★ ★ ★ ★ ★

"Okay, we're all set."

Even to my own ears, my voice sounds uneasy, strained. The past twenty-eight days have been trying, to say the least. But I persevered because that was the only way I knew I'd survive.

Saxon stayed true to his word, much to the horror of his mother. It's true what they say that in times of crisis, people's true colors emerge. Sadly, Kellie's colors are that of the darkest kind. I was half expecting Saxon to up and leave; I wouldn't blame him if he did, but he didn't. He put up with Samuel's daily outbursts and Kellie's constant cattiness with ease. The more they barked, the less he cared and his carefree attitude soothed my bubbling hysteria.

Sam's condition hasn't improved; he's still stuck—stuck not remembering who I am. And stuck being a complete jerk. Without Sophia's encouragement, I dare say I would be close to giving up. She said Sam's improving, but honestly, I think he's getting worse.

He barely acknowledges me and when he does, I wish he didn't. He's short tempered, indifferent, and just plain rude. But then sometimes, I catch him watching me musingly. I know he's lashing out in frustration because he can't remember me. He knows that he should, but he doesn't. I can only imagine how frustrating and scary it must be. But his mood swings are slowly driving me over the edge. I really can't keep up with him. He really is two different people—the perfect Dr. Jekyll and Mr. Hyde. But remembering my almost vows, I don't take his behavior personally because I know this isn't Sam.

Zipping up his duffle, I smile, hoping the gesture displays my excitement at Sam coming home today. Whether he notices or cares, I don't know, because he remains stone-faced and uninterested. "You ready to go home?" I ask, hoping for a signal other than this blankness.

He shrugs, turning to look out the window.

Counting to three, I remind myself of how hard this must be for him and don't take his response to heart. "Well, I am," I state, shouldering his bag. "I can't wait for things to get back to normal."

I refuse to believe that this staleness between us is our new normal.

Taking a moment to look at Sam, I still can't believe he's the same man he was weeks ago. Not only has his personality changed, so has his looks. He hasn't bothered to shave nor groom his hair. The longer locks on both his face and head have him looking more like Saxon. His clothes are no longer conservative or chic, and when his mother asked if he wanted to wear his favorite green polo, he told her to burn it and any others just like it.

He now sits in ripped jeans, black Nikes, and a plain black t-shirt. He told me that I was to replace his entire wardrobe with items just like these. I did as he asked because I just wanted him home. However, now that the day has arrived, I'm not so certain on what I wished for.

"When is Sax coming back?" Sam asks, finally making eye contact.

Fiddling with the strap on the bag, I shrug. "He had to go back to Oregon to take care of a few things. He didn't say when he'd be back."

"Lucky him," he mumbles under his breath. I do as Sophia says and brush off his lack of interest.

Saxon has been gone three days. He wanted to check on the garage and ensure things were running smoothly without him. From the brief conversations I've overheard, business is going well. I can't help but feel responsible that he's here and not there, but I'm selfish, and am glad he's stayed.

"I'll just have to do until he gets back," I tease, hoping to lighten the mood.

He smiles, but it's forced.

Sam has made no secret of the fact that he'd rather be going home with his mom and dad than me. But Sophia, Dr. Kepler, and Sam's parents agreed for things to go back to 'normal' he was to return home and fall back into his usual routine. But I wasn't so sure.

"C'mon, babe." I bite my lip, the slip making us both feel uncomfortable. Sam thankfully doesn't say anything and stands.

Time freezes as he reaches out and slips the duffle from my shoulder. It's the first contact we've made in weeks and my heart sings at the connection. He however remains untouched as he peers around the room sadly. I suppose this was the first new memory he made, and leaving it behind and venturing into the unknown is a scary feeling. Especially venturing into the unknown with a stranger.

I stand off to the side, giving him the space to say goodbye.

After a few moments of silence, he turns to me. "Okay, let's go." Those words should be filled with hope, promise, and joy. Instead, they're filled with dread.

We walk down the corridor and into the elevator, feet apart. To onlookers, we must appear to be complete strangers. Sam doesn't look at me, nor does he appear excited to be leaving. Regardless of his apathy, I'm ecstatic to have him home.

It's been nice having Saxon stay in the guest room, as the thought of going home to an empty house depresses me more than I care to admit. The thought has me wondering if Sam will be comfortable sharing our bed with me. I've been too preoccupied in ensuring he indeed was leaving this hospital with me, I skimmed over the minor details like whether or not he'll want his own room for the time being.

I want him to remember me, remember *us*, but I don't want to cram it down his throat.

In a way, we're sharing a bed for the first time and I don't want things to get any weirder. I can't handle any more weirdness.

The bright sun warms my Vitamin D deficient skin thanks to being cooped up inside for weeks. Both Sam and I are outdoorsy kind of people and being contained within those four walls was making me go a little stir crazy. I'm happy to finally be free.

Sam follows closely beside me, oblivious to what car I drive. Slipping the keys from my pocket, I sound the alarm on our silver Jeep.

The lights blink once in sync with Sam's eyes. "You own a Jeep?"

Opening up the door, I shake my head. "No, you do."

His mouth pops open.

"Welcome home, honey," I quip, unable to help myself as I get into the car.

I know I shouldn't be making jokes, but it's something I would usually say. And Sophia did say I wasn't to walk on eggshells around him. I was to act normal, as that normalcy was going to help Sam settle in. But I don't want him thinking I'm not taking this seriously.

But when Sam gets in a second later, a small smile touching his cheeks, I'm so glad I went with my gut. It's the best sight I've seen since the night he kissed me on the forehead, said, "Tomorrow you'll officially be mine," and beamed like he was the luckiest man alive.

He buckles up, the smile still present as he runs his fingers over the leather interior.

I don't make a fuss and start the car, feeling a little more optimistic than a minute ago. We drive in silence, the soft humming of the talk radio filling the air. The silence isn't uncomfortable however, as from the corner of my eye, I see Sam taking in the sights and sounds around him. This is no doubt all so much for him, as I don't know what he remembers, and what is all new to him.

"Are you okay?" I ask, glancing over briefly before focusing back on the road.

"I think so," he replies a moment later. "I just…I think I remember where we are?"

I almost sideswipe an oncoming car.

Quickly correcting, I swallow down my hysteria and ask, "You do? What do you remember?"

"I…" he pauses. "Up ahead is Paulo's, right?"

"Yes!" I reply, unable to contain my excitement.

"Their pizza is the bomb," we both say at the same time.

"Oh my god," I gasp, my hands shaking as I grip the steering wheel. That is their infamous catchphrase.

"Holy shit," Sam says, not masking his surprise. "That was so weird."

"What was? What happened?" I want him to keep talking in hopes it'll spark new memories floating to the surface.

"I could smell the richness of the freshly cooked pizza, and I could taste the herbs, the cheese. I could hear the snap of the crust as I bit into it. It was like I was there," he explains, baffled.

When he stops talking, I peer over at him to see him leaning with his head back against the rest, his eyes squeezed shut. His lips are pulled into a thin line as he places a hand over his eyes, blindfolding himself. I know he needs complete darkness, to shut him off from the real world and get lost in the past.

"I ate there after my basketball finals. Holy shit. I was fourteen." His hand drops into his lap as he slowly opens his eyes. "I remember."

I'm seconds from exploding in my seat, but concentrate on the road. "You remember what?"

"I remember we beat The Scorpions. Ninety-three to seventy-five. I was captain."

"That's right, Sam," I say, encouraging him. "You were. You were captain all through high school. You never left home without your ball. What else do you remember?" Fleetingly looking over at him, I hope it'll be me.

He stares out the windshield, his eyes never blinking. "A horse. Three horses."

A strangled wheeze gets trapped in my throat.

"Why do I remember horses? I never owned any," he asks, his tone littered with uncertainty.

Cleaning my throat, I reveal. "Yes, Sam, you do. We have three horses at home."

He spins to face me, not hiding his surprise. "We do?"

I nod. This is too much.

"Am I rich?" He sounds genuinely curious. "I know my parents are well-off, but am I? Are...we?"

The fact he just referred to us as *we* has me glowing from head to toe. "We do okay for ourselves. You work with your dad on the farm. It's been a good harvest this year."

"It's so surreal," he confesses, slouching low and shaking his head. "Why can't I remember any of this?"

I raise my shoulders in defeat. "I don't know, but you will." I tug at the necklace around my neck, hoping my good luck charm will work for me. Trigger some kind of memory. It doesn't.

"You think?"

"Yes, I do," I reply with poise. "And if any place can bring those memories back, it'll be your home."

As if on cue, I turn down a one way, graveled road, the tires crunching loudly over the loose stones. The sound instantly bathes me with a wave of nostalgia. I can only hope it'll do the same for Sam.

"Whispering Willows," he says, reading the wooden name plaque attached to the swinging steel gates.

"This is our home," I reveal, disheartened that he doesn't remember.

I ascend the pebbled driveway, our beautiful ranch in Big Sky County surrounded by nothing but lush greenery, vast countryside, and rolling hills. The dark wood exterior complements the large bay windows, framed by white panels, which allow the sunlight to stream in at every angle. Off to the right sits our big red barn and adjacent are the stables, housing our three beloved spirited Arabian horses.

The moment I saw this property, it was love at first sight,

akin to how it was with Sam. Our neighbors are two miles down the road, much to the delight of both Sam and I. It was one of the reasons we bought this property. Sam and I loved our privacy and Whispering Willows was our own secluded oasis where no one existed but us. Now I'm afraid that seclusion will lead to nothing but uncomfortable silences and complete loneliness.

Pushing those thoughts aside, I switch off the car and gather my wits. I pull up my big girl panties because I'm determined to have my life back. Not wanting to smother Sam, I grab my handbag and exit the car, giving him time to process everything at his own pace. The car door closes as I climb the porch stairs.

My fingers shake as I unlock the door, which is ridiculous, as I have no reason to be nervous. I have to pull it together. Slipping off my shoes, I toss my bag and keys onto the hallway table and make my way into the kitchen for a much needed drink.

Although it's twelve in the afternoon, I open the wine fridge and hunt for a bottle of Riesling. I'm not usually a big drinker, but lately I have been. Desperate times call for desperate measures and I can't remember a more desperate time than this.

Hunting through the drawers for a bottle opener, I pause when Sam strolls in, eyes wide and mouth agape. By his surprise, I know he doesn't remember where he is. "Would you like some wine?" I ask, the need for alcohol even more imperative now.

He scrunches up his face, my offer not interesting him in

the slightest. "Do you have any beer?"

I point to the silver refrigerator. "I'm not too sure. You can check, though." I hate that I'm giving him permission to look inside his own refrigerator.

He nods and walks over to the fridge while I continue my search for the bottle opener. When I find it, I practically saw off the cork, desperate to drown my woes. I pour myself a decent splash of the sweetness and take a desperate sip.

Thunder comes tearing into the room, jumping up on Sam, ecstatic to see him. Sadly, the same can't be said about Sam. "Get down," he snaps, pushing Thunder away and wiping down his clothes. Looks like Thunder fell through one of Sam's memory mines.

"That's our dog, Thunder," I explain, as Thunder sits at his feet, his tail swishing along the tiles.

"What happened to King?" he asks, referring to his childhood pet. He looks down at Thunder, uninterested.

Sighing, I take an even bigger sip of wine. "King passed away, just before we got Thunder."

"Oh." His face falls and my heart goes out to him. His sadness turns to query. "So, where's my room?"

This time, I toss back the contents of the glass in one long gulp. His room is *my* room, but looks like he has no interest in knowing where my room is.

When I think I can speak without crying, I place the glass onto the marbled counter and try my best to smile. "Saxon's taken the guest bedroom, but there are another three rooms for you to choose from." Feeling brass, I add, "But you're most welcome to stay in my room—well, our room," I amend.

Sam raises the Budweiser to his lips and takes a sip. The action reveals he's thinking before he answers.

"But if you feel uncomfortable, then I totally understand. I understand how hard this—"

"I'm happy to stay with you," he says, interrupting my nervous babble. "I just didn't want to presume, that's all. I don't want *you* to feel uncomfortable."

"I'm not!" I answer a little too eagerly. Oh god, this is so awkward. Why the sudden change of heart? I feel like I'm sixteen again as I say, "I meant, I wouldn't feel uncomfortable at all. It's your bed as much as it is mine. I think it would be good to try to do things that we normally would do."

"Do what things?" he asks, his tone turning husky.

My cheeks begin to blister when he makes no secret that he's checking me out. Is he still attracted to me in that way? The thought hasn't crossed my mind as I've been too preoccupied wondering if he hates me or not. The way his gaze is lingering on my chest, I dare say today he doesn't hate me as much as I believed he did.

Now I really feel like I'm sixteen.

Sam and I have never been overly adventurous in the bedroom. We both liked sex, but it never stemmed into the kinky stuff. By all accounts, it was relatively tame. But after being with the one person your entire life, the sex part, it fades, and you're content with companionship because at the end of the day, sex isn't everything. That emotional connection to another being is far more important and meaningful than having wild, sweaty monkey sex daily.

Well, that's what I thought until five seconds ago. I suddenly feel hot and bothered and incredibly…turned on. But I quickly quash down those thoughts as I don't want Sam thinking I'm an inappropriate pervert.

"Do you want to see the bedroom?" Sam cocks an eyebrow, while I almost die of embarrassment. "I mean, do you want me to show you to the b-bedroom so you can put away your things?" I quickly amend, tripping over my words.

My mind and the gutter are apparently best friends today.

Sam appears to like my trash talking however because he smirks. "Sure." He takes a long sip of beer, licking his lips once he's done.

Smothering the urge to take the bottle of wine with me, I turn on my heel and scurry out the door. Sam's heavy footsteps reveal he's following, and following close behind. The entire walk down the hallway all I can think is, *are we going to have sex? Do I want to have sex? I'm not sure. I definitely have missed having Sam in my bed, but having sex now would feel like having sex with a stranger. Sam doesn't know me, and I certainly don't know Sam. On the flipside, maybe we need to have sex to reconnect on that personal level? Maybe it'll help Sam remember?*

Scoffing, I doubt my genitals hold that kind of power.

Stopping at our door, I step to the side, deciding not to enter, as I don't want to give Sam the wrong idea. "So, this is our bedroom." I sweep my hand out, while Sam pulls in his lips, confused. He understands a moment later.

Peering inside, I observe him taking in the views of our large bedroom. Our king size bed is draped with a black duvet, which accents the dark gray throw cushions and the polished timber floors. Bedside tables sit on either side of the bed, and the huge stack of journals resting on the left side reveals which side I sleep on.

"I might take a shower and have a lie down." Sam's statement lingers in the air, a trail of innuendo following. Does he want me to shower with him? I've never been good with this sort of stuff. I'm completely oblivious when it comes to flirting. Not that I've had to worry, seeing as Sam and I got together when I was relatively young. But he was always the one who made the first moves, and I was more than happy to comply.

But right now, I want to run in the opposite direction as this feels forced and…wrong. "Okay, I'll be in the living room if you need me." I don't give him time to respond as I dash down the corridor, hoping to leave my gutlessness behind.

I detour and run into the bathroom, locking the door behind me. This is ridiculous. Having sex with my fiancé is absolutely normal. So why does the thought leave me an uneasy mess? I know the answer. It's because Samuel is as much of a stranger to me as I am to him. Sex is about celebrating your love, your reckless bond to be crazily in love forever. And at the moment, I don't feel that. Of course I love Sam, but the feelings, the butterflies, they've gone into hibernation. When he looks at me, there is no love behind his eyes, only confusion. And that confusion has tainted our innocent love.

It appears I too need to remember what the old Sam was like because this new Sam is nothing like the man I fell in love with. Sam may be in a good mood now, but I don't know when he'll change back into the cranky, impatient Sam—the Sam I've been dealing with since he woke up.

Needing to get that Sam back, I push off the door and splash some cold water onto my cheeks. Peering at my crazed reflection in the mirror above the basin, I tell myself I wasn't raised a quitter and I've lived through experiences far worse than this. Maybe rekindling our physical connection will help with the emotional blockage? It's worth a shot.

The mini pep talk is exactly what I needed. I apply a coat of lip gloss before opening up the door and charging down the hall. I'm going to show my fiancé that I fight for what I want, and I want him. Regardless of the fact that he doesn't remember me or us, I'll love him no matter what.

With that resolve in mind, I unfasten the elastic from my hair, freeing my long hair from the high ponytail. It tumbles around my shoulders. Just as I'm about to slip off my t-shirt, I stop dead in my tracks, muting my nervous, ragged breathing.

I'm frozen in the doorway of my bedroom as I watch Sam sleeping peacefully on our bed. It appears he only got as far as slipping off his shoes, as he lays fully clothed, sprawled out on top of the duvet. He looks peaceful, his features soft and restful. Looks like I'll have to prove my point another time.

Not wanting to disturb him, I quietly close the door and tiptoe down the passageway. Once I enter the living room, I take a seat on the sofa and let out the breath I was holding. I tie back my hair into a messy bun, seeing as my plan to seduce my fiancé just got shot to hell. But there's plenty of time for that.

My cell chimes, thankfully interrupting my pity party for one. Leaping up, I hunt through my bag and answer it quickly, as I don't want to wake Sam.

"Hello?"

"Why are you whispering?" Piper whispers.

I chuckle, needing her humor more than ever. "Sam just fell asleep and I don't want to wake him."

"Oh. How's he doing?" My silence answers for me. "That good, huh?" she says.

Slumping into the recliner, I lounge back and sigh. "On the way home, he remembered Paulo's, but that's all he remembered. He doesn't remember our home, or me."

"He will, Luce," Piper says encouragingly. But she doesn't know that. No one does. No one knows how long he'll be a stranger within his body. "Let's throw a party," she suggests when I remain pensive.

Her suggestion has me sitting upright, and shaking my head. "No way. What are we celebrating? My fiancé not knowing who he is?"

"No, we're celebrating life. What happened to Sam is awful, but it could have been so much worse." I know by worse she means Sam could be dead. She's right, but I've never been one for parties, especially now.

"I'm really in no mood for celebrating, Piper. I just got shot down," I share, needing her opinion on my insanity.

"What do you mean?"

Twirling my engagement ring, I explain. "Well, you know I suck at this flirting, girly stuff, but I think Sam wanted sex. So, I was going to initiate it."

Silence.

"Hello? Piper?" I ask, pulling the phone away from my ear to ensure she's still on the line.

"I'm here, sorry. My brain was just trying to process that last sentence. You were going to initiate sex? Wow, are you sure you're not the one with amnesia?"

I burst into laughter, but mute my outburst behind my hand. "I've got to try something."

"An even better reason to throw a party. What better way to seduce your man than by dressing up and shaking your tail feather."

"You're ridiculous." I chuckle, shaking my head. But she might be onto something. Maybe inviting Sam's friends will jog some memories, especially the friends he's had for years.

"You know I'm right, and besides, stop being selfish. I need Saxon to see me in my Sunday bests."

The mention of him has me smiling. "I knew there was an ulterior motive."

"Hey, two birds, one stone," she replies, her tone light. "Is he back?"

"No, not yet. Who knows if he'll come back? I texted to let him know Sam is home, so he might stay in Oregon."

"No, he can't! What about my diabolical plan for us to be married by fall? If he stays in Oregon, how's that supposed to happen? I'm his soul mate; he just doesn't know it yet."

By this stage, I'm cackling loudly, I'm certain I'll wake Samuel with my laughter. It feels nice to laugh. "I'll let you know the moment he returns."

"You better. I need to know if he feels as good as he looks."

"He does," I tease, quickly zipping my lips as I just fell into a really big hole.

"And how would you know?" Piper asks, not masking her interest.

"Because I cried in his arms more times than I care to admit," I confess. "And they felt nice."

"Nice? I think the word you're searching for here is un-fucking-believable."

They did feel unbelievable, but not in the way Piper thinks. Saxon provided me light when I was shrouded in darkness.

Even when I yelled at him constantly and acted like a complete basket case, he stood by me, allowing me to grieve in my own way. I'll never forget that. I'll also never forget that he stayed, just like I asked him to.

"Okay, fine, you can have your party," I say, surrendering. "It might be good for Sam to see his old friends."

"Of course it will. I think we all need some fun after the past few weeks."

She's absolutely right. We all need some fun. God knows I do. With that decided, we say our goodbyes, me promising to call her the moment Saxon arrives.

Feeling a little more like me after speaking to Piper, I decide to put on a DVD and wait for Sam to wake up. Nothing catches my eye until I run my finger over the spine of a case marked 'Memories.' This is probably not the best thing to watch as it'll probably just make me miss Sam more, but realizing that's not possible, I slip it from the rack and place it into the player.

The quality is awful, considering it was converted onto DVD from VHS, but that doesn't matter. I can remember each moment like it just happened yesterday. The first home movie is of Sam's basketball final—senior year. I'm perched on the edge of the sofa, watching Sam as his father proudly films his son tearing up the court like the skilled basketballer that he is.

His orange jersey highlights his tanned, taut skin and draws out the blond strands in his shaggy hair. When he bypasses two opponents and slams the ball into the hoop, the crowd roars in delight—me included. The seventeen-year-old me sounds completely smitten by her new beau. Sam runs backward, his eagle eyes landing on me as he points and winks cockily. I swoon now, just as I did then.

I continue watching, unable to tear my eyes away from the eighteen-year-old Sam, running circles around his opponents. He's fast, cocky, and skilled—no wonder he got offered a scholarship to Montana State. A scholarship he turned down because Greg's plan was for his boys to help him run the farm.

With a minute to go, Greg pans the camera sideways, bringing into view Kellie, Saxon, and I. I cringe when I see the adolescent Lucy because she looks like a complete geek. I have no idea what Sam saw in me—I was flat chested, not that that's changed, had a mouth full of braces, wore ridiculously huge glasses, and my clothes weren't exactly girly. But he never made me feel anything but beautiful.

Kellie hasn't aged a bit; she looks youthful, spirited, and fashionable in the latest threads. Her blonde hair sits in a side bun, her face painted in natural undertones, complementing her organic beauty. The camera then zooms in on Saxon.

"Are you excited, Sax? Your baby brother has won the finals for his team," Greg asks, the excitement evident in his tone.

Sax looks up for the briefest of moments, pinning the lens with an intense, unenthusiastic stare. I don't know why, but I unexpectedly have a pitter patter low in my belly. The seventeen-year-old me is oblivious to Saxon sitting beside me, too preoccupied by Sam's efforts on the court. But the twenty-six-year-old me is completely intrigued.

He looks untroubled, completely relaxed, reading a copy of *To Kill a Mockingbird* at a basketball game filled with cheerleaders and jocks. His hair is mussed, falling over his left eye, making him appear all the more enigmatic. He's wearing a ratty Led Zeppelin t-shirt and baggy skater shorts. The look isn't conventional for kids our age, but it suits him. He is utterly mesmerizing and I don't know why.

Before I can question myself further, Kellie angrily clicks her fingers in front of the camera, shouting that Greg film Samuel. A second before he complies, he inadvertently captures Saxon's frown, his expression conveying how Kellie's cruel words have affected him. But his feelings aren't anyone's concerns, not even mine because as the buzzer sounds, we all jump up and celebrate because Sam's team has won. The image ends on Sam being lifted onto the shoulders of his teammates, them singing his name.

A sinking feeling forms in the pit of my stomach and I suddenly feel like I'm missing something. I just don't know what.

I don't have time to delve deeper because the screen flickers and the next home movie is of my prom. The cinematographer this time is my dad. I could close my eyes and recite every moment, every word spoken because I've watched this a million times before.

"You look beautiful, sweetheart."

"Thanks, Daddy," the past and present me say.

"He's here! He's here!" my mom says, rushing over to the hall table to grab her camera.

I didn't know it then, but hours from this precise moment, I would lose my virginity to my prince charming. It went how any first time after prom was expected to be—rushed, clumsy, and awkward, but it was perfect. I wouldn't trade the feeling of knowing Samuel that way for anything.

A knock sounds on the door. "Daddy, be nice."

"I'm always nice."

I remember wondering if I looked okay, as the strapless blue gown showed off a little more skin than I was accustomed to showing. But when my mom opened the door and Sam's eyes widened and he gulped, I knew I looked more than okay.

"Mr. and Mrs. Tucker." Sam looked incredible. The simple black tuxedo clung to every plane of his athletic frame perfectly.

The white corsage he held was so pretty, so feminine, it brought tears to my eyes. I never felt more beautiful than I did that day. As he slipped it onto my wrist, I basked in his fragrance, anxious to get out of here so we could make out in his car.

"Now, son, let's go over the rules for tonight."

I laugh at Sam's horrified expression, although I certainly wasn't laughing when my dad started grilling Sam about having me home before midnight. Thankfully, Mom convinced him to let me stay out until one a.m.

I looked so nervous, and the same butterflies take flight within. I miss that feeling. That carefree, innocent first love is a love that compares to no other feeling in this world. I want that back. And I want that back with Sam.

The footage ends as Sam and I walk hand in hand to his old pickup, my dad mumbling, "He better take good care of my girl."

And he did.

He has ever since.

Ten

I WAKE WITH A START, convinced someone is watching me.

Jolting upright, my foggy brain takes a moment to process where I am. The familiar surroundings calm my racing heart and I groggily remember falling asleep while watching my home movies. Brushing the hair from my face, I see that it's peaking on dusk and the room is lit up by the gentle glow coming from the TV.

I rub the sleep from my eyes with the heels of my hands, but screech when the light flicks on, startling me.

"You do realize you snore like a freight train, right?"

"Saxon?" I almost tumble off the couch when I see him leaning against the doorjamb, arms and ankles crossed.

He pushes off the frame with a lopsided smirk. "Don't look so surprised. I told you I'd be back. I'm starving. What's for dinner?"

I dig at my eyes one more time just in case they deceive me, but nope, there he is, standing in my living room, all six foot four of him. Taking in his dusty jeans and boots, and windswept hair, I dare say he just rode in.

"It's okay that I came back, right?" Saxon asks, breaking my impolite gawking.

"Yes, yes, sorry, Saxon." I leap up, straightening out my clothes sheepishly. "I'm not a morning person."

Looking down at his watch, he smirks. "It's 6:07p.m." I can't help but smile. It's good to have him back.

Judging by the large duffle strapped to his back, I dare say he'll be staying a while. A sense of comfort wraps around me and I suddenly feel more optimistic than I did earlier. I don't know why, but Saxon, he levels me.

I know how that sounds, considering I barely know him, but he feels so familiar. Even though he annoys the living hell out of me at times, I like that he challenges me and I can be myself around him.

"I haven't even thought about food. Is there anything you'd like to eat?" I reply, addressing his earlier question as I'm still staring at him from across the room.

"Pizza," a voice announces from behind Saxon.

Sam.

When he comes into view, bumping Saxon with his shoulder playfully as he walks past. I can't help but smile at his sleep riddled hair and crumpled clothes. He looks adorable.

Sadly, when he fixes his eyes on the TV and sees footage of us swimming in Bali, he turns from cuddly to killer in seconds.

"What's this?"

"It's us on our five year anniversary," I explain, twisting my hands in front of me as his face falls blank. "We're in Bali."

"Bali? Why the hell were we there?" he asks, not hiding his disgust as he watches us frolic happily in the crystal blue waters. Unlike now.

I meet Saxon's aggravated stare over Sam's shoulder. He folds his arms over his chest, unimpressed. "I was over there for work, and after I was done, you flew over. It was your idea to celebrate our anniversary over there."

He scoffs. "I doubt I would ever suggest going over to that poor, filthy shithole."

I take great offense, as Bali is one of my favorite places in the world. The people over there are so generous, so happy, and yes, it may be a third world country, but it's a beautiful country nonetheless.

Sam slumps onto the sofa and watches the plasma intently while I repress my anger. He may not remember it, but this did happen—the proof is right in front of him. And he had fun. We both did. We all watch in silence, our eyes fixated on the TV.

"And what work?" Sam asks a moment later, turning to look at me smugly. "Please don't tell me you're a mail order bride. That explains a lot if you are." He turns back around, an arrogant smirk on his cheeks.

My mouth pops open. "*Excuse me*?"

"I'm kidding," he amends, but I don't actually know if he is.

"Lucy, can you help me unpack?" Saxon says, breaking through the palpable tension. I wordlessly nod, not sure what to do or say.

Saxon huffs angrily, glaring at Samuel before walking out of the room. I stand miserably, looking at the man I love more than life itself. But that man no longer exists. I leave Sam sitting happily alone on the couch as he perches his feet onto the coffee table.

I'm moving on autopilot as I ramble down the hallway and into the guest bedroom. The moment I see Saxon standing by the bed, his hands interlaced behind his neck, I burst into tears. I need to stop crying, I especially need to stop crying in front of Saxon, who no doubt is questioning his decision to return.

He makes a pained face. "Lucy, please don't cry."

I hide my tears behind my palms, attempting to mute my sobs. "I'm s-s-sorry." The action only makes me cry harder. I feel weak, silly, and embarrassed that I can't hold it together for more than five seconds, but these tears, they're laced with anger, frustration.

"It's okay, don't apologize." The floorboards creak as he steps towards me and rubs my upper arm. "He's just lashing out. He used to do it all the time when we were growing up. He's frustrated and annoyed, that's all."

"But he's b-being such an asshole," I stutter, choking on my sniffles. "He was never this mean before. It's like he's Dr. Jekyll and Mr. Hyde." The fact Saxon isn't jumping to his defense makes me think he doesn't entirely disagree with me.

My ugly sobs eventually die down and silent tears rack my body as I try and pull it together. I need to stop this emotional diarrhea. It isn't helping the situation one iota and it just makes me feel worse. When I think I can speak without choking, I pull my hands away, embarrassed to face Saxon after yet another breakdown. But what I see surprises me. He looks completely and utterly saddened. I was expecting maybe annoyance, not sadness.

"Are you okay?" he asks, dipping down to meet me at eye level. "I hate seeing you cry."

"I'm sorry." I quickly wipe away my tears, not wanting to upset him further. But he reaches out and gently secures my wrist. Looking down at our connection, I feel a strange sense of security seeing his strong fingers fixed firmly around me.

"I meant, I can't stand to see you cry. It tears me up inside."

My mouth pops open for the second time tonight.

He lets go of my wrist, shaking his head. "You don't deserve to be treated this way. It appears Sam's also forgotten his manners. But that doesn't surprise me. Decorum was never his strong suit."

I know Saxon doesn't want to hear this, considering he's still bitter towards Sam, but he's the only person who understands. He's the only person who can explain to me why Sam is being this way. "What does that say about me? About us? About our entire relationship, if he doesn't remember who I am?"

He looks torn, appearing to weigh up what to say. "Lucy, I wish I had the answers. At the risk of sounding like a complete asshole, Sam's behavior doesn't surprise me."

I cock a brow, intrigued.

"Samuel has always been a spoiled brat. He always got what he wanted. And now that he's being told what to do, he's acting out. I can feel his isolation," he reveals, pulling at his white t-shirt as if it's suffocating him. "He feels like he's drowning, and the old Sam, the Sam that *I* know, hates not having the upper hand."

I shake my head, jumping to Sam's defense. "That's not true. That's not Sam. I don't know what happened between you two, but—"

"That's right," he interrupts, angrily. "You don't know. So don't start making excuses for him. He may or may not remember, but I do, and I'll never forget it."

"He's your brother, Saxon." I keep my tone light, not wanting to wave a red flag in front of an already angry bull.

"I know who he is. I don't need reminding."

"What did he do that's so bad?"

"What didn't he do?" is his bitter reply.

I remain silent, hoping he'll at least share a small snippet of their past.

"It's all the small things, Lucy, that amount to the bigger

picture. Like him organizing that party the weekend my parents went away. He used my cell, without me knowing, of course, because if my parents ever found out, all they had to do was check the phone bill and see that it was my phone the calls were made from."

My mouth pops open. "It was *Sam* who organized the party that Fourth of July weekend?"

Saxon nods. "Yes. I tried telling my parents it wasn't me, but like Samuel predicted, they checked the phone bill and then there was no point arguing. I was grounded for a month because Kellie's precious crystal ornaments got used as bowling balls."

I always thought it was out of character for Saxon to throw such a huge party. But I never doubted Sam when he told me it was Saxon's idea.

"Or how about the time Sam thought it would be fun to get a fake I.D. in my name and then go out and buy beer."

"He didn't?" I shake my head, incredulous.

"Yes, he did," he confirms. "He was hanging out with his stoner friends and they had a bright idea to kill even more brain cells by getting wasted. Samuel paid that math nerd, Gordon, twenty bucks to make him a fake I.D. As it turns out, Gordon should have stuck to algebra because the I.D. may as well have come out of a cereal box. The clerk called my parents when Sam ran off, totally busted. I got grounded yet again because Sam was too chicken shit to own up and take the blame."

"Why didn't you tell your parents?"

"I did. When I told Kellie what Sam was doing, she would reprimand me for being a tattle tale," he states. "Not to mention, Sam was smart. He knew how to play my parents. Play the baby of the family card. He had them fooled. These examples are just a few in a long line of many. After a while, I just stopped explaining because they didn't believe me anyway. Sam transformed into the good kid, while I was the troublemaker. I was the older brother who should know better. Whenever a mess was made, it was always my name they called, not Sam's."

"You were only kids." I know it sounds like I'm making excuses for Sam's vindictive behavior, but surely Saxon can forgive something that happened years ago.

He indicates this conversation is over with by practically tearing the zipper off his bag. "You sound just like my parents." He yanks out handfuls of clothes and storms over to the walk-in closet, where he throws whatever he has in his palms onto the shelf.

I still don't know why he's so angry at Sam, but I do know now is not the time to ask. He stands in the closet, hands on hips, exhaling deeply. I don't say a word. I simply stand, chewing my lip, avoiding his annoyed glare.

If I want Saxon to stick around, I'm going to have to attempt to stop making him mad. And that's all I seem to be doing lately, as it appears we have a love-hate relationship. He presses all my buttons and it seems I do the same to him.

He steps out, taking one final breath. His presence is almost suffocating. "Lucy, I'm…"

But whatever Saxon is, I'll never know because we both pause when the sound of an engine roars to life. It takes us all of three seconds to realize it's my Jeep.

"No," I gasp, shaking my head, eyes wide. "He wouldn't?"

When the distinct sound of tires skidding over gravel pierces the air, we both know it *is* what we think it is.

"Motherfucker!" Saxon is out the door in seconds, charging down the hallway, fists clenched by his side. I chase after him because he's running towards the front door.

When he yanks open the door and bounds down the steps, screaming, "Sam! Stop!" I know it can't be good.

The cool breeze has goose bumps buttering my skin, but I ignore the bitter weather and spring down the steps, waving for Sam to stop. But he doesn't. My appearance only makes him drive faster as he fishtails down our driveway, flicking up stones and pebbles in his wake.

"Sam! No!" I scream, my shrill voice sending birds from their perches. "You're going to get hurt!" My advice falls on deaf ears as he accelerates and takes off faster than a cannonball on steroids.

I run after him, pushing forward with all my might, but as Saxon and I see the taillights grow smaller and smaller, we slow down our dead sprint and finally give up. We'll never catch up to him on foot.

I'm puffed and winded, but Saxon doesn't look like he's broken a sweat as he storms past me and charges into the house. Leaning over and placing my hands on my knees, I attempt to catch my breath, but the moment I hear a holler, adrenalin sings through my veins and I run faster than I ever have before.

"What?" I shriek breathlessly when I see Saxon standing in the hallway, pacing furiously.

"He took my fucking keys! That son of a bitch," he pushes out through clenched teeth.

A sense of dread passes over me when I realize Sam has no idea where he is. He may be able to distinguish some familiar places, but overall, he's literally driving blind. "Saxon, he doesn't know where he is! He'll get lost."

"I know," he barks, shaking his head. "This is so typical of him. This—*this* is Sam. This vindictive, selfish behavior is exactly who he is." He points towards the door as if to prove his earlier point that this current a-hole Sam is the true Sam.

But I refuse to believe it. He may have been that way with Saxon, but he never was with me. He treated me like a princess, like I was the only thing that mattered.

My sorrow is reflected on my face because Saxon's demeanor instantly changes and he takes a deep breath. "Let him blow off some steam," he states. "I'm sure he'll be fine. If he's not back soon, I'll call my father and go look for him."

"What set him off?" I ask, as his episode was definitely brought on by something. I see the change on Saxon's face immediately.

I follow as he walks into the living room, stopping in the center of the room. His eyes are riveted to the TV, suggesting my answer lies within what is paused on the screen. When I see the still image of Sam at graduation, draped in his cap and gown, I understand why he had the outburst.

Sam remembered Paulo's and then in turn, he remembered being the captain of the basketball team. Is it possible he remembered he was offered a basketball scholarship, but was forced to turn it down because his future was mapped out for him by his parents? Does he remember the disappointment and regret?

Yes, he graduated from college, but in marketing, a course he enrolled in to help grow his father's business. He told me it didn't matter, that this was his future, but I know that it did. I know turning down that scholarship was like turning his back on his dreams.

"He remembers," I gasp, unable to tear my gaze from the screen.

"It appears so."

I should be happy that memories are floating to the surface, but what if those memories are ones he wished stayed submerged?

★ ★ ★ ★ ★

It's now 11:30 p.m., and there's still no sign of Samuel.

Saxon is sitting calmly in the rocking chair, sipping his beer, while I'm pacing the deck, about certain I've worn a hole in the ground. Everyone has decided to be unreachable tonight, as I haven't been able to get a hold of anyone. Perhaps they're all trying to give us our space, but little do they know how much space is literally between us, seeing as I have no idea where Sam is.

"Should we call the police?" I ask for the tenth time.

"And tell them what? He's a grown man," Saxon responds, the same reply as five minutes ago.

"He's a grown man with amnesia," I correct, mid-pace. "I bet if I told them that they'd see how important this is."

Saxon doesn't reply.

I'm riddled with guilt for playing those stupid movies. It was too much, too fast. It was too overwhelming. Saxon said so himself. Sam feels as if he's drowning. And what do I do—throw him in the deep end.

"What do you do for work?"

I stop pacing and turn to look at Saxon, confused. "What?"

He smirks, a laidback, carefree smile as he rocks in his chair. "You said you were over in Bali for work. What do you do?"

Is he really trying to make conversation? When he continues staring at me, waiting for a response, I know the answer is yes. "Human aid," I reply. "Well, I actually graduated with a masters in human rights. I work for PFP—People for People. My role is to advise on human rights and enforce international humanitarian law and protection of civilians."

"In English, please," Saxon teases, sipping his beer.

Looking at the empty chair next to him, I give in. Taking a seat, I explain, "For my internship, I went to Ghana. I also went to Sudan for six weeks. My experiences have given me knowledge of the history of conflicts, and those presently arising within African countries. The time away was remarkable, as I met so many wonderful people. I made friends with many international militaries and UN peacekeeping operators. PFP works alongside WFP. WFP is the largest humanitarian agency fighting hunger worldwide. In a year, we reach ninety million people with food assistance in eighty countries. It's unbelievable."

When Saxon nods, remaining mute and picking at the label on his beer, I figure I'm probably boring him to death. I know Sam could only take so much before the subject was changed. "Sorry to bore you." I tuck my leg beneath me, rocking gently on the wooden chair.

But Saxon surprises me as he shakes his head. "You're not. I'm happy to hear you've stuck to what you love."

I purse my lips, not following.

"When you were like sixteen," he says, as if recalling the memory, "you kept talking about the Japanese hunting whales.

You gave me that flyer with all that gruesome shit they do. Made me turn vegetarian for a month. I always thought I'd see you on the news, hijacking one of those ships. Looks like I wasn't too far off the mark." He smirks playfully.

"I can't believe you remember that," I disclose, unable to keep the surprise from my voice. Thanks to Sam's temper tantrums, and being stuck at the hospital for hours, Saxon and I haven't really had the chance to have normal a conversation.

"Yeah, I do. I remember a lot of things." He scratches the back of his neck uncomfortably. Did he reveal something he wasn't supposed to?

"I remember too." I want him to know that even though we didn't share many moments together growing up, I recall fondly the few times we did. "I remember the time you took the blame for drinking your mom's last Diet Coke."

He chuckles, leaning back in his seat. "Never mess with Kellie's Diet Cokes."

"I'd just started dating Sam and I didn't know the protocols. Who knew she felt so passionately about soda." Saxon's gruff laugh shoots a tingle down my spine. "I don't think I ever thanked you properly."

"It's fine." He waves me off. "Annoying her is a favorite pastime of mine, so it's my pleasure."

Talks of Kellie give me the in I've been looking for. "Has she always been…"

"A bitch?" He fills in the blanks while I bite my lip. "Yes, she has. I learned early on that Samuel was the favorite. He was always the obedient one, while I—" he pauses, gauging the right word to use "—I've just been me. Too bad that was never good enough for Kellie."

I suddenly feel sorry for him, but I don't let it show, as I know that's not the reason why he shared this snippet of information with me. "I'm sorry I was so…absorbed with Sam," I settle with, thinking back to the video of Sam's basketball finals. I didn't even acknowledge his presence.

The twenty-six-year-old me is kicking my seventeen-year-old butt.

"Don't worry about it. You were in love," he quips, drawing out the word love. But I sense he's hiding beneath his humor.

"Maybe we can make up for lost time now?" I suggest, nervously tugging at the loose strands of my hair draped over my shoulder. I have no idea why I'm so nervy, so I stop fiddling.

When he shakes his head, I feel disheartened—like he's snapping my olive branch once again. However, I'm relieved moments later. "How about we just start fresh?"

"I'd like that." Feeling a surge of confidence sweep over me, I lean over the armrest and extend my hand. "Hi." Saxon looks down at the gesture, curling his lip in humor. I ignore him and continue. "My name is Lucy. Lucy Tucker."

"Nice to meet you. I'm Saxon Stone." When his warm palm swallows mine whole, an unforeseen, invisible charge coils around my arm and doesn't let go. The zap is so unexpected, I yank my hand away, a startled gasp escaping me.

I know Saxon felt it too because the hand I just shook sits bunched in a fist by his side. I suddenly feel my cheeks heat and I don't know why. I'm embarrassed, confused, and I think, a little flustered.

Saxon lifts the bottle to his lips, throwing back the contents quickly.

Before I have time to process what the hell just happened, red and blue lights flash across my front yard. It appears this night has just gone from bad to worse.

Saxon stands, shaking his head. "Looks like we know where Sam is." Offering me his hand, I accept, afraid my jelly legs won't hold me up without the support.

I want to run down there, hug, scream, and slap him, but I don't. Both Saxon and I watch the burly police officer get out of the patrol car and open the door for Sam. Sam exits, and the way he wavers on his feet hints that he's drunk. He looks dirty and disheveled.

"Great," I mumble under my breath. "His first day out of the hospital and he gets wasted." Saxon sighs. He takes the stairs and meets the officer in the middle of the yard.

I walk towards the railing and lean on it, watching rather than interfering. I seem to make things worse, so I decide standing this one out may be best for everyone. Samuel tries to high five Saxon, but Saxon doesn't humor him one iota.

"It would be pointless asking if you know this man because

I can see that you do," the officer says to Saxon. "He was up at the Pink Cat causing trouble with the girls. They aren't going to press any charges."

My stomach turns for so many reasons. At the forefront is the fact my fiancé was at a strip club. I'm not uptight, and under normal circumstances, I wouldn't care, but what I'm faced with is so far from normal that I do care—very much.

"Thank you for bringing him home, Officer." Saxon makes no excuse for Samuel's lewd behavior. "Did you happen to see a silver Jeep at the premises?"

"No, I did not." The officer passes Saxon Sam's wallet. "Your parents are good folks, son. If this were anyone else's son, I would have hauled his ass in and let him sleep off his drunkenness in a cell. You," the officer turns to look at Sam, who is peering up into the night sky, stumbling on his feet. "Don't let it happen again."

"Look at the Big Dipper!" Samuel cries, pointing to the heavens. He obviously doesn't appreciate the seriousness of the situation. The officer and Saxon shake hands, while Sam ambles off, oblivious to how lucky he is.

He wanders around the yard with his arms outstretched, his fingers brushing against theshrubbery as he chuckles happily. He stops occasionally to smell the flowers. Once the police car is down the driveway, Saxon storms over and yanks him around to face him. I push off the railing and stand at the top step, watching anxiously.

"Are you fucking high?" He doesn't remove his hand from Sam's forearm.

Samuel laughs manically. "Yes, I am. And very, very drunk," he slurs.

High? Samuel never smoked weed. But it appears I'm wrong. How did I miss this? Saxon's comment about Samuel fooling his parents sounds loudly in my ears.

"There was a time when you liked to smoke with Jonno and me. Remember?"

Jonno? As in Jonathan Whelan, his best friend from high school?

"We were sixteen, Sam. We were kids. We're now adults. How about you start acting like one?"

"Fuck you, man," Sam scowls, jerking his arm out from Saxon's grip.

"You can't just take off like that. Lucy was freaking out." He points at me. I appreciate his concern.

"What about you, Sax? Were *you* freaking out?" he asks disdainfully. Jealousy seeps from Sam whenever Saxon comes to my aid. That could be another reason why he sees me as the enemy.

The rage emanates off Saxon. "I couldn't give a rat's ass where you go. Your temper tantrums are old news to me. Get inside."

Sam sneers. "You're not Dad. You can't tell me what to do."

"No one can tell you what to do, Sam, that's the problem."

Saxon's tone is resolute, but Samuel doesn't seem to care.

"What happened to you? You used to be so fun. I hardly recognize you anymore." He shakes his head, appearing disgusted.

Saxon glares at him. "I grew up. Unlike you, Sam, I left this shithole and made a life for myself outside Mom's pussy!"

"Fuck you, you asshole! You're just jealous that Mom likes me better than you." Sam shoves at Saxon's chest, but thanks to his drunken state, he almost falls on his ass.

I run down the stairs, sensing a fight about to erupt. "Stop!" My demand is ignored.

Saxon snickers. "Jealous? Please. I like that my balls aren't rolling around in her purse."

Samuel's eyes narrow and he attempts to lunge at Saxon once again. He's too fast however, and Samuel ends up tripping over and falling face first.

Saxon laughs, crossing his arms over his chest. "Maybe Mommy can help you up."

"Stop it! Both of you!" I attempt to help Sam up, but he shrugs me off and stands on his own.

He's still unsteady on his feet, but his anger appears to have sobered him up some. "Fuck you both."

"Sam," I gasp, not understanding his constant anger towards me. "Stop being such a fucking jerk!" I'm seconds away from bellowing out in rage, but keep my cool.

"I'll be sleeping in the barn," he declares, staggering towards it.

"What? Why?" I chase after him, demanding answers.

All I get is indifference. "Because the farm animals don't talk back." He storms off.

I stop chasing someone who doesn't want to be caught. "You know what, fine, go! Screw you!" My temper finally boils over.

I feel Saxon at my back moments later. I shouldn't be upset at him, but I am. "Lucy…"

"No, don't." I spin around, glaring at him. "Thanks for making a messed up situation even worse."

"How am I the bad guy?" he rebukes heatedly, but he tersely backs down. "I'm sorry, all right?"

"Save your apologies, Saxon. I'm not the one who needs to hear them." My anger is misdirected, but he's the only one here. He's the only one who can handle it. "Samuel needs you right now. How about you stop being such an asshole and be the big brother he needs?"

"He needs a good slap in the face. How can you defend him right now?" He runs his fingers through his hair, pulling at the roots.

"Because that's not Sam!" I reply, feeling like a broken record. "He needs us to support him. To show him who he is. And you being a sarcastic jerk is not helping. I can't give up on him because he's never given up on me!"

He huffs, his chest expanding. This fight is one I feel has

only just begun.

"I'm going to bed. Goodnight." I push past him, a swirl of emotions rattling inside my head. I'm thankful when he doesn't follow, as I need time to digest what just went down.

As I stomp down the hallway, I'm saddened that the happiness and laughs that once reflected off these walls are now replaced with anger and tears. My happy place has just turned to shit.

Closing the door behind me, I crawl onto the duvet and tuck myself into a ball as I lay on my side. Things were going well this morning and I thought that maybe the old Sam was slowly reemerging—but it was premature.

I refuse to believe Saxon. This new Sam is not my fiancé. I know Sam, and he would never speak to me the way he has. I'm trying to put myself in his shoes, endeavoring to understand how frustrating and scary it must be for him to only remember pieces of who he was.

Anyone looking in would probably think I'm a fool for staying with Sam after the way he's treated me, but love, it isn't easy. What kind of a person would that make me, what would it say about my character and my love for Sam, if I deserted him when he needed me the most?

Love hurts.

Reaching out, I search the nightstand blindly, retrieving the journal from the top of the pile. I need these memories to help me remember. But most importantly, I need these memories to make me forget.

★ ★ ★ ★ ★

February 14th 2005

Dear diary,

I feel stupid.

Today is Valentine's Day and I totally screwed it up.

Samuel and I have been dating for about five months. He's been a complete gentleman, but tonight when things got a little heated in his pickup, I freaked out.

We were making out and it was nice. I love kissing Sam—I'd even go so far to say that he's the best kisser in the world. Not that I have anything to compare it to. But either way, I never feel more cherished than I do when I'm in his arms.

He had his hand up my top and down my pants, which was okay, but when he tried slipping off my t-shirt, that's when things were no longer okay. I haven't told Sam about my scars. I'm embarrassed he'll stop looking at me like I'm the most beautiful girl in the world.

I know that's silly—Sam isn't superficial that way, but I guess in a way, I am. I hate that those scars still have an impact on me. They remind me of everything I'm trying so hard to forget.

11:46 p.m.

I'm utterly in love with Samuel Stone. And it's now official!

I've just crept back upstairs after Sam texted me and asked I meet him around the corner from my house. Mom and Dad were asleep, so I snuck out, risking them waking, as opposed to me wondering why Sam wanted to meet in the dead of night.

I was so frightened he was going to call it off, but he surprised me when he pulled me into his arms and apologized for being so pushy. I explained there were things about my past which I wasn't ready to deal with, and he didn't push. He told me that whenever I was ready to talk, he was ready to listen.

A surge of confidence enveloped me and I reached for Sam's hand, allowing him to feel, rather than me telling him why I was so afraid. His eyes widened and for a moment, I was terrified he was repulsed by my deformity. But seconds later, as his fingers rubbed over the ridges, he declared, "I love you, Lucy, scars and all."

It was the first time he told me he loved me, and it was the best feeling in the world.

Eleven

THE NEXT MORNING, I'M SITTING at my kitchen counter, nursing my second cup of coffee. It's black thanks to Saxon drinking all the milk and putting the empty carton back into the fridge, giving the illusion we had milk—one of his many habits I've grown to accept.

I slept like utter crap, and have no doubt my unruly appearance reflects it. Sophia is due to be here at ten, but honestly, I don't even know if Sam will see her. I used to be able to read him like a book. But now, he may as well be written in Chinese.

"Hello? Anyone home? I bear gifts of the food kind." Piper's happy voice lifts my spirits and I unlatch the backdoor.

The moment she sees me, she frowns. "What's wrong, Luce?"

Looking down at her tray of Krispy Kremes, I reach for

them and sigh. "Let's talk about this while I overdose on sugar."

She doesn't argue.

I pour her a cup of coffee while she hops up onto the counter, watching me closely. "So, spill. What happened? I thought I'd come over and you'd be floating in a post-coitus bubble."

I scoff, passing her some coffee. "Hardly. The only coitus was Sam screwing me over by stealing my car, being MIA for half the night, then showing up in a police car after being kicked out of a strip club, drunk and disorderly. Oh, and he lost my car."

Piper's mouth hangs open, a look of utter disbelief on her face. "No!"

"Yes," I affirm. "I couldn't make this stuff up."

"This is messed up."

"Tell me about it. Then I yelled at Saxon for no apparent reason other than the fact he's Saxon," I confess, slumping onto the stool and rummaging through the box of donuts. "When did my life turn to shit?"

Piper looks stunned, which makes me feel even worse. I need one of her wise ass cracks. I need her to tell me this is going to be okay. But she can't. What she can offer me is some comic relief. "What a dickface. Where is he now?"

Tearing into my pastry, I reveal, "In the barn. Apparently he'd rather sleep beside our farm animals because they don't talk back."

"That fucking dickface!" she exclaims, slamming her mug

onto the counter. "I get he's having a hard time, but seriously, this is getting out of control. He's making the old, smart ass Sam look like a saint."

"I know." I sigh, my mouth stuffed full. "Sophia is coming over at ten. Let's hope she can try to find my fiancé under the layers of asshole he's currently buried under because I don't know how much longer I can deal with this bullshit. I'm trying to be patient, understanding, but enough is enough."

As Piper's mouth moves from side to side in contemplation, I'm almost afraid to ask what she's thinking, but I suck it up and ask. "What, Pipe?"

"Your patience is unbelievable, and you deserve some kind of a medal for putting up with his crap, but what if he never remembers, Luce? What if he's stuck being this gigantic dickhole forever? He was a little arrogant before, but this just takes it to another level."

"That's a lot of what ifs. Ones I can't accept right now." I scratch my fingernail over the handle of the mug. "I have to believe that he'll remember, Piper. If I don't…" I don't need to finish my sentence as she understands me clearly.

We chew in pensive silence, not needing any words to convey how we feel.

"Mornin'."

Saxon's arrival is exactly the distraction Piper needs. I, on the other hand, cringe and sink further into my seat. As he walks through the kitchen, making a beeline for the coffee,

I can't help but admire his good looks. My admiration of his freshly washed hair, white fitted t-shirt, and ripped blue jeans which hug all the right places has me thinking about our weird adrenalin punch last night.

One minute we were talking and the next I was questioning if my hand was on fire. I don't understand it. His confident, cocky touch is so unlike Samuel's, which is probably a good thing, seeing as he's not my fiancé.

"You sleep okay?"

His gravel coated voice snaps me from my thoughts. "Yeah, fine," I lie, meeting his lucid stare over the rim of his raised mug. Wisps of hair cover his left eye, the guise appearing as if he's guarding a secret.

Is he angry at me? He has every right to be. I lashed out last night, and he didn't deserve it. With that thought in mind, I push the box of sugar his way. "The pink ones are my favorite." He peers down at the box, grinning when he observes the lone pink donut surrounded by a sea of other colors.

I can't ignore this peace offering is similar to one that he offered me a few weeks ago. It appears we both need sugary goodness on hand to pardon our behavior towards each other.

He reaches for the pink frosted donut with colorful sprinkles, licking the gooey icing from his fingers. However, he surprises me as he passes it to me. I accept, as I would never turn down such an offering.

"You said they were your favorite," he explains when I

continue staring at him. I can't help but smirk as he then reaches for the yellow frosted one.

"Let's throw a party," Piper announces, breaking my gaze. When I cringe, she playfully wiggles her finger at me. "You said yes."

"I know, but that was before all of this—" I motion with my pointer around the room "—happened."

"What happened?" a croaky voice from behind me says. Does he not remember last night?

Piper stops chewing as she looks over my shoulder, not bothering to hide her distaste at Samuel's appearance. "Did you enjoy your stay in the barn? You sure as hell smell like you slept amongst the animals. Or maybe that's your natural stench."

"Piper!" I scold, my ponytail striking like a whip as I turn to face her. I play facial charades, begging her to stop.

She stops, but does a poor job at hiding her scowl. And Saxon does a poor job at hiding his lopsided grin.

When Sam rounds the counter, I suppress the urge to yell at him and be the bigger person. "Coffee?" He looks like utter shit in his crumpled clothes, snarled hair, and dark rings under his eyes. It appears we both slept like crap.

He nods while peering into the box of donuts. "Thanks."

I steady my hand as I pour his cup of coffee. His reply is better than a 'fuck you.' Maybe he's woken up on the right side of the bale. One can only hope.

When I pass him his coffee, I can't help but notice Saxon

standing off to the side, leaning against the counter as he quietly sips his coffee. Is he waiting for an apology from Sam? I know I owe him one, and I realize Sam owes us both one— actually, he owes us many. His behavior yesterday was really shitty, and then there's the fact of where exactly my car is.

But all of that can wait until after he's had his session with Sophia.

"So, party?" Piper says, cutting through the silence.

Just as I'm about to object once again, Sam's expression has me zipping my lips. "What party?"

"Thanks to your amnesia taking up everyone's life…" I close my eyes, shaking my head at Piper's tactlessness. "We have forgotten what fun is. No pun intended," she adds, waving off her comment. "So, I suggest we have a party to remind us."

"Sounds like a plan," Sam replies, a smile lighting up his face. "Who are you, by the way?"

Piper shrugs, not at all offended. "We're arch enemies. Quite frankly, I hate your guts right now." Saxon's laugh gets lost within the walls of his mug as he chokes on his coffee.

"She's joking," I amend, widening my eyes at Piper, telling her to quit it.

"No, I'm really not," she argues sarcastically. Sam doesn't seem offended, so I let it go.

With the party apparently going ahead, I decide to get ready as its already 9:30 and Sophia will be here soon. The problem is, how do I tell Samuel? I can't be sure if he remembers Sophia penciling in this appointment. It wasn't like he wrote it down or seemed remotely interested in the prospect of her seeing him after he was discharged.

I can sense yet another argument brewing.

Gulping down my coffee, I rinse my cup off in the sink, hoping someone will get the hint that it's time we all move. It shouldn't surprise me that that someone is Saxon. It appears he can read me a lot better than I thought he could.

"What time is Sophia coming over?" he asks casually.

"Ten o'clock," I reply, looking at Sam. I breathe a sigh of relief when he doesn't throw his mug against the wall in protest.

"Sam, go take a shower. You smell like shit," Saxon says, half joking.

I hold my breath, afraid World War Three is about to erupt in my kitchen. I'm stunned when Sam flips him off, but nods. "Fuck you, pretty boy. Are you sure you didn't use up all the hot water washing your hair?"

Piper snorts, muting her outburst behind her hand.

I am so relieved at their banter, as opposed to them cursing one another out like last night. It's these small snippets that have me not giving up on Sam. Underneath his anger lies the man I know and love. Here's hoping Sophia can bring him back to me.

Sam finishes his coffee and places the mug in the dishwasher. The simple gesture has me smiling. I want him to feel like this is his home again, and small things like this will help make that happen. He bumps Saxon playfully before walking down the hall. I refrain from asking if he needs directions to the bathroom as I'm trying not to smother him.

"So when is our epic party going to take place?" Piper asks, wiggling her eyebrows wickedly.

"I know that look, Piper Green," I reply, unable to keep the smirk from my face.

"What look?" She fakes innocence, but I'm not fooled.

"When I say party, I don't mean frat party, okay? Piper?" I press when she whistles and looks anywhere but at me. "Piper?"

Meeting my eyes, she grins. "Okay, I gotcha. Loud and clear. No frat party. What about a keg party?"

Saxon chuckles while I roll my eyes. This is a losing battle. A knock on the front door interrupts all talks of parties.

"This conversation is not yet finished," I tease, pointing at my conspiring friend.

"Bring it on," she replies, cocking out her hip.

I leave Piper shuffling closer to an unsuspecting Saxon. Poor guy.

As I walk down the hall, the glassed panel reveals that Sophia is standing at my front door. She's early, which makes me happy. She's just as keen as I am to get this show on the road.

"Hi, Dr. Yates." When she purses her red lips, I amend, "Sorry. Sophia."

She smiles. "Good morning, Lucy. I hope you don't mind that I'm a bit early."

"No, not at all. Please, come in." I open the door and step

aside.

She enters, looking like a complete runway model in tight blue jeans, red ankle boots, and a white silk blouse. Her black hair is tied back into a neat bun, exposing her natural beauty. Her beauty reminds me of my lack at the moment. I try and tame my bird nest, but the snarled strands protest and resist any grooming. I give up.

"How's Samuel?" she asks, pushing her glasses up the bridge of her nose.

"He's okay," I reply half-heartedly, closing the door.

"Just okay?" She reads through my bullshit instantly.

Not wanting Sam to overhear, I lower my voice as we walk down the hall. "Well, he's still moody, and he still hates me."

"I'm sure he doesn't hate you."

"I wouldn't be so sure," I reply, grateful for her efforts at attempting to play this down.

"We hurt the ones we love," she offers kindly.

I want to believe her, but I would be naïve if I didn't at least acknowledge the truth. "Thanks for trying to make me feel better, but Sam doesn't remember me, therefore he doesn't remember that he loves me. I like to think that a small part of him does, but lately, I'm not so sure." I'm proud I'm able to hold it together without bursting into tears.

I'm thankful when she doesn't give me false promises, or tell me that everything will be all right.

We walk into the kitchen, interrupting Piper fawning over

Saxon and his tattoos. The moment we enter, Saxon looks incredibly guilty, while Piper looks like all of her dreams have come true. He subtly removes his arm from her hold.

"Hey, Doc." When he addresses Sophia, I notice she tugs at her pearl earring.

"Hello, Saxon. It's lovely to see you again." Her customary confident voice wavers slightly, giving away her nerves.

I noticed their exchange at the hospital was also a little awkward, but didn't think much of it as I had other pressing matters to deal with, like trying to understand why my fiancé didn't remember me. But now that I'm not swimming in tears, I recognize this display as Sophia being into Saxon. Not that I can blame her—he's gorgeous.

I admire his ripped, muscled body, appreciating the way his tanned skin draws out the blond in his unkempt hair. His eyes are exceptional, the green swirling amongst different shades of blue and gray. But brilliant color aside, his eyes display a man with convictions.

His tattoos, which I've yet to fully make sense of, are vibrant and colorful, giving him that harder edge that Samuel lacks. Saxon is the quintessence of what a bad boy entails, and Samuel is, or used to be the total flip side of that coin.

I don't realize I'm staring until Saxon's lips twitch. The movement highlights the scar—another angle which screams revolt. I suddenly have an urge to run my finger over the smooth edges.

"Hey, Doc." Samuel's exact greeting for Sophia has me snapping out of my completely inappropriate and improper thoughts. I have no idea *where* they came from, but they need to go back there and never resurface ever, *ever* again.

I guiltily look over at Sam, who looks a little more like himself now that he's shaved and thrown on an old basketball t-shirt. For once, I'm pleased he doesn't acknowledge me, as he's oblivious to my raging internal war.

"Hello, Samuel. How are you feeling?" Sophia asks, while I sneak over to Piper, who looks at me inquisitively.

"I'm fine," he replies with a carefree shrug.

Sophia nods, her smile pleasant. "Lucy, may I use your study to conduct our session today?"

"Of course. Would you like me to show you where it is?"

Sophia's smile never falters. "No, it's okay. Samuel, I'm sure you can lead the way?"

I'm about to point out that Sam hasn't ventured into that part of the house yet, but keep quiet as I know what she's doing. It's ingenious really.

The hesitation is reflected on Sam's face for a split second before he pulls back his shoulders proudly and nods. No man, especially someone as proud as Sam, wants to admit defeat. She's forcing him to revert back to those memories that are locked behind closed doors. They may stumble along the way, but that's what she's here for—to pick him up when he falls.

Sam looks in the direction of the hallway and then briefly

at me. He's asking for guidance and the gesture warms my heart. I nod with a small smile. He leads the way with Sophia following, but not before she sends a flirty smile Saxon's way. It's not in any way sleazy. It's a subtle suggestion to show him that she's interested. And by the way he smiles back, I dare say he's interested too. I can't help but think their kids would be freaking supermodels.

"The back pasture is looking a little overgrazed. Do you want me to move the cattle?"

Saxon's kind offer reminds me that there are chores to do around here. My life has been put on pause, but it's time to press the play button. "That would be great. Thank you. Take your pick of where you want to put them. Just mind the field with the red fencing. There's a hole in the fence line."

"No worries. If I'm staying a while, I better earn my keep." His innocent comment has me beaming.

How long he'll be here hasn't really been discussed, and I didn't want to presume. But now that he's addressed the big fat elephant in the room, I couldn't be happier. "Well, in that case, you can make dinner," I tease, although I'm not kidding, as I hate cooking.

"Seems fair," he replies with a grin. "I make a mean enchilada."

I cock an eyebrow playfully. "Awesome, 'cause I have a mean appetite for Mexican. And it's even meaner when I'm not cooking it."

Saxon chuckles, shaking his head at my cheek. "I'll be outside if you need me."

The moment the backdoor closes, Piper curses. "That *bitch*."

Of course I know who she's talking about. I'm unable to wipe the smile from my face. "You have competition, my friend. And hot competition at that."

"She's not that hot," she interjects, but scowls a moment later. "Okay, fine, she's a freaking goddess, but she's too stuck up for Saxon. I mean, look at him and look at her."

That clears my smile as I *was* looking, perhaps too intently only minutes ago. "Looks like you're just going to have to stay for dinner and show Saxon why you're the better match."

Piper pulls up her sleeves with determination. "Damn straight I will. You don't mind if I hang around? I've got the day off work." Piper manages The Gap at our local mall. She's also studying interior design at the community college.

"Not at all. The past few weeks have been a nightmare. It'll be nice to actually do normal things like feeding my horses and wash my car." My sentence dies in my throat however when I realize I don't have a car to wash. "Scrap that. My normalcy can commence after I find my car."

As I reach for the phone, ready to call the police, Piper latches onto my wrist and smiles. "You're a brave, strong woman, Lucy Tucker. Don't ever forget it."

"Thank you, Piper. And I'm not brave. I do what I have to

to survive." And there is no greater need for survival than right now.

★ ★ ★ ★ ★

"Would you look at that ass," Piper dreamily coos. I don't need to look up to see whose ass she's gushing about.

I pat Potter along his mane while rubbing my cheeks along the bridge of his soft nose. I've missed my horses so much. Growing up, I was fortunate enough to own a couple of horses. I learned to ride early and it's something I enjoy immensely to this day. There is something indescribable about jumping onto the back of a strapping beast and trusting one another completely. The freedom of running boundless is liberating. It was also my form of therapy. God knows I now need that therapy more than anything.

It's coming up to twelve o'clock, and there's still no sign of Sophia. I don't know whether or not that's a good or bad thing.

Piper's inappropriate, but hilarious comments have kept me entertained, but at the back of my mind, I'm constantly thinking about Sam, and how his session is going.

"Do you think they're identical all over? Inside and out?"

Piper's odd question stops me in my tracks. "You're not asking me what I think you're asking me, are you?"

"That all depends."

"On what?"

She continues staring at Saxon, who is bent over the broken fence, repairing a missing panel. "On if you're talking about their dicks or not."

I burst out laughing. Stroking Potter's neck, I shake my head. "I'm not having this conversation with you, Piper."

"And why not?" She finally turns to face me, crossing her arms over her chest.

"Because I don't want to be talking about…Saxon's junk." I whisper the last two words, not wanting Saxon to overhear. My confession has me blushing.

She taps a finger against her lips, deep in thought. "Well, genetically speaking, Saxon's junk should be identical to Sam's. Therefore, it's kind of like you telling me about Sam's cock. So, I need details."

I cover Potter's ears, cackling loudly. "You are so inappropriate."

"No, I'm curious about my future husband's Mr. Happy, so quit holding out on me." I know Piper and she won't give up unless I tell her the gory details.

I guess she's right. Sam's bits are probably identical to Saxon's, so it's not like I'm envisioning Saxon's junk as I describe how amazingly perfect it is.

For some unexplained reason, my gaze fixes on an unsuspecting Saxon, making this easier to explain. Licking my lips, I grin, feeling utterly wicked. "It's big, like really big."

"How big?" she asks, leaning against the railing and

focusing on what I am.

"Big enough."

Piper squeals while I shush her, not wanting Saxon to hear. His sinewy body ripples in all the right places when he strikes a sledgehammer over his head and down onto the fencepost. A sheen of sweat coats my heated body, and I swallow.

"He's so… elegantly long and thick." I pause, my breathing mounting. "Sam's not a hairy guy, but he has a perfect dark, soft scruff painting his bellybutton which leads…down. The curls highlight his toned V muscle. But the scruff, it's groomed. It makes what he has so manly."

My cheeks heat, my body trembles, and I'm absentmindedly biting my lip as I focus on Saxon. "When we have sex, Pipe, he knows all the right moves."

"Holy shit," she pants. "I think I just had a mini orgasm."

"Me too," I lazily reply, my eyes still rooted on Saxon as he wipes the sweat from his brow with his inked forearm. "I know I'm no expert on the matter, but I think it's fair to say—" Piper shrieks "—everything is pretty damn perfect."

Even though I've known Piper since I was twelve, I've always been quite reserved and shy when it comes to talking about my sex life. Compared to Piper's sexual escapades, I guess mine was boring anyway. I've only ever had one partner, but that partner was more than enough. But talking about it now, it gives me a weird sense of sexual liberation.

I fan my cheeks, feeling an unfamiliar wave of…something

pass over my body. At that precise moment, Saxon lifts his head. I'm pinned to the spot when he affixes those eyes on me and doesn't let go.

I don't know how he knows, but he knows what we're talking about. His cocky, slanted smile reveals it.

"Luce, he is so hot."

"I—" I suddenly stop myself. What am I saying? I know? No, I don't know. It is highly inappropriate to be looking at my fiancé's twin this way. Identical or not, I shouldn't be checking him out, and that's exactly what I've been doing.

Thankfully, Piper is too caught up in Saxon's sex appeal to notice my guilt. But he isn't. He watches me, a hand shielding his eyes from the bright sun as he cocks his head to the side. He wears the perfect poker face while I'm struggling to breathe.

The door slams shut and raised voices are not exactly the distraction I wanted, but it's a distraction nonetheless. "Get out! You're not welcome here anymore."

I spin suddenly, my heart sinking when I see Samuel storming from the house. Sophia is following behind, her usual smile now replaced with a frown. I want to race after Samuel, but Piper latches onto my arm. "Leave him. If she can't talk to him, then I doubt you'll have any luck."

She's right. Every time I endeavor to console Sam, it blows up in my face. I can't deal with another shit fit just yet.

I watch with interest as Sophia stops trailing after Sam and stops by Saxon's side. I can't hear what she's saying, but I'm hoping its advice we can all use. Saxon nods, and she smiles.

I can't take the suspense any longer, so I head over to where they stand. "Hi, Sophia. How'd it go?"

Her grim expression says it all. "It's going to take time. Samuel is being extremely stubborn and if I didn't know any better, I'd say he was in no hurry to remember."

I can't keep the disappointment from my face. I stare at the ground without a sound. "What happened?"

She sighs. "It's always hard for someone to hear what happened to them. I told Samuel about the accident. He didn't take it well."

When I bite my lip, she reaches out to gently comfort me. "This is normal, Lucy. For the time being, I think it'll be best you don't mention the crash. For the sake of an argument, let's leave detailing his accident for therapy. It'll avoid him lashing out. He's going to have his good days and he's going to have his bad days. At the moment, it's normal for the bad to outdo the good. Some days you'll see a glimmer of who he once was. And others…" She doesn't need to continue as I know what she's trying to say. "I'll be back same time next week if that suits you?"

I nod, my eyes still averted.

"I've spoken to Saxon about trying to help pull those memories from him. I think you were right, Lucy. If anyone can help Samuel break through those walls, it's Saxon." Her reassurance means nothing to me because it leaves me feeling like chopped liver.

She says her goodbyes and I hear Saxon's boots crunch over the grass as he walks her to her car. Piper rubs my arm, but it's no use. Every time I feel a little better, something a hundred times worse happens and brings me back down.

"I'm going to take a nap." I know I've only been up for a couple of hours, but I'm suddenly dog tired.

Piper doesn't argue and sympathetically nods. "I'll bring in some tea."

I don't bother answering because the next thing from my mouth will be a heartbreaking sob.

I lumber up the stairs, suddenly needing my mom. As I shut the bedroom door, I pull out the cell from my pocket and dial her number.

"Honey, how are you?" Her sweet voice is an instant salve.

"Awful," I reply. There is no point sugar coating my feelings because she'll see straight through my lies.

"What's happened?"

"Oh, just the usual. Sam still hates me and now he won't even talk to Sophia." I collapse onto the bed, stomach first.

"He doesn't hate you."

"Despises then."

She turns off the water, as I think I've caught her in the middle of washing up. "This is normal, Lucy. The doctors have said this will take time."

"I know, Mom. You're right. It's just so hard. I want to hug him, tell him how much he means to me, but I know if I do, I'll be greeted with that blank, apathetic look. It kills me."

She sighs; my pain is her pain too. "I think you have to put yourself in his shoes. This is all incredibly new for him. You may remember, but he doesn't. Be patient. You know he'd do the same for you."

She's right.

"Do you want me to come over?"

"No, Mom, I'm okay. I think I'm just going to take a nap."

"Okay, honey. You call whenever you need us. Someday, you're going to look back and understand the reason why this happened. I love you."

As I snuggle under the blankets and welcome sleep, I hope that "someday" comes soon.

★ ★ ★ ★ ★

When I wake, I know I've slept the day away. It's now dark out and I feel even worse than when I cried myself to sleep.

I know I promised myself I wouldn't cry, but when will this end? It's only day two of Sam being home. How am I going to survive two more?

Rising slowly, I brush the matted hair from my eyes, looking around my deserted room. A room which once shared many happy memories is now filled with loneliness and despair. I suddenly have a desperate urge to move into the guest bedroom, but that won't happen, seeing as Saxon is in the room that has a bed.

Thoughts of Saxon have me remembering my weird reaction toward him. Each moment spent with him, I'm beginning to see him as just Saxon, not Saxon, Sam's identical twin. He's becoming his own person and I'm afraid of how much I'm coming to rely on that being.

Kicking off the blanket, I take the plunge and swing my legs, placing my feet onto the cool floor. As I stand, my whining muscles scream in protest. I stretch overhead and crack my neck from side to side. The house is deadly quiet and I figure everyone is either asleep or out.

Reaching for my favorite yellow knitted pullover, I slip it on and decide to face the world and whoever is awake in it. My bare feet scuff over the floorboards as I amble down the hallway, in no real hurry to get to anywhere fast. The mouth-watering smells of chili con carne and refried beans linger in the air as I enter the kitchen, sending my sudden ravenous stomach into a frenzy.

Opening up the refrigerator, I see that Saxon made his Mexican feast after all. Too bad I was passed out and couldn't enjoy it. The depressing thought makes me shut the door and have a glass of water instead.

Something shiny catches the iridescent moonlight as I stand in front of the window, downing my water. As I peer closer, a sense of relief surrounds me because I see that my Jeep is parked down the driveway. I know this was Saxon's doing. Unlatching the backdoor, I step out onto the porch, drawing down the long sleeves of my pullover over my hands. There is a certain chill to the air, but that could just be my mood.

"Mornin', Sleeping Beauty."

"Sweet mother of Jesus!" I yelp, clutching a hand to my racing heart as I whip my head to the right. Saxon is sitting in a rocking chair, puffing away on a smoke.

"Sorry." He smirks. "I didn't mean to scare you."

"It's fine," I reply, still trying to catch my breath. When I think I can speak without wheezing, I ask, "Where's everyone?"

"You just missed Piper, and the last I saw, Sam was chopping wood." I cock an eyebrow, but he shakes his head and shrugs.

I exhale loudly and slump down into the chair next to him. "Any luck breaking through those walls?" My tone is mocking.

"Nope." He pops the P. "Those walls are as hard as Sam's head. That doctor is crazy if she thinks I have any hope helping Sam."

Deciding to forget about Sam for the moment, I nudge him with my elbow playfully. "That doctor is sweet on you."

"What?" he replies. I can't decide if his expression is horror or disgust.

"Sophia's got a thing for you. Please don't tell me you haven't noticed?" When he sits blankly, scratching his temple, I know the answer is no, he hasn't noticed. "Are you blind?" I scoff. "She's been making googly eyes at you since the first moment she met you."

"Googly eyes?" he questions, scrunching up his face. "Is that chick codeword for something, because I have no idea what that means?" He takes a long drag of his cigarette.

I can't help but laugh at Saxon's adorability. "She's been checking you out, or in guy codeword, she's been eye...fucking you."

His tongue darts out to wet his bottom lip and I follow the movement, intrigued. "She's okay, I suppose."

"You suppose?" I chuckle, sitting higher in my chair. "She's freaking gorgeous." He shrugs, appearing unaffected.

Maybe I've misread the signs? But I'm sure there was chemistry there. There definitely was on her behalf. But by how unmoved Saxon currently is, maybe it's a one-way street? The thought makes me snicker, and I don't know why.

"Looks aren't everything."

"They sure are when they look like Sophia," I rebuke, wanting to get a rise from him. Instead, I get honesty.

"She's too smart for the likes of me." He places his butt into the empty beer bottle beside him.

His comment makes me instantly forget my iniquity. "Why would you say that?"

"Because it's the truth."

"No, Saxon, it's not," I reply softly. "You're incredibly smart. And incredibly kind, too."

A gruff laugh explodes from his chest. "Kind? What a way

to be put in the friend's zone."

We're quiet for a moment, me mulling over his words.

"Maybe that's my problem," he reveals a moment later.

"What problem?" I ask, tucking my foot underneath me as I get comfortable.

"Why I've never had a serious girlfriend before."

My mouth hangs open. Are the women of America blind?

"I don't know if I should be offended or not by your stunned expression," he mocks. "Do you think I'm some kind of manwhore? Actually—" he raises a finger "—don't answer that. I've dated, and I use that term very loosely, plenty of women. Just none of them did it for me."

I gulp as my curious mind wonders just how many women is "plenty of women."

"Maybe you've been looking in the wrong places," I suggest. I wish I'd kept my mouth shut however because it looks like I've just kicked a puppy.

He frowns, avoiding my eyes. "Maybe."

I want to know more about Saxon, as I hope to uncover the truth about why he left Montana.

"Where did you go after you moved out?"

"Which time?" he asks, smirking.

"The first time," I reply, wanting to go back to the beginning.

"The first time I moved out was when I turned eighteen. I moved in with Laura Rose."

I can't help but screw up my face in revulsion. "Laura Rose

was…" But I pause, as the next word out of my mouth was surely going to be a curse word.

But Saxon reads my train of thought. "A tramp?" he offers, while I nervously pull at an imaginary thread on my jeans, not confirming or denying his claims.

"It's okay, Lucy. We all know what she was. *She* knew what she was."

"And yet you chose to move out with her. Why?" I ask, unable to hide my confusion.

He shrugs, reaching for the pack of Marlboros off the arm of his chair. Lighting another cigarette, he replies, "Even though I had my suspicions that instead of working she was cheating with the entire staff at McDonalds, it was better than living at home. And besides…" He smirks. "I didn't have to put the hard yards in with her."

I choke on air. Gathering my composure, I ask, "How long did it last?"

He chuckles, peering off into the distance as if remembering the time. "Not long. Six months, give or take."

"I don't remember you coming home. Where did you go after that?"

"I moved in with Pauly. I lived there for three years. Fun times," he says, blowing out a cloud of smoke. "We used to jam in his shitty little garage. We thought we were the Rolling Stones." He chuckles, revealing this memory as a fond one.

"I didn't know you were in a band. What do you play?" I

ask, thoroughly intrigued.

"I wouldn't really call it a band. More like a clutter of noise," he replies, tongue in cheek. "I played guitar and sung."

"What? No way. Samuel has zero musical talent. I've heard him sing in the shower and honestly, I thought two cats were getting slaughtered in there."

A graveled laugh leaves Saxon's chest. "I never said I was any good."

"I bet you are."

He cocks his head to the side and the movement causes his hair to tumble forward, masking one eye. "How do you know that?"

"I just do. You've got this air of mystery to you. I bet that helped write songs."

When he falls quiet, I kick myself, as I hope he doesn't take offense. I'm thankful when a dimpled smirk touches his cheeks.

"Air of mystery, I like it. It's better than an air of disappointment." When his tone turns sour, it's not hard to guess why.

Taking a deep breath, I hesitantly ask, "Why don't you and Sam get along? I'm sorry to pry, but there's got to be a reason. I know he was a jerk to you growing up, but there's something more, isn't there?"

"There is," he confirms, his jaw clenched.

The fact he doesn't elaborate is my hint that he's not interested in sharing what that reason is. I don't want to spoil this moment, so I don't press. Saxon will hopefully trust me enough one day to tell me.

"That's it?" he poses when I remain silent. "You're not going to ask me why?"

"I could ask, but I doubt you'll answer, so why waste my breath?" I reply smartly.

"You assume correctly," he counters playfully.

Saxon is so easy to talk to. It makes me wish that we spoke more when we were growing up. But I guess we both lived our lives and followed the paths we thought were the right ones to take. It's hard to imagine where we would be if Samuel and Saxon actually got along. But I'm a big believer that everything happens for a reason. I have to remind myself of that as I see a dark figure emerging from the barn.

My mood instantly dampens and I exhale deeply. Saxon reads the mood shift and offers me a smoke. I chuckle, but decline.

Sam looks exhausted and he also looks filthy. I have no idea what he's been doing, and I don't bother asking, in fear of getting my head bitten off.

"Hey." Samuel addresses both Saxon and me. I smile, exultant he said hi.

"Hey," Saxon replies, rocking back in his chair. "There's food in the fridge if you're hungry."

"Starved. I could eat a horse." He looks at me and smirks. I'm thankful he's making jokes.

I'm desperate to ask him about his session today, but don't. The way he's lingering, it appears he wants to talk to Saxon alone.

Sighing, I stand, wishing he'd want to talk to me. "Well, I'm going to bed." Even though I just crawled out of it twenty minutes ago.

Sam looks relieved, while Saxon looks up at me, disappointed. He doesn't ask me to stay, however. "Goodnight, Lucy."

"Night, Saxon. Goodnight, Samuel." I'm hoping he'll say he'll join me soon. But he doesn't.

"Night, Lucy." There is no love behind his farewell. He's more interested in bumming a smoke.

I fall into bed, mentally exhausted and drained. I wonder how long it'll be until Sam comes to bed? Or the better question is, *if* he comes to bed?

Rolling onto my stomach, I reach for his silken pillow and inhale his familiar fragrance as I draw it up to my nose. His scent was one that used to comfort me, but now, it just underlines the reality that I've never felt more alone.

★ ★ ★ ★ ★

I can't sleep.

Every time I fall into a restless slumber, I dream. And those dreams turn into nightmares.

The space beside me is empty, as Samuel has once again decided that he'd rather sleep anywhere but in my bed. Sick of this constant ache, I kick back the covers and decide to make myself a cup of cocoa. It always worked when I was a child, so I can only hope it'll do so now.

As I slip into my robe, I hear the pipes whining as someone starts up the shower. Could it be Samuel?

Opening the door a sliver, I slip through and tiptoe to the bathroom. Light streams out from the ajar doorway, and I'm like a moth to a flame as I drift towards it. I don't know what possesses me, but like a thief in the night, I take a deep breath before peeking inside.

It takes my eyes a while to adjust, as plumes of steam fill the guest bathroom, but when they do, I jump backwards and press my back to the wall. A freight train is speeding through my veins, my blood soaring loudly in my ears, my body tingling and betraying me because in that shower is not Samuel—it's Saxon.

I need to turn away and go back the way I came, but I can't. My feet act before my brain can keep up and before I know it, I'm flat to the wall, my face peering around the bathroom doorjamb. I've never seen another man nude before. And I feel sinfully wicked that that man is Saxon.

The mist masks my vision, but I can make out enough. Water trickles over his hardened body as he unknowingly lathers up a handful of soap. His back is turned—it's golden and tanned and so very muscled.

The glass is caked with a thick fog, but when he turns to the side, I get a glimpse of a toned, firm ass. I never thought watching a man shower could be a turn on, but that was before I watched Saxon getting clean.

His hand slips lower as he begins washing over his stomach and down between his thighs. I instantly avert eyes, ashamed that I'm watching, but Piper's comment today about Saxon's junk has me curious. *Is* he identical to Sam—inside and out?

Knowing I'll never have this opportunity again, I give in to my inquisitiveness and shyly continue watching. My eyes follow each lithe movement, mesmerized by each droplet kissing his glistening skin. I'm lost in this erotic vision and don't realize what I'm seeing until it's too late to turn away.

His arm begins moving in a distinct manner, slow at first as he leans his head back, his wet hair sticking to the slope of his neck. As the strokes get faster and faster, the clear sound of his hand working his shaft bounces off the white walls. Water sloshes in time with his frantic speed, and when he slams his palm against the tiles and leans forward, I too mimic his movement.

Even under the water spray, I can hear his primal grunts, and the sound does something it shouldn't. I press my thighs together, hoping to suppress the tingle shooting all the way to my core. I'm with him every stroke of the way, watching in breathless anticipation, desperate to see how it ends.

His outstretched palm curls into a fist, hinting that he's close. Piper's comment plays loudly in my mind as I stand on tippy toes, desperate for one…little…look. He shifts and by some miracle, the fog clears and his glorious ass comes into full view. Its firm and shaped liked a peach. His dimples of Venus are perfectly symmetrical, just like the rest of him.

The frantic speed of his arm and his low, guttural moans has me biting my lip to mute my whimper. He suddenly turns to the left, and through the cloud of steam, I see his hand working his length madly. The sight of his strong hand wrapped around his thick, long, hard, very hard…cock, has me yelping and bashfully turning away.

My heart is galloping and I feel like I've just run a race. This is wrong, so very wrong.

What the hell am I doing?

I only saw him front on for two seconds, but it was two seconds too long. What I've just done hits home, and I race down the hall and into my room. It takes me minutes to calm my nerves and process what I just did. I'm appalling. No better than a peeping tom.

I crawl under my blankets, the comfort of cocoa long gone because I don't deserve it. I'm trembling and it frightens me because I don't know if I'm trembling in fear or excitement. Squeezing my eyes shut, I know another sleepless night is ahead of me. But somehow, I know if I dream, I'll dream about the fact that Saxon and Samuel aren't identical after all.

I WAKE WHEN A PERSISTENT nudging digs into my lower back.

Snapping one eye open, it takes me all of three seconds to realize that unrelenting prodding is Sam's erection pressed into my lower back. His lulled, heavy breathing displays that he's sleeping, but it's not uncommon for him to get a little frisky when sound asleep.

Under normal circumstances, I would reach underneath the blankets and wake him up to a nice surprise. But now, I'm afraid I'll lose a finger if I try. I also feel guilty after what I saw last night. But Sophia did say for him to remember we should try and revert back to our normal routine. So maybe a little action under the sheets isn't a bad place to start.

Rolling over slowly, I gasp when the light streaming in through the curtains draws attention to his dark stubbled jaw line and parted soft lips. Looking so at peace, I can almost forget that underneath that tranquility lies a man who loathes me.

However, focusing on the mission at hand, I nervously lift the sheet and slide my fingers underneath. I don't dare make a sound, afraid he'll wake and tell me to stop. I rest my hand over his boxer briefs, his hard-on hot and demanding.

With cautious fingers, I slide them up and dip under the waistband of his briefs, biting my lip as I feel the soft curls coil underneath my touch. I stroke his length gently, my eyes glued to his face, waiting for any signal that he's awake. He still appears to be asleep.

I lean up on my elbow, as this gives me more leverage to take control. I never miss a beat. I continue stroking up and down his shaft, increasing the speed and pressure as I feel a tingle beginning to build low in my belly.

His flesh is hot, scorching hot, and I feel empowered that it's hot because of me. As I rub over him, a soft moan passes through his lips, but his eyes remain squeezed shut. He stirs, but I assume he's lost in a wave of pleasure and happy to give over total control.

I cup the heavy weights beneath his length, rolling them gently while rubbing my thighs together, completely turned on. A sated sigh passes from both our lips as Sam arches his back, pushing himself into my palm.

"Oh, babe, that's it," he growls, his voice raspy and coated with desire. As I run my pointer over his tip, he howls, undulating. "You're fucking incredible, Alicia. I'm almost there.

You always know what I like." His words instantly extinguish my flame.

I remove my hand from his underwear at lightning quick speed, shaking it out as I suddenly feel dirty. When his eyelids flicker and a scowl replaces his pleasure, I jump out of bed and run straight for the door.

I can't stand to witness the apathy in his eyes when he sees it's me, and not his ex-girlfriend, Alicia, jerking him off. I yank open the door and slam it shut behind, resting my back against it as I try and recollect my thoughts.

Rapping my head against the wood grain, I hold back my tears. He doesn't remember anything about me. Not my touch, my love, my entire being—nothing. I'm a stranger to him. A stranger he'd rather imagine was his ex-girlfriend.

Pushing off the door, I take a steadying breath and sigh when I see Thunder trotting down the hallway. Samuel has hardly acknowledged him, and I know the feeling all too well.

"Hey boy," I coo, rubbing his head. "How about we get you something to eat?" He barks in consensus.

We both amble into the kitchen where I grab Thunder's food and make my way out the backdoor. As I serve up his tinned food, I feel inadvertent tears approaching. I can't remember a time when I've been more miserable. My childhood feels like a walk in the park compared to what I'm currently going through.

Thunder happily eats his breakfast, while I'm seconds away from losing it. I knew this would be hard, but I feel like I'm being torn to bits. I'm treading with caution, afraid I'll hurt Sam and his progress, but what about me? He doesn't seem to care that he's hurting me time and time again.

A tear slips past my crumbling walls, and I angrily wipe it away, frustrated at how hopeless I feel. When Thunder yaps excitedly, I lift my head to see Saxon jog up the driveway. He's topless and in black running shorts, which sit low on his slender waist. Images from last night flood my brain, and my cheeks heat hotter than the flames of hell.

His broad chest is tattooed with what appears to be an hour glass sitting over his heart with two huge wings extending up across his collarbones. Gazing down, I see he has cursive writing coiled around his ripped flank. I shouldn't stare, but I can't help it. He is pure masculinity—raw, ripped, and ruling.

His upper body is commanding, unyielding, and ordering total control. His pectorals are firm, a featherlike dusting of sleek dark hair running down between the dip of his collarbones, coiling all the way to his navel. His abdominals are an eight pack and his obliques pop, not an ounce of fat on him. His V muscle, my most favorite part on a guy, is like an arrow pointing to what I know is an incredibly impressive package. His shorts don't leave much to the imagination, either.

When I make no secret of my staring, Saxon comes to a slow stop before placing his hands on his narrow waist and gulping in mouthfuls of air. The action has me shamefully averting my eyes, horrified by my gawking. I did enough of that last night. Thunder drops a ball at my feet, and I'm grateful for the distraction.

As Saxon strolls over to me, I see that he's slipped on a t-shirt. I've probably made him feel extremely uncomfortable. If he were staring at me the way I was just staring at him, I would feel objectified, too. I need to pull it together, as Saxon being here is the only thing keeping me sane.

"Good morning," he pants, still breathless from his early morning run.

"Morning," I reply, feeling my cheeks blister.

"Why are you up so early?" The moment he stops in front of me, his signature, robust fragrance catches on the light breeze. My sense of smell cartwheels in delight.

"Couldn't sleep," I finally answer. I leave out the fact I was too afraid to sleep in case my very vivid imagination conjured up how his shower session ended.

He grins, the sight brightening up my morning. "Are you hungry?" My stomach growls, replying for me. I place my hand over it, blushing. "C'mon, I'll make you pancakes. One thing Kellie taught me which stuck was that pancakes make everyone happy."

I can't help but laugh. "Well, in that case, you better make double." He frowns.

I need to put a lid on my woes because I know I'm sick of hearing myself complain. I can only imagine how annoyed Saxon is.

Painting my face with a staged smile, I say, "So, are we going to eat, or what?" But Saxon reads through my façade instantly.

He captures my forearm within his warm palm and shakes his head. I choose to ignore the very vivid memory of his hand on something else. "Don't do that, Lucy. Don't pretend with me. Your honesty and the fact you wear your heart on your sleeve is a refreshing change from the bullshit I've been surrounded with. No one expects you to be holding it together." He loosens his grip from around my arm and brushes his fingertip along the apple of my cheek. "Just be you, okay? I don't want you to be anyone else but you."

I don't even know what to say, so I nod. He smiles, a smile which I've come to rely on to get me through the long days. We walk towards the house, Thunder following closely behind in comfortable silence. That's one of the many things I like about Saxon. We don't have to fill the silence with nonsense. I'm going to try and forget what I saw because I value our friendship too much.

As he opens the door for me, I beam, feeling a sheet of calm envelope me, unlike five minutes ago. That calm gets trampled on, however, when I almost bump into Samuel. He looks incredible in blue jeans, a checkered shirt, and boots.

"Shit, sorry," he quickly apologizes, steadying me as he plants his hands on my upper arms.

I look down at his fingers, then back up at him, wondering if he's okay, as he just said sorry and saved me from falling.

When a grin touches his cheeks, I'm certain he's running a fever.

Saxon's huge frame shadows me, and for some unexplained reason, I subtly shift out of Sam's hold. I'm still burned from this morning and I'm not comfortable with him touching me as all I can hear on repeat is being called Alicia.

"I was going to make coffee," he declares, that weird thing called a smile still hugging his cheeks. "Would you like some?"

My mouth hinges open. Is he actually being nice to me? His moodiness is giving me emotional whiplash. I don't know how much more of it I can take.

My non-receptive disposition must translate into a yes because he moves behind the counter and opens the pantry door to retrieve the coffee. Without thinking, he opens the cupboard above the stove-top and reaches for three mugs.

My attempt at being subtle is downright laughable as I spin to look at Saxon. He's a lot better being shrewd than I am and nods once, confirming that he saw Samuel reach for the cups of his own accord. Did he remember? Or was it innate? Whatever it was, I can't deny I'm excited.

"So, I was thinking, how about you show me what you—what I usually do around here?"

"W-what?" I wheeze, my voice displaying my complete surprise.

"Sophia said to help me remember, I should engage in activities I used to enjoy doing." When his gaze drops to my braless chest, my cheeks burst into flames.

No guessing what activities he's thinking of 'doing.' Is his change of tune because of this morning? Is he hoping I'll put out if he shows me that he's trying? I hate that I'm questioning him. I never would have before.

When he continues staring at me, hopeful, I give in. "Sure."

The room becomes as bitterly cold as winter. "I'm going to hit the shower," Saxon declares. I purse my lips, not understanding his sudden anger.

"I'll see you out there?" I ask with a smile as I turn to face him. "That fence ain't gonna fix itself."

I'm greeted with a blank stare and a grunt. And just like that, I'm transported back to being sixteen years old. He doesn't commit either way and walks out of the room.

I'm suddenly left feeling incredibly guilty and I don't know why. Samuel doesn't give me time to digest it, however. "So where do we start?" he asks excitedly. I raise a suspicious eyebrow.

Why is he so animated this morning? Maybe he used thoughts of Alicia to finish where I left off. I clench down on my jaw at that thought. "I too am going to have a shower. How about you go out into the barn and get the horse feed ready? It's clearly marked."

Sam nods. "Sure, I can do that. We can have our coffee to go." Today, he's Dr. Jekyll.

This is too much. His sincerity and kindness reminds me of the old Sam. A Sam I haven't seen in a very long while. A

Sam I've missed dearly. My fear however is, how long will it last? Pushing those negative thoughts aside, I focus on the fact that Sam appears to want to remember. Maybe his session with Sophia wasn't a complete disaster after all.

Without making a fuss, I leave and scurry down the hallway and into my en suite where I strip off. The hot water feels divine on my skin and I use this time to process the events of this morning. I'm happy Sam appears to want to remember, but why did Saxon freeze up at the thought? Does he not want Sam to remember?

Scoffing at such a thought, I quickly finish showering and head into my room to get dressed. I slip on a white fitted tank and blue denim overalls—my usual farming attire. I comb my fingers through my hair and reach for the straw hat sitting near my dresser. Looking at the minimal cosmetics scattered along the top, I decide to make myself a little more presentable, hoping the effort might encourage Sam's memory.

Sitting in front of the mirror, I reach for my fair foundation and apply a light dusting to my face. My green eyes look exhausted and restless, so I decide to liven them up a fraction by applying some mascara. Reaching for my cherry ChapStick, I coat my lips and then paint a light layer of gloss over the top. The red brightens up my lips, and gives my pastel cheeks a light glow.

Securing the hat onto my head and drawing my long hair forward to frame my face, I smile, as this is the first time I feel like me. With a small skip to my usual heavy step, I slip into my boots and look forward to a day of hard work and sunshine.

Thunder chases after me as we walk outside and down the back steps. Stopping, I take a moment to breathe in the fresh air and bask in the sunlight, warming my chilled skin. The rays are exactly what I need and I can't wait to feel the earth beneath my fingers, reminding me that I'm alive.

To my left, I see Samuel brushing Luna, appearing to be at home with the white beauty as she relishes in the grooming. She is a striking horse, and although Sam doesn't remember her, I know she remembers him. Seeing him tend to her reminds me of the time we purchased her, both falling in love with her elegance and spirited nature.

I'm lost in the past, a place I revisit often, and fail to notice Saxon working on the fence to my right until Thunder tears over to him, barking ecstatically. He jumps up on him, licking his face adoringly while Saxon pats him, grinning.

Looking from left to right, I can't help but feel exceptionally blessed to have these two remarkable men in my life. Although it took tragedy to bring us together, we're together nonetheless.

With that thought in mind, I go to work, excited to slip into normality—even just for a day.

* * * * *

As I'm raking out the stables, Cullen, our Alpine goat, bleats, hinting that she's hungry. Looking over at her enclosure, I see she's eaten all the freshly laid out hay and grain I put out for her this morning.

"I have no idea why the saying is as hungry as a horse. It should be goat," I mutter under my breath as Cullen begins gnawing on my pant leg.

Chuckling, I gently brush her away and go in search of more food. All of our supplies are low, which means I'll have to take the pickup and stock up soon. This actually may be a good idea for Sam to engage in simple, normal activities such as this one.

Throughout the day, it's taken every ounce of willpower to stop myself from helping Sam. His frustration could be clearly seen when he attempted to do something, but couldn't remember how or where the tools or supplies were kept to get the job done. Saxon made it clear he wasn't helping, which I knew was in Sam's best interests. But it still was hard to watch.

I guess we both have to be cruel to be kind. But judging by the satisfied smile on Saxon's face when his brother was cursing under his breath, I dare say he's not minding the hard love approach one bit. I know Saxon and Sam's relationship will most likely always be strained, but I think this time together will mend some of their broken bridges. Even if it means they can tolerate being in the same room with one another for five minutes, I'll consider that a win.

I'm unsure if Sam remembers what transpired between

them because the love-hate relationship applies to both Saxon and I. I wish I could ask Sam what he does or doesn't remember, but I know that'll just end in tears.

Cullen's feed is just out of reach, so I climb onto the first wooden railing and lean over the fence to pull it over. However, just as I bend forward to pick up the bag, the fence shakes with an almighty, unexpected force. I yelp, cursing Cullen for ramming the fence and before I can stop myself, I propel forward and brace myself for a painful fall. But the tumble doesn't happen. A pair of strong hands lock around my middle, stopping me from face planting into several bales of hay.

"I've got you." My body sags in relief when I feel Saxon at my back.

Bent over at an odd and not to mention unflattering angle, I'm grateful when Saxon effortlessly scoops me up into his arms and sets me to my feet. However, when I turn to face him, he doesn't remove his hands from my waist. Even through my overalls, the heat from his touch burns my flesh. My heart begins a steady climb and I'm suddenly breathless.

He peers down at me from under the peak of his cap, his eyes swimming in something I can't name. I'm unexpectedly lost for words and I lick my dry lips. The air is humming with an electrical charge which zaps me, and shoots a shiver down my spine.

Am I running a fever? As I draw my palm to my brow, Saxon smirks, a slow, confident swagger.

My palms get sweaty, my mouth gets dry, and I feel hot all over. I tingle. What is happening?

"Are you all right?" Saxon asks, sliding both hands to the small of my back.

No, I'm not all right. I'm quite certain I'm a second away from combusting, and I don't know why. But when the tip of Saxon's pink tongue darts out to wet his top lip, I know why. It's him. I'm breathless, on the verge of hyperventilating, and fairly certain my cheeks are seconds away from bursting into flames because Saxon's hands are on me. His touch is stoking a fire within me. And…I like it.

Horrified, I jerk out of his hold, ignoring the stabbing in my heart when we separate. This situation is completely unacceptable and I need to leave now. So why do I stand firmly rooted to the ground, unable to tear my gaze from Saxon?

Remembering him in the shower, I recall how commanding and consuming his naked form was. He radiated strength, protection, and control, and I realize I want to be wrapped in that sanctuary because it's the only place I feel safe.

I feel like I'm drowning. I need to leave. Now.

Just as I turn on my heel, a car's tires crunch over the pebbles in our drive. Cursing, I storm towards the door as I know whose car it is. Kellie waves to Samuel, who is moving some boulders that have fallen into the shallow stream which runs through our property.

Saxon is at my back, sighing when he sees his parents park

their Audi Q7 near his bike. This isn't really the distraction I wanted, but I'll take anything I can get.

"Well, today just turned to shit," he says. "I think I'll hide in here until they leave."

I still haven't said a word, as I'm afraid of what I'll say if I do. I need a moment to catch my breath.

We both watch as Kellie bounces out of the car, waving Samuel over. Greg appears to be checking out Saxon's motorcycle, nodding in approval as he looks at the black, shiny beast. Samuel wipes his hands on his jeans before Kellie throws her arms around him, holding on tight.

Has she always been this clingy?

She never made it a secret that she loved Sam, but I'm now curious to see just how she greets Saxon. Will he get the same warm reception? Something tells me no.

"I don't think they're going anywhere." I observe Greg pulling out grocery bags from the trunk. "The sooner we get this over with, the sooner they leave." I'm surprised that I actually mean it.

Saxon turns his baseball cap around and nods.

Kellie's curious eyes swing our way as she zeroes in on us walking up the hill towards her. I suddenly feel guilty. I feel like she knows that moments ago, I was freaking out over Saxon touching me, which is ridiculous on all accounts.

"Thank you," I whisper, afraid Kellie might hear.

"For what?" Saxon questions.

Turning to look at him, I smile, thankful when he returns the gesture. "For saving me," I reply, meaning that in every sense of the word.

He appears taken aback, but composes himself a second later. "Always." Why do I feel like that word bears the weight of so many different meanings?

And just like that, those overwhelming feelings return.

"Lucy, you look well," Kellie says, indicating she wants a hug. Her warm welcome has me snapping back to reality and I embrace her loosely.

"Thanks, Kellie."

When we pull apart, Kellie doesn't hide her distaste at seeing Saxon all sweaty and dirty. And he doesn't conceal the fact that he enjoys seeing her squirm.

"Kellie," he gushes, opening his arms wide. "What a surprise." Before she has time to protest, he throws his arms around her, rubbing his sticky, filthy body all up against her white pantsuit. His smug face is priceless and I stifle a laugh behind my hand.

She subtly breaks out of his hold, but the damage is done. Her outfit is now smeared with flecks of dirt and grime. She appears as if she wants to yell but stops when Greg walks over, beaming. He's no doubt happy Saxon initiated contact, even though that contact was premeditated to make a mess.

"You look right at home, son." Greg is blatantly obvious, implying he wishes this was a full time gig, and on his farm, working alongside him and Sam at *Stone and Sons*.

Saxon's broad shoulders raise, but drop when I inhale a deep, panicky breath through my nose. I can't take any hostility. My head isn't in a good place. I want to play happy families for just one night.

"What's on the menu?" Saxon asks, reaching for a paper bag from Greg's hands.

Greg reads the derailment loud and clear, but doesn't make a fuss. "Your mother wanted to make all of your favorites."

"Of course she does," he replies sarcastically, curling his lip when he glances over at Kellie, who is dabbing at her lapels with a wet wipe.

If Greg picks up on his sarcasm, he doesn't show it.

"Right." I clap my hands. "Who wants coffee?"

Both Saxon and Samuel surprise me when their lips tip up into that same mischievous smile. This was going to be one long night.

* * * * *

October 1st 2004

Dear diary,

Tonight, I met Sam's parents. They invited me over for dinner and no matter how nervous I was, I knew I had to go.

The Stones are one of Montana's

richest families, as they own one of the biggest wheat and barley farms in the West. I wanted to dress nice, as the few times I've been over there, I've always felt underdressed. Mom said my floral baby doll dress was pretty and appropriate, so I wore that with my black flats.

When Sam picked me up, I was so nervous. But the moment I met Gregory and Kellie, I instantly felt at home.

We sat down to a feast of every vegetarian dish I could ever wish for. Samuel didn't appear too pleased by the no meat menu, claiming he'd convert me one day soon. Just as we were about to begin, Saxon, Samuel's twin brother came home, not hiding his disgust at seeing me in his home.

I should be used to this reaction, as Saxon hardly hides the fact that he hates my guts. The thing is, I don't know why. I've tried on more than one occasion to talk to him, to try to find some common ground, but he doesn't want anything to do with me.

It upsets me that he feels that way because being Samuel's twin, I really want to try and get along. But he doesn't feel the same.

Dinner was pleasant and comfortable, apart from Saxon sitting through the entire evening with his ear buds in. If it weren't for Sam holding my hand underneath the table, encouraging me to answer his parents' questions, I think I may have been mute.

The night was fun, even with Saxon scowling at me. Although, when I pulled a funny face at him from across the table in secret and I saw a ghost of a smile touch his lips, I knew underneath his animosity lies something...more.

I don't know why he hates me, but I'll make it my mission to find out.

Thirteen

I'VE PROCRASTINATED LONG ENOUGH.

Hugging the tattered journal to my chest, I smile when thinking about the last entry I read. I certainly wasn't smiling when writing it, but now, it highlights how mine and Saxon's relationship has changed. Grown. It also confirms that what Sam and I had was real. And I'm certain we'll get it back.

Placing the journal onto my nightstand, I kick off the bed and slip into my flats. I smell a lot better than I did a couple of hours ago, as I took a nice long soak in the claw foot tub, and thanks to the journal entry, I've donned a floral babydoll dress. My hair is down and slightly wavy, framing my face.

Let's hope tonight's dinner will be just as fun as the first time we broke bread.

As I leave my bedroom, I look down the hall, towards Saxon's room. For some unexplained reason, I go left instead of right. I don't question it. Just how I don't question my strange reaction to him earlier. As I reach the closed door, a soft country song can be heard sounding from within. I can't help but smile. No matter how much of a badass he is, Saxon's still a country boy at heart.

Knocking softly, I wait, hoping he doesn't tell me to go away.

He doesn't. "Come in."

When I open the door, a small breath catches in my throat, as Saxon is sitting on the bed, topless. An open journal sits in his lap, while Thunder sleeps at the foot of the bed.

"Hey," he says, while I stand, admiring the picture perfect moment.

Clearing my throat and brain, I reply, "Hey yourself. How'd you know I wasn't your mom knocking?"

"She wouldn't knock," he playfully counters without missing a beat.

Walking into the bedroom, I appreciate the way the sunlight streaming in from the opened window kisses his bronzed skin. "You keep a journal?" I ask, jutting my chin out towards the book in his lap.

He grins, running his left hand though his hair, pen entwined in his fingers. "I could pretend I was doing Sudoku, but you got me."

I laugh. "I keep a journal, too. I have since I learned how to read and write."

He whistles. "That's a lot of words." Closing the black leather book, he places it on the side dresser. "Do you still write in it?"

Stepping forward, I run my fingers through Thunder's fur. "Not lately," I confess. "Those entries are ones I don't wish to remember."

I sound completely pathetic, but it's the truth.

Saxon weighs up my response. "No matter how bad your memories, it's still your history. It's your legacy. You should write it down. This way, you can always look back and remember that you survived. You lived." He sits up tall. "Life isn't all about happiness and good fortune. In most circumstances, it's the shitty memories that emphasize the good. Makes you appreciate what you have, and stops you from taking anything for granted."

"Wow." I smile, standing on tippy toes to look at the journal. "Are you sure that's not a philosophy book?"

He grins.

Jokes aside, he's right. I've been frightened to write in my diary because I don't want to document this time in my life. But Saxon has a point. Sometimes, you've got to experience the bad in order to appreciate the good. Like right now.

"So, am I in your diary?" I tease. When his face falls, I know the answer is yes. Just how he's in mine.

Reaching for a discarded t-shirt which lays by his side, he slips it over his head. "We better go. We wouldn't want to ruin Kellie's spectacular dinner plans."

Although he's being sarcastic, he's right.

I've been holed up in my room for the afternoon as Kellie insisted she cooked, hinting she didn't need any help. Sam seemed content talking to his father, catching up on lost time and memories. I only seemed to be the third wheel as he sat with his back to me, asking his father questions which he could have asked me. Once it was made more than obvious that Saxon and I weren't welcome to join the Stone family reunion, we crept off to our rooms like outcasts, booted off Happiness Island. I now understand how Saxon felt all these years. No wonder he left.

We stroll down the hallway, in no hurry to get there fast.

"I'm sorry, Saxon."

"You're sorry?" He curls his lip, confused.

I nod.

"Why?"

"Because I didn't realize how much of an outsider you were within your own home. I was so…" I pause, searching for the right word. "Infatuated with Sam, I didn't see it. But now, things are becoming clearer."

Just as we round the corner and enter the kitchen, my point is highlighted. Kellie is doting on Samuel, who is sitting at the counter, sipping ice tea.

"You look so well, Sammy. Before long, you'll be back on the farm with your father and things can go back to the way they were. The way they're meant to be." Her eyes flick up, landing on Saxon. She doesn't mask her direct tone, suggesting that Saxon isn't part of those plans.

"Smells good." I gently touch Saxon's forearm, encouraging him to move, as he's rooted to the spot.

He thankfully does.

The dining table is set out like its Thanksgiving, as the table is covered with every food imaginable.

"Wow. You've gone to a lot of effort," I say, avoiding using the term 'overkill' to describe her feast.

Kellie places a huge bowl of mac and cheese in the center of the table, beaming when Samuel expresses his delight. "Nothing but the best for my sons."

Saxon looks at the table before walking over to the fridge. I watch as he pulls out three bottles of beer.

Once Kellie is done dishing up the final plates of food, she takes a seat near Greg, who sits at the head of the table, unfolding his napkin and placing it into his lap. She pats the seat next to her, smiling at Sam. But he surprises me when he takes the seat opposite her. He looks at me, hinting that he wants me to sit beside him. I have no idea why, but I don't question it.

We all watch as Saxon slouches into the seat next to Kellie, not at all impressed to be sitting beside her. I give him a gentle smile across the table, but all I'm returned with is a stiff upper lip.

"Sam, I've made all of your favorites," Kellie says, standing and indicating she wants his plate.

"I can see that, Mom," he replies happily, passing her his dish.

As she begins piling mac and cheese, fried chicken, mini sliders, coleslaw, and fries onto his plate, I reach for the bottle of wine, feeling uneasy that she's treating Sam like a child. I understand she's happy he's home, but this is ridiculous. He's not an invalid. And he's not sixteen years old. If she wants him to remember who he is, she needs to start treating him like a grown man.

I throw back my Riesling, Saxon's grinning face distorted through the bottom of my wine glass. He reads my annoyance clearly.

"How's work, Lucy?" Greg asks, trying to make conversation.

"I haven't been there for a little while, but I hope to get back soon."

When Kellie attempts to serve Saxon, he shifts his plate away from her. She doesn't hide her scowl.

"This ongoing war in Syria is just devastating. All those millions of people affected. Will your organization be lending a hand?"

"Yes, we will. It's been a continuing battle for quite some time. I've worked quite closely with many humanitarian groups across the globe, trying to strategize a plan of action. After..." I pause, as I was going to reveal that after our honeymoon, I was scheduled to go over and offer aid to the war torn country.

Samuel knew this and supported me one hundred percent, but now, I can't be too sure what he'll think.

"I was actually scheduled to go over at the end of next

month for twelve weeks," I confess, nervously rearranging my silverware. "But I think I'll postpone. I can always be as effective here as I would be over there."

"It's awfully dangerous over there, Lucy. And besides, you're needed here," Kellie says as she cuts into her chicken.

She's right, but this is my job. This is what I love doing. This is *my* normal.

"I think you should go," Saxon interjects, leaning back in his seat, sipping his beer.

"Don't be absurd," Kellie snaps. "Samuel needs her here." Sam looks at his mom and screws up his face in dispute.

"And the homeless, famished people of Syria don't?" Saxon counters smartly.

"They're not my problem. Samuel is. I'm sorry they live where they do, but if they want to blow one another up, then good riddance, I say. They're doing our troops a favor. They should bomb that entire country. Nothing good comes out of there, anyway."

My mouth hangs open and I blink twice.

Saxon shakes his head, disgusted. "That's a lovely attitude to have, Kellie. Screw the needy because Sam bumped his head."

Samuel snorts besides me, but doesn't say a word. The old Sam would be reprimanding his mom for such unethical, prejudiced views. But this Sam finds the entire exchange hilarious. Greg picks up on the hostility and uneasily tugs at the collar of his Abercrombie polo.

I should chastise Kellie, but I don't. No matter how much of a bigot she is, she's still practically my mother-in-law and I was raised better than that. I simply smile bitterly and sip my wine.

I've lost my appetite, but can feel Kellie eyeing my empty plate. My mother's warm voice echoes in my ears to be the bigger person and let this go. I do. I serve up the smallest amount of food possible and pick at it like a sparrow.

We eat in relative silence, the TV filling the void. Kellie and Greg chat amongst themselves, laughing about whatever trivial bullshit fills their day. I have no idea why I'm so unreceptive towards them. I've never been this way before. I used to love hearing about their plans to travel, or what was installed on the farm. But has Kellie always been so annoying, and has Greg always been so…gutless?

As I peer across the table at an uninterested Saxon, I know the answer is yes.

"Sammy, remember this?" Kellie holds up her arm, a thin gold bracelet sliding down her slender forearm.

I have no idea why on earth she would ask him if he remembers. Has she forgotten he's suffering from amnesia?

Samuel looks at her, mid-bite, shaking his head, completely uninterested.

"Well, I do. You bought this for me for Mother's Day. You were nine. You couldn't wait and gave it to me a day before. Saxon, what did you get me again?"

He tips the beer bottle towards her wrist. "That bracelet."

Her face pales. "No, that's not right. Sam got me this."

I stop chewing, wondering if this is another one of those times where Sam totally screwed Saxon.

"He may have given you that, but I was the one who paid for it. I saved up all year, not spending a cent of my allowance to buy you a gift I thought you'd like. Sam found it hidden underneath my bed and then he gave it to you without me knowing. It was my fault for not finding a better hiding spot."

"That's impossible," she declares, shaking her head.

"No, Kellie, it's very possible. I'm pretty sure I told you this until I was blue in the face. You just didn't want to believe that Sam had forgotten to acknowledge you as his mother."

I bite my lip, while Sam watches on.

"How long will you be staying, Saxon?" Kellie asks, not even bothering to look at him.

"He can stay for as long as he likes," I answer for him, unable to hide my annoyance.

Kellie's eyes widen ever so slightly, not expecting my reply to be filled with such force.

"I just meant, the garage—who will look after it while you're gone?" she quickly amends. I'm surprised she knows where he works.

"It's under control, Kellie. Thanks for your concern." He doesn't take his eyes off me, which makes me nervous.

"Right, how about dessert, honey?" Greg says. He's forever the mediator. She nods and stands, clearing the table. I help her in silence, thankful that this nightmare is almost over.

She puts on some coffee and passes me a delicious smelling orange up-side-down cake. I place it into the center of the table, wishing I could pass on dessert. I slump into my seat, never feeling more alone as Sam talks to Greg about the latest basketball scores, totally ignoring me.

My wine is my only savior and as I reach for it, I steal a glance at Saxon. He's inclining back in his seat, his arms intertwined behind his neck. If he had ear buds inserted, I would compare tonight's dinner to the one we had so many nights ago. However, tonight we appear to both be uncomfortable.

He watches me closely, just as I watch him, and just as I'm about to turn away, he pokes his tongue out at me. I blink, unsure if I'm hallucinating, but when he places his thumbs to his temples and waves his hands out childishly while sticking out his tongue, I know that I'm seeing things clearly for the first time in a long time.

He's pulling a funny face at me—the same face I pulled at him. He remembers. And just like he did to me, a ghost of a smile touches my lips. My strangled giggle attracts the attention of the room, but Saxon is as cool as a cucumber as he sips his beer. No one saw the exchange but me. It'll forever be our secret.

I instantly feel better.

"Coffee is served," Kellie announces, just as Samuel's cell pings.

He turns the screen away so I can't see it. His action makes me instantly suspicious. He taps out a quick reply to whoever just messaged him and replaces the phone in his pocket with a smile.

A wave of dread passes over me.

"Samuel, how are things going with Dr. Yates?"

I spin to look at Kellie, shaking my head subtly. This conversation is not fit for a dinner table. Or any table for that matter. She doesn't get the hint however.

"She seems like such a lovely lady. Have you discussed with her…what happened?" She places a hand to heart dramatically.

I can feel Sam's good mood shift immediately. "Yes, we have. I hope that motherfucker fries," he snarls. "Or better yet, give me five minutes with him and I'll show him what it feels like to be in a coma."

"Sam," I whisper sympathetically, gently touching his leg. But he yanks it out from under my touch, scowling. And out comes Mr. Hyde.

"Samuel!" Greg scolds. "Watch your language around your mother."

But the warning sends Sam off. "I'm sure she's heard the word fuck before, Dad. And besides, in this circumstance, I think it's warranted. I don't remember who I am because that asshole took my life away from me! How is that fair?"

Sophia was right. This topic is one best left to therapy. I can hear Samuel's pain, frustration, but most of all anger at being in the situation he's in.

My heart bleeds for him. "You may not remember who you are, Sam, but I do. I'll never forget." My nostalgia has the opposite effect on Sam.

"Well, that's great for you, Lucy—" my name sounds dirty "—but I don't remember a damn thing. I don't remember you, or this house, or anything of my adulthood, for that matter." I can see his frustration at not remembering.

Saxon glares at Sam. "How about you stop whining and feeling sorry for yourself and man the fuck up? Sophia wants to help you, but of course you're being a stubborn asshole about it. We're all trying to help you," he concludes, angrily.

"I don't want your help," he spits, pointing at Saxon. "You can go back to fucking Oregon and live your perfect life."

"Fine!" Saxon kicks back his seat and stands. "I don't need this shit." Leaning forward and bracing his hand on the table, he pins Sam with a defiant stare. "Amnesia or not, you haven't changed. You wanted to know the reason why I left? Well, the reason is you."

"Saxon!" Kellie shrieks, standing.

But he ignores her. "I covered myself in tattoos, grew out my hair, and left this shithole dump because I needed to forget! I needed to forget *you*. Every time I look into the mirror, I'm reminded that you're my brother, and I fucking hate it. I fucking hate you. And I know you remember *why* I hate you."

Samuel shoots up, mimicking Saxon's terrifying pose. It's the ultimate standoff, and I'm afraid of what might happen when someone decides to move.

"Boys, that's enough!" roars Greg, thumping his fist on the table.

I look between Samuel and Saxon, my body trembling, horrified at this scene of pure hatred. What did Samuel do? I used to think their differences were a simple misunderstanding, but now I know that's not true.

When a tear slips down my cheek, Saxon's eyes rivet my way. His gaze softens. "You don't deserve her, you son of a bitch." He pushes off the table and storms from the room, while I'm left with my mouth hanging open.

The room explodes into pandemonium as Kellie flails over to Samuel to ensure he's all right. "This is just like Saxon to ruin a family meal." She looks over at Greg, who shakes his head, disappointed.

This isn't Saxon's fault. Kellie's cruel comment reminds me of the stories Saxon shared with me. It appears he's been taking the blame for all of their family troubles, and it's not right. I can't take it a second longer. I spring up from my seat and run to the bathroom.

Locking the door behind me, I slide down it, needing a moment to catch my breath. Once I slump to the floor, feelings of hopelessness overtake me. Reaching for a perfume bottle off the basin, I hurl it against the wall, it shattering into a million pieces, just like my heart.

For the first time ever, I want to console Saxon and not Sam.

I sink even further at the messed-up situation I find myself in. I'm so frightened that Saxon is about to leave. He has every right to. But if he goes, how am I going to survive this? Saxon is the only person who understands what I'm going through because he's going through it, too.

Does Sam really remember whatever transpired between him and Saxon? And if he does, what did he do?

Needing answers, I take a deep breath and swallow down my tears because crying isn't going to solve a thing. Standing, I splash some cold water onto my face and decide to get to the bottom of this rift once and for all.

Opening the door, I charge down the hallway, ready to kick hostilities' butt, but sadly, the only butt that gets kicked is mine.

"I hate being here, pretending to be someone I'm not. I'm trying, I really am, but I can't stand the sight of her. I have no idea what I ever saw in her and honestly, being here is just hindering my progress. She's constantly down my throat, forcing me to remember her. But you know what, there's a reason why I don't remember her. It's because she makes me sick. She's a reminder of a past I don't want to remember."

I sag against the wall, ensuring I stay out of sight as I mute my whimpers behind my hand.

"Samuel, just give her a chance. She loves you so much."

"That's the problem…I don't love her. And I doubt I ever did."

I can't hear another word. I can't stand here and listen to the love of my life renounce his love for me.

I tear down the hall, yanking open the door and soaring down the stairs, tears of betrayal burning my eyes. The moment the night air caresses my heated skin, I kick off my shoes and take off in a dead sprint, needing to get away from this painful ordeal.

I don't know where I'm running to; it just feels good to be free. My feet sink into the flourishing grass, but I push harder and harder, the burn in my entire body animating my every move. Spreading my arms out wide, I close my eyes. I wish I could take flight and leave my life behind. My life as I knew it is no longer and I don't know what to do.

The cool wind whips at my face as my hair catches on the breeze, trailing behind me. I push forward, the adrenalin kick helping me to run faster. The moonlight illuminates the stables, a silent suggestion of where I should go. I tear inside, working on autopilot as I jerk open the door to Potter's pen. He backs up, unsteady and frightened by my abrupt arrival, but when he senses it's me, he steadies.

Without delay, I quickly put on his bridle, before I mount him, bareback, and squeeze my calves around his muscular barrel. "Let's go!" I cluck my tongue twice, sending Potter into a high-speed gallop.

Loosely clutching the reins, I push my weight forward, allowing my body to become one with this magnificent beast as he dashes out of the stables and onto the vast land. I bounce in sync with his strides, squeezing my legs on his sides, encouraging him to go faster.

We have bonded and established a mutual respect and trust for one another. And we have also developed good communication over the years, so when I roar, “Hike!” he knows I want him to really stretch his legs and don’t hold back.

The full moon is the only light source we need as we ride through the fields, with no real destination in mind. As I lead him towards the back of the barn, an orange ember catches my eye, and I know without really looking who it is.

Saxon pushes off the wall, his eyes wide when he sees me sitting on the back of my horse with tears streaming down my face. “Lucy!” he calls out, throwing his cigarette to the ground.

But I don’t stop. I can’t. This is the first time in forever that I feel like I can finally breathe.

“Faster!” I yell, thumping Potter’s sides with my legs. He obliges. He runs faster and faster but yet, it’s not fast enough.

The world blurs around me and the fact I’m sobbing doesn’t exactly help either. But my mind is finally clear. There is no changing Samuel. He is what he is and he’s an asshole. I’ve tried my hardest to be understanding, to give him time to heal, but it’s not good enough. It’s never been good enough.

His cruel words sound over and over in my head, bringing on a fresh set of tears—tears of sadness, laced with a pinch of anger. If he doesn’t want to be here, then I’m not forcing him to stay. I only want what’s best for him. If he thinks I’m a hindrance to his progress, then he can leave. I won't be blamed any longer. I'm sick of being the scapegoat. I am done.

As Potter gallops towards the mountains, the ground becomes bumpy and our ride becomes unsteady as I've never ridden out this way before. But I keep urging him forward, as the further away I flee, the better I feel.

My dress is hiked up, my hair is flowing freely, and I'm barefoot, riding my horse bareback—it's an indescribable feeling of utopia. It's exactly what I need. Sadly, my need for freedom has me losing my good judgment and as I steer Potter through dense vegetation, he suddenly becomes spooked and panics.

I try and calm him down, soothing him with gentle words, but it's too late. The unfamiliar grounds, combined with the uneven earth and thick undergrowth, has him neighing furiously and suddenly slowing down his trot. He backs up as something I cannot see startles him.

"Easy, Potter," I affirm, but he doesn't listen. I try and steady him, but it's useless.

Without warning, he rears up onto his hind legs, bucking me off his one thousand pound body. I don't stand a chance holding on. I lose grip of the reins and get thrown feet away. I land with a painful thud, my body connecting brutally with the terrain.

Ignoring the stabbing pain in my temple, I automatically curl myself into a tight ball, afraid Potter will trample me. The stampede thankfully doesn't come.

"Potter, easy boy!"

I cautiously raise my head, almost crying in relief when I see Saxon charging through the scrublands like a madman. He's riding Luna, looking at ease on the powerful beauty. Potter neighs and gallops off in the opposite direction.

"Potter!" I scream, but the shooting pain in my temple has me dropping like a sack of potatoes.

"Lucy! Are you okay?" Saxon's words are jumbled, broken down into slow motion.

The world starts spinning and I close my eyes when something sticky trickles into my right eye. I'm lying on my side, collecting my breaths while counting the billion stars flashing before me. I lie still, at peace, to gather my thoughts and push out the static. But when a wave of nausea rolls over me, I sit up as I think I'm going to be sick.

"Lucy? Can you hear me?" Saxon's voice is my beacon of light and I hold onto it to stop myself from drowning.

"Y-yes," I stammer, my voice ricocheting off the walls of my brain. I try and focus, thankful when his strong frame becomes clearer.

"Fuck, you're bleeding." He ties Luna to a tree before running back over to me.

"I'm fine." I try and raise my hand to feel for blood, but my arm feels so incredibly heavy. It plops loudly into my lap.

"You're not fine," he rebukes, ripping off his t-shirt.

Before I can question if my eyesight is failing me, he drops to his knees before me and presses the garment to my forehead. The moment it connects with my brow, I yelp.

He recoils. "Sorry." He eases up the pressure, but continues holding it to my temple, his face hard, mixed with concern. "What were you doing riding like that? You could have gotten yourself killed."

Looking up at him from under my lashes, I don't hide my embarrassment. Now that I'm not riddled with anger, I know that he's right. "I know. It was stupid."

His signature fragrance seems stronger, wrapping me in a bubble of pure masculinity. I never want to leave.

"What happened?"

Saxon isn't silly. He knows for me to take off so irresponsibly, something heavy went down. "Samuel doesn't love me anymore," I pathetically reveal.

His eyes widen, but he shakes his head. "That's not true."

"I heard him, Saxon," I miserably confess. "He told your parents that I make him s-sick. That I'm hindering his p-progress." My lower lip trembles, but I refuse to cry.

He sucks in a hissed breath through his teeth. "He's an asshole. Don't listen to him. The only person hindering his progress is himself." His gaze never wavers from my injury as he tends to my wounds.

We're silent, our heavy breathing filling the still night air. I begin to feel better, no longer lightheaded, and my nausea slips away. But Saxon continues nursing me until he's satisfied I've stopped bleeding.

The moonlight paints his naked torso, the swirls of colors of his tattoos contrasting against the blackness of the night. With a need so fierce and unplanned, I shakily reach out and stroke my fingers across his collarbone and down his muscled bicep. I dare not look at his chest, only focusing on his face and arm.

"They're really beautiful," I whisper, my voice cutting through the sudden inner storm.

His flesh breaks out into tiny goose bumps. I'm mesmerized by each one. I want to run my fingertip over each ridge.

"Thank you." With slow, apprehensive fingers, he gently brushes a curl of hair from my brow. I whimper, his touch doing something it shouldn't. His words however, completely ruin me. "So…are you." He swallows. He's visibly nervous.

"Saxon…" I don't even know what I want to say. This entire time, I knew I felt something…more. More than I should. And it's wrong. I shouldn't feel anything but friendship for him, but I can't squash down this invisible pull every time he's near me.

Our eyes lock and I get lost in an ocean of tranquility. Saxon is my anchor, saving me from drifting away when uncharted waters become too rough.

I know what's going to happen. I need to stop it. But I can't. He closes the distance between us so painfully slow, I almost forget to breathe. My stomach begins somersaulting and my body heats with…desire. I want him to kiss me.

"Thus from my lips, my sin is purged," he whispers, licking his bowed upper lip.

He is asking my permission, but he doesn't need it.

"Then have my lips, the sin that they have took."

Reciting *Romeo and Juliet* to a book geek is the way to my heart. But he could say nothing at all and I would still feel this tsunami rolling within.

He smirks, the incredible sight taking my breath away.

This is the time to pull away, to say no, but as he edges closer, I find myself edging closer, too.

At first, I'm taken aback, and remain motionless at the unfamiliar sensation of the softest pair of lips lightly touching mine. They're apprehensive, testing the waters, and they're also afraid. Saxon's confident demeanor is now replaced with trepidation and longing. The sentiment has me tingling from head to toe.

Our lips are pressed together in a deadlock, but neither of us dare move. We're both afraid that whoever makes the first move will set off a chain reaction of uncontrollable catastrophe that will seal our fates forever.

The thought is the reality check I so desperately needed and I tug away, horrified at what almost transpired between us. But my sense of right and wrong soon fades away when Saxon's hand snaps out. He fastens his fingers around my nape, drawing my face to his. We're inches apart, watching one another, never blinking. His warm breath fans my cheeks. I can feel his desire in every breath he takes.

On his knees before me, surrendering everything that he is, he whispers, "Let's pretend tomorrow doesn't exist." Pressing his forehead to mine, he earnestly says, "Whatever happens now, it'll just be memories from yesterday." I can feel the tremble rumble throughout his entire body, and his uncertainty leaves me abandoning any lingering doubts. For this stolen moment in time, I just want to…feel.

Gently pushing on his bare, solid chest, he allows me to climb onto his lap as he nestles into the rocky terrain. Without a second thought, I wrap my legs around his waist and hold on tight, with no intention of ever letting go. His chest is rising and falling so quickly, I'm certain I can hear his heart hammering wildly within his body. The cadence matches mine as I seal my mouth around his. The touch of his full lips pressed to mine is complete perfection. But when he angles my mouth at the perfect slope and skillfully tangles my tongue with his, I know that *this* is nirvana.

The kiss at first is slow, like a roller coaster beginning its incline. But as we reach the pinnacle, it's an exhilarating head rush of fast, breathtaking passion. When he senses me coyly opening up, lowering my guard and losing myself in the moment, he growls into my mouth. He dominates me with a fierce desire and in this moment, I am his.

I can't keep up with the frantic pace, and finally, I surrender all I am. I allow him total control, melting when he sucks my bottom lip with a long, wet pull. I madly fuse our lips together, unable to get enough of this heady feeling, needing him to consume me, devour me, make me whole.

He is everywhere, engrained into my every pore, but yet he's not close enough. I cup his face, his soft stubble feeling like silk underneath my fingers. He moans into my mouth, the sound doing something to me I can't explain. Pressing my chest to his, I feel his heart still pounding frantically against mine. It pleases me to know he's just as affected as I am.

I wrap my arms around his neck and toy with the long strands of hair curling at his nape. When he moans even louder, I thread my fingers through his hair and yank hard, fisting his thick locks. He hisses, the sound striking straight between my legs. I'm so turned on, I can feel myself getting wet and I'm embarrassed that all it took was a kiss to get me so worked up.

Our mouths never miss a beat as we kiss recklessly, both appearing to live by Saxon's words of pretending there is no tomorrow. When I feel something firm stir between us, I whimper, shamelessly wanting to feel more. Flashes of what I saw in the shower flicker behind my eyes, and without a second thought, I rock my hips, gasping at the unforeseen awakening within. This is so unlike me, but I like it.

Each tango of tongues and sashay of lips drives us closer to crossing the line of no return. But who am I kidding? That line was crossed the moment I saw Saxon as someone other than Sam's brother. This should feel so wrong, but it doesn't. It feels right.

I continue kissing him until I can longer breathe without him. He becomes my life source—each kiss bringing me back to life. But when I hear my name catching on the wind, the reality of what I'm doing and who I'm doing it with douses my flames, reminding me that right now, right this second, I'm an adulterer. I've just cheated on Sam, and with this brother no less.

I feel sick.

Yanking away, I meet Saxon's startled stare, him not understanding why I stopped. But when I cover my cheating, dirty mouth with a wavering hand, he gets it. There is no remorse in his eyes, only regret. "Lucy…"

His deep, husky voice makes this real. Makes the fact I made out with Saxon and liked it so very real. I'm disgusting.

Pushing off of him, I almost fall backwards as I attempt to stand. He lunges out to help me, but I slap his hand away. My engagement ring catches the moonlight. "Oh my god. What have I done?"

Standing on my own two feet, I look down at a broken-hearted Saxon. My need to console him leaves me winded, but I can't. I'm afraid if I get too close, I'll kiss him again.

"Lucy!" There is no mistaking that its Greg calling out my name. I need to get out of here.

"I'm sorry, Saxon. This shouldn't have happened." My lip trembles as I know I've just lost my best friend. But I've also lost a piece of me.

I don't wait for him to reply. I can't. I turn on my heel and run. That's all I seem to be doing lately.

Too bad I can't run away from the colossal mess I've just made.

★ ★ ★ ★ ★

September 4th 2004
Dear diary,

One month ago, I met Sam. So it only seems fitting that one hour ago we shared our first kiss. I don't think I'll ever be able to wipe the smile from my face because I can't remember ever being this happy!

It was totally unplanned, which is completely ironic, seeing as I've been dropping not so subtle hints all month.

Sam won his basketball game and being on a high, his teammates decided it would be fun to throw an impromptu party at Jonno's house. Piper and I were excited to go, as it was our first real party. We've been to a few smaller parties, but this one was massive. There were over one hundred people there, and most were kids from our school.

Samuel was of course the star attraction. Everyone wanted a piece of him. Piper was off looking for Saxon, but I knew this wasn't really his scene. I know she's using Saxon as an excuse because she doesn't particularly like Sam, and I don't know why.

Every time I tried to talk to Sam, a new face would appear, congratulating him on his win. It was great seeing him being appreciated and acknowledged for the amazing athlete that he is, but after a while, I felt like the third wheel.

I never drink. Like ever. But tonight, I decided to try my first beer. It was awful, but after two sips, I felt buzzed. Boredom led to another beer and before I knew it, I was drunk. Wow, what a lightweight. The first time I drink I get drunk and off of two beers!

I noticed Alicia Bell loitering around Samuel for the majority of the night. She was his girlfriend before we started dating, and from the way she was hanging all over him, I dare say she wishes she still was.

I don't know if it was the beer or maybe the fact another girl was pawing my boyfriend, but I marched over to Samuel, pushed through the crowd of fans circling him, and kissed him, right there in front of everyone.

At first he froze, and I thought I was doing it wrong because I've never kissed anyone before. But when he looped his hands around my waist and drew me into the warmth of his body, I knew he was just as shocked as I was by my forwardness, as me instigating this kiss was kind of a big deal.

The kiss was perfect. Everything I thought it would be and more.

My head was spinning the entire time and I'm certain it wasn't the alcohol. I was drunk on Samuel. I still am.

We kissed for minutes. The crowd eventually grew bored by our frantic making out and left us to our heavy petting.

My heart is still racing because I

can still feel, smell, and taste everything about that first kiss—it was the kiss of all kisses, and I'm sure no other kiss can compare.

Fourteen

I CAN'T FACE HIM.

I can't face either of them.

What have I done?

After I was done assuring Greg I was fine, I ran back to the house and hid in my room. Samuel, of course, wasn't anywhere to be found, and I spent another lonely night in my bed alone. But for once, I didn't mind.

It's now after midday and I have no intention of leaving my room—ever. I've used the time to catch up on the real world as Kellie's comments last night had me thinking about how much I miss work. Now that Samuel has made his feelings perfectly clear, I guess there is no reason for me to stay. I could go over to Syria like I planned and lend a hand to people who actually need and want my help.

Groaning, I slam my laptop shut, as I'm in no frame of mind

to be helping anyone out. I'm the one who needs assistance at the moment, but I have no one I can ask.

I certainly can't talk to Piper or my parents about this, as I'm so ashamed by my actions. I don't want anyone to know what I've done. The person who I would usually go to in times of crisis is Saxon, but for obvious reasons, that option is totally off the table.

I don't know what I'm going to do.

A soft knock on my bedroom door has me falling back onto my bed and covering my face with a pillow. I know who's there. Samuel would have zero need to come see me and Piper is at work. When the knock sounds again, I reach for another pillow.

I vaguely hear the door whining open, revealing that I can't hide forever. But I can try. As I blindly reach for another pillow, warm fingers gently clasp around my wrist to stop my hunt. I squash down the happy feelings of him being in my room, touching me.

"Are you playing hide and seek? 'Cause if you are, you really need to find a better hiding spot." Saxon's voice is muffled, but it still sends a shiver down my spine.

Fingers walk down my arm, leaving a blaze of goose bumps in its wake. I don't bother trying to mask my response to him because my body is a complete traitor. Gently coaxing me to let go of pillow number one, I oblige, as I'm finding it hard to breathe in my cushioned cage. Pillow number two is a harder battle because I know once it's removed, I'll have no other choice but to face my infidelity.

Saxon doesn't give up and finally, I give in, but I keep my eyes squeezed shut. I can't face him. Not yet.

"Lucy, please look at me."

"No, I can't," I reply, red-faced.

He sighs, a sound of frustration. "So you're going to keep your eyes closed every time I walk into a room?"

He's right. I'm being absurd.

With a slow, measured speed, I open my eyes. They land on Saxon as he stands by the bed. His arms are crossed, but he doesn't look mad.

"Hey."

Sitting up, I brush the matted hair from my brow. "Hey."

This is so incredibly uncomfortable and I hate it. We never used to have any uncomfortable silences, but that was before I threw myself into his arms like the adulterating whore that I am.

My face obviously betrays my thoughts. "Lucy, stop it," Saxon says, sitting beside me.

I shift away, afraid of getting too close. I can't look at him. I lower my eyes, scared of what happens when I gather my wits and face him.

"Lucy, about last night…" His pause makes me groan.

"I don't want to talk about it."

"Well, too bad, because I do."

His stubbornness is what I need and I angrily raise my eyes, only wishing I didn't as I zone in on his bowed upper lip—lips that I kissed, and liked kissing very much.

"Ugh!" I slap my hands over my face. I really am not doing myself any favors.

He chuckles. "Seeing as you can't look at me, I'll do the talking. We kissed, Lucy, that's it. We didn't break any laws."

"Are you serious?" I cry, unshielding my face. "I broke about five hundred laws. The most important law was to remain faithful to my future husband!"

His grins, a telltale sign that he's pulling my leg. "Now that you're actually looking at me, can we talk?"

I nod because he's right. We need to talk about this as I like looking at him. Again, not doing myself any favors.

"I'm not going to tell anyone about what happened, if that's what you're worried about."

Pulling at a loose thread on the bedspread, I shake my head. "That's the least of my concerns. It shouldn't have happened."

"I know, but it did."

Silence.

"I did mean it when I said we can pretend that tomorrow doesn't exist."

If only it were that simple. "I can't pretend. I know what I did. How can I live with myself? I cheated on my fiancé who has amnesia with his identical twin brother. If that's not an episode for Jerry Springer then I don't know what it is."

He smirks. I'm glad he's finding my dilemma amusing.

"Look, you're under a lot of stress, Samuel is being a complete asshole to you, and not to mention, you hit your head. One can't blame you for doing something out of character. We all make mistakes. You were vulnerable."

But that's the problem. As I sit here, listening to Saxon make excuses for my epic sluttiness, I don't see what we did as a mistake. Yes, we shouldn't have kissed, I acknowledge that, but the act within itself, the kiss, it wasn't a mistake. It certainly didn't feel like one. It felt perfect.

This scenario, however, is not. "Friends kiss, it's no big deal. Anyway, I was drunk..." He continues talking but I don't listen to a single word he says because my head begins reeling. He was drunk? Since when? I didn't think he was intoxicated. He only had three beers at dinner.

Is he really disregarding our kiss? He's not playing the 'I was drunk and you were concussed' card, is he?

It appears that he is. "Neither of us was in the right frame of mind. You're right, it shouldn't have happened."

Saxon is giving me a get out of jail for free card and all I want to do is rip it up in his face. Wasn't the kiss any good? Is that why he can pretend it never happened? From my end, it was unbelievable, but Saxon obviously doesn't agree.

"I like being your friend, Lucy, and I wouldn't want a little thing like a kiss to ruin that friendship."

He needs to stop talking.

"Are you angry at me?" he asks, while I sit, grinding my

teeth.

Am I?

The way he's discounting what happened between us hurts. It also pisses me off. I'm a melting pot of emotion right now. I should be relieved that things can go back to "normal" between us, but I'm not. But I also don't want to lose Saxon as a friend.

"You don't want to be friends anymore?" The sadness breaks my heart.

"Of course I do," I reply, leaning out to touch his forearm, finally speaking. "I just…don't want things to be weird between us."

"Neither do I." He looks down at my fingers caressing his arm. I quickly snatch my hand away.

"I'll never forgive myself for what I did to Sam, but I don't think I can do this without you. So if pretending is the lesser of two evils then…okay." I feel like I've gotten off scot-free. I deserve some kind of punishment for my crimes. But all I get is Saxon's hand slipping into mine. "I'm an awful person, Saxon. I don't deserve your friendship. I deserve to be treated like the cheating tramp that I am. Sam hasn't even been home a week! I'm atrocious." I'll carry this guilt around with me for as long as I live.

"Hey, don't talk like that." He squeezes my fingers. "A week in this house feels like a hundred years. Not to mention, a lot has happened before this week. Samuel isn't who he once was. He hasn't exactly been Mr. Prince Charming since he woke.

And besides, it was just a kiss. One…simple…kiss."

The pause between each heated word has every nerve in my body standing to attention. I can feel that familiar fire building in my body. I need to stop it. Right now. Yes, he's absolutely correct. Being in this house feels like a time warp, but that doesn't excuse my behavior.

"Yeah, one kiss. One that'll never happen again." I can taste the regret the moment I say those words.

Saxon pulls in his lips and attempts a smile. "That's right, and under normal circumstances, if Sam was Sam, you wouldn't have kissed me, right?"

I freeze and my cheeks instantly heat. Why can't I answer with conviction?

As he watches me, the perplexity etching his brow, I remember what it felt like to be in his arms. How safe and at home I felt. I used to feel that way with Sam. Would I feel that way now? If none of this had happened, would I have responded to Saxon the way that I have?

I know the answer is no.

I don't need to answer his question, as my silence fills in the blanks.

"See, it was just a misunderstanding. Let's forget it happened." His words don't reflect the deflated look on his face. But I don't press. I squash down my disappointment to him referring to our kiss so flippantly because it's the right thing to do.

"Did you want to come into town with me? I noticed you're running low on a few things. I'm not sure what you feed that goat, but she's demanding more of it."

I smile, happy that he's making jokes.

"Sure. We need a ton of stuff, so we can take the pickup. I guess I should also think about getting a few things for this stupid party Piper insists we throw."

Saxon chuckles when my response to the party I don't want to host can be clearly seen on my face. "It might be good to try and be normal for a night," he suggests. "Although, I don't know how normal it'll be with the number of people Piper intends to invite."

I shake my head, not even bothering to ask who's on the guest list.

"I'll be out in a minute. Let me attempt to resemble the living," I say, tongue in cheek.

Saxon nods and stands. He looks down at me for a moment, a look of regret swarming around him. It's gone a second later.

Once the door closes behind him, I exhale loudly, somehow feeling more miserable than before. I should be relieved that things with Saxon have been somewhat resolved, but I'm not. And I don't know why.

★ ★ ★ ★ ★

"I don't think we can fit any more in here," Saxon says, tossing the last bag of feed into the truck bed. He's right. The Chevy pickup is overloaded with supplies.

I didn't realize how much stuff we needed until I made a list of things we were running low on. Usually, Samuel would be the one taking care of what's needed, but due to obvious reasons that won't be happening any time soon and besides, I have no idea where he is.

He's MIA—again. He seems to be making a habit of it and I wouldn't be surprised if he's packed up and gone to live with his parents.

Shaking those thoughts away, I focus on the task at hand. "How much do I owe you, Billy?"

Billy Campeer, the county's most trusted supplier, shakes his head. "I'll just put it on ya tab, Lucy," he says with his drawn out Texan accent. "There's no rush, ya hear? Y'all just focus of gettin' ya boy fixed up."

I nod, wishing it was that simple. "Thank you, Billy. I'll let Samuel know you say hi." He nods, giving Saxon a wave goodbye.

Saxon is tying down the bags with rope, looking completely at ease as he does so. He really would have been at home on the family farm, but I know his dream is not working alongside his brother and father. He's living his dream in Oregon.

I know eventually he'll have to go back, but a part of me is hoping that won't be any time soon.

"Are you hungry?" he asks, jumping down from the bumper

and wiping the sweat from his brow.

"I could eat," I reply, smiling, as the sound of food has my interested stomach growling in delight.

"Anna's BBQ is a few blocks from here," he suggests.

"BBQ sounds great."

We lock the car and walk down the busy street. It's actually nice to get out and about, seeing as my home has felt like a prison cell lately. I can't believe it's only been a few days. It feels like months. The thought has me wondering what it will actually feel like in three months' time. I really could do with a crystal ball.

Saxon's cell chimes and he excuses the interruption before answering. I don't mean to eavesdrop but its evident the call is work related.

"Just order the usual, Fred." Pause. "I don't know when. I understand that, but it's complicated."

No guessing what or whom is complicated.

The phone call lasts for a minute, with Saxon hanging up with a huff. "Sorry about that."

"It's fine." Waiting a moment, I sheepishly ask, "Everything okay back home?" I see no point pretending I didn't hear his exchange.

"Yes, fine."

His short response isn't convincing. As much as I hate to say it, I know this is the right thing to do. "If you need to go back, Saxon…I understand. I don't expect you to stay here. I've already gatecrashed your life. I don't want to jeopardize your business as well."

"You're not."

As I attempt to protest, he stops walking and grabs my wrist. "I'm where I'm meant to be, okay?" When I don't respond, he rubs his thumb over my mounting pulse. "Okay?"

"Okay," I reply, a sense of relief overtaking me.

Before I can scold my selfishness, a familiar voice greets us. "Hello, you two." Saxon instantly releases me.

Sophia stands before us, looking relaxed in blue jeans, a peach silk camisole, and ballet flats. Her good looks really make me feel like the ugly duckling, especially when I see Saxon smile broadly.

"Afternoon, Sophia. What are you doing here?"

"It's my day off and I wanted to visit Green Leaf Nurseries. My roses are looking a little worse for wear. Well, actually," she backtracks, "I'm pretty sure I killed them with my nonexistent gardening skills."

Saxon laughs. "Maybe it's best you stick to something less delicate. Like a cactus."

Sophia grins. "I think you may be right."

She's making no secret of the fact she's flirting with Saxon, and I don't know if my little talk has opened his eyes to it because it appears he's flirting back, which is perfectly normal. They're both single. Not to mention gorgeous.

I'm suddenly struck with an idea. "What are you doing

tomorrow?"

She shrugs. "Nothing really."

"Would you like to come to a party at my house? I understand it may be a little weird, considering you're Samuel's doctor, but my best friend will probably invite every man and their dog, so odds are you won't even see Sam."

She looks at Saxon, who is looking down at me, puzzled.

Yes, it's extremely weird that I'm setting him up with the gorgeous doctor, considering we kissed not even twenty-four hours ago. But this is what friends do. We both agreed to forget it and what better way for that to happen than for Saxon to be paired up with someone like Sophia. She matches him in all aspects. It's a match made in heaven.

I ignore the pang of jealousy when she says yes. "Perfect. I'll text you the details, if that's okay."

"Of course. Thank you for the invite. I look forward to it." She smiles at Saxon, who returns the gesture half-heartedly.

"Well, I better go salvage those plants," she says, picking up on the sudden weird vibe Saxon is throwing out.

"Maybe try some compost or peat moss," I suggest. "It might help." She thanks me for the tip and bids us both farewell.

Saxon remains quiet, guarding his thoughts.

"So, looks like we better stock up on beer," I say, trying to lighten the mood.

He replies with a stiff, upper lip smile.

★ ★ ★ ★ ★

I had a side order of awkward with lunch.

Saxon is angry at me, and I'm pretty certain it's got to do with the fact I invited Sophia over on Saturday. I thought he'd be happy, as he wasn't exactly recoiling in disgust when she was flirting with him.

This is exactly the type of awkward I wanted to avoid. I have no one to blame but myself.

"I'm going to call my mom. I should check in with her," I call out to Saxon, who is tossing bags of feed from the truck.

He replies with a nod.

As I drag my feet up the porch steps, I sigh at the predicament I find myself in. My life as I know it officially sucks. I thought I could have a do-over for my sins, but I should have known it wouldn't be that easy. But I don't deserve easy.

What I did to Samuel was unforgivable. I deserve every ounce of grief I feel. I also should have kept my nose out of Saxon's personal life because he clearly doesn't appreciate me playing cupid.

Feeling awfully sorry for myself, I open my bedroom door, deciding to keep out of Saxon's way for the rest of the afternoon. However, I yelp when I bump into Samuel. He's dressed in blue jeans and a black and white checkered shirt. His hair is wet and simply styled, but the heavy handed cologne reveals he's dressed to impress.

"I'm going out," he says, reaching for this wallet off the dresser.

That's it? No explanation to where he's going or who he's going with.

"Okay. What time will you be back?" I ask, hoping I don't sound like a nag.

"I don't know," he says dismissively, patting down his pockets to ensure he's got everything he needs.

His offhand attitude tips me over the edge. I've had enough. "Sam, this has got to stop. Your love-hate attitude is beyond confusing. Stop treating me like the enemy. I'm only trying to help you."

My words appear to fuel an out of control fire. "I don't know how many times I have to tell you this, but I don't want your help!" I recoil when he yells the word help.

"Sam…"

But he doesn't want to talk. "For the love of the god, Lucy, just shut up," he groans. "Your voice has got to be one of the most annoying sounds in the world. Aren't you tired of hearing yourself complain? I know I am."

The stress of the past few weeks, not to mention the past twenty-four hours, suddenly explodes out of me and I decide now is a good time to tell Sam how I feel. Sophia's words of wisdom can bite me. "You owe me like a hundred apologies! I've tried to be accepting. I've allowed you to lash out, but enough is enough! You can't treat me this way." I shove at his chest, he stumbles backwards, stunned. "I'm not your punching bag and your mood swings are giving me whiplash. You're a mean, selfish asshole, Samuel, and if this is the new you, then I want nothing to do with you!" I take a deep breath, my purge making me feel somehow worse.

He stands in the middle of the room, eyeing me. Maybe lashing out wasn't such a bad idea. I've tried to be understanding and to stay composed, but I can't do this anymore. Each dismissal is stripping away any shred of hope I have left.

We stand staring at one another, locked in a standoff. Just when I think I've gotten through to him, he tears down my optimism by being the cynical bastard he's become.

The room is filled with slow, loud clapping, as Sam sarcastically applauds my attempts to have him see how his behavior is hurting me. "Finally, we agree on something." I shake my head, not understanding. He happily clarifies, "I want nothing to do with you, either."

Tears fill my eyes, my heart breaking all over again. "Why are you being so mean? What have I done to you?"

"I'm not being mean. This is me," he affirms, jabbing his thumb into his chest. "Get used to it."

I clasp onto his wrist, shaking my head. "No, this isn't you."

"Yes, it is," he snarls, yanking his arm out from my desperate grip. "Forget the Samuel you thought you knew because that person is dead."

"No," I whisper, tears spilling down my cheeks. "That's not

true. I l-love you."

"You're pathetic," he cruelly spits, marching forward and backing me up until I slam into the door. "You're in love with a ghost! The sooner you get that through that thick head of yours, the better it'll be for the both of us."

I press my palms flat to the wood grain, turning my cheek, enraged. But I withhold my anger. "I'll never give up on you, Sam. No matter how hard you push, I'll push back twice as hard. I wasn't raised a quitter. You're still the same man who proposed to me, who loved me more than life itself. You're just lost in..."

But he doesn't let me finish. "Are you even listening to yourself? Lost? I'm not fucking lost. You're the one who's lost in a fantasyland." He grabs my left wrist and waves my floppy hand in front of my face. "Take this off. It was my grandmother's, not yours," he says, referring to my engagement ring. "This is embarrassing because I will never marry you."

"What? No," I gasp, squeezing my eyes shut.

He drops my arm, like touching me will pollute him somehow. "Get out of my way. I'm done with this conversation."

I stagger to the side, unsure if my legs will hold me up. He storms past me, uncaring that I'm hurt beyond belief. But that hurt quickly transforms into utter rage. I'm done being treated like dirt. I was done being treated that way when I stopped being M.

Memories of my childhood come roaring to the surface

and I visit a very dark place. A place I've kept locked away for years. My legs pound down the corridor as I chase after Sam, sniffing back my tears. He quickly turns, but I don't give him a chance to speak.

"How dare you!" I slap him so hard across the cheek, I'm almost certain I can hear his teeth rattle in his mouth. The sound is satisfying. "You know what? If it's so bad being here, then you can leave!" I point to the door. "You don't want to be here, and honestly, I don't want you here if you're going to act this way. Saxon was right about you."

His eyes narrow into slits as he rubs his reddening cheek. "I bet Saxon just loves being the good guy. It's a nice change from being a screw up."

"He is *not* a screw up. You take that back!" I'm quick to jump to his defense, which has Sam's mouth parting in insight.

"It is true," he ambiguously reveals. "I thought I was dreaming."

"What are you talking about? Dreaming about what?"

Before he has a chance to answer my questions, Saxon barges through the front door, his eyes darting between Sam and I. Sam's mouth tips up into a secretive smile, one I'm not privy to.

"What's going on here?" Saxon doesn't conceal his rage. "Well?" he presses when we remain mute.

"I'm going out," Sam declares, my speech falling on deaf ears.

"Are you all right, Lucy?" Saxon asks, his eyes searching my face frantically.

I nod unconvincingly. "What did you say to her?" he asks, glaring at Samuel.

Sam raises his hands in mock surrender. "She's the one who did all the talking." Why do I feel like there is a hidden message behind his words? "Don't wait up," Sam mocks, pushing past Saxon's unmoving frame.

"Sam, if you walk out that door…don't bother coming back." I can't believe I'm giving him an ultimatum because I know which path he'll choose.

When he stops dead in his tracks however, a breath hitches in my throat. Has he changed this mind?

Seconds feel like minutes as I anxiously wait for his reply.

With his back turned, he cruelly says, "Well, in that case… give Saxon your ring. I'll make sure Mom gets it." And with that he slams the door shut behind him.

"Fuck you, too!" No goodbye. I'm sorry. Not even a, thanks for the memories, not that he remembers me.

Saxon is by my side in two huge strides. When I peer up at him and see that his eyes are no longer filled with annoyance, a tear spills down my cheek. His face contorts in pain before he wipes it away with this thumb.

"What h-have I-I done?" I manage to choke out, the consequences of my actions hitting home. "I hate him!"

"No, you don't. Breathe, Lucy. It's just a bad day. Not a bad life."

"It feels like I'm having a lot of bad days lately." I sniff, biting my lip to stop the tears.

He sighs, his fists clenched by his sides. "We're going out," he suddenly declares.

"What?"

"You heard me. We're going to forget this bad day and the ones before it ever existed."

"The only way that'll happen is if copious amounts of alcohol are consumed."

Moving closer, he hesitantly brushes back a stray strand of hair which drapes across my brow. The contact feels good, comforting.

When the engine of my Jeep roars to life, Saxon smiles. "I'll drive."

Fifteen

I HAVE NO IDEA WHERE we're going, as Saxon is being awfully secretive about where he's taking me. The only hint he disclosed was I had to wear my cowboy boots.

It's a warm night so I've decided to wear my short denim shorts and blue and white plaid shirt. I've tied it Daisy Duke style because if I'm going to wear my boots, then I've got to go the whole hog.

My hair is loose and I'm wearing barely any makeup. As I reach for my cherry ChapStick off the dresser, I freeze, deciding to wear my peach one instead. Grabbing the essentials, I stuff everything into my bag and I head outside.

Locking the front door, I smile when I see Saxon leaning up against his bike. He's looking less festive in blue jeans, a gray fitted t-shirt, and motorcycle boots. As I bound down the stairs, I promise myself that tonight, I will try and forget about Sam. I know it'll be virtually impossible, but I'll try my best.

Saxon whistles as I walk towards him. He tips his baseball cap mockingly. "Howdy, ma'am," he says in the lamest country accent.

I can't help but laugh. "There is no way I'm riding that thing," I say, shaking my head.

Saxon smirks. "Yes, you are. Get on."

"You're so bossy," I mumble under my breath.

He passes me a black helmet before mounting the beastly bike with ease. I watch as he straddles it, shuffling forward to give me minimal room on the back.

"You want me to sit there?" I ask, horrified, pointing at the tiny space behind him.

"Don't worry, I won't let you fall," he confidently replies, removing his baseball cap and slipping his helmet on.

Taking a courageous breath, I slip the helmet on before very awkwardly climbing onto the motorcycle. I instantly press my chest to Saxon's back and grip around his waist like a spidermonkey, clinging on for dear life.

He chuckles, the sound vibrating through my fingers. "Ready?"

"No."

"Hold on tight," he sarcastically quips once the engine roars to life. I yelp.

With one last throttle, Saxon takes off and my body jars backward with the force. I can feel his hardened abs underneath my fingers, and the faster he goes, the tighter I squeeze, afraid I'm going to fall off.

He steers the bike down the driveway and before I know it, we're on open road. As we ride through the quiet streets, a sense of freedom overwhelms me, and I feel like someone other than me. It's similar to how I felt when riding Potter bareback and into the darkened night.

Every inch of my body is telling me to close my eyes, but I don't. Tonight is about forgetting because my woes will still be there tomorrow. I take in the sights around me, feeling like I'm flying as the night sky passes me by. Wheat, corn, and potato farms are our backdrop for the ride, however when Saxon takes a left, we're surrounded by fields filled with hundreds of sunflowers.

The towering yellow plants take my breath away, their beauty reminding me of a forever summer, mingled with constant happiness. It's absurd to think a simple flower can make me happy, but I'll forever associate them with this night.

We ride for countless moments, but I don't care. The further away we go, the easier it is to forget why we're here. Feeling a little more confident, I loosen my grip around Saxon, relishing in the way the air whips at my face, shooting a charge throughout my body.

I've driven this road a thousand times before, but somehow, it feels like my first time. When Saxon picks up the speed, I scream, but not in terror. No, I scream in excitement.

"Faster!" I yell to be heard over the whipping wind. Saxon obliges and pushes this beast to full speed.

I know it's incredibly dangerous riding this way, but I trust Saxon one hundred percent. The way he handles himself on a motorcycle is similar to how he carries himself—with confidence, elegance, and control.

As I'm nestled against his back, my arms secured around his strong form, I can't help but think back to our kiss. I shouldn't, but I can't stop. From the very beginning, Saxon has given me a sense of freedom. I was so busy comparing him to Samuel, but they are worlds apart. The way he makes me feel isn't the way Sam does, or did. With Saxon, I feel…alive. And I feel free.

Saxon turns down a dirt road, gravel kicking up as he zooms towards a glowing hue. The closer we get, I come to realize the glowing hue is actually a lit up old barn. The imposing wooden building however isn't your average barn. The tall white sign out front with red letters reveals just exactly where we are.

Sawbuck Saloon.

The patrons out front are dressed in cowboy boots, hats, and western style shirts, laughing rowdily while drinking beer. The loud country music cuts through the night air and as the door is an open panel, I can see people dancing inside.

Saxon pulls the bike over, reversing into a spot by a beat up old Chevy. Once he kills the engine, I take a moment to catch my breath. I attempt to dismount without falling onto my face. My head feels like it weighs a thousand pounds as I look around at my surreal surroundings. Peering inside, I see a horde of people in a line, dancing.

I turn around so quickly to look at Saxon, I almost give myself whiplash. "Is this a

honky-tonk bar?" I can't hide my excitement.

Saxon chuckles as he runs a hand through his mussed hair, reminding me that like an idiot, I'm still wearing my helmet. Before I have a chance to unbuckle it however, he strides forward and pins me with a heart stopping stare as he unfastens the strap from under my chin.

He works with deft fingers, the soft contact buttering my skin with goose pimples. I lick my lips, tasting peach. As he slips the helmet from my head, I smile, but his gaze is filled with a look I've come to know. It's a look that can only lead to trouble.

"First round's on me," I say, clearing my throat to break the palpable tension. This is not how friends behave. Saxon snaps from his lusty trance, and nods.

Sawbuck is exactly how I envisioned a honky-tonk bar would look. The huge bar, stocked with every alcohol imaginable to mankind, runs down the length of the wall to the right. Neon Budweiser signs sitting in cowboy boots with spurs and Bud Light signs are scattered around the enormous room, highlighting what the beer of choice is for these thirsty patrons.

When Saxon points towards the ceiling, I stifle a laugh behind my hand as I see tattered cowboy boots and hats dangling from the wooden rafters. Fairy lights are tangled amongst the creativity, setting off the lively atmosphere perfectly.

We wait in line patiently, while I can't stop taking in the sights. Wooden barrels line the front of the stage where a five piece band is playing an upbeat country song. Behind them are black and white photographs of John Wayne, Clint Eastwood, and Johnny Cash. Large wagon wheels are nailed to the walls, complementing the rustic vibe.

"This place is amazing," I shout to be heard over the electric banjo. "How on earth did I not know it existed?"

Saxon shrugs his brawny shoulders. He's too polite to say what we both know to be true. Samuel wouldn't be caught dead in a place like this, and because this isn't really his scene, it wasn't mine, either. Saying it aloud in my head, I realize how pathetic I sound.

"Is everything all right?" Saxon asks, narrowing his eyes playfully. "You look like you're about to punch somebody and seeing as I'm the closest person within reach—I won't lie, I fear for my life."

And just like that, I feel my rage lessening.

The pretty bartender wipes down the bar before asking what we want. "I'll have a Budweiser. Lucy?" Saxon looks down at me while I bite my lip.

Looking over at the specials board, I realize I may as well be reading Swahili as none of it makes any sense. Remembering an episode of *Sex and the City* I watched when Samuel was away for the weekend, I smile. "I'll have a Cosmopolitan. Thank you."

★ ★ ★ ★ ★

No wonder Carrie and the gang got hooked on these drinks. They are delicious. They are also very, very potent. That might explain some of Samantha's poor life choices.

"How about we get you some water?" Saxon suggests, subtly yanking the cocktail glass out from under me.

"Hey!" I yell, making grabby hands for it. "I was drinking that."

We're sitting around a barrel, my alcoholism openly staring at me as I give up on counting the amount of unknown glasses sitting inches away.

"Water," Saxon firmly repeats, but his lopsided grin tells me he's enjoying my drunken state. "You got a thing against coasters?"

I try and focus on the blurry Saxon, who points to the table. Peering down with one eye open, I see I've made confetti out of my coaster.

"Seriously, are you going to tell me what's bugging you? You go from happy to homicidal in point two seconds. What's going on?"

I shrug, reaching for his beer. When he attempts to stop me, I raise a brow. He raises his hands in surrender.

"You were right. Sam is a big, fat a-hole."

He sits higher on his stool, not masking his surprise. "I could have told you that years ago. Why the sudden change of heart?"

Sipping my stolen beer, I sigh. "I think I've been sleepwalking."

One of the many things I like about Saxon—he doesn't need a manual. "And now you've awoken from a very long sleep?"

I nod.

I'm unsure if it's the alcohol, or the fact I find talking to Saxon so incredible easy, but I decide to divulge it all. "This entire time, I thought Sam's bad behavior was because he was frustrated, confused, and scared. But now…I'm not so sure. What if you're right? What if this Sam is the real Sam and I've just been too blinded by love to see it? Both of you have said it. Am I just a hopeless romantic, desperate for my happily ever after?" I'm questioning everything and I hate it. I know Sam, the old Sam loved me, but why doesn't the new Sam remember me?

"No, Lucy." Saxon's tone is sympathetic. "You're just a girl who fell in love. Unequivocally and wholeheartedly. Sam *does* love you. He always has."

I wipe my eyes, brushing away impending tears. He's right, but I still feel helpless. "I'm a love struck fool, that's what I am." My engagement ring catches my eye, confirming my foolishness. Tugging at the ring, I attempt to slide it off my finger.

However, Saxon's hand gently rests over mine before I can

take it off. "Leave it. It's yours. When Samuel gave that to you, he wanted you to have it."

Looking down at his hand, I frown. "Why are you defending him?" I don't understand. I thought he'd be jumping at the chance to have a major bitch session about his brother.

"I'm not." He shakes his head. "I'm defending you."

"I don't get it."

He smiles. "You're drunk, you're upset, and you've been thrown a massive curveball. I want you to make that decision when you're sure. Right now, you're running on emotion. It's a dangerous thing."

When his fingers squeeze mine, my heart does a tiny flip flop. "Have you always been this smart?"

He smirks, and the sight, it takes my breath away. "I've always been the practical one, while Sam was always the pretty one."

I know he's joking, but the alcohol lowers my guard as I reach out to stroke his whiskered cheek. "You're pretty too."

The surprise is evident on his face. And honestly, it's on mine, too. But I don't question it. I accept and embrace. Just how I should accept and embrace Saxon's words of wisdom.

A loud roar has us both turning to see a group of people cheering and clapping as a young man rides a mechanical bull. He appears to have done this before, as he's riding the bull like a pro. Above him sits a sign stating anyone who can stay on for eight seconds wins unlimited drinks and a cowboy hat.

The grin reveals what I want.

"C'mon," I say, jumping up from my stool and dragging Saxon to where the action is. "That hat is mine."

He doesn't protest and chuckles as we push through the rowdy crowd. When we speak to the guy running the show, he initially thinks its Saxon who wants to ride, but when I tell him otherwise, he looks down at my small frame and laughs. His response has me even more determined.

"All right. Just wait here. I'll call on you when it's your turn." I watch as another cowboy takes to the bull like a duck to water. Maybe this wasn't such a good idea.

As Saxon stands beside me, arms folded as he watches on with interest, a group of girls to my right have deviously migrated closer to us, not bothering to mask their appreciation of the tall, dark, and handsome next to me.

"Ask him," I hear one girl whisper.

"No, you ask him," another says.

"He's gorgeous," girl number one says—the girl who is about to get her eyeballs gouged out. "Excuse me?" She rudely leans across me and taps Saxon on the arm.

He looks at her and smiles.

"My friends and I were just wondering if you were going to ride the bull." I bet they were.

"Not me, but this little cowgirl is." He playfully nudges me with his shoulder, while I try not to glare at the hand still attached to his bicep.

"You're up, pretty thang," the man at the controls says, snapping me from my uncharacteristic thoughts of ripping out the groper's long fingernails one by one.

The pretty brunette sizes me up, seeing me as competition. Well, I'm about to show her just how competitive I can be.

Guzzling down the last of my beer, I pass the empty bottle to Saxon. "Tell them I drink Bud Light," I boldly say from behind my hand, hinting I've got this in the bag.

I kick off my boots before stepping onto the inflatable red round ring where the bull sits dead center. The bouncy surface will provide all the cushioning I need when I fall face first. What was I thinking? Eight seconds is a long time when riding a crazed bull. Not to mention, I'm wasted.

I mount the bull as I would my horse, but the shoulder span of this thing is huge, so it takes me three attempts before I get on. Digging my heels into its wooly sides, I grip onto the handle with one hand and raise my other in the air for balance.

"All right, little lady. On three, two and one!"

The moment the deafening buzzer sounds, the bull begins moving underneath me like it's possessed. I scream, but that panic soon turns to determination when I realize I didn't fall off as soon as the thing started bucking. I grip on tighter, squeezing my thighs and finding my balance to stay afloat. My drunken state is long forgotten and I focus.

Looking at the clock counting down, I see that I've made it to three seconds without flying off. When four seconds ticks over, I know I've made this bull my bitch. I hold on tighter, refusing to let go. I won't let this bull, or any other *bully* beat me. I feel free.

I use my horse riding skills and athletic build to guide me and before I know it, the buzzer sounds, the bull stops throwing a bitch fit, and the crowd goes wild. My eyes search the spectators for Saxon, who smiles, giving me a thumbs up.

Jumping off, my inner thighs hurt like crazy, but I bounce across the floor and fling myself into Saxon's arms. He catches me, laughing.

"I did it!" I shout, unable to contain my excitement.

"You sure did," he says, hugging me tight. "You ready to claim your prize?"

Being wrapped in his arms this way, enveloped in his fragrance and warmth, I know that this, him, tonight, this is my prize. But I nod. I'm surprised when he walks with me still clinging to him, arms and legs wrapped around his neck and waist.

The controller doesn't hide his disbelief that I stayed on as he passes me a straw hat with a pretty turquoise strap. "Congratulations. Looks like I bet on the wrong horse."

"I've been riding since I was eight," I smugly reveal, before hiccupping—looks like I could only evade my drunken mess for eight seconds.

"Well, god damn, shame on me." Both Saxon and I laugh as we leave the next hopeful to try and conquer the bull. He doesn't put me down and carries me over to the bar. As I look over his shoulder at his posse of pissed off admirers, I can't help but smugly grin.

I feel silly being carried this way, but I also don't want him to let go. Talk about push and pull. "So," he says, reaching for the hat in my hand and placing it on my head. "What would the cowgirl like to drink?"

Adjusting the hat, I purse my lips in contemplation. He spins around so I can see the bar over his shoulder. Being pressed to his chest this way suddenly has me appreciating all the hard contours and muscular planes that make up Saxon Stone. I begin to feel that flutter in my belly—the flutter which leads to wicked thoughts.

A drink catches my eye, just for the name alone. I shouldn't, but it's out before I can stop myself. "I think I'll have a sex on the beach."

A choked breath gets trapped in Saxon's throat, while I grin.

★ ★ ★ ★ ★

"No, you can't leave her out here. She looks lonely," I say, pointing to what I thought was Saxon's bike. When he turns me around however, I realize I'm pointing to a Vespa.

"It'll be fine and she? Since when has my bike been a female?"

"Since forever," I reply, scoffing.

I have no idea what time it is because I lost track after my tenth shot. Saxon gave up with the water card after my third slippery nipple— the drink, I mean. I feel so educated in the world of spirits after tonight. I don't know how educated I'll feel tomorrow morning when I'm throwing most of it up, but I'll deal with that when I'm crouched over the bowl.

Saxon slips his cell into his pocket once he calls a cab. He refuses to ride his motorcycle home, afraid I might fall off. I told him I was fine. However, when I tripped over air while walking to the bathroom, I knew he was right.

I can't believe how much fun I've had. A shitty day has actually turned into one of the best days of my life. Fingering the woven straw in my hat, I smile, still on high from riding that bull and hanging on. It's silly, but accomplishing that put forward the notion that I need things to change at home. There is no doubt in my mind that I love Sam, but is the Sam that I love someone I've put on a pedestal all these years? Have I been too blinded by love to see the cracks beneath the surface?

My memories of him are filled with nothing but love, happiness, and fun times, but if I were to dissect each one, would they be as perfect as I believed them to be? I do know that my journals will help me find those answers.

"Are you cold?"

I look up at Saxon, snapping from my thoughts. He really is incredibly gorgeous, and I know that's not the beer talking. "A little," I confess, as the night has taken an unexpected cold turn.

He steps forward and gently rubs my arms.

Instantly, my traitorous body purrs at the contact and I'm too drunk to fight it.

"Better?"

My head wobbles as I nod.

The moonlight catches off his curved lip, highlighting his scar. Before my brain can reprimand my finger, I'm tracing the outline of his mouth He's visibly shocked, but he doesn't pull away. "What happened?"

I don't remove my finger to allow him to reply. His warm flesh feels too good to break contact.

"I ran into a door," he replies, smirking.

His response gives insight that he doesn't want to talk about it. But when I finger over the scar repeatedly, mesmerized, he knows I won't accept anything but the truth.

"I got into a fight."

"With who? Why?"

"With no one special and why, because…I needed to feel pain to know I was alive."

I freeze, pinning him with an inquisitive stare. His comment has me thinking about scars of my own. "Every scar means you were stronger than whatever tried to beat you." Tears prick my eyes, hating how closely I can relate to his remark.

Saxon watches me, reading between the lines. He's come to read me so well.

A horn honks, alerting us that our cab has arrived,

thankfully interrupting a moment that was filled with too much emotion.

The alcohol hits me on the way home, and I end up slipping in and out of sleep. Nothing can compare to seeing the sights of Montana on the back of Saxon's bike anyway, so I fall into a peaceful slumber. The car stopping and Saxon's hushed voice alerts my foggy brain that we've arrived home, but my heavy eyelids and even heavier legs refuse to budge.

"Lucy…" he coos, "we're home."

I groan in response and turn into my pillow.

Wait, pillow?

As my "pillow" shifts, I realize I'm draped all over Saxon. If I wasn't completely wasted, I would move. But the idea of moving hurts my pounding head and turns my nauseous stomach. So instead, I snuggle firmer into my makeshift cushion.

A graveled laugh soothes my aches and pains and I sigh, hugging into Saxon—the world's comfiest bed.

I'm certain I'm floating because all of a sudden, I feel weightless. My body sags and I allow myself to be swept away in total stillness. A thump…thump…thump against my ear is the most soothing sound in the world. Not to mention with every breath I take, I'm cocooned in the most comforting smell. I want to stay here forever.

Forever comes to a screeching halt however when my ride through the clouds ends. "I'm going to put you to bed, Lucy. Okay?" No, that's not okay. That sounds like an awful idea.

Forcing one eye open, I see the white stain of my bedroom door. I know I didn't walk here, therefore, I know I'm in Saxon's arms. I don't want to leave. I don't want to go in there because the thought of spending another night alone is too damn depressing. And then on the flip side, if Samuel is in there, I don't want to be sleeping next to him either. My bedroom holds too many memories, ones I don't want to deal with right now.

"Can I sleep with you?" I ask, my voice sounding like a garbled mess.

"W-what?" The hitch in Saxon's voice is unusual, as he's usually so poised.

"Can I sleep with you?" I repeat. "In your bed. Next to you. I promise…I won't touch. Your virtue is safe with me." I giggle at my own joke.

Saxon exhales loudly, and I'm too tired and drunk to decipher why. "Sure."

Relieved, I snuggle into Saxon's chest, sighing when that sense of comfort surrounds me once more. His boots sound against the floorboards as he walks towards his room. The door creaks as he opens it.

The moment he carries me in, I groggily open my eyes, thankful when he doesn't switch on the light. "Do you think you can stand?"

I'm pretty certain that I can, so I nod.

I can feel his uncertainty when he lowers my feet to the ground. Even when I'm upright, he doesn't remove his hands from my waist. The moonlight peeking in through the parted curtains basks us both in an ethereal glow, somehow adding to the magic of this night.

"Thank you." My eyes droop to half mast as I fumble with the buttons on my shirt. I also feel like I'm wading through choppy waters as I sway from side to side. At this rate, I'll get undressed by next week.

"Here…let me help you."

Before I can protest, Saxon's warm fingers overlap mine and he begins unbuttoning my shirt slowly. This is wrong, and so unlike me, but the need to crawl into bed and sleep overrides my modesty. His harsh breathing fills the still room. His face is hard, his jaw clenched.

I watch through a hazy cloud as each button pops free, revealing more and more of my skin. My flesh heats, part embarrassment, and part in craving. It's been so long since someone has touched me so intimately, I long for more.

Once my buttons are undone, Saxon slips the shirt from my shoulders, disrobing me as it falls to the floor. His chest rises and falls, making no secret of his thoughts as his gaze lingers on my chest. I have on a plain black bra, but the way Saxon is looking at me, I feel like I'm naked.

He swallows before dropping to his knees before me. The gesture for some reason warms my heart and I can't help but smile. He makes his intentions clear as he secures a hand behind my calf, indicating he's going to take off my boots. Placing one hand on his shoulder for balance, I lift my leg and watch in appreciation as his bicep flexes when taking off each boot.

I'm now standing barefoot and topless with Saxon still on his knees. He's looking up at me with nothing but admiration and I feel…beautiful.

He points to my shorts, timidly, asking permission. "Your, um, shorts."

I know I shouldn't, but I nod, lost in this moment between us.

His Adam's apple bobs as he swallows nervously before reaching forward. Looking up at me from under his long lashes, he unsnaps the button on my shorts. He stops, his hands singeing my flesh as they rest at my waist. He waits, again seeking consent if it's okay he goes on. God strike me down, I nod.

The heat from his fingers sends a charge throughout my body as he slowly unfastens my zipper and slides the denim down my legs. As they pool at my feet, I step out of them, feeling beautifully wicked.

Saxon is still on his knees, surrendering. I don't know why I feel that way, but his torn features reveal he's battling an inner war. Finally standing, I feel even smaller and fragile in his presence, only clothed in my underwear and cowboy hat.

The room is spinning, but it's not the alcohol. It's Saxon.

Feeling ashamed for such feelings, I hurriedly toss my hat onto the floor and turn, forgetting something which I'm usually so guarded about.

Saxon's gasp hints that he's seen my deformity. "Lucy, who did that to you?" The anger in his voice scares me.

"No one, just…" But he's on me in seconds, spinning me around so quickly, I almost fall.

"Who?" His hard eyes reveal he's not going anywhere.

My lower lip trembles and tears prick my eyes. "Let's just say before I was Lucy Tucker, I was a nobody."

Saxon's face falls and his lips dip into a saddened frown. "This happened when you were a kid?"

I nod sadly. "I'm adopted, Saxon. I'm not sure if Samuel ever told you, but I grew up in the system. I didn't even have a name. I was just known as M."

He loosens his grip around my bicep, but never breaks contact and for that, I'm glad.

Taking a walk down memory lane, I confess, "When I was four, I went to live with Nigel and Denise Martin. At first, I was excited to live in Hollywood. I mean, this is where dreams come true. But my dreams soon turned to nightmares when Nigel's true nature emerged. He was a mean man with a rotten temper. Denise was too busy rubbing shoulders with her socialite friends to notice. Or maybe she just didn't care. I still don't know why they fostered me. Maybe they thought it would camouflage their true nature, as people would see their act as charitable and kind.

It started out with little things. Nigel slapping me on the

wrist for making too much noise. Or yelling at me for dragging in dirt from the yard. I can't really remember much else, just flashes of him not liking me very much. But that one night, in his study, it's a memory I'll never forget. It's one that still haunts me to this day."

I don't know why I'm telling Saxon this. It's not an easy memory for me to share. But I know he won't judge me for something that wasn't my fault.

"There was a room next door to mine which was always locked. I was too young to understand then, but later on I found out that Nigel and Denise had lost a daughter to SIDS. The maid forgot to lock the door and the inquisitive four-year-old me thought it would be cool to see what was inside. When I stepped inside, I thought I had stumbled upon a goldmine. The pink room had every toy imaginable locked inside. To a kid who had nothing, this was the ultimate jackpot. Looking back, it was an untouched time capsule, a shrine to the daughter they lost."

Wiping my tears away with the back of my hand, I continue. "A teddy bear sitting alone on a rocking chair in the corner of the room caught my eye. He looked so sad, so lonely, kind of like me. I was so desperate for a friend. A stuffed bear was better than having no one at all. So I walked over, not understanding the consequences, and decided he was to be my new best friend. I still remember the feel of him, the smell. He was perfect. But our friendship was short-lived.

Nigel charged into the room, slapping me so hard across the cheek I lost two teeth. I'd been hit before, but never like this. I didn't understand what I had done wrong. I was four. I tried to give Nigel the bear, apologizing for touching something that wasn't mine. But it was too late. He grabbed me by the ponytail, ignoring my cries for help and dragged me over to the bed. He then threw me onto my stomach. I heard his belt being unbuckled."

Saxon's eyes turn murderous.

The near darkness makes my tale easier to tell. "I-I didn't understand what he was doing, but he made his intentions clear when he yanked up my dress and slapped me so hard across the behind with his belt, tears stung my eyes. He made sure he used the buckle. I don't know how many times he hit me. I'd passed out by strike number five, still clutching onto that teddy, needing someone to hold my hand.

I woke up in the hospital where a nice lady told me that the bad man was gone. Sadly, the scars from that night will remain with me forever. He whipped me so hard he tore the skin off my back and behind. I don't know how many stitches I got to piece me back together again. But it was enough to leave me looking like this." I gesture to my body, not hiding my disgust. "Not long after, Simon and Maggie came into my world, saving me from becoming another statistic.

"I've been keeping journals ever since. Obviously, when I was too young to write, I relied on drawing to express my sadness and fears. Maggie and Simon were told what had happened and Mom recognized my pictures as a form of therapy. She kept every one. And I'm glad she did. I went to therapy when I was old enough to talk about what had happened. That's when I began writing in my journals."

Saxon nods, appreciating their significance.

"On my eighteenth birthday, I burned that bear. I know it was kind of morbid me holding onto it, but he was a reminder of who I once was, and who I was now. My childhood wasn't easy, but I'm not a victim. Not anymore. And I'll be damned if I stand by and let another human being be treated the way I was."

"So that's why you do what you do," Saxon says in sudden understanding.

"Yes. I fight in the name of the four-year-old me. I was silent, but not anymore. Every time I help someone, I'm taking back a small piece of me. So you see, we've both got scars. My perfect life isn't so perfect after all," I say, referring to his comment at the hospital.

He turns his cheek, ashamed. "I'm so sorry. Please forgive me. I didn't know."

For once, I'm the one who comforts him, and it feels nice. After revealing my vulnerabilities, I feel strong. "Sshh, there's no need for you to be sorry."

The room is silent, heavy with emotion. It's a feeling I'm all too used to when I dig up the ghosts of my pasts.

"I'm going to find that motherfucker…and kill him." The

anger behind Saxon's promise displays that he's not joking.

His response is so different than Samuel's. Sam was understanding, and sorry for what had happened, but Saxon has launched into full-blown protection mode. He looks like he's about to jump on his Harley and ride to Hollywood and kill Nigel with his bare hands.

"He already did it for you. Well, a twenty gauge shotgun did," I say, revealing that Nigel took his own life. His clenched jaw whines in anger.

"I didn't tell you this expecting you to avenge my childhood, or for you to look at me differently. I told you because I…trust you, Saxon. I want you to know all there is to me, and I hope one day, you'll feel the same."

I know he too has skeletons in his closet, ones I hope he feels comfortable to release one day. But not today because suddenly, I'm dog tired.

"Thank you for listening to my story."

His face softens. "Thank you for trusting me with it."

A yawn escapes me and my eyes begin to droop shut. Saxon pulls back the woolen blanket on the bed. White sheets have never looked more comforting and my body sings in ecstasy when I slip inside. Saxon draws the blanket over me while I sigh, never feeling more at peace.

I'm not sure how long later, but the mattress dips besides me. I instantly let out a low hum, feeling safe and at home with Saxon by my side.

Caught between reality and the dream world, I whisper my fears aloud.

"Will you take care of me?"

His heavy breathing fills the night air.

"Yes," he replies after a drawn-out silence.

"You promise?" I know this can't last forever, and I'm afraid.

He counters with so much emotion, his sincerity brings tears to my eyes. "Yes, I promise."

"For how long?"

Pause… "For as long as you want me to."

As I fall into a deep sleep, the word "forever" replaces goodnight.

Sixteen

I WAKE, ALMOST CERTAIN I'VE been run over by a steam train. Twice.

I know it's bright out, and that fact has me turning into my delectable smelling pillow. When my pillow begins breathing, however, I know I've missed the memo.

Against my better judgment, I pry open one eye to hazily see my pillow is made of flesh—warm, supple, muscular flesh. The intricate tattoos reveal that chest belongs to Saxon.

Cataloging through what I can remember, I recall ending one of the funnest nights of my life in Saxon's bed, where I still remain. Something has shifted between Saxon and I, I can feel it. I don't know what, but I know it's something which makes me happy. My mood dampens however when I remember Sam.

I don't know where he is, or if he'll ever be back. He's made his feelings perfectly clear and I have to accept it, whether I like it or not. It hurts, but what other choice do I have? I can't force him to remember. And I certainly can't force him to love me.

"Mornin.'"

Saxon's hoarse voice reminds me of his promise—his promise to look after me for as long as I want him to. It wasn't fair of me to ask, but I can't do this without him. It concerns me that "this" is living.

"Good morning," I reply croakily.

"How you feeling?"

Considering the amount of alcohol I consumed and the fight with Samuel which triggered my alcoholism, I feel okay. "Better than I thought I would."

"Good to hear."

We're both very aware that I'm wrapped in Saxon's arms, snuggled tightly against his chest. I should shift away, especially since I'm wearing nothing but a bra and boy shorts. But I don't want to. The thought turns my stomach.

As if on cue, my belly grumbles.

"Are you hungry?" Saxon asks, chuckling.

"A little." Shifting slightly, I draw back so we're sharing the same pillow. We're inches apart, breathing in the same air, and it's nice.

The early morning light highlights the rolling green swirls in his eyes, which seems to complement the heavier beard lining his strong jaw. It's funny. When looking at Saxon, I no longer see Samuel. In my eyes, they're no longer carbon copies of each other, a fact which I'm sure Saxon would be thrilled about.

"I'll make us some breakfast. And coffee."

The suggestion of food and coffee has me groaning in excitement. "Yes, please. Feel free to serve up anything greasy or fried."

"I think I can manage that." I melt when a dimple hugs his left cheek.

He pulls back the sheet and slips out of bed, appearing unconcerned that the only thing he's wearing are a pair of black boxers. I avert my eyes, only for them to stubbornly rise back up again, zeroing in on his magnificent body.

He's lean, but muscular, his frame radiating nothing but strength. A true rugged, masculine body.

When my gaze lingers on his flank, he turns his back and quickly retrieves the discarded t-shirt off the floor. I scold myself for openly staring, making him feel uncomfortable.

"I'll meet you out there," he says, stepping into his jeans.

"Okay."

He gives me a final look before closing the door behind him.

Sighing, I throw an arm over my eyes, embarrassed and angry at myself for being unable to control my emotions around Saxon. We're friends, he's also Samuel's brother—I need to remember that.

I slowly sit up, the room spinning as I try and gather my bearings. When I think I'm steady enough, I pull back the blanket and stand. The room is a little lopsided, but I manage to walk across the room without bumping into anything or tripping over my two left feet.

I feel beyond wicked standing in Saxon's bedroom in only my underwear and decide to hunt through his drawers to borrow a t-shirt. My shirt and shorts have way too many buttons and zips to hurdle through. I find a Harley Davidson shirt which I recognize as the one he wore the first time I saw him at the hospital. I remember how happy I was to see him. How I threw myself into his arms without any reservations and how he caught me just as freely.

Drawing the shirt to my nose, I take a big sniff, relishing in his familiar, comforting smell. Slipping it on, I smile when it hangs to my knees. Just as I'm about to close the drawer, I see his journal sitting hidden underneath his clothes.

Peering at the door nervously, I slip my hand inside, inexplicably needing to run my fingers over the source of Saxon's most intimate thoughts. I wouldn't dare read what's inside, as I know how private a diary can be. I also know however, that inside lies the reason why Saxon and Samuel don't get along. I could sneak a peek and finally uncover why the two brothers are mere strangers. I could…but I won't. If I ever find out the reason why, it'll be because Saxon or Sam wants to share their story with me.

Quietly closing the drawer, I gather my clothes and boots off the floor, goose bumps painting my skin when remembering

Saxon undressing me so intimately. It's a memory I'll never forget. Tiptoeing through his room for some reason, I close the door behind me and pad down the hallway to my bedroom. I have no idea why I feel the need to sneak around. I doubt Sam is home, and even if he were, he wouldn't care where I slept last night.

With that thought in mind, I yank open my bedroom door, ready to shower and face another day of the unknown. My confidence takes a nosedive however when I step into my bedroom and see a sight I never thought I'd see.

Sitting in the middle of the room is Sam and sitting around him, scattered all over our hardwood floor are my journals. There are piles surrounding him, the boxes they once sat in overturned. In his lap sits an opened journal, and when he meets my eyes, there is nothing but guilt reflected in his.

"W-what are you doing?" I stupidly ask because it's fairly obvious that Samuel has no respect for me or my privacy.

He holds up my diary, shaking his head. "I'm sorry, I didn't mean…"

"You didn't mean to read my dairy?" I offer when he draws a blank. "It just jumped off the dresser and into your lap?"

He doesn't reply.

"You can't do that, Sam. You can't just read someone's diary. Not cool. It's an invasion of my privacy!" I think back to being in Saxon's room some thirty seconds ago. I was presented with the same temptation, but I resisted. I respect Saxon. Sadly,

Samuel doesn't feel the same way about me. "And why are you even back here? You made it quite clear you couldn't stand the sight of me yesterday."

His silence angers me further.

"Now is the time you apologize for being a gigantic dick! But I guess apologies aren't your strong suit. How many did you read?" I gesture with my chin towards my scattered memories.

"You love me," he says in a dreamlike voice.

"I…what?" I reply, scrunching up my nose, confused, my anger coming to a screeching halt.

"You love me," he repeats, waving my diary. "I'm sorry for reading it, but I can't remember you, Lucy, and the diaries, they were just sitting there. I was curious. I'm also sorry for being a complete asshole to you yesterday."

My mouth opens and closes like a stunned goldfish.

Why would he want an insight into my world? He made his feelings perfectly clear last night. How would my diaries be able to change his mind when I haven't succeeded?

"If you had any questions about us, you should have asked, not resorted to snooping. I feel so violated," I say, drawing my clothes up to cover my chest.

"I know. I'm sorry." He places my diary on the floor and stands. He doesn't move, however. We simply stand, staring at one another, waiting for the other to speak. But I don't know what he wants me to say.

"It was so weird seeing myself, a self I cannot remember,

through your eyes. I sounded like an all right kind of guy."

"You were," I affirm, sad we're talking in past tense.

"So all that stuff, it really happened?"

"Yes, it really did."

"Wow." His eyes widen. "I can't believe I didn't take the scholarship. I know my grades were good enough."

His comment has me cocking a brow. "You remember your grades?"

His mouth parts, appearing to be caught out and I don't know why. "I just meant..." he quickly backtracks, rubbing the back of his neck, "that I know I was always a good student."

That's not what he meant and we both know it. Alarm bells sound in my ears and I don't know why. Samuel wasn't a great student. He was an exceptional basketball player, and good at math, but he wasn't so good on the academic playing field. What am I missing? He did, however, do a lot better than I thought he would on the SATs. But if he put his mind to it, he could achieve anything.

But the reason why he didn't accept the scholarship was because of his dad. Greg and Kellie made it crystal clear that his future was working on the farm with Greg. He didn't want to disappoint them, so he finally caved. Saxon was the lucky one. He got out.

"I'm sure you read about why you didn't accept the scholarship," I sarcastically say. "I'm sure you read about a lot of things."

My head begins pounding, and I don't know if it's because I'm angry or if my hangover has decided to rear its ugly head. Either way, I want a shower. But more so, I want to brush my teeth.

Remembering I'm standing in Saxon's shirt, carrying my clothes as I crept down the hallway, I suddenly feel incredibly guilty. This emotional ping pong is sure to give me a nervous breakdown one day soon. "I'm going for a shower," I announce, choosing to ignore the fact that I just came from Saxon's bedroom.

Sam doesn't seem to care either way as he nods, watching me stomp across the room. "Can I make you coffee?"

I trip over a discarded diary, almost bumping my head against the dresser. "Coffee?" I squeak.

"Yes, you know. The black, delicious smelling liquid that comes from little beans."

Is he making a joke?

When he smiles, I know the answer is yes.

This is too much.

That breakdown is not too far away. "S-sure," I fumble, tripping over my words as I know Saxon is currently doing that for me, but I don't want Sam to know that, as he'll soon discover that I spent the night in Saxon's room. And more importantly, in his bed.

Sam appears happy by my response.

He looks at the mountains of diaries surrounding him,

then back up at me. I sigh and wave him off. "I've got them. Just go make coffee."

"Sorry again." When he appears genuinely apologetic, I push down my anger, as him being remorseful is better than him biting my head off. And I also see a glimmer of the old Sam breaking the surface.

I don't reply, but instead place my belongings on the floor and reach for an empty cardboard box. Sam watches me for a moment before leaving me to clean up his mess.

Looking around at my most treasured memories, I slump into the middle of the room and brush back my matted hair. I should be happy Samuel wants to remember me, but I'm not. Reading one's diary is not kosher, but considering Sam's situation, I guess I could cut him some slack. In a weird, completely messed up way, he was only trying to uncover who he was. Who *I* was. But why am I not happy?

This is the first real effort he's made since coming home, and although it's only been a week, it feels like a lifetime. It feels like I'm doing life without parole.

* * * * *

I shower in record time, feeling human once I dry off and slip on my jeans and PETA tee. The straw cowboy hat looks at me from the bedroom floor, presenting me with the option that it'll hide my bird nest perfectly. But wearing it around Sam feels wrong. Sighing, I pick it up and hide it in my closet.

The smell of strong coffee has my taste buds dancing in delight as I close the bedroom door and amble down the hallway. I have no idea what I'm about to walk in to, considering Sam and Saxon are in the kitchen, both making coffee. I don't hear any yelling, so that's a good start.

Both brothers turn around when I enter, which makes me feel a touch uncomfortable. It's Saxon's eyes I meet first and he thankfully smiles, before returning to the bacon popping on the stove.

"Sax was already making coffee and breakfast," Sam explains, pulling out three plates from the cupboard.

"Smells good," I say, standing on tippy toes to look over Saxon's broad shoulders.

From what I can see, he's working the stove like a whiz. Eggs, bacon, sausage, and flapjacks are on the menu, my ravenous stomach growling in excitement. Sitting on the stool, I watch in interest as Samuel quickly reaches for a mug and pours a cup of coffee.

"Do you take sugar? Cream?" he asks, looking directly at me.

I glance over my shoulder to ensure there's no one behind me. "Just black," I reply when I find my voice.

He places the mug in front of me and smiles.

I look at it apprehensively, wondering if it'll jump up and bite, as there's got to be a catch to why Sam is being so nice to me. Yesterday's Sam was a right royal asshole, who made his feelings for me perfectly clear, so why the sudden change of heart?

This predicament is not helping my growing headache and I rub my brow.

"Is there room for one more?"

"Piper!" I exclaim, jumping up from the stool, thankful someone else is here to make conversation.

My on edge behavior has Saxon turning to look at me over his shoulder, a smirk tugging at the corner of his lips.

"Sure, Piper," he says, gesturing to Samuel to grab another plate.

Piper narrows her eyes. She's onto me. "You okay, Luce?"

"Yeah, fine," I reply, sitting back down as I'm standing like an idiot. "Just tired."

Saxon's eyes meet mine, peering in on my secret silently.

"Where do you want these?"

Now that I'm semi-sane, I notice her hands are filled with paper bags. "What are they?"

"You're kidding, right?" When I shrug, pulling a guilty face, she shakes her head. "Have you forgotten what day it is?"

I scratch my temple. "Well…"

She looks at Saxon, then at Sam, who raises his hands in the air. "Don't look at me. I'm the one with amnesia, remember?"

Piper huffs, placing the bags onto the counter. "It's Saturday."

Oh, shit.

Before I can gripe that I'm in no mood to party, Piper points her fingers at me. "Luce, don't even. It's happening." I slouch low and sip my coffee, knowing that it'll be one of many.

Saxon dishes up the delicious smelling breakfast, but I've suddenly lost my appetite. The thought of having random strangers in my home does not sound appealing whatsoever. My head already feels like it's about to explode. I don't need to add rowdy partygoers to the mix. This is a bad idea on all accounts, but I don't stand a chance against party planner Piper.

We eat in relative silence, the TV filling the calm. To someone looking in, we would appear like a normal family eating breakfast together on a Saturday morning. But I know better. I'm a bundle of nerves, waiting for Sam to lose his temper over something small and storm out, claiming how much he hates being here. But he doesn't. He eats, trying to make conversation with Saxon, who looks just as puzzled as me.

What's going on? What has happened for Sam to start acting like…Sam? Like the old Sam I loved more than life itself. I should be over the moon, ecstatic that he's making an effort, but something doesn't feel right. I just can't place my finger on it.

"You don't like your eggs?"

"Huh?" I blurt out, looking up to see Saxon smirking. He gestures with his fork to my plate.

Peering down, I see that I've massacred my breakfast,

leaving behind a colorful mess. Pushing my plate away, I sigh. Saxon gulps down his coffee and places his plate in the dishwasher. "I'm going to pick up my bike."

His comment has me snapping out of my funk as I desperately want to talk to him and ask if Sam has said anything to him. Before I can offer to drive him however, Piper shoots up from her stool while shoveling the last of her breakfast into her mouth. "I'll drive you," she says around a mouthful of food.

Saxon's gaze flicks my way before he nods. "Thanks."

"Piper, if you want to stay here and decorate, I can drive Saxon," I offer, hoping she'll take the bait.

Of course she doesn't. "No, it's fine. I need to pick up a few extra things anyway." No she doesn't. The bags she bears are packed full. But I don't make a fuss.

Sam looks at me and again, that thing called a smile is directed my way. "Maybe we can get a head start on tonight?"

I can't hide my surprise. "S-sure."

Saxon runs a hand through his sleep mussed hair, narrowing his eyes. Piper let's him ponder for a second before looping her arm through his. "Ready when you are."

Her chirpy voice is filled with excitement, as I know she's eager to spend some alone time with Saxon. Knowing Piper, they'll take the longest detour possible. Rising, I scrape my untouched breakfast into the trash, hoping my uneasiness doesn't shine.

"We won't be long," Saxon says from behind me. "Did you

want to come for a drive?"

I know what he's doing and I appreciate it. He's acting on his promise to take care of me, obviously sensing my distress. Turning, I see Piper shaking her head animatedly behind Saxon's back, waving her hands in the air.

"No, it's okay. Sam is right. It's probably a good idea to get things underway." Saxon nods, but his usual poker face isn't as foolproof as it once was because I can now read him just as well as he can read me.

Once they're out the door, my palms begin to sweat and an awkward silence permeates the air. I'm filled with a heavy sadness when it becomes evident that I no longer feel comfortable around my fiancé. There was a time when I believed I could tell Sam anything, but things have changed. I'm now too afraid to talk in fear of getting my head bitten off.

When Sam clears his throat, appearing just as uncomfortable as I am, I decide to make the first move. Pushing down the past few weeks, I try my best to smile and mean it. "So, what's Piper got in there?"

Sam looks relieved that I instigated conversation as I have every right to tell him to shove it. But the fact that he's trying has me wanting to try too. I just have to remember that underneath his harsh words, bad attitude, and constant hatred lies the man I was going to marry. And besides, this is what I wanted, wasn't it?

As Sam begins hunting through the bags, pulling out every

known party supply possible, I can't help but think I should have been careful what I wished for. "How many people did she invite?" he says, whistling.

Looking at the loaded counter, I shake my head. "Knowing Piper, too many."

"Well, we're in for some night." I unexpectedly shiver and I don't know why. "Where should we start?"

Ignoring my weird premonition, I look at the twenty different color boxes of Jell-O and laugh. "It appears we'll be making Jell-O shots for the rest of the morning. Oh—" I pause "—but you can start with clearing the living room if you like." I have no idea if Samuel remembers what Jell-O shots are, and I don't want to make a big deal about it.

My attempt at being subtle however falls short. "I'm a fast learner," he offers, rolling up the sleeves of his sweater.

I hold my breath, waiting for some kind of explosion to erupt, but it doesn't happen. Instead, Sam begins opening the packets of Jell-O, waiting for me to instruct him further.

"Right," I say after a few seconds of collecting my thoughts. "We'll need a couple of big bowls and a measuring cup."

Before I can direct Sam to where the bowls are kept, he walks over to the cupboard near the fridge and opens it. My mouth drops open and I gasp. "You remember?"

His hand freezes on the handle. "Holy shit." The mixing bowls stare at us innocently, while I choke on my raspy breathing. "I don't know. I don't think I remember?"

"You've done this once before," I say, winded.

"I have?" He spins to look at me, eyes wide.

"Yes, you did it the other day. With the mugs." I point to the cupboard above the stove top.

He scans to where I'm pointing. "Un-fucking-believable."

My stomach drops at his comment as I can't make out his mood. Have I just ruined a "moment" by putting my foot in it? We were having a semi-decent conversation and now I've gone and…but I pause. This is exactly the type of attitude I refuse to relive. No more second guessing myself.

I am thankful however when he turns to me and smiles. "Maybe there's hope for me after all, then?" His optimism reminds me of the old Sam.

Whatever has triggered this response, I decide not to question it for now because even though I'm completely confused, I'm also…glad.

"Hello, anyone home?"

Sam cocks a brow, obviously not recognizing my mom's voice.

"It's my mom," I state, while his mouth falls open in understanding. "We're in here."

My parents walk into the kitchen, my mom unable to hide her happiness at seeing me standing beside Sam without tears in my eyes.

"My, my, what on earth have you got there?" Dad asks, looking at the endless Jell-O boxes as he kisses me on the top of the head.

"It's Piper's doing, sir," Sam replies politely.

I don't know how much he remembers of my parents, but he never once called my dad sir. Dad doesn't make a fuss, however, and smiles.

"We're throwing a party tonight, and no Dad, you're not invited." I giggle when he stops mid-tango.

This reminds me of the old days when Sam and my dad used to get a kick out of teasing me. But why does it feel so different?

"Honey, I have some of your things in the car. I cleaned out the attic and didn't know what you wanted to keep, so I brought it all over. Did you want to take a look?"

"Maggie, I can get that," my dad says, but when my mom shakes her head, I know this is her silent cue to get me alone.

Samuel smiles, none the wiser. "You can help me…"

"Simon." My dad fills in the blanks when Sam pauses, obviously not remembering my dad's name. Dad rolls up his sleeves and the boys get to work.

The moment my mom and I step aside, she gently rubs my arm. "What's the matter, Lucy?"

She can read me like a book. She always has been able to.

"Nothing, Mom. Sam is really trying."

"That's great news. Isn't it?" she adds when I remain quiet.

"Yes, of course it is. It's just…" How do I explain what's going on without sounding like a tart?

"Just what?"

"Things have changed. I've changed."

"Change isn't a bad thing," she says as we walk to her car. "I would be surprised if things didn't change."

"What do you mean?"

As she pops the trunk, she asks, "How's Saxon?"

I almost trip over my feet, giving away my dilemma. "He's okay."

"Just okay?" She stops by the car, giving me a knowing smile.

"He's really incredible. I never thought he could be so… caring and supportive and just a really amazing guy." She waits for me to continue. "Something has shifted between us, Mom," I confess, feeling so damn guilty.

I expect disappointment, but all I get is warmth. "Why is that such a bad thing? It's wonderful you two are getting along so well."

I lower my eyes, ashamed we're getting along a little too well. "He makes me happy."

"Honey, you're allowed to be happy. Whoever you find that happiness with is your choice. Don't feel guilty for living. Samuel's condition is a perfect example of grabbing life by the…"

"I got it," I interrupt with a grin. "Thanks, Mom."

I instantly feel better. I still feel guilty, but she's right. Life is too short to live in the dark.

As we're going through my things, my cell beeps, indicating that I have a text. As I see who it's from, I can't help but smile. It's a picture message of the fields of sunflowers we rode past. They look just as beautiful today as they did yesterday.

"Is that from Saxon?" my mom asks.

Snapping my head up, I nod sheepishly. "How'd you know?"

Wrapping her arms around me, she reveals, "Because you look happy."

Seventeen

"I REALLY THINK WE MADE progress, Luce," Piper says, switching from a red dress to a beige dress as she interchanges hangers while looking in the full-length mirror.

I peer up from the middle of the floor where I've set up camp, flicking through my journals.

Today went from weird to weirder. After my parents left, Sam and I cleared away anything breakable and made room for the army Piper has invited. This led to Sam asking about certain items and what meaning they have. I told him the porcelain horse was a statue he bought for me when I turned twenty-one. The photo sitting in the wooden frame on the mantel was taken when we visited New York to watch The Knicks. By the end, I had detailed the history of over twenty items, Sam appearing genuinely curious and interested while listening to each story.

It was nice reliving the happy moments between us because

there haven't been many of late. Well, not with Sam, anyway.

"He was on his phone most of the time though. I wonder who he was texting."

It was me, I silently reply.

Sam and I had transformed our home into a frat house in under three hours and it was fun. We actually chatted while doing it and in a weird way, it was like we were getting to know one another again. He asked questions about himself, about me, and about his future. It was just like the old times. But when I bounced down the hall and into my bedroom, my chiming cell revealed that the old times are dead and gone.

I had about twenty text messages from Saxon, all asking if I was okay and if Sam was causing me problems. His concern was really touching, but it made me feel guilty, like Sam was the bad guy.

I still can't help but think how long will this last? Or is this change for good? If so, what does that mean for Saxon and me? Will he go? Will we stop being friends? We've bonded because of what happened to Sam, and because of it, Saxon promised to take care of me. But what happens if I need to take care of Sam? What happens if things go back to the way they were?

Those questions plague my mind as I sit in the middle of my room, skimming through my diaries, discovering who I once was. I don't feel like the same Lucy Tucker. I feel like I've grown.

"Piper, have I always been so pathetic?"

Piper stops rambling about Saxon, her red dress pressed against her body. "What?"

"Pathetic," I repeat, waving my diary in front of me. "Have I always been so…needy?"

When Piper appears to be weighing up how to respond, I know the answer is yes.

"Oh my god. Why didn't you tell me? These diaries make me sound like I was following Sam around like a lost puppy dog. When did I lose my independence? Or the better question is, did I ever have any?"

Piper tosses the dresses onto the bed and sits down beside me. "You were never pathetic. Just in love. You were smitten by Sam, everyone could see that. There's nothing wrong with that. He loves you more than life itself. You're his, or were, his world."

Sighing, I confess, "But I feel like I've sacrificed pieces of myself to fit into Samuel's world."

"What do you mean?"

"I mean, I never ate red meat, but a year into our relationship, I was chomping on a steak like a famished caveman."

Piper giggles. "Choosing to eat red meat is hardly sacrificing your independence."

"I know, but it started out with little things. I only went to the college that I did because Sam went there. I never really explored my options. I would have loved to travel to places like Tibet, Nepal, or Peru and done some soul searching. But instead, I feel like I settled." I can't believe I'm saying this aloud, as I didn't even know I felt this way.

No one's relationship is perfect and that's the problem. I thought mine was. Sam was my perfect guy. He was the one guy everyone wanted and he wanted me. I felt privileged to be seen with him. How sad is that?

"For argument's sake, let's say that you did settle. Why the sudden epiphany? I know Sam has been a complete asshole to you, but there's got to be a reason why you're thinking this way," she wisely says. But I can't tell her. If I tell her, then I'll have to admit to myself that the reason is Saxon.

He's pushed my buttons from the get go, but in some strange, unexpected way, he's helped me uncover who I want to be. It makes no sense, but I feel that Samuel and I both woke up after his accident changed people.

Piper is still looking at me, waiting for an answer, but it's an answer I can't give. "I'm just being stupid," I say, dismissing my thoughts. Stretching out, I drag the red dress off the bed. "This is nice, except, where's the rest of it?"

Piper bursts into laughter. "Hopefully by the end of the night, on Saxon's bedroom floor." Her comment makes me feel uneasy, but I smile.

Looking at the lone dress sitting on the bed, I reach for it and finger the soft silk. The dress is actually a beige, sleeveless romper with a pretty floating feather print. The plunging neckline matches the short shorts, but it's tasteful enough that if I bent over, I wouldn't be flashing the entire room.

"Can I wear this?"

Piper doesn't hide her surprise. "I didn't think it was your style." Just as I open my mouth, she amends, "Which is exactly *why* you should wear it. Nothing like kicking off your newfound independence with some cleavage."

No matter my mood, Piper can always pick me up off the ground. I feel incredibly guilty for not telling her about what happened between Saxon and me. The thought has me wondering if he told her about why he left his bike at the saloon. I haven't seen him since his return, so I haven't been able to ask him.

"Did Saxon tell you why he left his bike?" I decide to ask, curious.

She pops her gum. "Just that he went out and had the best night of his life." I gulp. "He didn't tell me who he went with. Do you know?"

I pull at an invisible thread on the romper. "Nope, no idea." The moment the lie leaves my lips, I feel like the world's worst friend. There is no reason for me to lie, but I did. I'm too gutless to look at the bigger picture.

"Oh well. I'll just have to make sure tonight is the best night of his life, so all other nights pale in comparison." When she wiggles her eyebrows up and down, I shake my head, laughing.

"Did you want to get ready first? I really should clean up this mess," I say, referring to my diaries littering the floor.

"Yes, best to take the temptation away from prying eyes,"

she replies with bite, "Still can't believe he read them. He broke like some vow doing so." Her harmless comment has me lowering my eyes because *I'm* the one guilty of that.

★ ★ ★ ★ ★

"It's not too much?"

"Yes, it's way too much, but that's not a bad thing," Piper says, smacking my hand away as I try and wipe away the layers of gloss she's applied to my lips.

I would have never bothered dressing up in the past, seeing as there are more important things in the world, like feeding the hungry, but it does feel kind of liberating shedding the old me and starting with something fresh.

Piper curled my long hair, the honey blonde curls falling down my back, making me feel feminine and pretty. She then went to town on my face, plumping, primping, and painting every surface until I emerged looking like someone other than me.

My green eyes look huge, thanks to the warm bronze eye shadow Piper caked on. She ditched the black eyeliner and used a plum color instead. My long lashes look like they're on steroids with the layers of mascara coating them. I drew the line at hooker red lipstick and we settled on a clear gloss instead.

Piper looks amazing in a red tunic dress. She's got a runner's body with incredible long legs and not an ounce of jiggle on her. She's wearing black pumps which add about five inches to her small frame. She's dressed to impress and I know she's only interested in impressing one man tonight. Her long hair is straightened, not a strand out of place, and her red lips look wickedly inviting. Saxon doesn't stand a chance.

Thinking of another beauty that may be fighting for his attention tonight, I realize Saxon is going to be one busy boy. I still haven't spoken to him since this morning, and haven't replied to his texts either. I don't know what to say other than Sam has been fine—great, in fact. I feel like I'm rubbing his nose in something that isn't there.

"C'mon, let's go. Sam may not remember you, but he sure as shit will after he sees you in that outfit." I nervously brush my hands down my romper.

We walk towards the door and like predicted, I trip, thanks to the monster heels Piper insisted I wear. I may be on a path of self discovery, but in these shoes, I'll be tripping every step of the way. I'm certain they leave a dent in the wall as I kick them off. Piper watches in horror as I bend down and slip into my black cowboy boots.

"No."

"Yes," I reply, my feet singing in relief.

When she hears Bon Jovi blaring down the hallway, she gives up arguing and claps excitedly. "This is my jam!"

I follow behind her as she practically runs into the living room. There are about a dozen people mingling down the corridor, and I don't know a single one. When I round the corner however, that dozen is quickly replaced by a dozen more faces I don't recognize.

Piper is long gone, swallowed up in the sea of people, leaving me to fend for myself. At a guess, I would say there are roughly one hundred people mingling in my home. When I hear rowdy laughter from outside however, I know that number will multiply, as the night is still young.

Still feeling hung over, I decide to stick to water, which is a shame as alcohol would help make the night go faster. Politely pushing past random strangers, I enter my crowded kitchen but come to a screeching halt. A circle has formed around a young girl who barely looks twenty-one, sucking on a beer bong hose. She's in denim shorts and a bright pink bikini top, which only adds to the frat party vibe.

I have no idea who these people are, where they've come from, and how Piper knows them, but I smile as I duck and weave past them, adamant to have a good time. I grab a bottle of water and decide to sit out on the porch and enjoy the warm night, but when I turn around, I smack straight into Samuel.

"I'm sorry!" we say at the same time, smiling.

He looks incredibly handsome in black jeans and a white V neck t-shirt. His longer hair is styled messily, but it suits him. His jaw line is coated with a light scruff, giving him an edgier, non-Sam look.

He looks down at my drink and shakes his head, mockingly.

"You can do better than that."

"No, no, water is fine," I reply, still smiling. "My liver needs a night off." The moment I confess my sins, I zip my lips, kicking myself for the over share. Samuel has no idea what I did last night and I'd like to keep it that way.

"Ah, c'mon. One glass of wine can't hurt." When his eyes twinkle and a familiar dimple touches his right cheek, I cave. It's the same face he pulled whenever he wanted something in the past and then, just like now, it has worked.

"Okay, just one," I say, holding up my finger.

"Stay right here." He points to the spot where I stand.

When he pushes past a couple making out against the fridge, he gestures to them and pulls a mock disgusted face. I can't help but laugh. The wine sits at the end of the counter, and Samuel is having a hard time reaching it as a billion people stand in the way.

His fun, laidback attitude reminds me so much of whom he used to be. It's almost enough for me to forget the past few weeks—almost. One song ends and then another begins and that song suits the person who has just walked into the room to a tee. "Sex on Fire" by Kings of Leon fills the space between us as I lock eyes with Saxon Stone.

He stops, not caring that people are trying to get past. The only thing he seems to care about is me. His commanding presence fills the kitchen and, it fills my…heart. I've missed him. I don't know what is happening between Saxon and me, but I can't deny that something is there.

I wish I could control my emotions around him, but I can't. My lips hurt as I grin. I'm pretty sure I resemble the Joker. As he adjusts his backwards turned baseball cap, his biceps move in just the right way so I can admire the rest of him. He's wearing a white Santa Cruz muscle tank which hangs low on his flank, exposing his ripped obliques and scripted tattoo which I can't read. The wings from his chest piece peer out from under his tank, complementing the colorful artwork running down his arm. His hair is mussed, the dirty blond drawing out the sea green in his eyes. He is beautiful.

I can't take my eyes off of him, and he's making no secret of the fact that he can't take his eyes off of me either. I feel hot all over. As he scans down my body, his gaze heated and hungry, I shamefully press my legs together, turned on.

"Here you go." The familiar voice jars me from my very inappropriate behavior and I guiltily lower my eyes.

There was a time when I craved to hear that voice, but now I crave to hear another—the one which filled a hole when I needed Sam's familiarity. But now, I need Saxon's.

"Th-thanks, Sam," I stutter, angry at myself for thinking something which I shouldn't. This newfound independence is turning me into a tramp.

"You look nice tonight," he says, sipping his Budweiser. I gulp down my wine, wishing I could drown in it.

I don't know where Saxon is and I'm too nervous to look

up and seek him out. He no doubt saw Sam give me a drink without throwing it in my face, and the fact I haven't replied to his texts highlights that something is askew. But why do I feel guilty? This is what we both wanted, right? For Sam to remember. That's why he's here. The butterflies within hint otherwise.

"Do you want to dance?" Sam asks, again snapping me from somewhere other than here.

I crinkle my nose. "I'm not a very good dancer."

"It's okay, neither am I. I don't think?" he adds, smirking.

"You're right. You're a terrible dancer," I tease.

"Well, let's be terrible dancers together then." Before I have time to protest, he grabs my forearm and pulls me through the crowd.

The room spins as faces I don't know whizz past me and laughter fills the air. Everyone seems to be having a good time and so does Sam. He begins a ridiculous jig to some alternative rock song, making fun of his nonexistent dancing skills. Not that I can talk, as I'm not any better. I move to the upbeat tempo, trying my best to stay in time, but give up soon after.

Thankfully, the song ends, but when "She Will Be Loved" by Maroon 5 takes its place, I wish we were dancing to *anything* but this. Sam looks at me while I chew the inside of my cheek. I feel silly standing in the middle of the room, motionless, seeing as we have prime real estate in the middle of the "dance floor."

When Sam offers me his hand, I gingerly take it. Looking

up at him from under my lashes, I suck in a breath when he pulls me into his arms. I stand rigid, my heart racing and my feet feeling like lead. Everything about him is so familiar, but my reaction to him is not. He begins to sway slowly, and I hesitantly follow his lead. As Adam Levine sings about being loved, I can't help but see the irony of this particular song and my situation.

Weeks ago, I would have given anything to be loved by Samuel, but now, the love that once was shared between us isn't there. Warranted, Sam doesn't remember that love, but I do. And I don't remember it feeling this forced. I made peace with the fact that Sam and I may never go back to the way things were. But his change of attitude has just thrown a monkey wrench in the works.

I need to talk to Sophia. She's the only person who can explain to me what's going on.

Thoughts of her have me looking over Sam's shoulder, searching the room for Saxon. When I find him, I wish I had just kept my eyes glued to the floor. He's standing with his back pressed against the wall, watching me—watching us. Piper is talking to him, but he isn't listening to a word she says.

I loosen my grip around Sam's shoulders, feeling guilty—always guilt. Why am I riddled with this constant shame? But it's too late. Saxon's hard jaw, folded arms, and cold eyes reveal that he's seen it all. Seen my fiancé get me a drink and ask me to dance. Why is that so bad?

I know why. I've known all along—I was just too afraid to admit it.

I'm torn between my past love and…Saxon. It doesn't make any sense. But none of it does. Sam being in the wrong place at the wrong time doesn't make sense. Nor does him waking from a coma and not remembering who I am. What does that say about our relationship? What does that say about me?

I suddenly feel like the walls begin closing in on me. Struggling to breathe, I push Sam away. He looks at me, confused. "Sorry, Sam, I just…need some fresh air."

"I'll come with you," he offers, but I shake my head, making it clear I want to be alone. He doesn't argue as I run from the safety of my home and out the back door.

The night air feels wonderful against my skin and I take three much needed deep breaths. Tilting my head to look into the clear, star-filled sky, I curse the universe. Such beauty can also be so cruel.

I've somehow found myself in a predicament I cannot explain. I'm changing, I can feel it. Every breath I take brings me closer to where I think I'm supposed to be. I just don't know where that is yet.

"Lucy?" I hate myself for feeling this way. I hate that I crave him near me.

Closing my eyes, I continue blindly looking into the universe. The blades of grass sound under his boots as he walks towards me. His heavy stride hints at purpose behind his steps.

The hair on my arms stands on end when his unique fragrance catches on the breeze.

"Is everything all right?"

"Yes, Saxon, everything is surprisingly fine."

"Then why do you look so sad?"

Sighing, I open my eyes and look at him. "I don't know what that means." But I do. Sadly, I do.

Approaching me with caution, he slips his hands into his pockets, appearing just as lost as me. "You're standing in a room full of people, but you're still alone."

I lower my eyes, embarrassed by his accuracy.

He keeps walking closer and closer and instead of backing away, I stand my ground, titillated to discover what happens when he reaches me.

"Why didn't you text me back? I was worried about you."

"Everything was fine," I reply, still staring at the ground.

"I made a promise to take care of you. And I meant it." My heart begins pounding as he stops a hair's breadth away.

"Sam was great today. He actually wanted to speak to me, which is a nice change. Then he got me a drink and asked me to dance," I reveal on a rushed breath. Why am I telling him all this?

"So why are you crying?" he asks, his voice soft, concerned.

Angrily wiping at my tears, I laugh a maniacal cackle. "Because I don't want him to be nice to me. How messed up is that? I've become so used to him being the cold, heartless jerk that he's become, I don't know how to take this new attitude."

"But this is what the old Sam was like, right?"

Saxon isn't stupid. He knows what's going on. "Yes, Saxon, he was. But things have changed."

"Why, Lucy? What's changed?" He takes a step closer. The heat from his body warms mine.

"Never mind. Forget I said anything," I jumpily say, finally meeting his eyes.

I see confusion, sadness, anxiety, and fear swirling in his depths—it's apprehension which I put there. Saxon feels what I feel. We both appear to be standing in a room full of people, feeling utterly alone…until we find one another.

"I can't do this." I turn, needing to run away before I do something so terribly wrong because I won't regret it.

But he doesn't let me flee. He latches onto my forearm, spinning me around. "Do what?" His chest is rising and falling so quickly, his rough breaths fan the hair from my cheeks.

"This," I clarify, motioning with an unsteady finger between us. "I don't know what "this" is, but I just can't. Please let me go."

But he doesn't. My words only inspire him to pull me closer and closer until not a breath of air can pass between us. "I can't let you go, Lucy. I'm afraid you'll run away if I do."

"Saxon…no." My protest is weak, contradictory to my request. And my actions betray me as Saxon swallows before lowering his lips to mine.

I'm lost in the epitome of this heartfelt moment, looking

into the soul of the man who somehow has opened my eyes when I wasn't even aware they were closed. But that man is my fiancé's brother and another wave of guilt crashes over me, dragging me under.

"No, I can't." I press against his chest before we take yet another step towards our undoing.

"Lucy…" he cries. But I pull out of his hold and walk back towards the house, not turning back.

The party is in full swing, while I'm ready to call it a night as I push my way past the crowd. Piper bounces over to me, shaking her head. I instantly think she saw my almost exchange with Saxon, but let out a breath of relief when she says, "Why is Sam's doctor here?"

"Oh, shit, sorry, Piper, I forgot to tell you. I sort of invited her."

"Why would you do that? You're totally cock, well, cooch blocking me. Lucky for you, Saxon promised me a dance. Or two," she adds with an over-exaggerated wink. She's obviously very drunk.

"When?" I blurt out.

She cocks an eyebrow. "Just now. He came in looking awfully huffy, so I decided to take advantage of his testosterone."

Great.

"I need a drink."

"Everything okay?" she asks, concerned.

No, everything is not okay, but I nod.

Making a beeline for the kitchen, something catches my eye and I have to look twice to ensure I'm not seeing things. Sam is pressed against the wall, talking to the one and only Alicia Bell. She looks exactly how she did in high school—a gigantic slut. And she's acting just how she did in high school—a gigantic home wrecker.

Her long, brunette hair is pulled back in a high ponytail, highlighting her heavy handed black eye shadow and pink glossy lips. She's wearing a blue dress, which I'm unsure if it's a man's oversized shirt or indeed a dress. Either way, the silver glitter pumps she's wearing all add to the stripper vibe.

I can't believe Samuel is talking to her. A thought suddenly punches me in the guts. Does he remember her? If so, that's not saying an awful lot for me. Deciding to find out, I pull back my shoulders and walk over with my head held high. When she sees me, her face twists in disgust, just how it did when we were kids.

"Hi, Alicia." Her name feels like acid sliding down my throat.

"Lucy," she replies, just as impressed as I am. "Samuel and I were just reminiscing about the good old days. Weren't we, Sammy?"

I grit my teeth, knowing using her old pet name for him will get a rise out of me.

Sam nods with a grin. "Yeah, we were. We got up to some crazy shit."

His comment cements my worst fears. "So you remember her, but you don't remember me?" My voice is raised, but I don't care. I'm sure everyone is talking about it behind my back anyway.

Alicia raises a hand to her gaping mouth, muting a giggle. "You don't remember her?" I close my eyes for a second, cursing my temper.

Sam scratches the back of his neck, pulling an uncomfortable face. "Yeah, I'm sorry. It's not like I'm doing it on purpose."

He appears genuinely repentant, but it's too late.

Alicia purses her collagen pumped lips cruelly. "Oh, how sad. I guess you didn't make enough of an impression to be remembered."

Tears prick my eyes because no matter how spiteful her words are, they're the truth. Sam dated Alicia for mere seconds compared to our relationship, but he seems to remember those trivial seconds quite clearly. But with me, with us, I may as well be a stranger, just how this room full of people are strangers to me.

"Excuse me," I choke out, not giving Alicia the satisfaction of seeing me cry. Sam calls out to me, but he doesn't follow. His actions confirm that he doesn't care for me at all.

I shove past the partygoers, desperate to get to my room and forget this disaster of a night ever happened. But when I round the corner and see Saxon pushing a giggling Piper into his room, I know forgetting this night will be impossible. That image is forever charred into my brain. The door slams shut behind him, reflecting how my heart feels.

I amble down the hallway, feeling numb. When I enter the bedroom, I don't even bother turning on the light. I walk blindly to my bed and collapse on top of it, face first. I sniff back my tears, as crying won't change anything. It won't change the fact that Samuel remembers his high school girlfriend, but not me. And it doesn't change the fact that right this second, Saxon is probably having sex with my best friend.

Images of him taking off her beautiful red dress and laying her gently on the bed assaults my masochistic brain and I groan into the pillow. Then another image flashes behind my locked eyes of Saxon throwing her against the wall and devouring her whole. I don't know why, but this image hurts the most. If Saxon were in love with Piper or even the slightest bit interested in her, then I wouldn't care. But it feels like he's doing this to get back at me. To hurt me.

But I scold myself for such thoughts. Saxon can have sex with whomever he wishes. He owes me nothing. After he's done with Piper, he could rightfully seek out Sophia and go for round two. The thought makes me sick.

The bedroom door squeaking open puts an end to these god awful thoughts and I spring up, brushing the hair from my cheeks. Straining my eyes to see in the near dark, I'm hoping the figure illuminated by the hallway light is Saxon, but it's not.

"Lucy?"

"Go away, Sam," I groan, falling back onto the mattress. He's the last person I want to see.

The door closes but his footsteps sounding off the hardwood floors tell me he's not going anywhere. "No, I won't. I really am sorry. I don't know why I remember Alicia and not you, it's not like I have a choice. From your diary entries, I know I should remember you, but I don't. I've been so angry since I woke up, and I've blamed you for what happened to me because it's always easier to blame a stranger than someone you—"

"Love?" I fill in the blanks when he pauses. It makes sense.

"I'm sorry, Lucy. I want to remember, I really do."

"It's fine, Sam. I know it's not your fault. You can't force love." I lay on my back, staring up at the ceiling, tears spilling from the corner of my eyes.

In a way, I'm glad Sam has explained his behavior. He woke, stuck in a universe where I don't exist. I tried pushing my memories onto him, desperate for him to remember, but in turn, I ended up pushing him away. And by doing that, I pushed myself closer to Saxon.

I don't realize what's happening until Samuel is crawling onto me from the foot of the bed. I freeze, forgetting to breathe when I feel his weight settle on my body.

"Maybe we could make new memories?" he offers, his breath bathing my flesh. He lowers his lips to my neck and kisses over my frantic pulse.

The touch feels nice, but it doesn't send a tingle to my toes.

It doesn't have me pawing at Sam, needing to feel him against every inch of my body.

"I know what you like. I read it in your diary," he thickly says against my throat. "I read how you loved me touching you." As if on cue, he runs his hand down between the valley of my breasts, slipping his fingers inside my plunging neckline. "I read how I was the only man who made you come." I gasp, his fingertip circling my left nipple.

I'm struggling to breathe and I don't know if I'm robbed of air because I'm turned on, or because I'm desperate to flee.

Sam flicks the front clasp on my bra, it peels away, uncovering my breasts. He doesn't waste a second and replaces the cup with his palm. His hand is hot against my skin, his fondling feeling desperate and rushed.

"Sam," I protest, attempting to push his hand away, but my plea dies in my throat when he sucks over my carotid pulse in a long, wet pull. I arch my head back, exposing more of my neck as this is one of my most favorite places to be kissed. I have no doubt Sam knows this because he read about it in my diary.

I should feel betrayed that he read so much of my personal thoughts, but as he continues cupping and kneading my breast, sucking on my neck as he slips a hand between my thighs, all I can think about is how long it's been since he touched me like this.

I feel him growing hard against my stomach as he heats up the contact, circling over my core with two skillful fingers. My starved body is responsive to his touch and I whimper, needing more. Sam reads my desperation and quickens the speed of his fingers.

I need to stop this before it gets out of hand, but Sam's hands all over me reveal that it's too late. A niggling thought scratching at the surface seals my fate. Saxon is down the hall doing the exact thing to Piper. Why do I need to stop? Having sex with my fiancé may just be what I've needed to find my way through the storm and make things right again.

"Make love to me, Sam," I frantically whisper, my fingers fumbling over his belt buckle. Those words seem to be the key to unlocking the hostility we've found ourselves in.

Our impassioned moans fill the air as I yank open his jeans, dragging them down his thighs as he almost rips the belt off my waist. Just as I grab a hold of his red hot erection, he roughly flips me onto my stomach and tears the romper from my body. The material is stretchy, with no buttons or zips, so he maneuvers it off with ease. He doesn't bother taking it all off, satisfied when my back and ass is exposed.

He scoops a hand under my belly, positioning me on all fours. I feel incredibly exposed displayed this way, especially since it showcases my scars. Just as I attempt to turn over, Sam wraps a hand around my waist and positions his blunt head at my entrance. I'm not ready yet. He hasn't even dipped in his toe to test the waters. But it appears he doesn't care and is happy to dive straight into the deep end.

"Sam, wait!" I cry when he presses against me.

"Oh, shit, sorry," he says, easing up the pressure.

He's still pushed against, but thankfully, he runs a hand over my behind and then dips low. The moment he inserts a finger into me, I gasp, as the intrusion isn't exactly gentle. I'm not even halfway there, as he didn't prep me, or ensure I was ready to go.

He continues trying to warm me up, but I'm not with him. My muscles aren't receptive of his efforts, and I don't know why. I was into the heavy petting, but when the pants came off, it's like my body shut up shop.

"Do you want me to stop?" he asks, sensing my complete lack of excitement.

I'm angry at myself for not meeting him in the middle, as he's trying. For the first time since this nightmare began, he's actually trying. With that thought in mind, I shake my head, determined to make this happen. "No, but maybe I could turn around?" I don't like this detachment. I never have.

He instantly withdraws his fingers and lets me go. I flip around onto my back and timidly take off my clothes so I'm now completely nude. It's thankfully dark and the only light source is steaming in from the curtains as the moonlight peeks out from under a cloud.

Sam slips off his t-shirt. The jeans follow soon after. We're now both completely nude and I have never felt more awkward. He lies on top of me, shifting to get the position right. I don't remember him being this heavy and a winded breath escapes from my lungs. I also move, trying to place my arms and legs at a comfortable angle, but all I manage to do is get us tangled into a limb pretzel.

He glances down at me, appearing to be waiting for permission. I don't blame him, considering the last time he instigated anything I froze up like the North Pole. I take charge and wrap my arms around his neck, drawing his face towards mine. It dawns on me that we haven't even kissed. We're completely naked and haven't even shared a simple kiss.

I seal my mouth over his and we come together as two strangers in the night. We're both reacquainting ourselves with one another, testing what the other likes. I have the upper hand and kiss Sam the way he used to like to be kissed. I start out slow, but Sam takes charge and sticks his tongue so far down my throat, I almost gag. He doesn't read my aversion and continues digging around in my mouth as if he's panning for gold.

The kiss is sloppy, messy, and clumsy, nothing like our first kiss. And nothing like my first kiss with Saxon. I really should *not* be thinking about that, but it's hard not to when I have what's currently going on in my mouth to compare it to.

Saxon's mouth melded perfectly to mine, his tongue stroking not prodding and his lips were warm, soft. Thinking about that kiss has me losing myself in the memories and taking control. Thankfully, Sam follows my lead and we kiss like adults, not teenagers making out for the first time.

His looming bulge is hinting that he wants in and as I shift my leg to the side, he nudges against my entrance eagerly. The kiss has made me a little more receptive, and Sam can feel it. "I don't have any protection," he says regretfully.

"It's okay, I'm on birth control." I can sense his relief.

My admission has him breaking the kiss and nibbling down my throat. This is Sam's move, a move he obviously read about in my diary. But I focus on his lips and what he's doing down below. He's nudging himself into me, and when I eventually let my guard down, he slips inside.

I gasp, my unaccustomed muscles adjusting to the intrusion as Sam moves within me. We've been connected timeless times before but this somehow feels different. Our bodies move out of time, both dancing to a different song. Sam is listening to heavy metal, while I'm dancing to the beat of my own drum.

His length stabs at me as he increases his strokes, grunting and bucking wildly, while I'm wondering where I put my hands. This is hardly romantic or even any good.

"You're so wet, babe," he moans happily while I cringe, feeling like a B-grade actress in a bad porno.

This awkwardness continues on for what seems like hours and when Sam looks into my eyes, I turn away, burying my face into the pillow. I can't look at him, afraid he'll see my lack of excitement. I resemble a starfish, lying there, waiting for him to finish. This isn't like riding a bike because now that I've fallen off, I don't think I ever want to get back on.

This act was once filled with love, but now, it's filled with nothing but boredom and regret. Whether he can read my detachment or not, I'll never know because it doesn't seem to bother him either way. He pumps into me, his forceful strokes moving me up the bed. I bang my head on the wooden headboard, yelping on impact. Samuel misinterprets my pain for passion.

"That's it, babe. Work with me."

I try and get involved, to make this a team sport, but I can't. He resembles a bunny, sprinting towards the finished line, while I never began the race. When he groans and finally collapses on top of me, I'm actually thankful it's over. I keep my face turned, unable to look at him because he'll see I'm about to cry. When he pulls out, his seed spills down my leg. He doesn't bother to clean up after himself as he rises and closes the bathroom door behind him.

Rolling onto my side, I hug my pillow into me, never feeling more alone. An act which should unite two people has driven us further apart. I feel dirty, coated in shame. I thought sex could save our relationship but instead, I think I've just made things worse.

★ ★ ★ ★ ★

22nd May 2005
Dear diary,

This entry is probably going to be the shortest one yet because there are simply no words to describe how I feel. Tonight was prom. And it was the night I lost my virginity to Sam.

I don't regret a single moment because it was perfect.

He was gentle, caring, attentive, and patient—all the things a girl could ever ask for. I don't know what I was expecting, but it wasn't that. It was better. It hurt, but the pain...it felt good after a while.

I still can't believe it happened.

Once I come down from cloud nine, I will detail every second, but for now, I just want to appreciate the reality that I'll be connected to Samuel forever.

Sex really does change everything.

Eighteen

I WANT A DO-OVER.

If I could take back the last twelve hours, I would. I would take it all back.

The empty place beside me has long since cooled as Samuel rose quite early. I, on the other hand, plan on staying in bed forever.

I can't believe we had sex. And I don't mean that in a toe curling, hot, and bothered way, either. Piper has shared many of her horror sex stories with me, and although I felt for her, I didn't understand because sex with Samuel was always good. But last night, it was bad. So very bad.

Once he emerged from the bathroom, I pretended I was asleep, as I couldn't deal with talking or cuddling or worse still, him wanting to do it again. He snored contentedly beside me, while I didn't sleep a wink. It's the first night he's slept beside me, and I've never felt more alone.

Saxon's comment rings loudly in my ears because in this circumstance, it's true. I've never felt more alone than I do right now. I was stupid to think that having sex could somehow miraculously fix what is so broken between us. What happened wasn't making love because there is no love between us. There is no emotional connection. It's gone. I really *am* in love with a ghost.

I can't swallow down this ball of regret because there is another reason why I did what I did. I'm so ashamed of myself. I don't even know who I am anymore. I slept with Samuel to prove to myself that I don't have feelings for Saxon. But it's backfired. It's only proven that I do.

When I saw Saxon take Piper into his room, I was jealous. And I was hurt. I know I have no right to feel this way, but I've finally discovered what that "something" is. I have feelings for Saxon, feelings I shouldn't have. But thinking back to our first encounter, I believe they've always been there.

I don't know what to do. The person I would usually go and spill my heart and soul to is the person who is driving my regret. I can't have feelings for Saxon; I know that it's wrong. But I can't help it.

Stewing alone is making me feel worse, so I decide to face the music. If luck is on my side, Piper and Saxon will still be asleep, caught in a post-coitus bubble, and I can disappear for the day. Or maybe the week.

I take a scalding shower, wishing I could scrub the shame from my skin. Sadly, it's still there when I open the door and try not to trip over discarded cups, empty beer bottles, and half-eaten packets of Cheetos.

The living room looks like an atomic bomb has exploded and in its wake, it's left behind debris of the party kind. It's going to take all day to clean this mess up, but it's a good way to keep occupied.

The kitchen looks even worse, and as I hunt through my drawers to find the garbage bags, I find a dildo instead. It's evident the world was on crazy drugs last night.

Deciding to start with the kitchen, I roll up my sleeves and begin collecting all the bottles from the counter. I have no idea how many people were here last night, but judging from the mess, I'd say a lot. I'm surprised no one crashed, seeing as a ton of alcohol was consumed, but I still have the rest of the house and outside to clean.

I'm in the process of filling bag number three when someone announces their arrival by scraping the barstool along the tiles. Looking up, I see Piper slumped on the chair, cradling her brow. "Kill me," she moans into her palms.

Usually I would smile, but now, I just feel sick. "Rough night?" I cringe the moment the words leave my lips.

"Like you wouldn't believe. Is there any coffee?"

"Coming right up," I reply, trying my best to mask my emotions.

The bottles rattle as I dump the bag onto the floor. "Ah, not so loud," Piper gripes, placing her cheek against the counter.

"How much did you have to drink last night?" I ask, washing my hands.

"I don't remember. I don't remember much of anything, actually."

With my back turned, I question, "Oh? Where did you crash? In one of the spare rooms?"

She is silent, which is never a good sign. "In Saxon's room."

My hands tremble as I dry them on paper towel. "Wow. That's…great, Pipe." Before I can interrogate her further, the back door swings open and in strolls Samuel.

The moment I see him, I feel even sicker than I already feel. I roll the paper towel into a tiny ball and clench my fist around it. "Hey, babe," he says, giving me a kiss on the cheek. Piper half raises her weary head from the counter and cocks an inquisitive brow. "I'm just going for a quick shower. Any coffee?"

"I-I was just making some," I reply, fumbling over my words.

"Awesome, I won't be long. Better make it strong. Mr. Personality out there needs a hit of caffeine, stat," he jeers smugly.

I blanch.

Sam walks down the hallway whistling happily while I tighten my fist. The moment he's out of earshot, Piper lifts herself from the counter and wiggles her pointer at me. "You had sex."

It's not a question, but rather a statement. I see no point denying it. "Yup." But that's all I can say. I don't want to elaborate, or talk about it in general because I just want to forget it happened.

But of course, Piper has other ideas. "That's it? Yup?"

"Yup," I reply, spinning around. I fumble with the coffee maker as she presses.

"Nah-uh. What happened?"

Hoping to evade her with humor, I commence, "Well, when a man likes a woman, he sticks his…"

"Luce, cut the crap. What aren't you telling me?"

There are a lot of things I'm not telling her, like how I have feelings for the man she just hooked up with. "It was fine, Pipe. Can we change the subject?"

"Fine?" she says, disgusted. "Fine is what you say when things are not fine. Fine is not the word you use to describe sex. What happened? I thought you'd be out there singing, 'the hills are alive with the sound of mmm I just got laid?'"

"Looks like you thought wrong," I reply with bite. I really don't want to talk about this because the more she pushes, the more I'm bound to breakdown and tell her everything.

"Lucy Eva Tucker, look at me." Sighing, I turn around, proud of myself for keeping the tears away. "What's wrong?"

I shrug. "I don't know. We had sex and well…it was kind of, sort of very, very awful."

Her mouth hits the floor. "What do you mean?"

"I mean…I feel like I had sex with the Energizer Bunny."

"Ooh." She makes a pained face. "Sex sprain?"

I rub my head. "No, more like a brain sprain."

"I don't understand. What happened? I thought he was stellar in the sack?"

"He was, but…" I draw a blank because I can't tell her it sucked because there was no feeling behind it. It was mere screwing to get off. Well, for Samuel, not for me.

She fills in the blanks. "But what? He forgot how to fuck, too?"

"Piper! Not so loud." I gesture with my hands for her to lower her voice.

"Screw him. Actually, on second thought…" She backtracks, scrunching up her nose.

There is a big, fat elephant in the room that needs addressing but I don't know how. While we're on the topic of sex, I suppose I could ask her how it was with Saxon. But do I really want to know? Her rumpled appearance points to one hell of a night.

That has me turning back around and silently making our coffee. As I'm waiting for it to percolate, I gaze out the wide, triple paneled window above the sink, lost in thought. A figure stalking across the yard catches my eye, ending my moment of serenity.

Saxon looks livid. He has a garbage bag draped over his shoulder but makes no use of it as he kicks a beer bottle across the grass. As it hits the wall of the dining room and shatters, I jerk back, stunned. I watch as he slams the bag onto the ground, mumbling something under his breath.

Sam did say he was cranky, but this appears to be beyond cranky. I quickly reach for a mug and pour the boiling contents into it. Just as I turn and ask Piper if she wants sugar, I see that she's sound asleep on the counter. That explains why the questions stopped.

Composing myself as best as I can, I push open the backdoor, carrying Saxon's hot coffee in hand. The early morning sunlight is blinding, so I squint, shielding a hand over my eyes. The closer I come to Saxon, the clearer it becomes that he's incredibly mad. Did he have a fight with Samuel? And if so, over what?

"Good morning." I stop a few feet away, watching Saxon as he wordlessly picks up trash. "I brought coffee," I say when he doesn't acknowledge me.

When he continues picking up bottles, ignoring me, I know his anger is directed at me. I've never been more terrified than I am right now. "Saxon? Is everything all right?" He turns his broad back, a silent fuck you.

He must be angry about our almost kiss, but why would he be? He welcomed Piper into his bed, and I…welcomed Sam into mine. I remember Sam's smugness, his quip that Saxon was crabby. The universe tilts on its axis and a sense of dread surrounds me. I feel like I'm about to drown.

He knows. I don't know how he knows; I just know that he does.

Placing his untouched coffee on a log, I press, "Saxon…"

"Did you have a nice night?" he sneers, his back still turned.

I'm caught with my mouth hanging open. "It was o-okay."

"Just okay? I'm sure you can do better than that." His voice is angry, bitter, and pained.

"I went to bed early," I reply, which earns me an incensed laugh.

"The festivities not exciting enough for you?"

"What's that supposed to mean?" I bark, not appreciating his tone. "And the least you can do is look at me."

He turns around so quickly I take a step back, afraid he's going to bowl me over with his wrath. He radiates nothing but pure rage as he pins me with a stare that is laced with hate. "I owe you nothing."

I bite the inside of my cheek to stop the tears. "Why are you so angry at me?"

"I'm not angry!"

"You could have fooled me!"

Something big is about to happen—I can feel it.

We're at a standstill, waiting for the other to confirm what we both know to be true. We're both holding onto secrets, but I won't stand here and be made to feel guilty for having sex with my fiancé.

"If you've got something to say, then say it, Saxon." I'm

done playing. Yes, I had sex with Sam, but he had sex with my best friend who he doesn't even like. Or maybe he does. Either way, he has no right to reprimand me.

His lips pull into a thin line "Oh, I don't think you'll want to hear what I've got to say."

"Funny that, because you probably won't like what I've got to say, either."

My comment knocks him off his high horse, and he blinks once. "I highly doubt that. Say whatever you've got to say. I'm a big boy. I can handle it."

His arrogance is pissing me off and I suddenly explode. "I saw you."

"Saw what?" he replies, expressionless.

Images of him taking a giggling Piper into his room play on repeat, fueling me to yell, "I saw you and Piper!"

"Saw me and Piper what?" he has the gall to question, enraging me further.

"I saw you take her into your room, where you no doubt fucked the living hell out of her!" Those words are ones I would never use, but I'm driving on pure emotion, fire behind the wheel.

He looks stunned for a fraction of a second, before he howls out a throaty snigger. Why is he laughing? His aloofness sets me off, and I storm forward, shoving at his chest with both hands. The laughter dies in his throat.

"Do that again and see what happens," he warns, his jaw

clenched.

"Oh, what are you going to do, you big macho man?" I mock, thrusting my palms against his chest once again. This time however, his hands snap out and lock around my wrists. The pressure is firm, almost punishing, but the tremble in his fingers betrays the fact that he's just as crazed as I am.

He tightens his grip and draws me towards him so we're inches apart. His breath feels like an out of control tempest as it lashes against my face. "So that's why you had sex with him, because you saw me take Piper into my room?" I gasp, his confession leaving me winded. "You got back at me for wanting someone…other than you."

I'm left speechless, tears of anger pricking my eyes. He wants me? The lowered brow, thinned lips, and flared nostrils all point to one thing—he's wanted me all along. And I…I've wanted him.

Every moment we've spent together comes roaring like a tidal wave, memories overtaking my rage and nothing has been clearer. What have I done?

"Was it good for you? Because damn, it was good for me!" he shouts vulgarly. "That Piper, hmm—" he hums, licking his lips "—she's a real pistol. Went right off when I…"

But I don't allow him to finish a sentence I have no interest hearing. I yank my wrists from his hold and slap his cheek so hard, I'm almost certain I've broken my hand. I clutch it to my chest, tears pricking my eyes.

"You're disgusting!" I spit, ready to hit him again for speaking that way about Piper.

"Well, better that than a liar." He rubs his reddening cheek.

"A liar?"

"Yes, Lucy, you're a liar."

"How am I a liar?" I cry, not understanding what I've lied about. I never denied sleeping with Sam.

He shakes his head, exasperated. "Figure it out yourself. I'm done." He's done? Is he leaving? For good? Well, good riddance. I don't want him here anyway.

The moment those thoughts float to the surface, I realize that Saxon is right. I *am* a liar. I've been lying to myself this entire time.

The backdoor swings open and out charges Sam. "What's going on? I heard yelling. Is everything all right?" Something the old Sam would say, but that Sam is dead. And so are my feelings for him. I don't know what I feel for the new Sam.

"Go back to living your memories of yesterday," Saxon spits into my face, "because you're too afraid to live for today." With that, he storms off while I choke back my tears.

Sam is by my side, rubbing my arm. "What's his problem? Are you okay? You're shaking."

"I'm fine," I unconvincingly state, brushing his hand off of me as I watch Saxon stampede into the barn.

He has no idea what's going on as he stands clueless before me, waiting for answers. Answers I can't give. "Coffee is on the counter," I say in a zombie-like voice, turning towards the house.

"Hey, you're not going to tell me what happened?" he says, stunned.

"There's nothing to tell," I reply, and walk towards the backdoor.

Piper is still drooling on the counter, oblivious to what just happened—lucky her. The moment I burst into my bedroom, hot tears slide down my cheeks. I lean my back against the door, drumming my head against the wood grain.

I remember when we were all having breakfast and I couldn't quite place my finger on why I wasn't over the moon that Sam was making an effort. Something didn't feel right, and I didn't know why. But now I do. I don't want things to go back to normal. Too much has happened.

I don't fail to see the irony in all of this. I wanted so desperately for Sam to remember, but now, I want him to forget.

Nothing makes sense anymore. My endless diaries look back at me from their boxes, taunting me with what once was, but that's no longer. It'll never be again. Angrily wiping away my tears, I storm through my room and kick over a box, the contents spilling all over the floor. Dropping to my knees, I frantically rip open each diary, flicking through the pages, desperate to find a blank page—a blank canvas to start new.

After tossing diary after diary over my shoulder, I finally find a fresh page. Hunting through my bedside dresser, I find a pen.

Ripping out the sheet, I use the front of the leather-bound journal as my support and draw my knees to my chest.

Here's to new beginnings.

★ ★ ★ ★ ★

June 14th 2014

Dear diary,

I've done a bad, bad thing. I've fallen for the wrong man.

Yes, call me every scandalous name that there is—it can't be any worse than what I've already called myself.

My life was perfect, or so I thought. But now I know there is no such thing. Life isn't about perfection; it's about experiencing imperfection, to appreciate every imperfect breath you take.

Saxon Stone is my fiancé's identical twin brother and I think...I'm in love with him. I don't know how it happened, it just did. It certainly wasn't planned and if I could take it back...I wouldn't.

The Samuel I once knew is no longer, but if today, right this second, he "woke" up and remembered who he was, who I was, would I be happy? Would I want to go back to the way things were? I don't know.

I've swam in rough waters. I've treaded high tides. And I've survived. I've found myself in unpolluted recklessness, but I've never felt more alive. I am who I am because of this god awful nightmare, but sometimes we have to experience loss to appreciate what we have.

I have Saxon, or had, but now—I don't know what I've got. Samuel seems to want to try, but is it too late? Has that ship sailed?

There are so many questions, ones I don't have the answers for. But there is one answer which is clearer than any others, and that is, I can't let Saxon go.

* * * * *

For the next four hours, I sit in front of the bay window, searching for any sign of Saxon. I've looked high and low, but he doesn't want to be found.

Samuel drove Piper home, sensing that I needed space.

And he's right. I need space from everyone but Saxon. I need to talk to him. I need to find out what this all means.

I'm biting my nails anxiously, watching the yard for any movement, hopeful that Saxon will come back. He does.

The moment I see his tall figure crossing the yard, I leap up from my seat and run through the house and out the back door. Saxon sees me running towards him, but he turns up his lip and continues walking with no intention of stopping.

"Saxon! We need to talk!" I don't keep the panic from my tone; I want him to know that I'm afraid—afraid of losing him.

"I've got nothing to say," he bites back, his eyes hard.

"Cut the bullshit!" I cry, running after him as he stalks past me. "You're angry at me for having sex with Sam. Why? You had no qualms sleeping with Piper, so why am I the bad guy?"

"I don't care, Lucy. You can fuck whoever you want." His venomous words are contradictory to his claims.

"And you call me a liar. I think you need a long, hard look in the mirror. I'm sorry if me sleeping with Sam hurt your feelings. For the record, it wasn't any good. Terrible, in fact. The whole time I was thinking, why am I doing this?" I confess, not caring that I'm sharing it all.

"Why did you do it then?" he screams, finally stopping and turning to look at me.

"I don't know!" I cry, pulling at my hair.

"Liar," he counters, shaking his head. "I thought you were different, but you're not."

"Please, don't go. Stay here with me."

He scoffs, his face contorted. "Stay here and watch you play happy family with Sam? No thank you. Been there, done that." He closes his eyes the moment his confession passes his lips.

"What?" I gasp. "What are you talking about?"

"Forget it. Forget I said anything." He storms off, but I refuse to let this be.

"Saxon! What does that mean? You were what…into me when we were kids?" I ask, hating how conceited I sound, but what else does this all mean?

"Get over yourself, Lucy," he sniggers, yanking the door open and stomping through the house. I follow in hot pursuit.

"Talk to me, you stubborn asshole!" I grab his forearm, forcing him to look at me, but he's stronger than I am. Before I can retreat, he's got me pinned up against the wall.

His chest is pressed to mine, our breaths are ragged and rough, and his darkened eyes reveal he's about to pounce. "When you look at me—" he growls "—do you see him?" He doesn't need to clarify who he's referring to. "What about when I kissed you? Did you think about him?"

My mouth opens and closes, gasping for air, as Saxon's heated words are robbing me of breath. However, as he reaches between us and cups my mound, I choke, almost certain I'm seconds away from passing out.

"What about if I *fucked* you, Lucy? Do you think you'd compare who the better fuck was?"

My cheeks heat, my body trembles, and I get so incredibly turned on by his sexual aggression, I know he can feel it through the thin cotton of my shorts. I want him to kiss me. To tear off my clothes and take me right here, but I know that won't happen because he's waiting for me to answer him.

"I d-did at first," I confess, my voice small. "But not anymore."

"What do you see now?" He begins boldly massaging his fingers over me, into me, the pressure shooting straight up to my core.

I can't speak. His hands are the only things I can focus on. This is so terribly wrong, Samuel will be back any moment, but I can't stop. "I see…you," I whimper, biting my lip.

"Good," he hums, increasing the speed of his fingers between my legs. "You better hold onto those memories, because that's all you'll ever have."

He rubs over my center with two fingers in a wide circle before kissing me dismissively on the lips. The kiss is short, a mere peck, but I read it loud and clear. This is goodbye. He drops his hand and cruelly pulls away.

Tears prick my eyes, my high long gone. "Saxon," I plead, "I don't know what this is, but…"

"This…is over," he interrupts, not giving me a chance to finish. Not giving me a chance to confess that I have feelings for him.

He backs away from me, his eyes deadpanned. "I'll catch

ya later."

"Where are you going?" I ask, unsure if I want to hear the answer.

"I'm going out."

"Are you coming back?" I sadly say, following him as he strolls to his room.

"Not sure yet." He hunts through the drawers, looking for a clean t-shirt.

The doorbell sounds, giving me a reason to leave the room because I wouldn't go away otherwise. As I walk down the hall, I squint to ensure the person I think I'm seeing at my door is really there.

"Sophia?" I can't hide my surprise.

She looks beyond stunning in a maroon dress which hugs all the right places. Her hair is out, her makeup is heavy but tasteful, and she smells lovely. She looks, smells, and is dressed for a date—a date with Saxon.

"Hi, Lucy. Nice to see you. I missed you last night." I'm staring at her, unable to speak. She clears her throat. "Is Saxon home? He told me to come at five. I'm a little early," she says, looking at her silver watch. She's always early. Always eager. But in this circumstance, I wish she was neither.

I'm standing in the doorway, blocking her entry as I don't want her inside. I don't want her anywhere near Saxon.

"Hi, Sophia." Saxon's energized voice is like nails running down a chalkboard, and I recoil, inching the door shut. But it's pulled wide open as he welcomes Sophia into my home. She steps in, but I don't move an inch, a barrier between her and Saxon. She looks over my shoulder, grinning flirtatiously.

When did Saxon arrange this date? Was it before or after he slept with my best friend?

"Don't wait up," he jeers, pushing past me and guiding Sophia out the door as he places his hand on her lower back.

I stand, watching speechlessly as they get into her Honda. I'm feeling so much—anger, regret, sadness, confusion, but most of all, I want a do-over.

Nineteen

I WAKE WITH A START, as it sounds like an elephant is tiptoeing through my living room. Reaching for the lamp on the side table, the darkness is replaced with light, highlighting a very drunken Saxon attempting to be quiet. He's frozen to the spot, his arms and legs mid-stride. If it wasn't two in the morning, and if two days hadn't passed since I saw him last, then I might be able to see the humor in it. But now, I'm just mad.

"Where have you been?" I whisper heatedly, not wanting to wake Sam.

"I told you not to wait up," he slurs, pointing to a spot on the wall behind me where he most likely thinks I am.

"That was two days ago!"

"Oh." He chuckles, slapping his leg.

"Saxon, this isn't funny." I jump up, irritated that he's taking this so lightly.

Two days ago, Saxon walked out the door with Sophia and never came back. I tried calling his cell, her cell, Greg and Kellie's cell, I even called the hospitals, almost certain he was lying in the ER. But no one knew where he was. Sophia offered to help look as she hasn't seen him since their "date," but I politely declined.

Sam had his weekly session and just like always, Sophia gave me a rundown on how things were going. But this time, instead of listening to a word she had to say, all I wanted to know was how her date with Saxon went.

One snippet of information which happened to make it past the Saxon barriers was that Sam was ready to give it his all. Sophia said his standoffish behavior was all part of the grieving process because in a way, the person he knew was dead. Once he worked through the five stages of grief, he was ready to move forward and accept his situation—it makes sense. It appears Sophia is smart *and* beautiful—doesn't seem fair.

But now that Samuel was ready to accept and move forward, *I* was the one stuck in the past—a past where Saxon and I were still friends. I can't stop thinking about him and what transpired between us when he had his hands all over me. I can still feel his touch—I crave it. And I hate myself for it.

But looking at him, I know I'll never feel his hands on me again. He made it clear that what we had, whatever that was, is now over. His comment, however, still eats away at me. He said he wasn't interested in watching Sam and I play happy family because he's seen it all before. What does that mean? Was he jealous of our relationship? And if so, why?

I have more questions than answers, but with the state Saxon is in, I know I won't be getting any clarification any time soon.

"You look awful." I sigh, his shabby appearance hinting that he's been doing it rough.

"So do you," he replies, swaying. "Have you been crying?" His concern has me hopeful that maybe he's come around. Maybe he's needed some time away to clear his head.

I know the time apart has made things clearer for me. There is no denying that I have feelings for both brothers. And it kills me to confess that I don't know who I feel stronger for. I do love Sam, but I don't love this Sam as much as I did. And Saxon…I don't know what I feel for Saxon. It's an indescribable feeling that I've never felt before.

"I'm fine," I reply, heavily. "Let me help you to your room." I wrap my arm around his waist, ignoring the way my body responds to being within five feet of him. I'm thankful when he doesn't push me away and sags against me.

We begin a slow, unsteady journey through the living room where Saxon manages to bump into every piece of furniture I own. He's absolutely wasted, and if I didn't know better, I'd dare say he's been on a bender for two days. He certainly smells and looks like he has been.

As we turn the corner and stagger down the hall, he bends

low and takes a big whiff of my hair. I've showered, even remembered deodorant, so I wonder what he's smelling. "You smell like butterscotch," he mumbles, sniffing the top of my head.

"It's my new shampoo," I explain, securing my hold around him so he doesn't fall.

"I like it. It smells nice. Makes you even more edible." Now I'm the one in fear of falling, as his comment catches me off guard. "You always smell nice, though. And I like your hair. It reminds me of roses and sunshine."

"Roses?" I know this is merely drunken talk, but they do say one reveals all their secrets while under the influence.

"Yes, you've never seen or smelled an ugly rose. They're classic, timeless, and beautiful—just like you."

I don't know what to say.

As we pass my bedroom, I hear his jaw clench. "But you're not my rose."

All talk ceases as we stumble to his bedroom, unscathed. I steer him to his bed, where he flops onto it, face first. With unsteady fingers, I slip off his dirty boots. There is no way I'm going to be able to move him, so I find a blanket in the closet and drape it over him.

A contented sigh fills the room as he rolls over, snuggling into the pillow. I take a moment to look at him and appreciate all that he's done for me. I can only hope when dawn breaks, he too gives me the chance at a new day.

Taking one last look at his peaceful form, I tread softly towards the doorway. However, I stop dead in my tracks when he mumbles something under his breath. These words are my dawn.

"You may not be my rose, but you'll always be my sunshine."

★ ★ ★ ★ ★

After Sam's failed attempt at getting me naked, he's decided to walk Thunder and probably blow off some steam. The thought of him touching me makes me physically ill. I know it's all psychological, but I need to sort out my head before I even think about going down that road with him again.

It's nine a.m., and I'm not so patiently waiting for Saxon to arise. I know he'll be incredibly hung over, but he doesn't have to do the talking. All I ask is that he listens to what I have to say. I don't have a speech planned, but I want to tell him what I should have told him nights ago. That I feel something for him that has no labels, and I'm pretty certain he feels the same way about me.

Needing someone's advice, I quickly dial my mom.

Before she even has a chance to say hello, I blurt out, "Mom, I think I've fallen in love with…Saxon."

"I know, honey."

"You…what? How?" My mouth hangs open. Am I that obvious?

She sighs. "Lucy, baby, I think it would be unnatural if you didn't feel something for him. He's been your savior, your rock."

"What am I supposed to do about it, though? He's Samuel's brother. It's wrong."

"No, it's not. The only thing that's wrong is you lying to yourself. Be honest. Be honest with yourself. Be honest with Saxon. You both deserve that."

She's right. "What if he doesn't want to hear what I have to say?" I'm frightened he'll throw it back in my face, punish me for finally revealing my feelings.

"Honey, listen to your heart. Tell him."

Sniffing, I wipe my eyes. "Thanks, Mom. I hope you're not disappointed in me."

I can feel her gentle touch through the phone. "You could never disappoint me. You're my miracle. You're everyone's miracle. Don't forget that."

Heavy footsteps thumping down the hallway have me quickly saying goodbye. I nervously sip my coffee as I stand behind the kitchen counter, using it as a shield. I don't know what mood Saxon will be in, and I don't fail to see the irony of that. Sam's asshole role has now been filled by Saxon. When he stomps into the kitchen, I know he hasn't had a hard time filling his shoes.

He doesn't bother acknowledging me as he heads straight for the pot of coffee. He pours himself a cup before walking past me, and out the room, just as quickly as he entered.

Hell no.

"Saxon!" I cry out, chasing after him. When he doesn't slow down, I sprint ahead of him and turn, placing a hand against his chest to stop him from taking another step. "What was that?"

"What was what?" he asks, blankly.

"Don't play dumb. You know exactly what I'm talking about."

"Lucy, if there is a point to this story, please get to it, otherwise, I'm going back to bed." His vacant stare hurts more than his words.

"I thought we could talk. You've been gone for two days."

"I'm sure Sam was more than happy to keep you company," he barks, challenging me to dispute his claims.

"This isn't about Sam, it's about…"

He sniggers, shaking his head incredulously. "This *is* about Sam. It's *always* been about Sam."

When he attempts to push past me, I stand my ground. Listening to my mom's advice, I plead, "Talk to me, please. What does that mean?" I grip his t-shirt in a desperate fist, begging him to stop with the attitude and talk to me like an adult.

He slaps my hand away. "I'm done talking."

I refuse to cry as I confess, "Saxon, I don't want to lose you."

I'm openly begging he at least listen to what I have to say. But I may as well be talking to a brick wall. "You can't lose what you've never had."

"Why are you being so cruel?" I whisper, my lower lip

trembling.

He shrugs, the detachment complementing his words. "It seemed to work for Sam." I turn my cheek, his contempt an invisible slap.

He doesn't console me, or even look back as he walks to his room.

★ ★ ★ ★ ★

I'm working alongside Sam, but it's not by choice.

After Saxon's brush off, I decided to occupy my time with something other than him. Before Sam's accident, we would spend hours outdoors, tending to life on the ranch. It was cathartic as well as rewarding, and I could do with both right now.

Sam is prepping, oiling, and checking the haying equipment to ensure it's in good working order. Our first cut of hay will happen in the next couple of weeks, so he wants to be prepared. I'm checking over what seeding we have, as I want to begin leveling the ground.

We work in silence, but every so often, Sam looks over and smiles. I know he wants to make conversation, but after this morning, I think he's nervous to initiate first contact. Weeks ago, I would have given anything for him to do so, but now, I just wish he would go away.

"So, I was thinking…" I gulp because this is how this

morning's conversation commenced. "Did you want to grab dinner tonight?"

A better proposition than sex, but still not inviting at all. "Dinner?" I vaguely say, continuing to look over my supplies so I can avoid eye contact. "I'm not really hungry."

"It's 1:30 in the afternoon," he replies, not concealing his hurt.

"I had a big breakfast," I counter.

"Lucy, please look at me." His pained tone has me sighing and meeting his grief-stricken eyes. "I really am sorry for the way I acted, but I'm trying now. It feels like you're not even meeting me halfway."

He's right, I'm not, but just like he did, I need time to grieve. I had no other choice but to be the strong one, but now, it's my turn to be a little selfish. "You're right, Sam. But you have to understand, you really hurt my feelings. It's going to take some time for me to forget what you said and did. How do I know this change will last? You're like two people at times, and I don't know which one I'll wake up to."

It feels good to express my fears because it's the first time he's really wanted to talk.

"I understand that, but how many times do I have to say sorry before you cut me some slack?"

"For as long as it takes," I quickly reply. "You owe me that. I was patient with you…it's now your turn to do the same."

He nods unhappily, but doesn't argue.

The rest of the afternoon we work in silence, both wishing we were anywhere but here.

★ ★ ★ ★ ★

True to my word, I didn't go to dinner with Sam. I did go to dinner with myself, however. I couldn't stand to see him moping because although I don't know how I feel about him, I hate seeing him sad.

I could have called Piper, but I've been avoiding her because I can't stomach to hear about her sexcapades with Saxon. The only person I want to be around is me, as I need to do some serious soul searching, and I can't do that at home.

I'm being pulled in so many different directions—I don't know which way is the right way to go. I really want to talk to Saxon, to get it all out on the table and then see how I feel. But how do you talk to someone who doesn't want to listen to what you've got to say?

One thing I've decided is that I'm no longer eating meat. I used to be a happy, healthy vegetarian, and I intend to be one once again. Too bad I decided this the moment I walked into Anna's BBQ. This place brings back fond memories of when Saxon and I ate here after our kiss. Regardless of what happened, we were still able to break bread and be civil towards one another. Now, I doubt he can stand being in the same room as me.

As I'm pensively picking through my salad, a familiar, magical laugh catches my ear. Turning to my right, I choke on my half chewed tomato when I see Saxon and Sophia sitting two tables away from me. Their hands are entwined on top of the red and white checkered tablecloth as they look longingly into each other's eyes.

I thump my chest, wheezing for breath quietly, as I don't want to draw any attention my way. Finally, I swallow past the lump in my throat and huddle low in the booth, turning my back so they can't see me. I need an escape route and I need one now.

Looking ahead, I see a middle aged, robust woman with rosy cheeks, flipping burgers in the kitchen, smiling broadly and looking at home. I'm assuming this is Anna. Most days, I would appreciate what she's done to the place as she's definitely brought Texas to Montana. But today, all I can appreciate is the exit.

Behind me are the bathrooms, so that means the only way I'm getting out of here is walking past Sophia and Saxon. From the brief look I got, it appeared they'd only just arrived, as there was no food on the table. The tablecloth looked way too clean, as Saxon would have caked it with remnants of his ribs if they'd already eaten.

A small stage is set up next to the bar and when I hear a twang of a banjo, and see the lights dim, my heart leaps, as this is the distraction I need. "Don't be shy, folks," a man with a long southern drawl says over the microphone before he begins playing a Hank Williams song.

Peeking over my shoulder, I see cheerful diners taking to dancing by their tables. I scan over to Sophia and Saxon. He's smiling at something she just said. I suppose I should be happy that he's smiling. I can't help but wish I put the smile there instead of her.

Turning back around, I psych myself up, certain that I can blend in with the crowd. If worse comes to worst, I'll just dance my way out the door. Counting to three, I take a deep breath and leap out of the booth and…into a wall of muscle.

Dang it.

Saxon steadies my arms, a gut reaction to someone barreling into him. But when I raise my eyes and curse whatever gods are looking over me, he drops his hands. "Lucy?"

"Hi."

The music is quite loud and the lighting a blue tint, but I can see and hear him perfectly. Nothing else exists but us. "What are you doing here?"

"Eating," I reply, grimacing. "I was just leaving."

"Where's Sam?" he asks, raising an eyebrow, looking behind me.

"At home."

"You're here by yourself?" He doesn't seem to believe me.

"Yes, Saxon, I am." I want to talk to him, to blurt out how I feel. But I'm not doing it with his date a few feet away. "Enjoy your date."

He appears guilty for a fraction of a second, before the smug, offensive Saxon emerges. "I will. I don't plan on coming home, so don't bother leaving the porch light on."

My heart dislodges and sinks downward in a spiral of despair. I know he's trying to get a rise out of me, but I bite my tongue and decide to be honest. "I liked being your friend."

Not the reply he was expecting. And his response is not what I expected either. Stepping forward, he blankets me with his rage as I walk backwards, trapped between the booth and him. "We were never friends. Stop kidding yourself."

An acknowledgement, a cruel one, but an acknowledgment nonetheless. This is the first time he's said aloud what I've been feeling all along. He sees the hope in my eyes, but crushes it a second later. "Go back to your lies, Lucy, and I'll go back to mine."

He turns his back, leaving me slumped against the wooden booth. I watch in horror as he reaches his table and swoops forward, kissing Sophia on her perfect mouth. She jolts back, stunned by his aggression, but doesn't question it as she matches his passion a second later.

I'm going to be sick.

Running through the crowded room, I push past happy patrons, wishing I could dance my troubles away. The crisp breeze is exactly what I need, and my need to vomit subsides—for now, anyway. Leaning against the brick wall, I'm half hoping

Saxon will come to my rescue, apologizing for being a gigantic asshole and that he wants to talk. He does neither.

A concerned passerby asks if I'm okay, the worry in her warm eyes is enough to set me off. I sprint to my car, tears leaking from my eyes. I feel helpless, useless, and so alone. I don't know where to go. I can't go home because home isn't where my heart is anymore. I left my heart in Texas.

Starting the Jeep, I tear down the road, wiping the avalanche of tears with the back of my hand. I sob harder than I've ever sobbed before. I sob for me, for Sam, for Saxon—I sob for the Lucy Tucker who no longer knows who she is.

I drive on auto pilot to the only place I can call home.

I kill the engine, but don't bother to turn off the headlights or close the door as I run across the green, manicured lawns. The white home set amongst the hills is my palace, my happily ever after.

"Lucy?" my mother says, the door opening wide. "What—"

The wind gets knocked from her lungs as I throw myself into her outstretched arms.

She comforts me for several minutes while I stay nestled in her embrace, weeping. I can't stop. I know how irrational I'm being, but I'm crying months' worth of tears.

When I hear my parents' hushed, concerned voices, it reminds me so much of when they delivered the news about Samuel. The day this all started. Choking back my heaving breaths, I will myself to calm down.

"Honey? What's the matter?" I don't know what it is about a mother's soothing voice, a tender touch that provides her child a medicine that cures all wounds.

I don't feel better, but I feel human. "Mom, I made a big mistake," I mumble into her shoulder, afraid to look at her. I'm ashamed.

"Simon, can you make us some hot cocoa? Lucy and I are going up to her room."

My room.

And just like that, I know I'm where I'm supposed to be.

We amble up the stairs to my bedroom, a place which was my sanctuary, my safe place—a place I need to be right now. We sit on the bed, my mother giving me all the time and space I need.

Looking around, I realize I haven't been here in months. I haven't felt the need to, because my home, Whispering Willows, *was* my safe place. But now, it's just a vacant house filled with regret.

My pastel pink room hasn't changed a bit. My iron cast queen bed still has the same pink butterfly print duvet, the one I chose when I turned thirteen. Stuck to the walls are posters of horses, and places I so desperately wanted to visit—India, China, Australia. So many dreams, but none of them lived.

A small desk sits against the wall. Travel brochures, poetry books and my copy of *The Catcher in the Rye* are strewed on top of it. I remember sitting at the wooden desk, dreaming about my encounter with Samuel the night it happened. Everything seemed so simple back then. But now, nothing makes any sense.

"Did you talk to Saxon?" my mom asks gently.

Sniffing back my tears, I nod. "But it's too late," I confess. "I've lost him, and I feel like I'm dying inside."

She reads my shame instantly and her face falls. "Oh, Lucy."

"I didn't mean for it to happen," I cry, "it just did. It's not an excuse and I'm disgusted at myself." I cover my face with my hands, unable to look at her and see the disappointment.

After a poignant silence, she speaks. "Your father and I fell in love with you the first moment we saw you. I may not have given birth to you, but you are my child. I know you. We have watched you grow into a beautiful, caring, considerate young woman and your heart, Lucy, it's so big. It's always been too big. So it doesn't surprise me that you find yourself in this predicament. In love with two people."

The moment she says the words I've been dreading to accept, I uncover my eyes. I'm afraid I'll see disappointment in hers, but I don't. All I see are the same kind, gentle eyes that rescued me when I needed saving. Just like I do now.

"What do I do?" I ask, desperate for the answers.

Leaning forward, she brushes the hair from my face. "Follow your heart, honey."

"My heart is torn, Mom. Right down the middle. I love Sam, I always will. But I don't know who I am anymore." I fall into her arms, sobbing.

She rubs my back, reassuring me that everything will be all right. “Love doesn’t make sense. Love happens when you least expect it. It’s inconvenient, messy, and reckless, but that’s the beauty of it. It isn’t a decision; it’s a promise—a promise to chase inconvenient, messy, and reckless love with someone who embraces the chaos with you.”

I continue crying, her wisdom cementing what I’ve known to be true. “Can I stay here tonight?”

“Honey, you can stay for as long as you like.” Settling into her arms, I close my eyes and allow sleep to overcome me. I can only hope when I wake, the chaos subsides and I can see through the confusion.

Twenty

My head feels clearer when I wake. I even feel semi-human when I shower and sit at the counter and enjoy my cup of coffee.

Mom's words were exactly what I needed to hear. Love *doesn't* make sense. It doesn't make sense for me to love Saxon, but I think that I do. I thought I knew what love was. But when I met Saxon, he turned my beliefs upside down.

I know I can't hide out here forever, but it's nice to pretend that I can. Mom and Dad have gone to run a few errands, so I have the house to myself. My family home is a stunning, old-world style house set on five acres. After growing up in squalor, this home was a palace—my real life castle.

As I roam from room to room, still in awe of the arched walkways and barrel ceilings, I stop when a picture hanging off the feature wall in the family room catches my eye. It's a photo of Sam and me at our engagement party. The day was perfect.

Stroking over the glass, I smile, remembering how proud I was to be wearing his ring. Now, however, looking down at it, I feel foolish.

A car's tires crunching over the gravel makes me walk to the bay window, wondering who it could be. When I see the red Chevy pickup, I do a double take, incredulous when I see Samuel emerging from inside.

What's he doing here?

I want nothing more than to hide, but I've done enough of that. This problem isn't going to solve itself and the sooner I try and walk through it, the better. Exhaling, I wait for Samuel to ring the doorbell before I answer the door. The moment I open it, I get hit with a serious case of the guilt's.

He looks visibly upset, which is a nice change from looking visibly pissed off. "Hi."

"Hi, Sam." I lean against the doorway, trying my hardest to stay strong.

His sea green eyes peer up at me from under a black beanie, which is a new look for him. "Is everything okay? You didn't come home last night."

"I thought it was my turn to stay out all night," I reply, directing my comment at him and Saxon.

He lowers his eyes. "Are you coming back?"

Am I?

Instead of answering, I cock my head to the side in interest. "How'd you get here?" I know he doesn't remember, which can only mean one thing.

"Saxon is in the car." I look over his shoulder and see Saxon sitting in the driver's side. I'm surprised he agreed to drive Sam, seeing as he's the reason why I'm here in the first place. "He's worried about you, too."

His comment has me scoffing, folding my arms defensively. "I highly doubt that. I know you can't remember, but I'm sure my diaries alerted you to the fact that Saxon hated me. Not much has changed," I add, unable to hide my sadness.

"There's something I want to tell you, Lucy. I didn't remember it; well, I didn't think I did until the other day when you were so quick to jump to his defense." He's captured my full attention and I nod, silently beckoning him to go on.

"When I was in a coma, I was neither here nor there. I was floating. I could hear voices, sounds, but I couldn't distinguish who they were, or where they were coming from. But there was one voice which I'd always recognize. It kept me grounded."

"Saxon's," I whisper. He nods.

"All the days, hours, minutes, seconds—they all melded into one. But one night, my voice sounded back at me. It said I was to come back to you, Lucy. I didn't know what that meant, but I now know my voice was Saxon's, begging me to come back to you because you needed me."

I cover my mouth with a trembling hand.

"The pain was so clear in his tone, I felt like maybe he was the one who had lost you. He said that you were a good person, and that I was to take care of you because he couldn't. He cried. I've never heard my brother cry. And then, he was gone."

Saxon went to talk to Samuel before coming to see me, knowing that I believed he was the key. He did that for me. Even though we fought and his family treated him like shit, he still did all of this for me.

Saxon brought both Sam and I back to life. He didn't believe he could make a difference, but he did. He changed our lives forever.

"So you see, he doesn't hate you. Neither of us do." Samuel's apology is heartfelt.

"Thank you for telling me that." I sniff back my tears.

"I haven't told Saxon."

"Don't worry, your secret is safe with me," I quickly reassure.

I don't know what all of this means. There is something I'm missing. Just like Samuel, I'm missing pieces to a puzzle which becomes more unclear with time. And hiding away isn't going to help me solve the mystery.

"Let me just grab my things," I say, stepping backward and welcoming Sam into my home.

He stands in the foyer, waiting politely for me to return. It reminds me too much of prom. Writing a quick note for my parents, I stick it to the fridge with a horse magnet. It's ambiguous, but I know my mom will understand.

Gone to chase the chaos.

Grabbing my things, I lock up and follow Sam to the truck.

The closer we get, the clearer it becomes that Saxon is still angry at me, which pisses me off. If anything, *I'm* the one who should be angry at him for sleeping with Piper and then discarding her like some random fling. But I squash down those feelings as I open the door and slide across the bench seat and sit near him. It makes sense for me to sit in the middle, I'm the smallest, but being sandwiched between the two brothers feels awfully wrong. Sam closes the door, sealing my makeshift prison.

There is a gap between Saxon and me, as I can't stomach touching him without wanting to scream or cry. But as Sam's leg touches mine, I quickly scoot over. It really is the lesser of two evils. Our legs press together, and I whimper at the contact. This is ridiculous. I pull my leg away and curl in on myself so I'm not touching either brother. I'm now Switzerland.

Saxon doesn't acknowledge me as he starts the truck and speeds down the driveway. Johnny Cash blares over the speakers, hinting there is no room for talking in this truck, which suits me just fine. Sam thankfully keeps his distance, looking out the window, taking in sights which should look familiar to him, but don't. Saxon keeps his eyes focused on the road, his fingers gripping the wheel, his nostrils flared.

It appears he can't even stand being in my presence. I can't help but compare his response to how it was when we were growing up. No doubt, if he decides to acknowledge me, it'll be with a grunt or blank nod. I absentmindedly toy with the necklace around my neck, deep in thought. Saxon peers over, looks down, and scowls.

The rest of the trip home is traveled in silence and when we pull into the driveway of Whispering Willows, Saxon leaves the truck running, indicating he's not getting out. His empty stare out the windshield also reveals he has no intention of telling me where he's going.

Samuel opens the door, also getting the hint and offers me his hand as he jumps out. I accept. The moment my hand slips into his, I feel nothing. No fireworks, no butterflies, nothing. Unlike when I merely brushed against Saxon's leg.

"You coming back for dinner?" Sam asks, looking at Saxon.

"No," he replies, leaning over the seat and slamming the door shut. I shudder at the harsh sound.

He takes off down the drive, never looking back, and for once, neither do I. If I'm going to chase the chaos, then I have to embrace the silence first. And there's only one way I know how.

★ ★ ★ ★ ★

Two weeks later

"What time is Sophia coming over?"

"Ten." Samuel's sigh is a common occurrence these days. But I suppose that's better than hearing him yell. The past two weeks have been about me embracing the silence, much to the horror of Samuel, who has wanted to embrace the noise.

He's trying, he really is, and sometimes when I see snippets of the old Sam shine through, I think that maybe today is the day I go back to loving him. But that day never arrives. And neither does Saxon.

I've seen Saxon no more than fifteen minutes over these past two weeks. He comes and goes as he pleases, and honestly, I'm surprised he's still coming. I have no idea why he's still here. I refuse to believe it's got anything to do with Sophia. They barely know one another. It's impossible they're already attached. They've only known one another for a few weeks. But that's all it took for me.

"Did you want to grab lunch after my session?"

"Maybe," I reply, not raising my eyes from my iPad. I'm emailing work about something very important. Something which will hopefully help me see past the storm.

My detachment isn't intentional. Sam and I have made peace. He's apologized countless times for his behavior, and for the fact he still doesn't remember me. He's asked to watch our home movies, even begged I take him to all of our favorite places, and I have, but it's just not the same.

I look back at these events, places with fond memories, but I have no desire to make new ones. All I can focus on is my future, but the question is, does that future include Sam?

The thought of leaving him tears out my heart, but so does the thought of staying. I want to support him, to help him remember who he once was, but in doing that, I have to remember who *I* was. And those are memories I wish to forget.

"Have you seen Saxon?" he asks, sitting on the arm of the sofa, watching me type out the email.

"Nope." If he's trying to make conversation, best he chooses another topic.

"I think it's weird they're dating."

"They're not dating." I'm quick to jump in and contest his claims.

"I'm pretty sure I still remember what dating is, Lucy," he says with a grin. "We can only assume he's spending most of his time over there, and he doesn't have time for his brother—they're definitely dating."

"Looks like he missed the memo then," I mumble unhappily. When Sam waits for me to continue, I state, "Bros before hoes."

He splutters up his coffee. "I don't remember you being this funny."

I don't bother amending that he doesn't remember me at all because his uncomfortable face reveals that he knows what I'm thinking.

"I still think it's weird, and maybe a little unethical." He has my attention. I place my iPad on the table, implying I'm listening. "Well, Sax *is* my identical twin. Does she find *me* attractive?"

I cock an eyebrow. Is he fishing for a reaction? Of jealousy, maybe? Is he testing to see if I go all medieval and beat her ass for looking at my man? The sad part is, I don't know *who* my man is.

I'm saved by the bell, literally, as the doorbell sounds. Although the person seeking entrance is someone I'm not excited to see. I stand, leaving Sam's question unanswered as I answer the door. Why can't this woman have an ugly day? Every strand of hair sits perfectly straightened. Not a blemish or imperfection in sight.

"Good morning, Lucy." She's always in a good mood. Would it kill her to have a bad day once in a while? I don't want to question why she looks overly chirpy this morning.

I open the door, begrudgingly welcoming her in. "Hi, Sophia."

Usually, I would make small talk, but today, the only talk I would make is hounding her about Saxon's whereabouts.

"It's been two months since Samuel's accident and I really think he's making wonderful progress. Have you noticed he's been more receptive of wanting to remember?" I stare at her ruby tinted lips, wondering if she left a mark on Saxon's cheek when she kissed him goodbye.

Shaking my head to dislodge those thoughts, I reply, "Yes, definitely." And that's all she's getting out of me.

I lead her down the hallway where Sam is happily waiting for her. It appears her milkshake brings all the boys to the yard. I need to stop this cattiness…now. "I'll be in the kitchen if you need me."

I make a new pot of coffee and idly scour the internet on

my cell. Piper's text is a grateful distraction.

Wanna catch up? Miss you. ☹

I miss her, too. Since that night with Saxon, I've purposely been staying away. She has been busy studying and working double shifts, but every time she suggests we catch up, I've always made an excuse not to.

I need my best friend.

Yes! Come around for dinner? Around 7?

I'll be there!

She doesn't ask who will be there because she doesn't have to. The few times we've spoken, I've let drop that Saxon is never around.

My thoughts bite me in the ass however when the backdoor swings open and in strolls the devil. The cell slips from my fingers and scuttles along the kitchen floor. Did he come here with Sophia? The cell only stops once it bounces off his dirty boot. He peers down at it, unimpressed.

His distaste, as always, hurts my feelings and I quickly drop to a squat to pick it up, hoping to hide my sadness. But he gets there first. When he offers me the phone, I look at it, and then up at him suspiciously. What's the catch?

He waves it at me, a half a smile tugging at his lips. A sight I haven't seen for a long time. The cell lights up with a text message. He looks down at it. "Piper wants to know if she should bring cake." The casual mention of her irritates me, and

I snatch the phone from his hand.

"So you're having dinner. How nice." And out comes the asshole Saxon I've come to dislike. I don't bother answering him and stand.

Opening the fridge, I reach for the carton of milk, which thanks to Saxon being MIA, is full. I make myself another cup of coffee, but don't bother asking if he'd like one. "What time is dinner?"

The coffee goes down the wrong pipe and I choke. Tears sting my eyes as I thump my chest, attempting to breathe. "You want to come?" I ask, my voice croaky and winded.

"Sure." He steals my coffee.

"Why?" I don't hide my surprise.

"Why not? It'll give you a chance to get to know Sophia better."

I see red. "I know Sophia just fine. And besides, Piper is coming."

He shrugs, unruffled. "The more the merrier."

That's it. I've had it with his carefree, offensive behavior. "You're unbelievable."

"That's what she said," he has the gall to reply.

He's looking for a fight. I can read his body language. But I'm all out of fight. This person standing before me is not the man I believed him to be, so fighting him would be pointless… because I don't know who I'm fighting for anymore.

"Dinner is at seven. It'll be vegetarian."

My admission catches him off guard. "You're a vegetarian again?"

"Yes, there are a lot of things about me that's changed," I bite back confidently.

He's speechless as I snatch back my cup of coffee from his hand and leave the room with my head held high.

It's the first time in forever I've felt like me. And I like it.

★ ★ ★ ★ ★

At 6: 59 p.m. I curse my confidence because there is no doubt in my mind that this dinner will be a complete disaster.

Needing to add a splash of color in my life, I decided to wear my favorite pastel green lace dress. It's cut off at the sleeves with a high collared neckline. My makeup is minimal—nothing but powder on my cheeks, mascara, and peach ChapStick. As I slip on my cowboy boots, I hear the front door closing and the unmistakable bubbly voice of Piper.

I've missed her more than I thought possible.

I gave her a heads up about Saxon, thinking she'd cancel, but she didn't seem concerned. I don't know how she can remain so calm. But that's Piper—-always the optimist.

My boots tap on the floorboards as I walk down the hallway, a sense of anticipation trailing behind me. I just want this dinner over with.

"Please tell me you made vegetarian lasagna?" Piper says,

hands interlocked in front of her as I enter the kitchen.

I laugh. "Yes, I did."

Her lips smack together. "Puts my store bought Key Lime to shame." I look down at the pie, which looks delicious.

Sam opens a bottle of red, pouring us three glasses. When he fills my glass halfway, I indicate to fill it right up. He doesn't argue, nor does he question my need to get wasted before dinner.

"How's school, Pipe?" I ask, beginning to prepare the garden salad.

"It's okay. Happy it's my last year. Looking forward to earning some real cash."

"What do you do?" Sam asks, genuinely curious.

"Interior design," she replies. When she smirks, I know nothing good can come from this conversation. "I still think it's so weird you don't remember anything at all."

"I remember some things," he disputes.

"Just not the important things," she counters.

Silence.

Well, this dinner has commenced just how I predicted it would. And when the backdoor swings open, it just goes from bad to worse.

"Hello my nearest and dearest," Saxon quips, starting the night off on an uncomfortable note. I don't bother turning around and busy myself with hacking into the tomatoes.

Sam plays the hospitable host, offering Sophia a drink, while

I try not to imagine I'm slicing and dicing her head. "Smells delicious, Lucy," she says, attempting to make conversation.

Putting on the bravest face I can muster, I turn and smile. But when I see a bunch of sunflowers sitting innocently in her hands, I wheeze.

"Saxon told me they were your favorite." She unknowingly offers me the bunch, not realizing the memories these flowers hold—the memories of when I rode on the back of Saxon's Harley, never feeling freer. But Saxon does. Why would he do that?

"Th-thanks," I stutter, accepting the flowers. "Dinner is almost ready." It's a subtle hint to get out of the kitchen.

My eyes flick over to Saxon, who is standing by Sophia. They look so…perfect together, and it makes me sick. What also looks perfect is him. He's in blue jeans and a light blue button down shirt. The sleeves are rolled up, exposing his taut forearms. His hair is styled with some product and he's clipped his scruff, but he still looks edgy. And so very hot. She looks stunning as usual in a simple coral dress and gold gladiator sandals.

The biker and the doctor—somehow, a match made in heaven.

With that thought in mind, I turn back around and pretend to busy myself by looking for a vase before I burst into tears.

Sam leads them into the dining room, while Piper stays behind, watching me closely. "Are you okay, Luce?"

"I should be the one asking you that," I reply, ignoring her question, as the answer would be no.

"It's okay," she says nonchalantly. "It wasn't meant to be."

"But it doesn't bother you?" I ask.

"No, it's cool. It's not like I was in love with him or anything." So it appears casual sex is all the craze this year.

Not wanting to think about this further, I give Piper the garlic bread and salad, while I dish up the lasagna. It looks like slop, as I take no care in serving it up. Presentation is the least of my concerns. I try not to slam Sophia and Saxon's plates down in front of them, but when Saxon moves back to avoid flying projectiles of mozzarella and marinara, I know my efforts to remain civil are diminishing by the second. I take my seat near Sam, who is at the head of the table, facing opposite Saxon. What a way to ruin my appetite.

We eat in silence, the air surging with an undercurrent of uneasiness. I don't fail to notice Saxon's eyes on me, watching my every move. Annoyed, I meet his stare, silently questioning what his problem is. He responds with an egotistical smirk.

"So Saxon mentioned you've turned vegetarian," Sophia says, breaking through the staleness. "I think that's really great. I was vegan all through college. It really made a difference to my wellbeing." Of course she was. If she told me the sun shined out of her ass, I'd believe it, because little Miss Perfect can do no wrong.

"Yeah, I have," I reply when she waits for me to elaborate. "I guess I fell off the band wagon, but I'm back on." I can't help but direct my comment to Saxon, who sips his Budweiser.

"That's fantastic. I really admire that you're sticking to your beliefs."

"Lucy is passionate about a lot of things," Samuel kindly says, cutting into his meal. "She's just been assigned to help in Syria for three months."

All eyes swing my way, as I haven't told anyone that I've offered to go on the three month aid tour of Syria and its surrounding cities. Taking my mom's advice on board, *this* is the only way I can follow my heart. To see what true chaos is to appreciate the calm. I know the time away from both Saxon and Samuel will do me good and I'm hoping once I return, I'll know what I want to do.

"I'll miss her, but they need her more than I do," Sam concludes. He's been awfully supportive, but it's not his choice. I'm going either way. I won't let him stop me. Not again.

"When are you leaving?" I'm surprised when it's Saxon's saddened voice I hear.

"If all goes well, I leave in two weeks. I have my passport. That's all I need," I reply calmly.

He is anything but calm as he states, "It's a warzone over there. Worse than it has been in years. What with air and land bombings, kidnappings, and unspeakable treatment of foreigners if captured, it's not a place for—"

"For what?" I question, cocking my brow as I rest my fork

against the side of my untouched plate.

"It's just dangerous," he amends, sensing I'm close to boiling over.

"I know what it is. But sometimes, the unseen dangers are far more hazardous than the seen," I bite back, no longer talking about going overseas. Saxon reads my innuendo and clenches his jaw.

Sophia clears her throat. "That's really commendable and brave." Of course she'd say that—she just wants me gone.

"It's not brave, it's stupid," Saxon snaps, still glaring at me. Piper shifts beside me, sensing an argument brewing.

Tossing my napkin onto the table, I snap, "Nice to know you think helping people in need is stupid. You really are your mother's son." Low blow, but his comment reminds me of Kellie's bigotry. It also reminds me how not that long ago, he was all for me going over. What's suddenly changed? I thought he'd be happy to see the back of me.

Sam stiffens up beside me, and I instantly feel remorseful for being so nasty to his mom. "Sorry, Sam." I reach for his hand, squeezing lightly.

The table rattles and when I look to see what's caused the commotion, I see Saxon white knuckling it. He's scowling at mine and Sam's connection. He's…jealous? He's a mixed bag of emotion, and I don't know what comes next.

"I'm going out for a smoke," he announces, kicking back his seat.

Sophia looks up at him mid-bite, while I defiantly match his stare. He can't come in here and tell me what to do. It's my life, and he's made it clear he wants no part of it. The front door slams shut, ending all talks of me going overseas.

I pick at my food, a bystander to the conversation going on around me, as I have nothing I want to say. All I want to do is find Saxon and slap him. "I'll just put on some coffee," I say abruptly, interrupting Sam's story of him trying to shoe Potter.

The table looks up at me, but no one comments on my crazy-eyed look. I collect my plate and make a mad dash for the kitchen. Once inside, I place my hands on the counter and bend low, taking three deep breaths.

"Luce, what's going on?" Piper's slow footsteps expose she's worried I'm seconds away from losing it.

"How can you sit there and not want to…to…punch him in the face?" I exclaim, unable to hide my feelings any longer.

"Who?"

"Saxon," I reply, standing tall and facing her. "How can you stand seeing them together after what happened between you two?" There, I said it, and it felt just as I thought it would—terrible.

Her brows draw in, confused by my comment. "What are you talking about? What happened?"

The walls begin closing in on me as I scrutinize her bewilderment. "I-I saw you go into Saxon's room the night of the party."

"Yeah, and?" But her brows lift, almost shooting up into her hairline. "Oh my god! You think we slept together?"

"You did," I affirm, wanting to expose that I know. "Saxon told me you did."

Her mouth parts and she shakes her head. "No, Lucy, we didn't."

"*What*?" I gasp, the word catching in my throat. "B-but Saxon said you did."

"Well, I'm flattered, but he's a liar."

No.

This entire time I thought that he slept with her, and when I confronted him, he never set me straight. Why?

I suddenly feel sick.

Seeing Saxon and Piper together was one of the main reasons why I had sex with Sam. Not one of my proudest moments, but I was so angry that he was sleeping with someone…other than me.

Oh my god. What have I done?

Thinking back to our heated conversation, I realize that Saxon didn't confess he slept with Piper. I assumed, then I accused. Yes, he didn't deny it. But what good would it have done? I was adamant it happened—I used it as an excuse to justify my actions. But even if he did tell me the truth, it couldn't erase what I did with Sam.

Slumping onto the bar stool, I run a hand through my hair, tugging at the roots. "What happened?"

"Well, I was pretty drunk, but from what I can remember, I tried to kiss him." My fingers curl into fists. "He politely said no, and when I asked was it because he didn't like me, he said he liked me just fine. When I questioned why he wouldn't kiss me then, he replied he was in love with someone else, and he has been for a very long time. I then proceeded to throw my guts up for the next hour—nothing to do with his comment, by the way."

I gasp, tears stinging my eyes. Piper turns serious when she sees my reaction. "I thought that person was maybe Sophia… but that person is…you, isn't it, Luce? Saxon loves you. He has all along." She's found a missing piece to this ever-growing puzzle.

"I don't know," I cry.

"Is that why you slept with Sam? Because you thought I had sex with Saxon?" Piper has always been the bright one in our relationship. "Oh, Luce. No. Is that why you're running away to Syria? You're in love with both of them, aren't you?"

"I-I need to find him." I snivel back my tears, standing. "Stall them. Whatever happens, make sure they don't come find us. Lie, do whatever you have to." Piper nods. She's always got my back. "I'm sorry I didn't ask you first. I just thought—"

"It doesn't matter. Explains the cold shoulder these past few weeks."

"Sorry, Pipe. I'll make it up to you." I quickly kiss her on the forehead before tearing out the backdoor.

This misunderstanding has cost me so much. If I hadn't jumped to conclusions, none of this would have happened. It's all my fault.

I know where he is, without even needing to look for him. I run towards the barn, a plume of smoke hinting he's behind the wall. My ragged breathing alerts him to my presence, and he ducks his head around to see who's there.

When our eyes meet, everything changes and it's game on.

"Why didn't you tell me?" I demand, charging over to him.

"From where I stand, I don't think you're in any position to be asking me that," he barks, flicking his cigarette to the ground.

I come to a halt, surprised. "Why do you care if I'm going anyway? You've made your feelings for me quite clear. I still don't understand why you're still here? It's obvious you don't want to be, so go back to Oregon."

"I like it here. Sophia—"

The moment her name leaves his lips, I scream. "And you call me a liar!" I'm certain he's using her as an excuse to stay, but I want to know why.

"I thought this is what you wanted," he snarls, pointing to the house. "Isn't that why you invited her to the party? To get me out of your hair."

No, this most certainly is *not* what I wanted.

"Are you guys dating?" He's silent. "Are you dating her?" I demand once again.

"No," he finally replies. It appears things are definitely not what they seem.

Hurtling forward, I shove at his chest with both hands. He stumbles backwards, caught off guard. "Why didn't you tell me you never slept with Piper?"

"What difference would it have made? You believed what you wanted to believe. And it wouldn't have changed the fact you *fucked* him."

I pull back, stunned by his fury. "What else was I meant to think? You were taking her into your room."

"Where I held back her hair and watched her be sick for an hour. Then I put her to bed." His chain of events corroborates with Piper's. "Once she fell asleep, I went to look for you. I wanted to apologize for upsetting you. However, when I couldn't find either you or Sam, it was obvious where you had gone. And what you were doing."

I've never seen him angrier as he pushes past and storms into the barn. But this isn't over. Chasing after him, I latch onto his arm, spinning him, forcing him to look at me. The barn is dimly lit with rustic sconces.

"Why does it matter if I had sex with Sam? What difference does it make to you?" He turns his cheek, his jaw clenched. "Why?" I scream. "For once, be honest and tell me the truth!"

His face contorts as he pounces forward, gripping my upper arms firmly. His anger takes my breath away. "Because…I fucking love you!" He shakes my limp form, my body sagging like a ragdoll. "I can't stand being around you…you rip out my heart…time and time again. But I can't stand being away from you either!"

Too much is happening. The world is spinning, and I'm afraid I'm about to move with it. He loves me? Since when? Piper said he's loved someone for a long time. Is that person me?

"You l-love m-me?" I whisper, my eyes locked with his.

"Yes. I do. God damn it, I do!" he confesses, appearing plagued by the truth. "Ask me again why I've stayed."

I know he's referring to our conversation all those weeks ago when I asked him what reason is there for him to stay. I remember thinking that when I do ask him, his response will change everything I believe in and love. And I was right.

"Why did you stay, Saxon? What reason is there for you to stay?"

Releasing his grip around me, he drops his hands by his side. He is saddened, defeated by this entire confession, and I don't know why. "The reason is you, Lucy. It's always been you. All I wanted was you…but you never wanted me back." I now understand his heartache. He doesn't know if his admission will make a difference, but it has.

Suddenly, everything falls into line. "I-I want you now."

"What?" he wheezes, his chest rising and falling quickly.

"I want you. God help me, I've wanted you from the moment I threw myself in your arms and you caught me. I thought you felt that too… but you were so quick to dismiss our kiss," I reveal, finally understanding why I was so hurt.

He rushes forward, securing a hand to the side of my neck, begging me to listen. The contact is like a red hot poker to my heart. "I was scared of losing you. Of you running away from me. I saw the look in your eyes. The look of guilt, uncertainty. I'd prefer to pretend than lose you again."

"Again?" What does he mean by that?

But he ignores me. His eyes turn a molten, dangerous blue, and I gulp. "You want me, and not him?"

I know what he's asking, but I can't answer truthfully because I don't know. When he reads my indecision, he strokes his thumb over my sprinting pulse. "It's simple. You either want me or you don't."

This is it. D-day. Time to face what I've been too afraid to confront all along. I'll deal with the repercussions tomorrow because right now, right this second, I just want to be free. "I want…you. All of you."

He's on top of me before I can protest, not that I would because I want this as much as he does. We slam our bodies together, a union of chaos and madness. He drags me closer by the hips, while I wrap my hands around his nape, smashing my lips to his. The kiss is frantic, uncontrolled, it's the inconvenient, messy, and reckless kind of love that I've been missing, craving since I first saw Saxon.

His mouth is wicked, soft and hard in all the right places as he kisses me with a ferocity I desperately need. I tug at his long strands of hair, fusing our lips together, needing to feel every part of him ingrained into my entire being. He grunts low, his tongue tangoing with mine, unbending to be in control as he cups my cheeks into his palms. But I surrender, happy to submit and be devoured.

His impressive length pushes between my legs, sending an uncontrollable quiver to my toes. I remember watching him jerk off in the shower, and how taboo I felt. I want to feel that again.

As he dominates my mouth, I pull at his belt buckle. It unclips, allowing me to snap open his button and thrust my hand inside of his jeans. I gasp when I feel he's hard, hot, and ready for me, utterly exposed, as he's not wearing any underwear. I don't waste a second and wrap my hand around his long, torrid shaft and begin moving up and down. I'm never this sexually aggressive, but I feel if I don't consume him this instant, I just may explode.

He growls, a hungry, primitive sound which spurs me on, giving me the confidence to stroke him faster and harder. His skin is like velvet, his arousal coating his thick head. "Oh, fuck," he curses, tearing his mouth from mine and throwing back his head.

The veins in his neck are tensed, his Adam's apple bobbing as he swallows deeply. With my hand still down his pants, I lunge up and suck over his pulse, biting and licking, desperate to leave a mark—to show the world he's mine.

He cries out, his length pulsating in my palm—I hold the power and it's a heady aphrodisiac. "I watched you," I confess around sucking his throat.

"Watched what?" he forces out, bucking his hips in time with my riotous rhythm.

"In the shower. I watched you get yourself off." I should feel ashamed for confessing such sins, but I don't.

"Did you like to watch?"

"Yes," I reply, feeling myself grow slick.

"Good," he growls, quickly reaching for my hand and yanking it from his jeans.

I stagger back, confused, but he makes his intentions clear as he roughly grips the hem of my dress and tears it over my head and off my body. "Now it's my turn to watch."

I don't question it because nothing has felt as good as this. I reach around and unclip my white lace bra. It falls to the ground a second later, my nipples hardening as his eyes devour me whole. I'm not big busted, but Saxon's hum of approval erases my fears. He reaches out and cups my breast with trembling fingers, hissing and cursing. He fondles me until I'm mewling for more.

He gives me more, so much more as he bends down and sucks my pebbled nipple into his mouth while massaging my other breast with his hand. I feel so full, so alive; I don't know how much longer I can endure this sweet torment.

My underwear is soaked, my core so needy and hot, every

suck, lick, and pull is like a slap to my clit. When I can't take it anymore, I boldly slip my hand between my legs and commence putting out the uncontrolled fire within me. My flesh is slick and ripe, ready to be picked and consumed.

I toss my head back, squeezing my eyes shut, focusing on his hands, mouth, and body as I work my fingers deeper and deeper within me. I'm so close, I can taste the inevitable, and I know when I do, I'll be addicted to the taste.

Just as I rub over my center in a wide circle, Saxon secures my wrist and jerks my hand out from my underwear. I scream in protest because I was so, so close, but his deep, throaty chuckle reveals it's only just begun.

"That's my job," he hums, drawing my hand to his lips and suckling my fingers. They're coated with my arousal and I blush, embarrassed. "You taste incredible." He continues lapping my fingers, not leaving an inch untouched.

This action alone has me rubbing my thighs together, so desperate to come, I'm ready to beg. With a possessed passion, I grip the lapels of his shirt and rip them apart, sending buttons scattering all over the barn. His lips coil, happy with my aggression.

My action sets us both off and before long, we are madly pulling and yanking at one another's clothes, anxious to get them off. The moment we're both naked, he lifts me up like I weigh no more than a feather, and carries me to a mountain of straw bales. He tosses me onto them, his eyes hungrily watching my breasts bounce up and down. I crawl backwards, the straw tickling my ass and thighs. The feel is a mixture between pleasure and pain.

I wait for him to climb on top of me, to connect us in a way I so desperately crave. But he doesn't. He just stands and watches me. I subconsciously cover my chest, but he shakes his head, quickly leaning forward to expose myself to him.

"Reality is so much better than what I pictured it would be. You're fucking beautiful, Lucy. I don't deserve you."

His heartfelt confession has me kneeling forward and wrapping an arm around his nape, drawing him on top of me. His weight is perfect, and we align like we were meant to be one. We kiss, but this kiss isn't passion filled, it's laced with love—a kiss which I've longed to share.

I'm ready, I want him, so I scissor my legs, needing to feel him inside of me. He dips a hand between us, running two fingers along my slippery opening. I mewl into his mouth, opening my legs wider, needing him to bring this home. And he does. He works a finger into me, us both crying out at the sensation.

He's gentle, but he's also impatient, like he's reining in his passion because he wants to take it slow. But I don't want slow. I just want him.

I bite his bottom lip while gripping his thick length, guiding him where I need him to be. He grunts when we touch, pulling his lips away to look into my eyes. I brush the hair from his brow, yearning to be lost in his sea green depths and never be found.

"Are you sure? This changes everything." He's trembling and I don't know why, but nothing has felt sweeter.

"I've never been more certain of anything in my life." Sealing my mouth over his, I arch my back and just like that, we become one.

He works his way in slowly, he's big, massive in fact, and it takes a while for my muscles to accept him. But when they do, I'm in heaven.

We continue kissing as he rocks into me, careful not to take things too fast. But we learn this dance quite quickly, our bodies falling in sync with each other as he speeds up the momentum. I'm with him every step of the way, pushing when he pulls and acting as a yin to his yang.

He fills me to the brim, his girth bringing tears to my eyes. As he bucks into me faster, I yelp, and he instantly freezes. "I'm sorry. Have I hurt you?" The panic is clear on his face as he wipes the tears from the corner of my eyes.

"Don't stop," I reply breathlessly, hooking my leg around him to deepen the angle. He grins, and continues a controlled, steady rhythm.

I know he's holding back. I can feel his deliberate strokes are poised and restrained. But I don't want poised and restrained. I've lived my life under that pretense for far too long. I clench my muscles around him, rocking my hips and meeting him thrust for thrust. He groans and gives into my needy demands.

As he pumps into me ardently, all barriers between us slip away and all that's left is Saxon and Lucy—nothing exists but us, and it's beautiful. I place my palm over his hammering heart, right over his hourglass tattoo, appreciating the significance of it. Time will never change the fact that I love him, too.

He grips my thigh, pulling my leg out further so he can drive into me at a punishing speed. But I want it. I take everything he gives me, throwing my head back, my body lax. The bundle of nerves are treading so close to the surface, I can taste it.

He watches where we're connected, the satisfaction that I'm finally his showing as he grins. "You don't know how long I've wanted you this way." My eyes roll into the back of my head as he sinks into me over and over again.

I'm seconds away from coming but almost scream in protest when he stops moving and withdraws from me quickly. My muscles clench and spasm, missing his skillful shaft, but they purr in pleasure when he scoops a hand around my belly and turns me, arranging me to rest on all fours.

He glides his fingertips over my scars, tracing each jagged one. I attempt to shift away, conscious and ashamed, but he doesn't allow me to move an inch. A strangled sob and sigh gets trapped in my throat when he presses his lips to the ugliness, making me feel beautiful and loved.

Each lash of his tongue erases away the past and before long, my ass is high in the air as I arch my back, desperate to feel him inside of me once more. What I feel however is his pointer running down the pleat of my behind before his hands spread me open like a rosebud in bloom. When he buries his face between my backside, I try and scamper away, mortified and self-conscious, but he hooks a hand underneath me and draws me even further backwards so I'm bucking onto his face. I'm burning up from embarrassment, but also yearning. I feel downright desirable.

His tongue and mouth are in places no one has ever ventured before. He leaves no part of me untouched, leaving me squirming and shamelessly begging for more. The sound of his hand rubbing up and down his length fills my mind with erotic images, which has me letting go of restraint and riding out this feeling of pure bliss.

He is in tune with my impending release as he reaches between us and rubs over my swollen bud. The moment his deft fingers play me like an instrument made only for him, I scream, my hips bucking wildly, ready to ride out my release.

A startled cry escapes me as he slaps my ass cheek before pulling his mouth away and replacing his shaft where his lips once were. He pushes into me so deeply, I'm certain I can feel him imprinted into every part of my body. He rides me hard, punishing, and I like it. I slam back onto him as he thrusts into me over and over and over again.

He secures a hand around my waist, holding me prisoner, while the other coils around my hair, using my locks as reins.

I feel him everywhere and I never want him to leave. That thought has me buckling, and I ride out a release so great, I can't help but choke back a sob. I've never felt this way before and whether it's in the throes of passion, or in happiness that I'm finally free, I roar, "I…fucking love you, too!"

My words have Saxon humming, almost howling in relief. He drives into me, ensuring I feel every slow stroke. He's dominating, confident, and possesses every part of me, and I love it. I love him. After what seems likes hours, he bellows out his climax with an earth-shattering howl as he collapses on top of me.

We're both trembling, still locked as one, and nothing, nothing has felt more perfect. I'm where I should be. I've finally found where I belong.

Twenty-One

I WAKE WITH A SENSE of clarity. Or it could be the sunlight streaming in from the undressed window.

Tossing an arm over my eyes, I block out the daylight, not quite ready to face the harsh light of day just yet. What happened between Saxon and I was…I don't even know. There are no words to describe how I feel. It was nothing short of amazing.

After we collapsed, fully satisfied and complete, I fell asleep in his arms. I woke during the night, snuggled underneath a rug Saxon had draped over us. His heartbeat thumps robustly and warmly underneath my ear—a sound which almost lulls me back to sleep. But I know sooner or later we have to face what we did.

He said things would change between us and they have—they've changed for the better. I know I cheated on Samuel—I have both physically and emotionally, and for that, I will never forgive myself. But I'll never be sorry for what transpired between Saxon and me. But before we confront Sam, we have to uncover what "this" is. We both expressed our love for one another, but that doesn't automatically mean we're a couple. Or does it?

The ring feels heavy on my finger, and for the first time in so many days, I know it's time. I can't wear Samuel's ring any longer. We're no longer the same people we once were. I can't help but think that through losing Sam, I found myself. I found who I want to be.

Never feeling closer to another human being my entire life, I slowly rise, wanting to look at Saxon before he wakes. His mussed hair is sleep ruffled, flicking rebelliously in all different angles. His strong jaw line is covered with a dark scruff, complementing his bowed lips. Lips I so desperately want to kiss.

Leaning forward, I give into temptation and seal my mouth over his. Memories from last night flicker before my eyes, leaving me winded and craving more. He moans, the sound husky, rough, and so incredibly sexy.

"Good morning," I whisper from around his lips. I don't give him a chance to reply however as I slip my tongue into his warm mouth. He hums, surrendering, as I roll on top of him, our lips never breaking cadence.

When I feel him stir between my legs, although I'm a little

sore, I'm eager to feel him inside of me again. As I sit up, the blanket pools around us, the sunlight highlighting Saxon in all of his glorious, naked beauty. The vision has me realizing I've never seen him completely bare before.

He is an exquisite creature.

Tracing the sharpened planes and contours of his body, I decide to share something with him. Bare to him, I bare my soul. "When you first came to the hospital, I remember thinking you were here to save Sam." He lowers his eyes, appearing saddened by my revelation. Placing a finger under his chin, I beckon him to look at me. "But now I know…you were here to save me."

Tears prick his eyes as he shuts them, and nothing has ever looked more beautiful.

We don't speak, as our silence speaks volumes. I continue tracing over his cheeks, down his sharp jaw, outlining his collarbones, before gliding my fingers down his chest. As I detour to his flank, the elegant script tattooed on his side catches my eye. I've never been able to read it and when he shifts, I know there's a reason why.

I read the words over and over, not understanding what I'm seeing. There must be some mistake. My fingers clutch at his side, pleading that there is some mistake. But when his eyes pop open and nothing but guilt lies in their depths, I know I've at long last found the final piece to my puzzle.

My heart begins a deafening march, and I'm finding it hard to breathe. I'm suffocating—suffocating on something that I can't explain.

"W-why do you h-have that tattooed on y-you?" My voice breaks as I point to his side. He frowns, shaking his head regrettably. "Saxon, why?" I scream when he doesn't answer me.

The air is sour, stagnant. "You know why." Those three words seal my fate, along with his tattoo.

Ask her if she still keeps all her kings in the back row.

That line is from *The Catcher in the Rye*—it's the line which brought Samuel and me together. Those words left me a love struck fool. But why does Saxon have them tattooed on him?

My mind flashes back to that exact moment, that exact moment in time when Samuel and I first met. Looking down at Saxon's hands, I remember the flecks of dirt underneath Sam's fingernails—just like someone would have if tinkering around under a hood.

No...it can't be.

I shift off of him and slump to the ground. "Lucy, please, let me explain." Saxon raises his hands as he sits up, worry etching every corner of his face as he slips into his jeans.

"It was you?" I gasp, not needing him to draw a diagram. "It was you in the library...and not Sam, wasn't it? It was you who gave me this?" I yank at the chain around my neck.

"Lucy..."

"Wasn't it?" I shout, tears filling my tears.

"...Yes."

I suddenly feel so naked. I reach for the blanket and cover

myself, feeling utterly exposed and humiliated.

"Please let me explain." He sits beside me, but I shift away.

I can't speak, so I listen, hoping that some part of this will make sense.

"It *was* me you met in the library, not Sam. I understand how you could mistake us, especially since I didn't correct you. You never said Sam's name, but deep down, I knew you thought I was him."

"But I saw the basketball inside your backpack," I reveal, one of the reasons why I assumed he was Sam. "And you were so cocky. So Sam like."

"I did that to impress you. I saw the way girls flocked to Sam. I was trying to mimic his confidence. And the basketball? I had Sam's bag. It wasn't uncommon for me to pretend I was him."

"What?" I wheeze, as I feel there is so much more to this story.

Exhaling, he reveals, "I've loved you since the first moment I saw you." He looks embarrassed by his admission. "You radiated so much warmth and sunshine. I was drawn to you. But I was a shy kid, thanks to being told I was never any good. After being told that your entire life, you start to believe it.

I used my journals as a way to express myself because I could never voice my feelings to my mom, my dad, Sam, or to tell you how I felt. Sam read my diaries. That's how he knew I liked you. I also spoke to him about you, after that day in the library, asking for advice because I didn't know how to talk to girls. I told him everything we spoke about, naively thinking he'd help me get the girl. Instead, *he* got the girl. *My* girl."

"No," I whisper, tears spilling down my cheeks. "It can't be true."

"It is true, Lucy." Closing his eyes, he exposes his soul to me. "August fourth, two thousand and four. Today, I spoke to the girl of my dreams—little Lucy Tucker."

I gasp, shaking my head. Sam's nickname for me wasn't his after all.

"I followed her to the library, adamant that today was the day I was going to finally speak to her. I was tired of looking at her from afar. She was even more beautiful up close. Long honey blonde hair, and the greenest eyes I've ever seen. Eyes which encompass innocence and hope.

When she asked to borrow my copy of *The Catcher in the Rye,* I tried my best to act cool. But when we touched, I felt alive. No one has ever made me feel the way she does. When I offered her the book and told her she can keep it for as long as she likes, I wanted to add the same could be said about me.

"Lucy Tucker is my queen and I can only hope that one day, I'll be her king in the back row." He opens his eyes, a melancholy smile touching his cheeks.

The narration of his journal entry has me weeping, choking on my strangled sobs. It *was* him. This entire time, it was Saxon. I stroke over his queen chess piece tattoo on his forearm. Did he get this for me? Am I still his queen?

"Why didn't you tell me? You let me believe you were Sam. Why didn't you correct me, Saxon, why?"

"Because I saw the way you looked at Samuel. You liked him. When we first spoke in the library, I knew you felt the same spark that I felt for you, but I didn't know if it was genuine or not—if you felt that for me, or for Sam. I wanted to tell you, but I was afraid you'd stop looking at me the way that you did. I wanted so desperately for you to want me; that's why I didn't tell you. I didn't want to believe that when you looked at me you saw Sam, so I made you see *me*—and you did. But I was too late.

The person you returned the book to and had coffee with was *Sam*, not me, Lucy. He knew about you because like I said, I had confided in him about how much I liked you. I even asked for his advice on how to talk to you. That's why he fell into the role of being me, well, him, so easily. He knew everything."

"What?" I gasp.

"When I saw you a week later holding hands, I felt betrayed, hurt beyond belief. I thought that regardless of our connection, you still wanted Sam. I never knew you had coffee until Sam told me when we turned eighteen. He apologized and told me that you had approached him, thinking it was me, well, him. He didn't mean for things to happen. He said he was just intrigued by the girl who had captured my heart. But in turn, he fell in love with you. He's always been in love with you. Sam may have been an asshole to me, Lucy, but his feelings for you have always been real. You changed him."

We're both silent, deep in thought.

"By trying to act like Sam," he scoffs. "I inadvertently made you think I *was* him. I wanted to believe you thought it was me, but everyone wanted Sam. It made sense you wanted him too."

"I wanted *you*, Saxon. I fell for the boy who gave me this." I sadly look down at the necklace which now represents all I've lost. "Why didn't you tell me?"

He shrugs, helpless. "It didn't matter. I could see that you loved him, and you were happy. I was so hurt that you couldn't tell us apart. Stupid, isn't it? We're identical, for fuck's sake. But regardless, I couldn't be around you and be reminded of what I lost. And I couldn't be reminded of what Sam did. He betrayed me, even if he said he didn't mean to, causing an even bigger rift between us."

This explains everything. His hatred for me was caused by the fact I hurt him. I unintentionally hurt him, but tell that to a seventeen-year-old kid. But as we got older, he surely understood that I was just a child. I deserved to know the truth. "Why didn't you tell me when we got older? Or why didn't you tell me the day that we kissed?"

I'm beseeching him to tell me the truth because I need to understand.

With shaky fingers, he reaches out and brushes a strand of hair from my forehead. His touch still sends shivers down my spine. "Because I wanted you to want *me*. Not the seventeen-year-old me you met in the library. Yes, it was me you first met, but it was *him* you fell in love with. I wanted a chance to prove myself. To show you that the spark between us has always been there."

A thought hits me, leaving me winded. "You stayed away because of me. I ruined your life." He sacrificed his happiness for me.

Shaking his head vehemently, he cries, "Lucy, no. This isn't your fault." He wipes away my torrent of tears with his thumbs. "This is why I never wanted to tell you. It resolves nothing. It only brings up bad memories, ones I wish I could forget."

I thought I had all pieces to the puzzle, but I don't. There is still one remaining. "Is that why you hate Sam? Because he stole me away from you?"

Saxon sighs, his face forlorn. "It's part of the reason why."

"But there's something else?"

He nods.

I dig through every word he's spoken, looking for a clue, a minor sign which will piece this all together. It's there; it's on the tip of my tongue.

It comes to me so quickly, I nearly double over in disbelief. "Oh, god, Saxon, no—what did you do?"

He runs a hand through his hand, closing his eyes ashamed. "Being someone's twin allows you to be a doppelganger. And Sam asked me to be his. Numerous times. When he got into trouble with Kellie, I always took the blame. Perfect Sam could do no wrong. She could never tell us apart, so in the end, even when she caught Sam red handed, it was always my fault. Sometimes, I think she knew it was Sam, but it was always easier to believe one child was a failure, and not both her boys.

I hated Sam, but he was my brother and I naïvely hoped that maybe one day he'd need me as much as I needed him. But then I grew up. I realized there are bad people in this world, and my brother was one of them."

I gulp.

"We were always competing for Kellie's affection. She shouldn't have had one child, let alone two. But she loved Sam. He excelled at sports, something my parents could understand. But me, they thought I was weird, different. I was set outside the Stone mold.

"So the answer to your question is if Kellie, our own mother couldn't tell us apart, what hope did our teachers have? Sam was a great basketballer, but he was a lousy, lazy student. Dad was on his back to get good grades, set on him graduating and helping him on the farm. But Sam didn't want that. He wanted that scholarship to Montana State. But for that to happen, he not only had to excel at basketball, but in all his other subjects, too.

"He begged me to help him, saying I was the smart one, while he was the one who was supposed to turn pro. That was his dream, Lucy. And as his older brother, even after all the shit he pulled, even after Kellie favoring him throughout our entire childhood, I wanted that for him. And a selfish part of me wanted him gone, hopeful he'd leave you behind."

I don't make a sound, lost in a past I always knew was there.

"I sat his SATs for him, and I aced it. He was getting that scholarship, no questions asked. The makeup test was the following week, which I was going to sit. I made up some lame excuse that I had the flu and couldn't get out of bed to sit the original test. The excuse stuck, as no one upset the Stones. But that never happened because Sam told me the wrong date. I trusted him, but he lied. I was a day too late. The story of my life."

This is too much. "Why would he lie? It doesn't make any sense."

Saxon looks wounded as he confesses, "Because he wanted to ensure that I stayed here and looked after the farm with Dad while he went off to college and lived the dream. If not both, then one of us was expected to stay—no guessing which child my parents preferred. Sam wanted to make sure there was no hope of me getting into college and moving away. He was looking after himself. Better I stay here than him."

I shake my head. "But he didn't accept the scholarship. He stayed here, and he did what your father wanted anyway. And your mom and dad, they seemed so proud of him. I don't understand."

"I told him if he didn't tell mom and dad what we did, then I would. He always feared the wrath of Kellie, so he finally agreed. Deep down, I think he knew she'd never believe me. But Greg did. He knew Sam wasn't a good student, and that his top marks must have been my doing. Kellie and Greg feared what this would do to the Stone name if I ever spilled. And they knew that I would. So behind my back, they made a deal. Sam was to graduate, but as punishment for his actions, he would no longer be offered a scholarship."

"And your punishment," I whisper.

"I was to graduate bottom of the class, with no hope of ever getting into a decent college. My mistake was their reward as I had just doomed Sam and my future. To their friends on the school board, they looked honorable, teaching their sons a lesson. But in reality, they were only doing this for themselves. Yes, they were proud he was a great basketballer. But that stopped the minute high school ended. It was always expected Sam and I were to work with Greg. 'I can't have *Stone and Sons* without my sons,' Greg would state, saying he would be the laughing stock in Big Sky County and beyond. And this was his way to ensure we never left. All hope for the future was gone. Sam at least had a chance at going to college. But me, I was stuck regretting the biggest mistake of life."

"Why didn't you fight them?"

"Kellie and Greg would have no doubt manipulated the situation to work in their favor. There was no point fighting them. I did that my entire life and lost. My parents fixed the system so their kids failed. How messed up is that? Loving parents would want the opposite for their kids. But my parents are one of a kind. The results were kept secret, of course. Couldn't tarnish the Stone name. It appeared that Sam and I stayed here by choice. But we never did have a choice."

This explains Kellie's hatred for Saxon. In her eyes, he was trying to take Sam away from her.

"That's why you left?"

"Yes. It was time I made my own destiny," he says with conviction.

"Sam ruined your life," I cry, gripping the edges of the blanket, huddling beneath it. "You could have gone to college. You could have been anything you wanted to be." Sam was right, Saxon was the smart brother. But because of one simple mistake, his future was taken away from him.

No wonder Sam never wanted to talk about college or the scholarship. Always brushing it off like it was his choice. But in reality, there was never a choice to be made.

Kellie, Greg, and Samuel were happy to see Saxon gone, as he took their secrets with him. "None of them deserved your help," I exclaim, outraged at them. "But yet, you still came."

"I came because you asked me to," he simply replies. "I stayed because I knew how much you loved him. As much as I didn't want him to remember, I was going to try because I couldn't stand to see you cry."

This man has always had my best interests at heart—it's too bad I was blinded by something that was all lies. "I don't even know w-who Sam is. He never l-loved me. It explains why he doesn't remember me," I stutter, choking on my grief.

His face turns soft, affectionate as he looks at me. "Yes, Lucy, he does. How can anyone not love you? At first, he did it because he was curious. But then he saw what a compassionate, extraordinary person you are, and he fell in love with you. And you fell in love with him."

I choke back my sob. I don't know what the truth is anymore.

A weight appears to be lifted off his shoulders, but I can still see his pain. "So that's the Stone family secret. You now know it all. I wouldn't blame you if you went running for the hills. I did. When I finally stopped feeling sorry for myself, I packed up my shit and moved from town to town. I got a job at a garage in Oregon, working for a guy named Gus. He was like a father to me. When he passed away to lung cancer, he left me the shop. Nicest thing anyone has ever done for me."

I've missed so much of Saxon's life. But I've also missed so much of mine. I can't help but think what person I would have grown into if I had spent my life with Saxon and not Sam. Would I still be the same person I am now? Would I live where I do? Go to college where I did?

I could have been an entirely different person, and I suddenly feel cheated that the decision was taken away from me. I know Saxon had my best interests at heart, but he took away my choices. He made a decision for me which wasn't his to make.

"You should have told me," I press, my lower lip trembling.

My words appear to crush him. "I know. I'm sorry, Lucy. I was a dumb kid, angry at the world. And when I got older, it was too late. Looking in on your life, it was perfect, and I wanted that for you. You deserved that. I couldn't offer you that. I still have nothing to offer you," he confesses, lowering his eyes.

"Don't say that." His sadness hurts my heart.

"Regardless of what Sam did, you loved him. If I had told you, would you have believed me?" he poses.

Now I'm the one to avert my eyes, as I'm afraid to face the answer.

Remembering Sam's comment about his good grades has me thinking he remembers bits and pieces. But I'm certain he doesn't remember his parent's sabotage—lucky for him. "Does he remember he did this?"

Saxon raises his shoulders. "I don't know. I thought that he did, but now, I'm not so sure. He might have the luxury of forgetting, but I don't. I live with the memory of what could have been, but never will, every day."

Recalling Sam's confession, I reveal, "He told me you spoke to him the night he woke up from a coma."

"He heard that?" he asks, stunned.

"Yes."

His mouth parts and an impressed 'humph' leaves him. "You *were* right."

But my correct forewarning doesn't make me feel any

better. "He told me you said you couldn't look after me. Why?"

"Because I've lived with the regret of not telling you the truth my entire life. I failed you. I failed everyone."

I know I shouldn't be angry, but I am. I can't help but feel cheated. "You had no right to choose that for me. I fell in love with a lie. I fell in love with Sam because I thought he was the one who sent my heart into overdrive. But it was you. It's been you all along."

A tsunami of emotion rolls through me and I am beyond the point of no return. I'm so angry that the choice was taken away from me. "I feel like I don't know who I am anymore," I confess, blinking in disbelief.

He strokes over my eyes, my lips. "You're you, Lucy. My little Lucy Tucker."

Those words only make things murkier. I need to breathe. "I need time to clear my head." I stand, shivering.

"Time? Why? This changes how you feel about me?" He's on his knees, begging me to stay.

"This changes everything!" I cry out. "Sam should have told me. You both should have."

His face falls and he blinks once. "It doesn't change my feelings for you. It'll always be you. But I understand if you hate me."

His uncertainty and pain tears out my heart. "I don't hate you. I just need time."

"Are you still going to Syria?" he asks, holding his breath.

"I don't know, Saxon! Nothing makes sense anymore."

He nods, his eyes overflowing with nothing but sadness. Unleashing his secret hasn't given him freedom. It never will.

I need to find my clothes and get out of here. I can't make any decisions with him looking at me the way that he is. I need time, space, and silence. But just as I slip my dress over my head, a stale silence rips through the barn, resonating all the way to my soul.

"Saxon?" I spin around and gasp as I stare into the eyes of my true love—Samuel Stone. Saxon is still on his knees, the sight too monumental.

"Lucy?" His voice isn't laced with the usual anger, hostility, or hatred, it sounds like my Sam—the old Sam.

"S-Sam?" My skin pricks with tiny goosebumps, and it has nothing to do with the gentle wind. Rays of sunlight kiss his face, highlighting the bright red collecting at his temple and trickling down his cheek. "You're bleeding!" Finally finding my feet, I run over to where he is standing dazed, in the doorway. He appears confused, fearful, and dejected. "What happened?" I avoid his gaze, brushing back the matted hair at his brow.

He sniffs and raises his broad, bare shoulders. "I don't know. I think I blacked out. When I came to, I was lying on the shower floor. I can't…remember…"

"You can't remember what?" I wheeze, my heart in song with a steady staccato. When he reaches for my wrist and secures his bitter cold fingers around me, I hold my breath. His touch feels so wrong.

"Can't remember much of anything," he replies after a sluggish silence.

I still can't meet his eyes. "What's the last thing you remember?" I let out the trapped breath as he releases me.

"I-I…" he falters. Gathering whatever courage I have left, I lift my eyes and meet his lost, vacant stare. "I remember getting ready for our wedding day," he replies in a distant tone. "But I have a feeling I never made it?" I nod, envious that he has the luxury of forgetting the past few months, while I'm forced to remember every single heartbreaking detail.

"You honestly don't remember a thing?" I can't believe he gets given a fresh slate.

He shakes his head. "I remember nothing. Everything is so muddled. I must have hit my head harder than I thought." He raises his hand and rubs at his brow. When he pulls away, blood coats his fingertips. His cheeks turn a deathly white. He hisses in a pained breath through clenched teeth.

He remembers. But how much does he recall?

"What happened?" he asks, begging me to appease his pain. When he reaches out to touch me, I can't help but shrink away. He shakes his head, frowning. It appears he only just sees Saxon, on his knees, partially nude, when he shifts his gaze to the floor. His nostrils flare. "It appears a lot has happened."

I'm suddenly wrapped in a blanket of culpability. I should be happy, but I'm not. This time, when he reaches out to touch me, I don't recoil, but I should. Sam looks at me and I almost feel naked. I feel the need to cover my nudity and hide my sins from his knowledgeable eyes.

"I feel like I haven't seen you in years. I feel like something has…changed."

The burning guilt eats away at my stomach and I wrap my arms around my trembling body. We're silent, the staleness between us reflecting where our relationship stands. I remember who I *am*, but Sam remembers who I *was*.

Saxon finally stands, his naked chest pronouncing what happened between us. Sam looks between us, his eyes suddenly filling with hot, angry tears. "No," he gasps, "please god, no. Lucy, please, baby…tell me this isn't what I think it is." His raw plea breaks my heart.

I want to say so many things, but where do I start? This wasn't supposed to happen, but it did. My silence is the answer Sam needs. The blood whooshing through my ears is deafening, it's almost painful to breathe.

"Sam…" I'm unable to finish however because Sam storms over to where Saxon stands and slams his fist into his jaw. Saxon's head snaps back with a sickening crack as he staggers backward. He spits out a mouthful of blood and grins murderously.

"You motherfucker!" Sam roars, advancing forward, hitting Saxon over and over and over again. Saxon appears to take the beatings, not fighting back.

"No!" I try and break them up, but Sam pushes me aside,

intent on drawing more blood. I fall on my behind, a hand flying to my mouth as I watch Sam beat Saxon to a bloody pulp.

"Fight me!" Sam shouts, delivering an uppercut that knocks Saxon to the floor. He kicks him in the ribs, the stomach, the face. Saxon remains silent however, and if I didn't know better, I'd say he was accepting this beating as punishment for what we've done. But if that's the case, then I deserve this beating as much as him.

"Sam, stop! Please! You'll kill him! No!" My plea falls on deaf ears as Sam continues beating him, only content when he's dead. The sound of Saxon's pained grunts as he bravely accepts his fate is my undoing.

I can't stand by and watch this act of violence. Without a second thought, I run over to Saxon and shield his curled body with my own. I throw my arms around him, protecting him just as he has protected me.

"Lucy, move!" Sam bellows, his anger burning all the way to my center.

"No!" My reply comes out muffled, as I'm cocooned around Saxon's limp form. "Stop it. Leave him a-alone." I frantically kiss his temple, his cheeks, his hair, I need to feel him, need to make sure he's okay. When he inhales deeply, my body sags in relief. "I'm sorry," I whimper into his ear. "This changes nothing between us." It's what I should have said when he asked me this question before. "I…love…you. Please forgive me."

"I…love you… too." Those broken words are all I need to

hear.

I'm hugging Saxon with all my might and only become aware that Sam has left when a bloodcurdling scream fills the heavens and my name is repeated with an agonizing howl. I know I have to let go—just for now. I remove my body from Saxon's and cover my mouth as Samuel's anguished wails break my heart. It's ripped from the center of my chest and stomped on as he begs for me to explain what's going on.

But how can I choose? I'm torn.

Saxon makes the choice for me. "Go to him." He limply raises his hand, gliding his pointer along the apple of my cheek.

I blink back my tears. "*What*?" Surely I didn't hear him correctly.

However, when he attempts to sit upright and stubbornly points to the door, I know I heard him just fine. "I'm…okay." The pause between his affirmation highlights the deception. So does the fact he's clutching his side, breathing heavily through his nose.

"You are not okay," I just as determinedly state. "Let me help you." I'm thankful he allows me to steady him as he sways to the left. He squeezes his eyes shut, swallowing hard. The deep furrowing along his brow reveals he's in a lot of pain, but he breathes through it, planting his palm on the floor to ground him. I wait, never breaking contact, never wanting to let him go.

Saxon's eyes spring open and he looks at me, forlornly. "I'm not leaving you," I exclaim, shaking my head as I recognize that look. He wants me to choose. Well, I choose him.

He reads my grim resolution and of course, fights me. "I'm fine. Samuel needs you more than I do right now. I just need to catch my breath. I'll be out there in a minute."

"Saxon," I gasp, eyes widening. Why is he pushing me away? "I'm not going a-anywhere." I fumble over my words, a breakdown looming.

"Lucy, just go. Go…before he does something stupid." The guilt of what we did slashes at his face. Regardless of Sam's sins, Saxon will always look after his little brother.

I reach out for him, tears stinging my eyes. "Saxon—"

"Lucy, please…" A tear trickles down my cheek when I hear Sam's pleas. "He doesn't remember. He has no idea what's going on. If he hurts himself because of us…because of what I did… I will never forgive myself…and neither will you."

We both understand that regardless of our feelings, Sam needs us. He may not deserve our compassion, but we'd never forgive ourselves if we abandoned him when he needed us the most.

Bending forward, I tenderly kiss Saxon's cheek. A heavy weight settles in the pit of my stomach because I know now that Sam remembers— this is the beginning of the end.

"I love you."

Saxon smiles, but it's bittersweet. "I love you, too…little Lucy Tucker."

Sniffing back my tears, I charge outside. The harsh sunlight stops me in my tracks. Shielding my eyes, I desperately search for Sam. I don't have far to look. He's slumped on his knees in the middle of the yard, looking completely and utterly alone as he turns his head from left to right, searching the grounds for…me.

This is the moment I've been waiting for—for Sam to remember who I was, to remember what we had. I just wanted things to go back to the way they were. But now that my wish has been granted…all I want is for him to forget.

Acknowledgments

This book was a rollercoaster ride, but the blood, sweat, and tears were all worth it.

My wonderful husband, Daniel. I love you. Thank you for believing in me even when I didn't believe in myself.

My ever-supporting parents. You guys are the best. I am who I am because of you. I love you.

My brilliant agent, Kimberly Whalen. You believed in me from the very beginning. Your constant support, advice, and encouragement helped me when times were tough and I'll never forget it. Thank you for being so incredible and never giving up. This is just the beginning!

My exceptionally talented and amazing publishers, especially Heyne—Random House. Thank you so much for believing in me.

My editor, Toni Rakestraw—thank you!

My proof-readers—Lisa Edward, Catherine Brown, and Alissa Glenn. You saved my ass. Thanks for working on such a tight deadline with a smile.

Melissa Gill from MG Bookcovers & Designs. This cover was everything I wanted and so much more. Thank you for your patience. You're a true genius!

Tina Gephart— thank you for holding my hand when times were tough. You'll never know how much your support means to me. You're one in a billion and I freaking adore you! Duce forever, baby! #ottersbff

Lisa Edward— thank you for being there time and time again, and for offering me priceless advice. I don't know what I'd do without our talks.

Louise Mercer—my beautiful angel. You are my most treasured friend. We have been through so much together and it's been a crazy journey. Thank you for being my forever light.

Gemma Cawley—my bff! Thank you for being my biggest cheerleader and supporter. I can't wait until we open Cat Island! <insert cat mermaid scream>

Christina and Lauren—I adore you girls so much. Thank you for being you.

SC Stephens— You're one in a million.

Natasha is a Book Junkie, Maryse's Book Blog, Aestas Book Blog, Angie's Dreamy Reads, TotallyBooked Blog, All Is Read, Talkbooks, AC BookBlog, WickedGoodReads, Monique Tinline, Lisa Pantano Kane at Three Chicks and their Books, Two Book Pushers, Maria's Book Blog, Penny Rudge, Ariana McWilliams, Marisa-Rose Shor, Kylie Scott, Mia Sheridan, Audrey Carlan, Lexi Ryan, Geneva Lee, Kristen Dwyer, Jaz Menta, Meire Dias, Donna Cooksley Sanderson, Kathy-Jo Reinhart, Romance Writers of Australia, My French Sinners, Bradley Cooper, Jared Leto, Zac Efron, PLL—I cannot thank you enough for everything.

My beautiful family —Mum, Papa, Fran, Matt, Samantha,

Amelia, Gayle, Peter, Luke, Leah,

Shirley, Michael, Rob, Elisa, Evan, Alex, Francesca, and my aunties, uncles, and cousins—I am the luckiest person alive to know each and every one of you. You brighten up my world in ways I honestly cannot express. Samantha and Amelia— I love you both so very much.

My fur babies— mamma loves you so much! Buckwheat, you are my best buddy. Dacca, I will always protect you from the big bad Bellie. Mitch, refer to Dacca's comment. Jag, you're a wombat in disguise. Bellie, you're a devil in disguise. And Ninja, thanks for watching over me.

To anyone I have missed, I'm sorry! It wasn't intentional! So to make amends, this part is for you! Please insert name for your personalised acknowledgment.

Monica James thanks ______________________________ so very much! She's owes you a coffee and a billion trillion hugs.

Love M x

Last but certainly not least, I want to thank YOU! Thank you for welcoming me into your hearts and homes. My readers are the BEST readers in this entire universe! Love you all!

About the Author

Monica James spent her youth devouring the works of Anne Rice, William Shakespeare, and Emily Dickinson.

When she is not writing, Monica is busy running her own business, but she always finds a balance between the two. She enjoys writing honest, heartfelt, and turbulent stories, hoping to leave an imprint on her readers. She draws her inspiration from life.

She is a bestselling author in the U.S.A, Australia, Canada, France, Germany, Israel, and the U.K.

Monica James resides in Melbourne, Australia, with her wonderful family, and menagerie of animals. She is slightly obsessed with cats, chucks, and lip gloss, and secretly wishes she was a ninja on the weekends.

Connect with Monica James

Facebook: facebook.com/authormonicajames

Twitter: twitter.com/monicajames81

Goodreads: goodreads.com/MonicaJames

Instagram: @MonicaJames

Website: monicajamesbooks.blogspot.com.au

Made in the USA
Lexington, KY
11 March 2018